COMMENTS FROM READERS

I was intrigued from the first sentence to the final sentence of your book. I commend you for writing this book and the story of a very brave nurse who changed the focus of WWI.
~ Capt. Irene K.Weaver, NC, USN

I just finished your book on Edith Cavell. It was excellent! I have not enjoyed such a good book in a long time.
~ Marilyn Asselin, PhD. RN-BC, Assistant Professor, College of Nursing,
U. Mass. Dartmouth

This book is truly a gift.
~ Catherine Dicker, RN, Wellness Coach

The way you have presented the narrated the story of Edith Cavell blew my mind away. Something inside me changed forever. I was so inspired.
~ Narendra Goidani, Life School, India

Finished it last night. Stayed up to 2:00 a.m. 'cause I couldn't put it down.
~Gina Keller, Falmouth, MA

Fatal Decision is an absorbing novel. The large cast of characters, from the other nurses & staff at the clinic to the escaping soldiers to the German authorities, are all beautifully portrayed.
~ Lyn Baines, Book Critic, I Prefer Reading, Australia

It is gripping because of the story itself and Arthur's extraordinary ability to tell it.
~Beth Boynton, RN, MS, Consultant, Confident Voices

Arthur does a remarkable job of making Cavell and her world come alive.
~ Book review by Lucia Hwang, Editor of the National Nurse, National Nurses United

Finished your book last night! Loved it! Do you mind if I use Edith's story for my sermon this Sunday?
~ Rev. Nell Fields, Congregational minister, Waquoit Congregational Church

You have done such a good job of drawing the reader into the story.
~Major Patricia Taylor, Salvation Army

I am on my second reading of the book. I have so enjoyed it and am so inspired by it.
~ Peggy Diane Ischy, Leander, Texas

FATAL DECISION
EDITH CAVELL
WORLD WAR I NURSE

Second Edition

Other books by Terri Arthur:

Fatal Destiny: Edith Cavell, WWI Nurse
(British Version)

9/16

To Jim —
May This further
your knowledge in responses
to evil.

FATAL DECISION

EDITH CAVELL

WORLD WAR I NURSE

Second Edition

Terri Arthur

TERRI ARTHUR

Milwaukee, Wisconsin

Published by
HenschelHAUS Publishing, Inc.
2625 S. Greeley St. Suite 201
Milwaukee, WI 53207

All HenschelHAUS titles, imprints, and distributed lines are available at special quantity discounts
for educational, institutional, fund-raising, or sales promotion.

ISBN: 978-1-59598-354-1
E-ISBN: 978-1-59598-355-8 (Kindle)
E-ISBN: 978-1-59598-361-9 (e-pub)

Based on the 1st Edition, originally published by
Beagle Books, LLC, under ISBN 978-09841813-2-2

Publisher's Cataloging-In-Publication Data
(Prepared by The Donohue Group, Inc.)

Arthur, Terri.
Fatal decision : Edith Cavell, World War I nurse / Terri Arthur. -- Second edition.
pages : illustrations ; cm
Originally published: Beagle Books, 2011. British edition published with the title Fatal destiny :
Edith Cavell, World War I nurse.
Issued also in Kindle and e-pub formats.
Includes bibliographical references.
ISBN: 978-1-59598-354-1
1. Cavell, Edith, 1865-1915--Fiction. 2. Nurses--Belgium--Brussels--Fiction. 3. World War, 1914-
1918--Medical care--Belgium--Brussels--Fiction. 4. World War, 1914-1918--Underground
movements--Belgium-- Brussels--Fiction. 5. Biographical fiction. 6. Historical fiction. I. Title.
PS3601.R84 F38 2014b   813/.6   2014953853

Printed in the United States of America.

The road to the future is paved
on the ashes of the past.

To my Nursing Colleagues:
Save a life and you're a hero.
Save a hundred lives and you're a nurse.

And in loving memory to my mother, Pearl Matko.
The bravest woman I have ever met,
my heroine, and inspiration.

Edith Cavell in the garden behind her home in Brussels
with her two dogs, Don and Jack.

ACKNOWLEDGMENTS

Milly White, RN, who is a wonderful writer, supported me through the difficult and good times in the writing of this book. She was my confidant, travel companion, draft manuscript reader, cheerleader, and sounding post.

Evie Bain, RN, who encouraged the writing of this book, listened to my ideas good and bad, read my manuscript draft, and made helpful suggestions.

Steve Babitsky, Esq., my business partner and friend, for his professional literary advice, for allowing me to cut my novel-writing teeth at his writing programs, and encouraging me by repeating the words, "Write the book."

Vicky Wilson-Schwartz, Ph.D., my editor, who had the patience of Job, the wisdom of Solomon, and the ability to see what I meant to write.

Julia Watling, RN, BSc, PGC Medical Education (Leadership) Training and Development Manager of the Norfolk and Norwich University Hospitals NHS Foundation Trust, who helped me edit the American version of the manuscript into a British version for UK readers.

Nick Miller, Administrator of the Edith Cavell memorabilia, Swardeston, England, who welcomed me into the activities involving Miss Cavell and helped me edit the American version of the manuscript into a British version for UK readers.

Dawn Collins, RN, Assistant Director of the Nursing for Nurse Development and Education Norfolk, and Norwich University Hospitals NHS

Foundation Trust, who welcomed me into the activities involving Miss Cavell and kept me informed.

Sara Holmes and Andra Kurlis, Cardiff, Wales, who traveled with me during the research in the UK and Brussels, provided helpful materials, and coached me on British speech characteristics.

Dr. Gail Lenehan, RN, former editor of the *Journal of Emergency Nursing*, who guided me to the publication of my article, "The Life and Death of Edith Cavell, English Emergency Nurse Known as the 'Other Florence Nightingale,'" and encouraged me to "put it in the book."

Bernard Roper, Norwich, England for helping with the details of Cavell's life, referrals, and general information about Norwich, and speech characteristics of Norwich, England.

Jonathan Evans, expert on Edith Cavell and Curator of the Edith Cavell Museum at the Royal London Hospital, for his expertise and never failing to respond to my questions.

Thérèse Halflants, of Brussels, Belgium, who helped with local information, geographical details, editing, and French translations.

Françoise Rocher, RN, who helped me with French speech characteristics and translations.

Rita Thornton, RN, who traveled with me while I was doing research in London.

Gail Matko, who was my cheerleader and promoter throughout this process and beyond.

Tucker, my malamute lab, who stayed at my side during the entire writing and helped me write the sections on Edith's dogs, Jack and Don. He lost his life to cancer after the book was published.

Also my thanks and appreciation for assistance from:

Fiona Bourne, Archives Specialist, Royal College of Nursing of the United Kingdom, London.

Frances Woodrow, Archives Assistant, Royal College of Nursing Archives, Edinburgh, Scotland.

Wendy Lutterlock, Archivist, Imperial War Museum, London.

A. Ramos, Public Services, British Library Newspapers, London.

Kate Thaxton, Curator, Norfolk Regimental Museum, Norwich, England.

Edith Cavell's Statue near Trafalgar Square.

PRELUDE

OCTOBER 11, 1921
NEAR TRAFALGAR SQUARE, LONDON

"**D**id you know her?"

"Pardon?"

Elizabeth turned to look at the man who stood behind her. He repeated his question.

"Did you know her? The woman of the statue. Sorry for the intrusion, but I saw you standing here when I went into the National Portrait Gallery a while back. When I came out, you were still here, so I thought that she must have meant something to you for you to be here so long."

Elizabeth saw that the man was young, in his early twenties, trimly built with sandy blond hair and an open expression on his face. She looked back at the two wreaths of poppies placed at the foot of the statue.

"Yes, I knew her quite well, actually. At least as well as anyone could really know her. We worked together to build a school of nursing in Brussels before the war."

He hopped on one foot to shift his weight and leaned heavily on a cane. "That's quite an ambitious goal. So did you?" A few seconds passed without an answer. "Build the nursing school, I mean."

From his speech, Elizabeth guessed he was American. She tightened the belt around her woolen coat to keep out the chilled air. "It faltered a bit during the war and after Miss Cavell..." She stopped, looked up at the forty-foot white marble statue of Edith Cavell, resplendent in her nursing uniform and cape. "...was lost to us. But now that the war is over, it has recovered and become quite successful. They have since named it after her."

The man hopped up a step to stand level with Elizabeth. "It survived no doubt with your help."

"No, not really. I did go there to work with her, but when she left us... Well, the other nurses were convinced she was arrested because of her British heritage. Since I am also British, they feared the Germans would

---

1

arrest me next." She sighed and leaned over to straighten the bow on the wreath of poppies. She saw the man watching her gesture with intense eyes.

"So I did as they suggested and left a month later. I brought with me a young English woman who had been under Edith's care. After the war, I traveled a bit. Now I am the Matron of a hospital in Somerset." She held out her hand to him. "I'm Elizabeth Wilkins. And you are?"

"I'm so sorry. Where are my manners?" He shifted the cane into his left hand and held out his right. "David Trembly, from the States." He smiled. "But you already knew that."

"So, Mr. Trembly..."

"David, please."

"So, David, what brings an American over to this side of the Atlantic?"

"Nothing very exciting, I'm afraid. I fought beside a few of your English Tommies in the war. We agreed to see each other again after it was over. I'm to meet up with them this afternoon by the Lord Nelson statue, which I believe is over there." He jutted his chin in the direction of Trafalgar Square.

"Ironic, isn't it? Both Lord Nelson and Edith gave their lives for England during a war against a foreign invader. Both were shot, and both died in their forties," said Elizabeth.

Leaning on his cane, he bent over and read the inscription carved into the base of the statue.

"It should read, '*Patriotism is not enough.*' That was what she firmly believed and said in her last hours,' said Elizabeth.

That's a pretty bold statement to make during a war. What do you think she meant by that?"

Elizabeth looked away for a moment, thought, and then turned back to the man.

"She believed in the common humanity of all mankind. She loved her country just as you love yours, and the Germans loved theirs. But in the end, we all killed each other for the same high-minded principles—duty, love of family, and belief of our rights. Her belief in the welfare of all people transcended patriotism. She felt it was her duty to care for anyone who was in need, regardless of their nationality. This belief was woven into the very fibre of her being. It was as instinctual as breathing, and nothing could sway her from it, even when it put her at risk. She never wanted to be a martyr. She would be shocked at the response her death has caused worldwide."

As she spoke, the breeze brought to him an aroma of lavender rose perfume. He fingered a scar over his eye.

"I was just thinking, it's getting chilly and my feet are aching from walking about for hours. You must be cold from standing here for so long. There's a small café next to St. Martin's. Could I interest you in sitting with me for a few moments to warm up with a cup of coffee or tea?"

"I don't know," she hesitated until she saw the expectant expression on his face. "Well, why not? Just for a little while. I have another hour before I catch the train to Norwich. There's a ceremony in memory of Edith tomorrow at the Cathedral there."

Elizabeth watched as David limped down the steps away from the statue. "You are injured." It was half a statement and half an inquiry.

"Trench foot and frost bite. Lost a part of my foot on the left and a few toes on the right. It was an ugly war. I was lucky to get out alive with nothing worse than this. Most of us never came back. But don't worry, I get around just fine with my trusty friend here." He waved his cane in the air, then leaned conspiratorially toward Elizabeth. "Just between you and me, it's an excuse to carry a secret deadly weapon and be ready to knock the noggin off of anyone who is up to mischief."

Once they were seated in the café, he hooked his cane over the back of his chair. Elizabeth ordered tea and a fruit scone while he ordered coffee and a piece of pie.

"I remember my mother reading about Miss Cavell in the news. She was quite upset about how your nurse was treated. She said that her women's group—they called them women's clubs, but they were really about getting voting rights for women—wrote to President Wilson about doing something. I heard he got thousands of letters like hers. Some say he was more afraid of their pen than of the Republicans."

Elizabeth smiled at his joke. "When a group of strong women put their minds to it, there is no limit to what they can achieve." She loosened her belt, shrugged the coat off her shoulders to the back of the chair, removed the pin in her hat, and carefully set it aside on the empty chair at their table. "That was true of our Nursing School and Clinic, but it was never the same without Edith. We retreated into ourselves afterwards, and it took some time before we could think of how to carry on without her. She asked that I handle her belongings, few as they were. I tried to do everything as she wished, but it was best for everyone that I leave. It was fitting that a Belgian nurse should be put in charge."

"You live in London?"

"No, Somerset. It's west of here."

"Sorry, you did say that before. I'm sure your husband was glad to have you back."

"I am not married, but my family did breathe a sigh of relief when I returned. They had heard of Miss Cavell's fate and feared for my safety."

Their conversation was interrupted when the waitress placed their food on the table. Elizabeth broke off a piece of the scone and was about put it in her mouth when a small terrier dog pushed its way around the tables, sniffing for a stray morsel or a handout. She held a piece below the table for the hungry animal. David looked at the gesture with amusement.

"You must like animals. I'll bet you have a dog."

"No, but it reminds me of Edith's dog, Jack. She had two actually, but one disappeared.

"What happened to him after Miss Cavell…after she was gone?"

"The house boy, José, took Jack for a while. Then, a wealthy Belgian Princess named de Croÿ took him. He went from pauper to prince, roaming about in her chateau. During one of my visits, I noticed that he ran to the door when anyone arrived. He never stopped looking for Edith." She stared into the steam rising from the cup. I can understand that. I felt the same for years—expecting her to appear at any time."

Realizing she had spoken more to this stranger than to many others, Elizabeth felt a little embarrassed and directed the discussion to him. "But I am rambling on. What made you join the army to fight a war that was not yours, on another continent?"

"Like I said. My mother never stopped talking about what the Jerries did to 'that Nurse Cavell.' That was how she would talk about her. 'That Nurse Cavell' took care of those wounded Jerries and look what they did to her. Someone should do the same thing to them. Did you know that Nurse Cavell saved over two hundred men? She should get a medal for it."

"That was the number she admitted to the Germans in her trial, but my guess is that working with the Underground, she helped closer to a thousand escape to the Dutch border."

David gave a low whistle. "My mother was right! She should have gotten a medal, like a Medal of Honor, or something like it, in Britain."

Elizabeth wrapped both hands around her teacup. She felt the soothing warmth seep into her hands. It was difficult to discuss Edith this way with a stranger, but she found it comforting to see his appreciative reaction. She had been holding so much of this inside her. The pain of her loss was always with her, like a smoldering ember that could be inflamed by almost anything—a tune Edith had played on the piano after supper— roses like the ones Quien handed to Edith while he planned his treachery. Or—Elizabeth looked down at the chip in her tea cup—a chipped tea cup like the one she drank from when she had her first interview with Edith.

"Did she?"

The abruptness of the question startled her. "I'm sorry. Did she what?

"Did she ever get a medal for what she did?"

"She was awarded medals from France and Belgium after the war. England gave her formal recognition, but the Victoria Cross is only awarded to soldiers. There were no British medals of honor for women in her time. The truth is, while she was alive, the only medal ever awarded to her was for her work in the Maidstone typhoid epidemic while she was still a nursing student."

Just then, the waitress rushed over, flapping her apron at the dog, which was making his rounds to each table. "Out! Out with you, now!" The dog's nails skidded on the slippery stone floor as he rushed out the door.

David continued. "Her story was all over the front pages of the news, you know. A lot of letters were written about her in the opinion pages. It struck home to many of us because she sort of represented all women. There isn't a red-blooded man who doesn't want to protect our women. Truth was, many Americans were already fighting over there under other flags. So many of us secretly hoped something would happen to bring America into the war so we could sign up and fight under our own flag.

"We thought the sinking of the *Lusitania* would do it, but it didn't. People weren't ready to get involved. By the time the news about Miss Cavell came our way, opinions had changed. So in a way, your Nurse Cavell was responsible for our getting into the war, and my buddies and I signing up.

David took a sip of his coffee, and went on, "One Brit told me he joined the army after he heard what the Jerries did to 'his British nurse,' as he referred to her, and later found out that thousands of Brits from all over joined up. Not just from the UK, but also from Canada, Australia, and New Zealand. I met another soldier who came from her hometown, and he said every able-bodied man in that town enlisted within a few weeks after the news came out about her. Poor man never made it home.

"I heard that enlistments increased three times because of her. I read that so many of them joined up, England had to ask America to help with war supplies, uniforms, guns, food, and the like, forcing America to get involved, although, like I said, many of us were already anxious to kick a few Jerry asses. Sorry for the word, ma'am, but you know what I mean. Truth was that up until the new recruits signed up, the Allies were losing the war and America was in a depression. You needed our help, and we needed ways to put people back to work."

The waitress appeared. "Anything else?"

Elizabeth and David looked at each other and shook their heads. She slipped the bill onto the table. "No hurry, Luv."

David grabbed the slip of paper. "Please, let me. I feel so honored to have this time with someone who knew Miss Cavell so well."

Elizabeth reached for her coat and hitched it over her shoulders. "Thank you. I accept your kind offer, but I must be going now. I must go to Liverpool Street to catch the train to Norwich to attend a ceremony in her honor there."

A whiff of lavender rose wafted by him as she stood up and reached for her hat. David grabbed his cane and struggled to his feet. "May I call you sometime? I mean, while I'm still in England."

"You are a kind and dear man. I did so enjoy our little chat together, but it's best we say goodbye."

PART ONE: THE MAKING OF A NURSE

— 1 —

LEAVING HOME, 1896

E dith held her umbrella in one hand and a black leather snap purse in the other. She breathed in the cool Norwich air and pulled her tweed overcoat tighter about her shoulders. Dark clouds formed over her head, threatening rain. Gripping the handles of the canvas bag, she tugged it off the ground. It contained all she would have for the next year. She packed, unpacked, and repacked it again. Finally, she had decided on one ankle-length dress, two long skirts, two white blouses with puffed sleeves and high collars buttoned at the neck, a blue woolen sweater, a chemise, and a few undergarments.

She was still thinking about her choices when she hefted up the bag. *I'll be wearing a nurse's uniform most of the time so it won't make much of a difference what I bring.* Bag in hand, she stood on the platform with her mother and stared at the side of the train where large black letters against a yellow background spelled "LONDON." *It's too late to change my mind now.*

When her mother reached for her with outstretched arms, Edith dropped the bag. Wrapping her arms around Louisa Cavell's boney frame, she felt the warmth of her mother's cheek next to hers. Struggling to hold back tears, she gave the older woman a farewell hug and kiss. For the first time, she noticed lines around the corners of her mother's mouth and eyes. Louisa's translucent skin was lined with blue veins, thin enough to be etched by a pencil.

"I promise to write to you every week," Edith said, holding the knobby fingers of Louisa's hand in hers. Seeing her mother's sad expression, she quickly added, "And I'll return home every holiday I can. Especially on your birthday."

"Do you really have to go to nursing school in Whitechapel? There are other places for you to train. Whitechapel is no place for a woman to be wandering about. I read about young women being murdered there all the time, and they can't find the killer," Louisa murmured.

"I know, but those women were prostitutes. Besides, I will be too busy with nurse's training to be wandering about."

Louisa put her hands on her daughter's shoulders and stared at her. She tried to memorize every detail: the blue-gray eyes that stared back, the plain white high-collared blouse decorated with a colorful striped neck tie, the Celtic Tara brooch that had been passed down from mother to daughter for generations in her family, the long, dark blue skirt just short enough to reveal a glimpse of ankles covered in black silk stockings, and the black lace-up shoes with thick heels. She decided this was not the time to chide her daughter about the shortness of her skirt.

"I knew that some day I would have to give you up, and that day is now."

Edith met her mother's eyes. "Please be happy for me. I know this is difficult for you, but I feel that this is the right path for me. I have never wanted to do something as much as this. You and father have prepared me well all these years, and now I will make you proud, I promise." She kissed her mother's cheek and smiled. "Don't worry so much."

"I am already proud of you, my dear. You have nothing more to prove."

Louisa watched her daughter tug the heavy cloth bag up the train stairs and disappear through the doorway. Her mind whirled back to earlier times when her high-spirited daughter laughed and ran with her two younger sisters and brother down Brownes Lane with hoops and sticks. She remembered how her daughter went from a child playing with dolls to being a fierce competitor at lawn tennis. Louisa knew even then that this daughter would be different from her other three children.

Edith found a seat near the window and pulled her bag close her. She snapped open her handbag and took a quick inventory: one pound, three shillings, a farthing, her train ticket, the address of the London hospital, and a letter of acceptance from Miss Eva Luckes, the matron of the nursing school, whom she was to meet.

She flipped up a wisp of hair that had come loose from the thick brown plait pulled back behind her head. At the sound of the train whistle, she looked out the dusty window. A cloud of steam billowed over her window, blocking her view of the platform. A second whistle sounded and the train suddenly lurched forward and began to move. Metal wheels screeched over metal tracks until it rolled into a rhythmical clickity-clack, clickity-clack.

Edith Cavell looked back and saw the dark-clad, lonely figure of her mother grow smaller and finally disappear in the steam and cloudy grayness. At the end of her mother's outstretched arm, like a symbol of truce between mother and daughter, she saw a white hanky waving back and forth.

— 2 —

MEETING MATRON LUCKES

"**C**ome in," called out a voice from inside the office. Edith looked at the imposing figure on the other side of the desk. "Please have a seat," said the barrel-shaped woman. "Good to meet you."

My God! She looks like Queen Victoria, Edith thought.

Matron Luckes patted the folder on the desk. "I have reviewed your files. Your application and references are excellent."

Edith unfastened her coat but kept it draped about her shoulders as she eased into the chair opposite the large wooden desk.

"Miss Cavell..." started Luckes, emphasizing the last syllable.

"It's CA-vell. It rhymes with gravel," Edith quickly corrected. "Not Ca-VELL, which rhymes with hell." Edith saw the matron's eyes flash a sting of irritation and she immediately felt embarrassed for making the correction.

"Miss CA-vell," said Luckes. "Your references say that you are intelligent, well educated, and capable. You are a little older than the other probationers, but I consider that to be in your favor. It is important to me that my probationers learn to be disciplined. We expect you to conform to all rules. Will that be a problem?"

Edith surveyed the woman. Luckes was about a decade older than she, had a high forehead, deep-set eyes, and thin, wispy eyebrows. Every part of her was heavy and round. She was dressed in a black uniform dress with a narrow, white-starched collar that seemed to cut off circulation to her apple-like face. Her brown hair was pulled tightly behind her head and plaited. A gauzy white muffin cap sat on top of the mound and bobbed back and forth as she spoke. There was a faint odor of perfumed soap about her. Edith cleared her throat.

"I learned discipline and rules from my father, who is an Anglican priest."

Luckes noticed Edith's high cheekbones, aquiline nose, and elegant long neck. She had a royal bearing that reminded Luckes of a painting she had once seen of the Egyptian Queen Nerfertiti. Edith's pale complexion stood in stark contrast to the thick, rich, brown hair piled neatly on her head.

"That's good. Very good," said Luckes. "We can teach you skills, but character and morals are taught at home. You must be an honest woman before you can be a decent nurse. A proper woman can bring order and goodness to nursing."

Miss Eva C. E. Luckes was appointed Matron of the London Hospital at the age of 26, and served there from 1880-1919.

Edith returned an agreeable smile. *I've listened to my father preach to me for years. What's another sermon or two?*

"Nursing at The London will be difficult. You will work long hours and have little time to yourself, but if you love to help others, and I mean with all of your heart, you will be compensated with the satisfaction that you are making a difference in people's lives."

Luckes paused to gauge the effect of what she had said. "We expect you to be punctual and reliable. There is only one way to do things and we will teach you that way. You must pay absolute attention. Only by constant repetition can you truly learn how to nurse satisfactorily. By performing drills, every soldier learns efficiency and order. Nurses must do the same."

Edith had the feeling that these introductory comments were not impromptu but had been said many times before. *How many other women have sat here and heard these very words? How many others had actually learned the "one way to do things" and completed the training?*

"You will have little or no social life. Frivolity will not be tolerated. Pranks are also frowned on. Neither alcohol nor tobacco is allowed. Men are never allowed in the nurses' quarters. If you are caught flirting with a physician or medical student, you will be immediately dismissed. No appeal on your behalf will help. It is also improper behavior to get too friendly with the domestics. They have their duties and you have yours. Were you planning on getting married at some time?"

The question caught Edith off guard. "I, well..." she stammered. "I hadn't thought of it just yet. I have no one in mind, if that's what you mean."

It was the first time Luckes had seen her new pupil lose her composure. "That's exactly what I mean."

I can tell by her tone of voice that she doubts my ability to comply with her rules. But I am here, and I plan to stay here. I can't go back. Edith locked her steel-blue eyes straight into those of Matron Luckes.

"I have long prayed about my choice to train as a nurse. I left my home after I cared for my father when he was ill. I am here because I want to be here. It's not a dalliance until I find a husband or another

The Royal London Hospital, known as "The London"
when Edith Cavell attended it .

career. My character and discipline have never been in question. I spent three months at the Fountain Fever Hospital doing preliminary nursing in preparation for this work."

Glancing up, Edith saw a sign on the wall behind Luckes that read, "PATIENTS COME FIRST."

Edith's voice softened. "I appreciate all that you are telling me, Matron. I believe I am answering a calling to work among the sick and those needing my help, and I am willing to dedicate myself and practice the self-denial necessary to fulfill that calling." She paused and added, "Just as you and Miss Nightingale have done. I want to follow the examples you both have set for me."

"Good. Good," said Luckes, obviously pleased with this response. "A few more things. You are not to wear your uniform off hospital grounds. You are to keep yourself and your uniform clean at all times." She stopped, raised her eyebrows, and stared at Edith's muddy dress and shoes. "Will that be a problem?"

"No," said Edith, following Luckes gaze. "I had a bit of an accident out on the road. A cart rode..." She was not allowed to finish.

"I see. It's quite obvious. You are expected to attend all tutorials and do well on your tests. There will be times when you may be too busy to eat. You will get tired. If you get sick, we have an infirmary for you to recover. Is there anything I've said that you do not understand or feel you cannot do?"

"It is all quite clear."

"I am very careful with whom I choose to be a probationer at The London, Miss Cavell. Miss Nightingale and I have developed a rigorous training program. More than half of those who enroll do not finish. The population we serve is very demanding. Here is an outline of our expectations." She slid a typewritten paper over the desk to Edith.

Regulations for the Training of a Probationer

1. *A personal interview.*
2. *A letter from the medical officer stating you are physically fit for duty.*
3. *During the probationary period, board will be provided but not laundry.*

4. *After the probationary period board and laundry will be provided at the hospital nurse's quarters.*

5. *Salary for the first year is £12, £20 for the second.*

6. *Night duty will be an essential part of the training.*

7. *Work hours are from 7:00 am to 9:20 pm with thirty minutes for supper.*

8. *Training will be for a period of two years, after which there will be a test of competency.*

9. *If character and qualifications are acceptable, a certificate of efficiency will be awarded. (There will be further instructions concerning this if the State Registration of Nurses is instituted.)*

Edith read the list and looked up. "This is all quite clear."

"Then please report to Tredegar House for your preliminary training. I will instruct the matron there to show you to your quarters and provide you with a uniform."

With that, Luckes planted her hands on the desk, pushed up her bulky frame, and then extended a puffy hand to Edith. "Welcome, Miss Cavell, to our family at The London. Consider this your new home. We will get to know each other better in the months to come. Every Tuesday night, I hold a tea with my students. I will see you there."

Edith smiled and gave the hand a strong grip. "I look forward to it."

As Luckes watched the back of Edith's muddy hem slide out the door, she felt uneasy. Was it defiance or strength she saw in Cavell's eyes? Was it self-possession or too much self-assurance? *If she can't take direction, she won't survive the probationary period at Tredegar House. That will be her trial by fire.* Matron Luckes prided herself in her ability to sense early on if a novice would be able meet her standards.

The London was Luckes' life. She lived, worked, and fought for support for the Nurses' Training School. In a recent meeting with the hospital board, she had dared to speak boldly. "The hospital is defined by its staff. You should be moving away from putting out fires to lighting them. The best way to predict the future is to create it—and you create it by strategy, structure, and resources." After this speech, they gave her enough authority to create the kind of nursing school she envisioned.

Edith was led to Tredegar House, where novice nurses began their training. Down the hallway, the silhouette of a matron moved toward her, and the shape held out her hand to Edith. "Welcome. I've been expecting you. Follow me to your room."

Edith was led down a dark hallway and then up two flights of narrow stairs. They passed a few doors before the matron stopped in front of one. She opened it and gestured for Edith to enter.

The room was small with peeling gray paint on the walls. Tall windows that rattled in their frames emanated a damp chill. In the middle of her bed sat a pile of neatly folded linen. Edith thumbed through the pile: two sheets, a pillowcase, a thin cotton blanket, a pink cotton uniform, and a starched apron.

"The toilet is down the hall. You will be sharing it with ten other probationers."

Edith looked about the tiny room, where three other beds were pressed against the walls. "We'll be falling over each other."

"Not to worry. After you are through with your work assignments and studying, you will only need enough room to fall into bed at night. Unpack and report for the tutorial downstairs in one hour dressed in your uniform. Do not be late. Miss Luckes hates lateness."

— 3 —

PROBATIONER

Matron Luckes entered the room. Lifting her wire-rimmed spectacles, she scanned the roster of her seven probationers. She already knew their background and personal details. Luckes fancied her role as their teacher, mother, drill sergeant, and disciplinarian. Her eyes lingered on each face as she called out the students' names. After the roll call, she addressed them.

"Before Florence Nightingale, there was no formal training for nurses. Now, thankfully, all that has changed. The work will be hard. You will have to perform some of the most difficult tasks that can be asked of anyone. To do this, nursing must be the most important thing in your life. If you can't make this commitment, you might as well leave now."

No one moved.

Luckes continued, "It is important that we train nurses who are not only technically proficient, but also have the proper moral and womanly traits. We are moving away from the days when nurses were ignorant, slovenly, drunken, and uncaring. We fully expect our nurses will religiously follow the four Ds of nursing: discipline, devotion, dedication, and duty. Next to address you is Dr. Swingle, a respected surgeon at The London."

Edith tugged at the tight waistband of her pink uniform. Her wrists and neck felt irritated from the starched cuffs and collar. *I wonder if he is the famous surgeon also known as Jack the Ripper.*

Dr. Swingle, moved to the front of the room and leaned against the heavy oak desk. "Welcome to one of the most reputable hospitals in East London. We are pleased that you have chosen to train here. We believe that all our nurses are Florence Nightingales. Women who are trustworthy, loving, and motherly make good nurses."

Edith noticed the light flash off his gold and onyx ring as he gestured. He wore a dark suit; a gold watch fob dangled from the waist to his pocket. His thinning hair was slicked back. Bushy muttonchops flared out from each cheek. He jingled coins in his pocket with one hand and gestured with the other as he spoke.

"Novice nurses are like raw army recruits. Both are untempred steel and must be moulded by the right amount of pressure. That is what we do here: develop good nursing soldiers. To keep order, all soldiers must understand that their officers have the ultimate authority. Officers give the orders and soldiers follow them. The same is true in the medical profession. The physicians are the ultimate authority and must be obeyed by the entire staff, especially the nurses. Disobedience is a serious error and may result in dismissal."

Dr. Swingle fell silent for a moment, as if searching for something else to say, but finally finished with, "I look forward to working with all of you," and moved to the side of the room.

Luckes' stiff black uniform swished as she stepped back to the front of the room.

"Thank you, Dr. Swingle, for taking your very precious time to come here and address my nurses." She turned back to the probationers. "I will be lecturing you on the topic of general nursing, but you will also learn about anatomy, physiology, and the causes and symptoms of diseases. When you are not in a tutorial, you will work on the wards. We will try to coordinate your lectures with your work.

Matron Luckes took a breath, gazed out at the young women sitting before her, and continued in her stern, deep voice, "Since cleanliness is the basis of health and good care, you will all be assigned to general cleaning duties when the ward work is slow. That will include such duties as washing the soiled dressings, sweeping, dusting, polishing, tending to the fireplaces, and laundry. Miss Nightingale believes cleanliness is the key to good health."

One novice leaned over to Edith and whispered, "I hope that doesn't include washing out Luckes' knickers." The vision of those knickers made Edith smile so broadly that she covered her mouth with her hand.

"There will be no talking while I am lecturing," said Luckes. She stared at the girl who made the comment and then went on. "In an effort to get to know you all better, I encourage you to join me every Tuesday night from seven to nine in the evening for what I call 'At Home' because this is your home now. We are all a family and must act like one. We will talk together and share tea and cakes. During your training here, I also require you to keep a diary of your thoughts and progress." She handed each girl a notebook.

Edith found that writing in her diary became a daily ritual. Every night before she went to sleep, she would rest the book on her knees and think about what to write. The first entries were more about the daily routine.

> *I have settled into the routine of a novice nurse. The wake-up bell sounds at 6 a.m. and I and my three roommates are dressed in fifteen minutes after our feet have touched the cold floor.*

She discovered that the hardest thing to write about was how nursing affected her emotionally. She didn't want to admit to any weaknesses, but neither could she lie. One night after a particularly difficult time with patients she wrote,

> *Every night now I sleep fitfully. My sleep is disturbed with sights of sickness. I can see people yellowed with disease, swollen bellies, and festering sores floating before me. I can smell the stench of their diseases. I have come to recognize many of them by the odor they give off. I am awakened to their cries of pain. I try to hold on and give the illusion that I am maintaining control. To relax, I think back to when I walked through my mother's garden as the wind blew through my hair and the scent of lilies and roses wafted about. But this is another world — I must learn to accept it. I will ask if any of my friends here suffer from the same nightmares.*

A month later she wrote,

> *I love learning the physiology of the body. It unlocks the secrets of how life functions within us. It helps me make sense of what we are doing and why.*

And in another entry,

> *We work under the strict scrutiny of more experienced nurses who demand perfection. Three novice nurses have already left. The sight of acute illness and death was too much for them.*

— 4 —
THE DRAWING

During these first few months, Edith formed two friendships. One was with Fanny Edgecomb, another novice nurse. They met the day Edith was assigned to a 56-bed ward. Edith had taken a few moments to kneel and pray over a patient who had had spinal surgery for paralysis the previous day, when she heard a voice come up behind her and felt a hand on her shoulder.

"Edith." The voice was soft, almost a whisper. "Have you been back to your room since yesterday?"

Edith raised her head and saw Fanny standing over her. "There's a time to sleep and a time to pray. This is a time to pray," answered Edith.

When the patient saw Fanny, he held out his Bible to her. "Look what she has done for me. Open it."

Fanny took it and opened it to the flyleaf. Beautifully etched on the page was a picture of an apple blossom. Beneath it were the words,

> *If thou canst hold thy peace and suffer, then shalt thou see*
> *without a doubt the help of the Lord.*

Fanny looked at Edith. "I must warn you that I am prepared to like you very much. I hope you approve."

"I do, but I must warn you. I have a made a hash of previous friendships."

Fanny, a lithe and attractive young woman, put her arm under Edith's arms and pulled her to her feet. "Not this one. You look awful. Let's go and get you washed and into a clean uniform."

A few days later, while at supper, Fanny confessed to Edith that she had wanted to get to know her before meeting her that day on the ward. "I hesitated to approach you because I was told you were a...well, a bit of a cold fish and that you had no sense of humor." Realizing how unkind it sounded, she quickly added, "I'm so sorry. Not that you weren't a nice fish. Oh, that's not what I meant to say either." Both laughed at the awkwardness. Fanny's eyebrows always reminded Edith of two brown caterpillars that moved nervously about when she was upset.

"Fanny, it's all right. I've always considered myself to be rather boring. I'm so glad you went fishing and reeled me in. Never mind all this. Let's have a glass of stout. The Crossman Brewery just donated a few kegs to us, and I managed to get the last two glasses from the barrel."

While sharing a glass of the dark amber ale, the two women learned more about each other. Fanny discovered that Edith was 30 and the oldest of four children; Edith learned that Fanny was 22 and one of 14 children.

Another probationer, Bessie Leonard, became Edith's second friendship. She was assigned with Edith to polish the brass plaques over each bed, the two large tea urns, and the brass banisters.

"How long did it take you to get used to the smell of yellow soap and carbolic acid on the wards?" asked Bessie while reaching inside a large brass urn and scrubbing out the brown stains.

"It doesn't bother me as much as the cabbage cooking in the kitchen," said Edith.

"How about the smell from those maggots in the big German longshoreman's leg?"

"You're right," said Edith. "That rotten flesh smell is worse than the cabbage. He'll lose that leg if he doesn't die of a blood infection first."

"Or if Dr. Swingle gets his hands on him."

Edith rubbed hard on the other brass urn. "After I made thirty beds last week, the ward nurse came by and ripped them all up. She ordered me to make them all over again."

"Why? Whatever for?" Bessie queried.

"She said the blue and white bedspread squares were uneven on each side because there were eight squares on one side and ten on the other instead of nine on each side." Edith shook her head in disbelief.

"Last Friday, I couldn't even find any bloody bedspreads," said Bessie. "By the end of the week, supplies are sparse around here."

"Maybe I should sign up for ward work on Fridays so I won't have to deal with the number of squares are on each side," said Edith.

The two women smiled and continued to share stories until both urns were gleaming. Edith learned that Bessie was a 25-year-old Roman Catholic from Australia. Although her thick brown hair always appeared frazzled with wisps sticking out all over, Edith thought Bessie attractive. But what Edith loved the most about Bessie was younger woman's hearty sense of humor and need for adventure.

"Soon," said Edith, "we'll be done with our probationary training. Then we'll have a day to ourselves. How about taking the tram into London and troll around the city?"

"A tram to London?" exclaimed Fanny, walking up to the two urn polishers. "If you two are going to bustle around the city for a day, count me in."

"Brilliant," said Edith. "You're in. What are you assigned to today?"

Edith was amused at the way Fanny pursed her lips before she spoke. "I'm to sweep and dust the wards today. They started using the fireplaces last week. Makes everything rather sooty. I'm going to collect some fresh rags."

"You know, I heard the other probationers have given the three of us a title," Edith shared with her friends.

"A title? You mean like some kind of Dickens' characters called Scrub, Rub, and Flub?"

"No, nothing like that. They call us 'The Three Graces.'"

"Like 'Hail Mary, full of grace'?" asked Fanny, folding her hands in a gesture of prayer.

Edith shot a glance over to Fanny. "I've been called worse." She reached into her pocket and pulled out a single sheet of paper. "I have something to show you."

The other two stared at a cartoon ink drawing of a probationer with a broom under one arm and a bucket spilling water on her feet. Stuffed under a Dora cap, her hair was skewed to one side and disheveled. Her starched apron was stained and she had a harried look on her dirty face. Underneath the drawing were the words, "A slave."

Bessie looked up. "And which of us is this, Edith?"

"It could be any of us, but can't you tell by the hair that it's you?" said Fanny.

"A slave," read Bessie, holding her head sideways to see the paper in Fanny's hands. "Brilliantly done."

"What is brilliantly done?" asked a stern voice behind them.

A large hand belonging to the ward sister reached between them and grabbed the paper out of Fanny's hands. Many of the ward sisters were senior nursing students who felt they were doing the probationers a favor by berating them to make them tough. They were encouraged to report all infractions to the Matron. This ward sister was particularly feared for her over-zealous monitoring. She looked at the drawing and back at the three flushed faces. "Who is responsible for this?"

Frustrated by the menial work she was required to do as a probationer, Edith Cavell drew this cartoon depicting her role as "A Slave." (From St. Mary's Church, Swardeston, England.)

No one moved. The room fell silent. Finally, Edith spoke up. "I am. It was just a bit of fun after all the cleaning we have been doing."

"If you have time to do this, obviously we aren't keeping you busy enough. I'm giving this to Miss Luckes. You can discuss your joke with her." The ward sister marched away with a firm grip on the drawing.

Bessie stuck her hands in her pockets. "What do you think Miss Luckes will do about it?"

"I never thought a simple drawing could create such a stir," said Edith, stunned at the ward sister's response.

"She will probably just make you scrub out a few more brass urns," offered Fanny.

Edith's throat tightened. "Or dismiss me for insubordination."

— 5 —
LONDON HOLIDAY

Finally, their initial probationary period was over and the three young women—Edith, Fanny, and Bessie—had a free day to themselves. There had been no word from Luckes about Edith's offensive drawing. They guessed that the ward sister might have had a change of heart and not given it to Matron Luckes. They still had to face her for a post-probationary evaluation, but for now, they were free.

The three met in front of the hospital to begin their day in London. They climbed up the narrow metal stairs of the horse-drawn tram. When the three excursioners reached out to hand their penny fares to the conductor, he withdrew his hand and smiled, "You nurses do enough. This ride is on me."

Once seated on top of the tram, they giggled and pointed out what interested them as they looked out over the busy streets. After much discussion, Fanny wanted to go to Trafalgar Square, Bessie to Leicester Square, and Edith to Westminster Abbey.

By mid-afternoon, as they emerged from Westminster Abbey, Fanny noticed dark clouds moving in from the north. When they got to Charing Cross, thunder rolled over them, bringing in heavy drops of rain. They ducked into a shop doorway and watched a cyclist, anxious to get out of the rain, bump past them over the lumpy street. The wind flipped and folded the newspaper he precariously held over his head with one hand while trying to steer with the other.

"We can't walk about Leicester Square in this," said Fanny, shaking rain off her shawl. "And besides, isn't this Tuesday, when we should be attending Miss Luckes' homey gathering of weak tea and stale buns?"

Edith said she hadn't been to tea in a few weeks and needed to get back into the good graces of the Matron. They agreed it would be best to leave the theater district for another day and take the tram back.

On the way back, a thick fog drifted in. It swirled around the street lamps in great smoky patches. All color was sucked from the landscape and everything turned into murky shades of black and gray. Dark shadows of people, buildings, and lamps appeared and then disappeared. A dog came to the side of the street, sniffing the air as their horses passed by, and was then swallowed up into the thickness. A man was visible and then disappeared down a side street, the sound of his boots muffled on the stones.

"A devil of a fog," muttered Fanny as she huddled closer to her friends. A cold mist formed moist droplets on their faces and hair. The dark hide of the horse pulling the tram glistened silver as they passed under the gas lamps.

Edith again thought of the women who had been strangled and mutilated here. They had been found with their throats cut, their abdomens slit open, and their kidneys and wombs surgically removed. She shuddered at this thought and felt comforted by the hollow sound of the horses' hooves clopping on the cobblestoned streets as they pulled the tram in a slow, rhythmical pace back to Aldgate Station in Whitechapel.

Bessie turned to Fanny. "What did you think of Trafalgar Square?"

"I never thought Lord Nelson's statue would be on a column 18 feet tall. Did you know he only had one eye and one arm?"

"Looks like Dr. Swingle got hold of him," said Bessie, wiping the dampness from her face with her white handkerchief. "I wonder what someone would have to do to get a statue like that in Trafalgar Square."

"Oh, nothing much," said Edith, pulling her coat closer around her shoulders. "Just fight a country that was trying to take over all of Europe and get shot by the enemy." She looked over toward Bessie. "And die young. He was only 47 when he died."

"No, thanks," said Bessie. "I'd rather marry Swingle."

Fanny laughed. "After a year of being married to him, you might prefer being shot. You might even shoot yourself. What about you, Edith? Fancy yourself being in love?"

Edith felt awkward when the subject of men came up. She had never learned much about the culture of courting and all that came with it—its own special language, gestures, and behaviors. She liked men well enough, but felt as if they had their place and she had hers. She looked into the faces of her friends, who waited for her answer, and then out into the fog.

"I can't see myself tied to some man who thinks my brain should be as thin as my waist. Men seem more concerned with what's on a woman's head rather than what's in it."

Fanny smiled. "But you have a fair face and slender figure. Any man would be keen to marry you."

Edith chuckled. "Nonsense. I don't think there's a man who would tolerate my wish to be independent. Anyway, we would probably drive each other daft. So I shan't torture some poor chap by marrying him. Florence Nightingale never married. Look what she accomplished by being devoted to her calling. I'm not Miss Nightingale, but I plan to follow her example, challenge myself, and see what I can accomplish on my own without having to waste my time catering to the needs of a man."

"But don't you want to have children of your own?" asked Bessie, eyebrows raised, not believing what she had just heard.

"I have resigned myself to the fact that I will probably not be a mother, but I will be satisfied to mother those who need nurturing."

The tram stopped. "Aldgate," called out the driver.

* * * * *

Once back in their rooms, the three young women changed clothes and went to the dining room for supper. After eating, they entered the living room, where Miss Luckes would be coming to sit in her substantial upholstered chair.

A large silver teapot and small white teacups with simple fluting around their edges had been placed on the side table. Scones and teacakes were set out on silver plates. Each woman took a cup of tea and a single cake. Fanny and Edith sat together on a small, hard sofa, but Bessie plopped herself on the floor, spreading her full skirt over her outstretched legs. A few times, she turned to Edith and Fanny, scrunched up her shoulders, and gave them an impish grin. More probationers entered, took their tea, and found chairs or couches to sit on. Some sat on floor rugs and others on cushions, as there was never enough furniture for all of them.

A tall mahogany grandfather clock stood in the corner. As the gold hands of the clock clicked past the VII, Miss Luckes walked boldly into the room. The hum of quiet conversations silenced when she entered. Her hair was piled up under her cap and fixed with multiple hairpins, daring any strand of hair to stray out of place.

The stout matron sat on her designated chair, crossed her thick ankles, and forced a smile at the probationers. The faint, sweet odor of perfumed soap emanated from her. Everyone waited for her to begin. She always set the agenda and mood for these "visits," as she liked to call them. Sometimes she spoke about how best to handle a difficult patient. Other times she would open up the conversation to the group and let them ask their questions about a rule. Often the conversation centered on the difficulty of dealing with certain physicians. Occasionally Edith or someone else was allowed to play the piano, and they would all sing. But this evening, everyone sensed something was different.

With her eyes focused on Edith, Miss Luckes pulled out Edith's drawing. Her eyes were like flames. Edith's cheeks turned crimson. Luckes held the drawing high in the air for everyone to see. A few giggled and others smirked.

The Matron's breath came in catches.

She waited until the room became silent. "It would appear that some of you think this drawing is amusing. Does anyone here think this truly represents what nursing is all about?"

Nobody moved or spoke. Only the slow ticking of the grandfather clock broke the silence.

"Tonight we are going to discuss how symbols define our profession to society. After we are done here, I want the talented artist of this drawing to stay and have a private chat with me."

— 6 —

THE IMAGE OF A NURSE

Instead of the usual casual evening discussions, Miss Luckes lectured about the importance of maintaining the professional image of nursing. She explained how she had diligently worked to overcome the public's perception that nurses are not like the Sairy Gamp character Charles Dickens described in his book, *The Life and Adventures of Martin Chuzzlewit*. There, he depicted nurses as repugnant domestic servants who worked with a dust rag in one hand and a bottle of booze in the other.

When the clock chimed nine, everyone was relieved to be dismissed. There were a few quiet words spoken among the women before they left the room.

"What are you going to say to her?" whispered Fanny to Edith.

"As little as possible. I'll just let her rant at me; then I'll apologize and leave."

"But what if she dismisses you from the school?"

Miss Luckes' voice interrupted their conversation. "Miss Edgecombe, you may leave now. Miss Cavell, I will talk to you privately. We need to have a little chat."

Edith and her friend gave each other stiff looks. "I'll talk to you later," whispered Fanny.

Miss Luckes looked into the penetrating azure eyes of her probationer. She held up the cartoon drawing with the words "A Slave" written across the bottom. "This drawing tells me you have not grasped the important concepts of nursing. I thought you came to us with a keener understanding and a higher level of maturity. This indicates a somewhat superficial nature. Do you think the work of nursing is something to be joked about?"

Edith felt a cold knot in her chest. "Miss Luckes, I apologize if my drawing offended you. The truth is that we all came here to learn how to care for the sick and dying, but so much of what we do is scrub, wash, and polish."

Miss Luckes reached over and picked up a small book. "I want to read you something." She opened up to a passage from Florence Nightingale's *Notes on Nursing: What It Is and What It Is Not.* She cleared her throat.

It cannot be necessary to tell a nurse that she should be clean, or that she should keep her patient clean,–seeing that the greater part of nursing consists in preserving cleanliness.

The matron looked at Edith and flipped to another passage marked with a piece of paper.

The duty of every nurse certainly is prevention. Fever, or hospital gangrene, or pyoemia, or purulent discharge of some kind may else supervene. If she allows her ward to become filled with the peculiar close fetid smell, so apt to be produced among surgical cases, especially where there is great suppuration and discharge, she may see a vigorous patient in the prime of life gradually sink and die where, according to all human probability, he ought to have recovered. The nurse must ever be on the watch, ever on her guard, against the want of cleanliness, foul air, want of light, and of warmth.

Luckes continued, "Miss Nightingale has developed this manual to define what a nurse must be, what she must do, and what she must know. If you cannot agree with her, nursing is not the right career for you."

"Surely you won't dismiss me over one drawing," Edith blurted.

"Miss Cavell, I want you to understand why we do what we do. We are struggling to present the image of nursing in the most positive way possible. If we do not succeed in this, we will lose the faith and trust of the public. Everything we have worked for will be lost. Do you understand this?"

"I just thought a touch of creativity would lighten the load a bit."

"We are not looking for creativity. We are looking for conformity. I expect my nurses to follow the rules and be more reconciled to their duty than you seem to be. I want to see more self-control and dignity from you. You are not working up to your capabilities. I expect you to put your whole heart into this work."

"Your trust in me has not been misplaced, Matron Luckes. May I please borrow Miss Nightingale's book?"

The book was handed over to her. "You will have another evaluation, Miss Cavell, during which time we will discuss your progress." Then, with a single wave of her hand, "You are dismissed."

"Thank you, Miss Luckes," said Edith. "I appreciate your time."

Edith went to her room and took out her diary. In it, she wrote,

I try very hard to fit in, when the truth is that I seem to be made to stand out. There are codes of behavior to which I must learn to conform. With God's help, I will walk closer to the path of Miss Nightingale and will show Miss Luckes that I can stay the course and make her proud.

Then she wrote,

Lives of great ones all remind us
We can make our lives sublime,
And departing leave behind us
Footprints in the sands of time.
                    —From A Psalm of Life, *by H.W. Longfellow*

Edith was about to open Nightingale's book when Bessie bounded into the room.

"You won't believe it! While I was sewing up a tear in my uniform, I dropped the needle. Suddenly, I felt a prick in my foot and realized I had stepped on it."

"Oh, no," said Edith, "Should I try to pull it out for you?"

"No, I mean, thanks, but it was stuck in so deep I couldn't see it. So do you know what happened?"

"It's still in there?"

"No. I mean it was there, so I went to the infirmary. You won't believe this. They found it by putting my foot in a new machine. They called it a..." Her eyes rolled up as if she could find the word on the ceiling. " A...Roentgen machine. That's what they called it. Strange name, don't you think? The hospital just purchased it. They turned it on, with my foot in it, of course, and took a picture. They could see the needle as plain as day. I mean, they could see right through my foot to where it was, and then they just poked with the forceps and pulled it out. Just as nice as you please. Can you imagine, actually seeing inside someone's body? They said it had just been invented."

Bessie suddenly stopped talking when she saw the flat expression on her friend's face.

"Are you all right? You didn't let Miss Luckes get you down now, did you? You aren't dismissed or anything of the sort are you?"

"No, I'm not dismissed, but she gave me a stern lecture about the professionalism of nursing and said she would evaluate me again at a later date. I'll be all right. Let me see your foot."

Bessie removed her shoe, stuck her bare foot in Edith's face, and wiggled her toes. "See! It's gone!"

"Who invented it? A doctor?"

"What doctor?" Bessie looked puzzled.

"The one who invented the machine, silly."

"They said it was a German man named Roentgen. I don't think he was a doctor, but some kind of scientist.

Edith found the tiny puncture mark. "Did it hurt?"

"The needle?"

"Bessie, I'm sure the needle hurt. I mean the machine."

"Oh, no. It didn't hurt at all. There was a bright flash–like they had taken a picture. You could see the bones right through my flesh." She removed her foot from Edith's face and examined the tiny puncture. "I should like to work with a woman doctor for a change. I'll bet they aren't so pompous and don't yell at the nurses."

Bessie pulled on her stocking and fitted her broad foot into her sturdy shoe.

"Or pinch your bottom and stare at your bosom," said Edith.

Bessie smiled. "Oh, that's all right with me–if the doctors are handsome." She winked and left with a flourish. "Ta, ta."

* * * * *

From that day on, Edith's friends noticed a change in her. Edith scrubbed, washed, and polished without a word of complaint. Once, while she was washing dressing cloths in soda crystals and soaking them in carbolic acid, Fanny noticed her hands. Edith's fingers were red and cracked at the knuckles from the harsh soaps and disinfectants; her nails were ragged and worn down.

"Edith, you have to ask the matron to take you off dressing duty. Your hands are breaking down from too much washing and disinfecting."

Edith did not look up. "They will heal in due time."

Her two friends worried about her. They wondered if Edith was having an emotional breakdown. They noticed she was working late into the evening on the wards, often missed meals, lifted, and turned patients by herself.

"She barely weighs more than five stone," said Bessie murmured.

"You are right," said Fanny. "She's not a very sturdy woman." But neither friend could persuade Edith to see a doctor or take a day of rest.

Finally, the day came when Edith and her friends completed their probationary period and passed the dreaded examinations.

Edith still had to endure Miss Luckes' final evaluation. A graduation ceremony was held to officially recognize the success of the probationers. During the ceremony, Edith stood with her class in the center of the great hospital hall. She raised her right hand and along with her classmates, recited the Florence Nightingale oath:

> *I solemnly pledge myself before God and in the presence of this assembly to pass my life in purity and to practice my profession faithfully. I will abstain from whatever is deleterious and mischievous, and will not take, or knowingly administer any harmful drug. I will do all in my power to elevate the standard of my profession and will hold in confidence all personal matters committed to my keeping; and all family affairs coming to my knowledge in the practice of my calling. With loyalty will I endeavour to aid the physician in his work and devote myself to the welfare of those committed to my care.*

At the end of the ceremony, Edith's eyes glistened with pride as Matron Luckes pinned a badge to her uniform, officially identifying her as being past her probationer status.

Graduates were allowed a few days of vacation, but Edith continued her daily schedule without taking a break.

She wrote in her diary,

The nurses refer to us as "Probies." No matter. My favorite clinical rotation is on the paediatric orthopaedics ward. My previous experience as a governess has helped me be proficient in paediatrics. Now that London Hospital has a Roentgen machine, the surgeons are developing new methods to correct paediatric deformities. I think I have progressed well enough in my training so that Miss Luckes accepts my capabilities.

I find it interesting that each nurse has something in particular in their work that they find bothersome. For some, it is the sight of a purulent abscess or draining fistula. For others, it is the handling of gelatinous sputum that gets coughed up by those afflicted with pneumonia and consumptive lung diseases.

Most of us still get choked up with the odor of defecation or vomitus. I must confess that although I have come to accept the difficulty of those maladies and more, I am still fearful of being with those who are afflicted with various infectious diseases like tuberculosis, scarlet fever, cholera, and typhoid. I know that nurses seldom acquire these diseases, but I am still hesitant. I must set about to conquer this fear if I am to succeed and graduate. But can I overcome this fear? Will I be strong enough to pass the test when it comes?

THE MAIDSTONE TYPHOID EPIDEMIC

I t was six o'clock when Miss Luckes entered the dining room where the nurses were eating breakfast. She stood at the head of the table, waiting until all eyes focused on her.

"We have a difficult situation on our hands. Miss Plowman has come from the town of Maidstone with some troubling news. I will let her explain it to you." She stepped aside, allowing the tall, slender woman to come forward.

Miss Plowman was dressed in a royal blue nursing uniform and had a military bearing. An insignia on her uniform marked her as a nursing superintendent and made her look smartly official. She wore other medals Edith could not make out from where she was sitting. Plowman spoke with confidence.

"This August, during the hop-picking season, two migrant workers got sick and were brought to our hospital in Maidstone. They were diagnosed with typhoid fever. By the ninth of September, we had 117 cases on our hands. Now our hospital is overwhelmed with more than 600 typhoid cases. If we cannot quickly make the water supply safe, we are expecting that number to double. Thirteen have already died. We expect there will be many more."

There was a collective gasp from the students.

"We have patients lying on stretchers in schools and in mission rooms provided by the Salvation Army, and we are now relying on tents. We desperately need volunteer nurses from the various London hospitals to help us care for these patients until we can get this epidemic under control."

Miss Luckes took over. "I needn't remind you that Maidstone is only 40 miles southeast from here. It is very likely that the migrant workers who caused this may have come from the Whitechapel area. If this epidemic is not contained, we can expect it to reach London and cause death in disastrous proportions. I am asking for volunteers to help Miss Plowman and the physicians to treat those poor souls and keep this disease contained."

Edith looked around her. Everyone sat upright and stared at the two speakers, but no one moved. The aroma of eggs, hot cereal, coffee, and tea hung in the air.

Edith stood up. "I will go."

Luckes smiled at her and nodded. Another nurse stood and then another. Six in all from The London volunteered to join the nurses recruited from other London hospitals.

After breakfast, the new nurses were given only a few moments to gather some personal belongings. They then boarded a bus that stopped at other hospitals to pick up volunteers and proceeded on to Maidstone.

The first thing they noticed when they arrived was that the streets were deserted. There were yellow notices with the bold headings "Warning to the Inhabitants!" pinned to the walls of the buildings. Underneath the heading was an announcement of the typhoid epidemic.

All water and milk is to be boiled before drinking. The town council has opened a public laundry to wash and disinfect all clothing and bedding from houses in which there are cases of typhoid.

A dormitory for the nurses had been set up in a grammar school. One nurse looked at the thin canvas army stretchers and single army blanket folded on top. "It's the middle of October. Looks like we won't be any warmer here than we were in the nurses' quarters."

A physician walked in. He was business-like in his manner and spoke without emotion. "Welcome, ladies. Please follow me to the West Kent Hospital across the street."

He took them to a meeting room in the hospital. While they were still standing, he moved to the front of the room, turned, and addressed them.

"I want you to know what you will be dealing with. The typhoid epidemic we are experiencing is most likely due to drinking water contaminated by the feces of migrants who come seasonally to work in the area. The Medical Officer of Health will explain how that could have happened. "

He peered at the young women. " Be sure to drink only the water we provide. How many of you have worked with typhoid fever before?"

Half the nurses raised their hands. "I see. That's good. For the rest of you, here is a brief explanation. If you need to know more details, I am sure the more knowledgeable nurses will fill you in. Typhoid has an incubation period of two to three weeks. The first symptoms are fever, general malaise, abdominal pain, diarrhea, and mental confusion, most likely from dehydration. As the disease progresses, there will be rose-colored spots on the abdomen. Once they appear, the patient usually progresses to intestinal perforation and hemorrhage and death."

He took a deep breath, and continued. "Ladies, you need to brace yourselves for what you will experience. We expect that at least ten percent of the population affected will die. The most at risk unfortunately are the children and the elderly. Are there any questions?"

"Where will we be assigned?" asked one of the nurses.

"Some of you will be assigned to the hospitals and the schools where we have cots set up, and others will be assigned to tents and homes. If you have a preference, please let us know. Now, we must get you to work straightaway."

"Is there any chance that a vaccine may be produced to stop the spread of the disease?" asked Caroline Bell, a nurse who had sat on the bus beside Edith and had placed her bag on the stretcher next to hers.

"Possibly. Professor Almroth Wright is close to perfecting one. In addition, we have cut off the water supply at what we believe is the source of contamination, although we are unsure of how widespread it really is."

Edith was assigned to the children's ward. One of the children she noticed was a five-year-old girl named Lillian, who was particularly distressed. Edith bent down to calm the child.

"Lillian, I am Nurse Edith, but you can call me Edie. I am here to help you get better."

The child's skin was bright red with fever. She spoke through dry, cracked lips in a thin voice. "I'm...I'm burning up, Miss Edie. Thirsty. So thirsty."

She shook with rigours so intense the stretcher rattled on the wooden floor. Edith dipped some towels in cold water, folded them and placed them on the child's brow and neck, and armpits and groin. She gave the child sips of cool water. A rancorous, watery, brown liquid oozed from between the child's legs and down onto the floor.

"I'm...I'm so sorry, nurse... I mean, Edie. I...couldn't help it. If my mum knew, she, she... would spank me proper. Please...you won't tell her will you?"

Edith brushed the child's matted red hair back from her forehead. "Lillian, as long as you are here with me, you are my child. No one will be spanked. Once I get you cleaned up properly, I will get some sugar water for you. Would you like that?"

"Y...Yes, Thank you...Edie. Do...d...do you think I will g...get better? I don't w...want to m...m...make them s...sad."

This was difficult for Edith. She had seen death often enough, but it was so different with a child. Children usually worried less for themselves and more for their parents. Edith continued applying cool cloths and hummed in hushed, soothing tones. When Lillian's fever subsided and the tremors stopped, she fell into a deep sleep.

The nurses worked fourteen to sixteen hours a day, bathing the children, taking their temperatures, charting their pulses, cleaning their night clothes and bedding, and preparing what little food they could eat.

Miss Plowman came to the grammar school dormitory and found Edith sitting on her stretcher with her elbows propped on her knees and her head resting in her hands. The nursing supervisor didn't know if she was resting, sleeping, or praying. She put her hand on Edith's stooped shoulder.

"Edith, are you well?"

"Oh, quite so. I just haven't had much sleep and I must go back to the children's ward tonight. One of the night nurses is sick and can't work."

"Edith, this may not be a good time to ask you this, but..."

"Is there a problem with my work? Because surely if there is..."

"Just the opposite. I noticed the remarkable work you have done on the children's ward and how you managed the patients and staff. Many of the nurses refused to work the children's ward for, well...for obvious reasons."

Plowman sat down beside Edith. "Actually, I have another assignment for you. Since you come from The London and are familiar with the East End population, I'd like you to take charge of another unit. We have set up three hospital tents in which we are placing some of the hop-pickers. Since many of them come from your area, I hoped you would take the assignment. You will have a mix of new and experienced nurses to help you."

"But the children trust me now. I would hate to leave them. Surely it would be easier to find nurses who could work with these people than to find nurses who want to work with the children," Edith protested.

"We do have a few nurses who just arrived who are willing to care for the children. It's just that we need someone with your abilities to manage the care in these tents."

Edith sighed. "Miss Plowmen, are we getting any closer to stopping the epidemic? We simply can't continue at this pace. Is it slowing down at all?"

"The British Institute of Public Health has approved a new treatment that they believe will purify the water. It's an experiment using chlorine of lime. They were not quite ready to use it publicly, but we are in such dire circumstances that they are willing to push on and try it here. As for Professor's Wright's vaccine, they are trying it out first on the staff at the local asylum, and if it is successful, we can inoculate the rest of the population. In the meantime, they have closed the schools and churches and have transferred all court sessions to Canterbury. We are not allowing any public gatherings except where patients are being treated."

Plowman looked at the pale, weary figure sitting next to her on the stretcher. "I will find a nurse to cover the children's ward for you tonight so that you can get a good's night rest. Will you consider this new assignment and report back to me in the morning?"

"I will take the assignment, Miss Plowman," Edith said in a firm, quiet voice.

The next morning Edith went to the children's ward to say goodbye to her young charges. She first went to Lillian.

"Hello, Lilli." She crouched beside the child's cot and stroked the disheveled red hair away from her face.

"Oh, Edie, you are late today. I've been waiting for you. The doctor said my mum can come and take me home in a few days. I want to so much to go home, but I will miss you and…"

"Lilli, I too have some news. I will be working at another place and must leave you and the other children. Not to worry, though. There will be other wonderful nurses who will take care of you and the others. You will always be safe and never left alone."

The child took Edith's hand and stroked it with the tip of her fingers. "Will you come to see me again?"

Edith hugged Lilli's thin body. "I will, and I promise to bring a toy, that is, if you haven't left for home by then."

* * * * *

O utside the hospital's entrance, three heavy brown canvas tents were set up and filled with stretchers. When Edith opened the tent flap, the odor of rotting flesh, vomitus, diarrhea, urine, festering sores, and carbolic acid made her draw back. She gagged and took some deep breaths to regain her composure. She felt her pulse race.

This will be the ultimate test of whether I can overcome my fear of infectious diseases. If I can do this…no, I must do this.

Beads of sweat formed on her brow. Looking up, she saw a dozen nurses standing to the side of the tent. They were watching her and waiting for her instructions. She stared back at them. Then she heard a her father's voice quoting a Bible verse to her: "In God I have put my trust; I will not fear what flesh can do unto me."

Edith straightened up, took a deep breath, flipped open the tent flap, and with a flourish and a smile, she strode inside.

It took a minute for her eyes to adjust to the dim light. Oil lamps dangled from ropes tied to braces in the ceiling, sending shadows over the rows of emaciated bodies lying on stretchers. She bent over one man.

His skin was peeling and his mouth was covered with oozing sores. Crusts around his eyes prevented him from opening them. He lay in a dejected heap. Flies circled around the soiled rags that covered his body.

In the stretcher next to his, another man was raving in Irish. Edith recognized the word "thirst" in his rambling speech. Groans and cries for help came from various areas of the tent. Some were too weak to cry out.

Her eyes caught sight of two men who looked familiar to her. She bent over one cot. "Are you Henry?" she asked him, then pointed to the man in the next stretcher. "And is that Jack?"

The man strained his sunken, hollow eyes. "You're Miss Edith. I remember you from home. From..." He choked, gave a racking cough, and spat out a bloodied lump of sputum on the tent ground cover. He regained his breathing and rasped, "...from St. Mary's, where your father is the vicar. Me and Jack...came here to work, there being no work in Nor'ich to speak of." He looked at the man, built like a bull, strapped to the stretcher next to his and then back at Edith.

"He's in a bad way, isn't he?"

Edith looked over at Jack. He was delirious and tugging at his restraints. She removed the sheet from Jack's abdomen and saw blotchy, red spots. "Henry, I'm afraid your brother is very ill."

Henry grabbed her arm as if he were drowning and it was his lifeline. "You have to help him make it. He's got a wife and two children at home. He's my twin brother. He can't die."

When he saw the look on her face, he knew what it meant, and put his head down and wept.

"Jack, I'm so sorry. I'll send a nurse over to be with you and your brother."

Edith left the pair, walked outside, and organized duties for her nurses. She assigned one nurse to the Norfolk men. "Right now," she said pointing to Jack. "He's the sickest, and I fear he will soon die. Keep me informed of his condition."

She set up a tentative routine for shift changes, assigned a nurse to take inventory of the supplies and food, and arranged for all the others nurses to take turns emptying the waste-filled buckets next to each stretcher.

Once Edith had her staff in place, she walked about to match her roster of names to the patients on the stretchers, making notes of their condition. When she got to the two men from Norwich, Jack was being carried out on a stretcher with a sheet over his body.

Henry was sobbing. He repeated over and over. "Oh, God, no! What will I do now? What will his wife do?"

Edith sat beside the distraught man, held his leathery hand, and offered a prayer for Jack's soul and Henry's healing.

* * * * *

By Christmas, new cases had slowed, and many of the emergency quarters, which included the tents, had closed down. The new water treatment of chlorinated lime had been successful. Professor's Wright's vaccine trial had also been effective and many of the population were inoculated. The following three-week period, only one person died. Some of the nurses had already left, and Edith knew it was time for her to do the same. When Miss Plowman found Edith, she was packing.

"Please, Edith," the nurse supervisor begged. "Stay just one more night. We are having a reception to honor the nurses who volunteered here. Dress in a clean uniform and please come. I promise you won't be disappointed."

The town indeed put on a grand affair for the nurses. Each nurse was received by the Mayor of Maidstone, and directed to a prominent place on the second balcony. Looking down onto the stage, Edith recognized the Mayor of London, but did not recognize the eight additional mayors from surrounding towns who flanked the London mayor on each side.

To start the ceremony, the Mayor of Maidstone stood to make a speech. "These women," he said, pointing to the uniformed nurses in the balcony, "took care of 1,847 cases of typhoid."

The audience gave a collective gasp.

"Of those, 130 people died."

The Mayor waited until the murmur settled down. Then his voice rose and he took on the cadence of a preacher. "It is only because of these dedicated nurses that more did not succumb. This could have been an epidemic of unspeakable proportions but..." he made another sweeping gesture with his arm, pointing to the balcony, "...because of the dedication of these wonderful women, the Maidstone typhoid epidemic was dealt with and contained.

He allowed his words to float out over the room. "Were it not for their tireless work, the whole country might have been infected. They prevented a total and devastating disaster."

The Mayor motioned to Miss Plowman. "Miss Plowman is the supervisor who went out, recruited, and managed this team of nurses. She will now come to the podium and individually award them with the distinguished Silver Medal of Maidstone."

Miss Plowman walked to the center of the stage and called each nurse by name, asking them to step to the stage to accept their awards. When it was Edith's turn, she recognized the medal as being identical to the one Miss Plowman had worn on her uniform the first day she came to recruit them.

Caroline Bell, who had become Edith's friend, sat next to her during the ceremony. After each nurse had received her award, Caroline leaned over to Edith and whispered.

"A bit pompous, all of this, don't you think?"

Edith inspected the round, bronzed medal attached to a ribbon with brown and yellow stripes. She flipped it over and read the inscription etched into the back: *With gratitude to E. Cavell- for loving services, 1897.*

Keeping her face pointed toward the stage, she talked out of the side of her mouth to her friend. "I don't feel that what we did merits this much of a ceremony. We were just doing what nurses are supposed to do. But at least we will have the medals to decorate our uniform as a remembrance."

Caroline answered back from the side of her mouth. "I heard they are going to have music and refreshments after this and they are going to show us a cinematograph." She paused. "What's a cinematograph?"

"I don't know," said Edith, "but I can't wait around to find out. I have to be back at the hospital tonight by nine. I leave tomorrow morning. Before I leave, I must visit a little friend of mine and give her a toy I promised."

* * * * *

The following morning, Edith made her way to Lillian's home. When the door opened, the little girl ran to Edith and flung her arms around her.

"Oh, Edie! Edie! You came back just like you said you would. Look at how much better I am," said the child as she twirled around on her toes.

"I brought you the toy I promised," said Edith holding out a toy doll dressed like a nurse. "This is for you to remember me by."

Lillian hugged her new doll. "I will always remember you. Will you promise to remember me?"

Edith returned the hug. "I will never forget you, but now I must return to London."

The child's eyes widened. "Will you see the queen?"

"Oh, no, my little friend. But I can assure you that I will be seeing someone very much like her."

The Maidstone Medal awarded to Edith Cavell for her work
with the typhoid epidemic in Maidstone, England (front and back).

— 8 —

THE MAKING OF A CAREER

"You should have left it alone? Now I'll have to feed it," said the mother, staring at the newborn baby girl, kicking her tiny pink feet in Edith's arms.

Edith had just removed a mucous plug from the minutes-old baby and watched her skin turn from a bluish tinge to a healthy pink. She wrapped the squirming child in a soft blanket and nestled it in the mother's arm.

"Why would you say that? Look at her, she's perfectly beautiful."

"There's no hope for her or for me. I'm destitute. My husband couldn't find work, so he took to drink and then disappeared. Last winter, both my girls died of pneumonia. The only thing good to come out of this birth is that I get to lie in a clean bed in a warm room and eat decent meals for a few days."

Edith had heard this story recounted many times before in her maternity rotation.

"Alice, the baby is beautiful…"

She was interrupted by the mother's sobs. "Oh, why couldn't we both have died? It would have been the merciful thing for both of us."

"I know this is hard, but give me a day to try to sort this out for you. I'll be back."

Edith went to Miss Luckes and explained the pitiful situation.

"I'm willing to have a part of my salary taken out to support them if we could take the mother and child in. The mother can work in the laundry and linen room."

Luckes had been approached many times before by students who pleaded on behalf of a destitute patient. "Edith, we can't save them all. We do what we can, and I know it sometimes isn't enough. I'm hesitant to set up a precedent for this. Every patient in this hospital lives in poverty." Edith's eyes locked onto Luckes.'

"Isn't there a difference between just caring *for* a patient and truly caring about a patient? I would think that Miss Nightingale would choose the latter, and judging from the sign in your office that reads, *Patients come first*, I believe you would agree with her."

Miss Luckes looked away.

Edith continued. "I know this requires some thought. May I approach you about it again this evening during tea at Homes?"

Miss Luckes looked back into Edith's steady eyes and could not turn away.

"I'm not sure... maybe we can find some temporary arrangements until we work this out...," Her voice trailed off and then came back stronger. " But I must warn you that your tendency to get over-involved with your patients will be a problem for you. There are rules of behavior between patients and nurses. You cannot be a good nurse if you become emotionally attached to them. You can't take them all in."

Edith glowed. She ran back to the maternity ward to give the good news to the mother.

"But what good is it? I can't stay here forever. Where will I go next?"

Edith had already thought this through. "When you are well and the baby is old enough, I will arrange for you to live with a family in Nor'ich. I grew up there. It's the country. The air is clean and you will be out of the city slums."

The mother was no fool. She had spent her childhood in the country. It was her husband who had wanted to come to the city to find work. She knew when an opportunity was being handed to her and she took it.

"Thank you, Miss Cavell. My little one is so fortunate to have such a generous godmother. I can't repay you enough, but I know God will bless you for this." She cradled the baby close. "I will name her after you."

* * * * *

E dith was just getting used to the routine on the maternity ward with active new mothers and crying babies when it was time for her to move on to the next clinical rotation, which was the surgical suite.

A few weeks after her surgical training started, she wrote in her diary:

> *Surgical nursing is very different from my previous work on the wards. I so miss the interaction with my patients. Although there was a nursing supervisor in the operating setting, the surgeon rules. Every day I start with scrubbing my hands in chlorinated lime, sodium bicarbonate, and alcohol. The alcohol is the worst. It creeps into every crack and raw area created by the scrubbing and induces an icy sting that lasts for minutes.*
>
> *I am watched very closely by the nursing supervisor and graduate nurses in the surgical amphitheater. If I make a mistake, I am directed to remove myself, rescrub, and reenter the operating room. It is quite embarrassing but not as embarrassing as when I hand the wrong instrument to the surgeon or in the wrong way. One surgeon yells at me and then raps me on the knuckles. They have all taken to flinging surgical instruments past my face.*
>
> *Yesterday, a student nurse was deliberately stabbed in the hand with a scalpel. I am in constant fear that one small mistake under such delicate circumstances could harm the poor fellow under the sheets. They are quite right to chastise me until I perform perfectly.*

Just before she finished her surgical training, the nursing supervisor came to her. "Miss Cavell, you have become quite a proficient surgical nurse. One of the surgeons has requested that you return after graduation to assist him."

"Who might that be? I can't think of any of the surgeons who was particularly pleased with my performance."

"You are quite wrong and much too modest. Dr. Swingle has requested that you assist him after you graduate."

Swingle! I would rather polish coffee urns. He's asking a new graduate nurse because none of the trained nurses will work with him., thought Edith, though she said not a word.

The supervisor's eyes narrowed on Edith's dismayed expression. "It's quite a compliment, you know. There are many surgical nurses who would consider it a privilege to work with him."

She saw a twinkle of mischief in Edith's eyes the supervisor had not seen any time before in the last three months. *Right. Then ask one of them.*

"Please thank the good Dr. Swingle for his generous offer, but I must develop my own career before I settle into one place."

The supervisor's voice rose higher and louder. "As a new graduate nurse, you won't have this opportunity again."

Nor would I want it. "Thank you ever so much. Should I change my mind, I will let you know, but for now I must get ready for my final tests or I won't get a position anywhere," Edith stated in a calm voice, yet grinning inside.

* * * * *

F anny, Bessie, and Edith often studied together, and now that it was time for final exams, each hoped the other would have a better idea of how to pass them.

"Do you think they will ask many questions about physiology?" asked Bessie. "I've already forgotten most of that. Fanny, tell me again about how the blood gets from one side of the heart to the other, then down to the feet and back again. I should think it would all get stuck down there."

Without looking up from her textbook, Fanny yawned, "It's explained in chapter 5."

Flipping through a manual entitled *Medication Administration*, Fanny added, "I'm more worried about remembering all the medications for each disease. There are too many to remember. For instance, what's the bloody difference between sodium salicylate and sodium sulphate, or is it sulfite?"

Fanny groaned and flopped backwards on her bed, drawing her slender hand over her forehead. "I mean, why bother learning them? As soon as I learn them, some new medication gets discovered, and then we have to start all over learning about that one."

She turned to Edith. "You haven't said a thing. Are you prepared for finals?"

Edith was writing her daily entry into her diary. She looked up at her two distraught friends. "I'm not as worried about the examinations as I am about Matron's evaluation. We can get the best grades possible, but if she gives us a poor evaluation, we will never get a nursing position and all this work will be worthless. Her evaluation will be our first job referral."

* * * * *

"I can hardly walk," said Fanny, shaking out the cramps in her sturdy legs. "The Three Graces" were leaving the room where they had spent the day writing their final exams.

Bessie rubbed her buttocks. "I don't think I will ever want to sit down again—unless, of course, it's on the lap of a handsome man."

"It will take weeks before we know if we've passed," said Edith, hunching her shoulders up and down and twisting her head from side to side. "Ow! That hurts! I think I shall be in a hunched position for the rest of my life."

Bessie went over and massaged Edith's slender neck and shoulders.

"Don't think I'm going to massage your sore bottom in return," said Edith with a chuckle.

The following day, each graduate was called in alphabetically by last name for a private evaluation session with Miss Luckes. When she came to the Cs, she called Edith in.

Luckes noticed how different Edith appeared compared to her first interview. Edith was now thinner, paler and there was a vague sadness about her. Luckes now saw a woman who was quietly composed but something else as well. She found herself wondering, just as she had during that first encounter three years before, if she was seeing defiance or determination.

"Miss Cavell, you and I have been down many roads together over the last three years, haven't we?" Luckes began.

If I just agree with everything she says, I will get through this. "Yes, Miss Luckes."

"I have seen many changes in you, but I do not believe you have yet reached your full potential."

"I'm sure you are right."

"I rarely give an excellent evaluation to new graduates because I believe that in doing so, it weakens their motivation to do better. And every new graduate should strive to improve herself, don't you agree?"

"I do."

Luckes then handed Edith her evaluation typed on a single sheet with The London Hospital letterhead. She watched Edith intently as Edith took it from her hand and read it.

Edith Louisa Cavell is somewhat superficial, and this characteristic naturally impressed itself upon her work, which was by no means thorough. She has a self-sufficient manner, which is apt to prejudice people against her. She has plenty of capability for her work when she chooses to exert herself, but she is not very earnest, not at all punctual, and not a nurse that could altogether be depended upon.

She did good work during the typhoid epidemic and had sufficient ability to become a fairly good nurse by the end of her training. Her theoretical work was superior to her practical. She attained an average standard in the latter, giving a general impression that she could reach a higher standard if she put her whole heart into the work.

Edith was stunned. *This can't be. How could Luckes have written this about me after I worked so hard to follow the rules and dedicated myself to my work on the wards? Who will hire me with this evaluation on my record?*

Her mind raced. What will I do now? Surely no hospital will accept me now. Maybe I can do private nursing in patients' homes. The chimes of the nearby church clock interrupted her train of thought. Don't let her know how I am feeling and especially don't let her see me cry.

"Thank you, Miss Luckes," Edith managed.

"Now, then, Nurse Cavell," said Luckes, resting her elbows on the table and tented her fingers together. Her voice took on an air of mastery. "Whatever faults you may have, I am offering you a position here at The London, and I hope you will seriously consider taking it."

Edith looked up from the evaluation.

"A position?" *Is she daft? Or is this her way of forcing me to work here? I know they are very short on nursing staff.*

"I am offering you a staff nurse position on Mellish Ward." The matron watched Edith closely for a reaction. Seeing none, she continued. "Will you take it?"

"I will. Thank you." Edith stood on shaking legs and left the room.

When Edith got back to the nurses' room, she handed her evaluation over to Fanny, but Bessie grabbed it out of Fanny's hand and read out loud. Her voice rose higher with every word.

"*Superficial*! You? Edith Cavell–superficial?"

Bessie looked up at her friend. Edith shrugged her shoulders in agreement. Bessie continued reading, "*Not very earnest*? And...*not a nurse that could altogether be depended upon?*' What was she kocking back when she wrote this? I mean, I know some of these wards have been donated by ale makers–maybe she gets free samples."

"She said she wanted to encourage me to improve."

"Improve?" said Fanny. "You have set a capital example for all of us."

Bessie was still taken up by the evaluation. "*Not punctual*? How stupid; no one is ever on time. How can we be on time for supper when we must report at hand-over next shift nurse on 50 patients in 20 minutes? We can't be in two places at the same time." She looked up. "What are you going to do, Edith?"

Edith gave a sly smile. "She offered me a staff nurse position on Mellish."

"Ha!" cried Bessie. "I knew that old bat had an ulterior motive. You know what they say about Mellish. It rhymes with 'hellish' for a reason."

"It's a job. That's all I need right now. After a year, I will get an evaluation from someone else, and hopefully, it will get me a better position."

* * * * *

After working for a year on the Mellish Ward, Edith found that its reputation as being "hellish" was indeed well founded. Many of the patients were veterans of the Boer War in South Africa and came in with crushed limbs and gaping wounds. Worse were the amputations and the despair these procedures brought to the men. It took all of Edith's training and fortitude not to turn away from the disfigurements. In addition, the supervisors were regimented and often unreasonably harsh in their demands.

While working on Mellish, she met Eveline Dickinson, a nurse two years younger than herself and the daughter of an Anglican priest. Sensitive, intelligent, and a lover of music and literature, Eveline understood Edith in ways others did not. She was known to be clever, well-educated, and pleasant.

The two women formed a strong friendship. A vibrancy seemed to flow back into Edith when she was with Eveline. When Edith confided in her about the poor evaluation from Luckes, Eveline listened intently and smiled.

"Do you find this amusing?" said Edith. "I gave every fibre of energy and dedication I had to please Luckes and this is what I got after all that."

"I'm not laughing at you, or at your evaluation. You see, I thought I was the only one who got a poor evaluation from Luckes. Everyone admired and respected you. If that's what she wrote about you, then there was no chance that any of us would do better."

"Luckes wrote you a bad evaluation? I thought it was a personal issue she had with me."

"Edith, it wasn't personal. She had disparaging words for all of us. She said I was clever but narrow-minded, and had a profound belief in my own judgment of people and things, which she said was seldom sound."

She saw Edith raise her eyebrows at this and went on. "She also said I was hasty and impatient and…" Eveline cleared her throat as if to make a great announcement. "…and that I was conceited and self-centered. I believe that about covers it."

Eveline looked over at Edith and found the older nurse chuckling and shifting in her seat in an attempt not to laugh outright. "So what do you think about that?"

"I think it's the biggest piece of nonsense I've heard in years–that is, next to what she wrote about me."

— 9 —

NEW OPPORTUNITY—1901

After a year of working on the Mellish Ward, Edith accepted a position as night supervisor at St. Pancreas, a hospital that served a population similar to that of The London. Once she had gained supervisory experience, other offers came her way.

Eager to move into a higher position, she accepted a supervisor's position at the Shoreditch Infirmary. It was another Poor Law hospital, but was known for the work of a well-known physician named James Parkinson. It was there that Edith learned new treatments for a debilitating disease that caused muscle weakness, drooling, and a tremor called "paralysis agitans."

One day, the matron at Shoreditch called Edith to her office. It seemed to Edith that whenever she was called to the matron's office, it wasn't for anything pleasant, so she had barely entered the office when she blurted out, "If I have done anything wrong…"

The matron put up her hand. "Oh, heavens no, Edith. On the contrary, my dear. I have been observing you. Your clinical expertise and supervisory skills are exceptional. I believe you have skills that have not yet been tested and that you are ready to take on something new and different. Do you agree?"

"Possibly, but I am truly satisfied with…"

"I called you here to make a proposal to you. After much consideration, I am offering you a teaching assignment in our nursing school. We believe you are quite ready for this and have abilities in this direction."

Edith was stunned. *Did I hear this correctly? Teach in the nursing school? Of course, I could!* She realized that she had been holding her breath all this time and quickly exhaled.

"Yes, I accept. Thank you so much for offering this to me. And thank the school faculty for their trust in me. I will do my best. You won't regret this."

Reaching out to shake the matron's hand, she knocked a cup of tea over onto papers that were strewn about the desk. The matron gave a sigh of resignation.

"Not to worry. That will be all. Report to me tomorrow and I will assign you to your teaching mentors."

Edith left the office and walked down the long hospital corridors that led to the nurses' quarters. She mused, *Matron is right. It's a welcome change from working on the wards. I will miss the patients, but I'm ready to try something different.*

She struggled with the continual inner longing to challenge herself. As Edith looked over at the picture of her father's parish in Swardeston, she thought about how proud her parents would be when they heard about her new position. She remembered when her parish desperately needed a new Sunday school building. Her father had said a new building was impossible because the parish was too small and the communicants too poor.

Edith had taken this as a challenge. When the vicar of Norwich Cathedral refused to pay for the new construction, she negotiated with him to match whatever funds she raised. She set about local tradesmen for materials and volunteers for their time. Then she hand-drew cards with lifelike pictures of flowers and birds and distributed them with a letter from the Bishop inside.

At first, everyone was amused at Edith's efforts, but people did buy the colorful cards, read the letter for donations, and contributed something, however small. When she had collected enough money, promises of materials, and help, she returned to the Bishop and reminded him of his promise. Within a year, her father's church had a new Sunday school building.

Now Edith put all her dedication and energy into her new teaching position. The supervisor often dropped in on her classes to monitor her progress. "I miss seeing you on the wards. The patients often ask for you, but this was a good decision for both of us. Your work here is going well," then added, "Be careful you are not too harsh with the students."

* * * * *

A fter years of teaching, it seemed to Edith that academia kept her away from the real world. Every day blended into the next. It was as if she lived in a cloister and the outside world was just a memory of another life. One day, she overheard two of her students discussing their plans after graduation.

"I'm going to travel all over Europe," said one student. "I want to eat *brioche* in Paris and *cannelloni* in Italy—anything rather than sausage, mashed potatoes and mushy peas."

"My parents are taking me with them on a trip to Switzerland. Can you imagine picking edelweiss off the side of a mountain?" said the other.

Their conversation touched a longing in Edith that she had been ignoring. She had worked for ten years without a break and was now forty years old. *Maybe I should take some time to experience new adventures in new places.* She wrote a letter to her friend Eveline:

> *I am keen to take a long vacation with you. My finances are looking hearty as I have not had much to spend my money on, so I am thinking of visiting France, Italy, Switzerland, and Belgium. I should so much like to show you around Brussels, having lived there as a governess some time ago. Can you come?*

Two weeks later, she received a letter back from Eveline. "*I am in such a good place, I can take as much as six weeks off to travel with you.*"

Edith was ecstatic! She hugged the letter and danced around her room. She scheduled a meeting with her supervisor to ask for the time off.

Sitting in her supervisor's office, Edith tried to find the right words. She looked down at her hands and then up at the mahogany eyes of her superior. "I...uh...I have been working for eight years now. I went into nursing a little late, as you know. I thought that if I took a break, I could renew myself and rethink my career."

"Are you dissatisfied with your work? I'm sure we can make other arrangements..."

Edith interrupted. "I love teaching, and your pay is generous. I was thinking if I took a break for a few months, I could return refreshed and maybe with a new idea as to what else I could do. My class is finished and there's a new teacher who is quite willing to take on the next class for me."

"Are you rethinking your career? I thought you were quite satisfied with your work here," said the supervisor.

"The truth is that I don't really know. There must be something else. Something different. I need to explore other possibilities before I am too old to have other avenues open to me."

"But you are doing so well here. Do you really want to throw all of this away?"

"No, but there have been some changes in my life. Two of my best friends have married. My other friend, Eveline, is still very much a part of my life, but soon she too will be thinking of marriage, and I will be alone. I've saved enough to afford a holiday with her. I believe God leads us step by step. When I return, I pray He will show me what the next step should be."

The supervisor pointed a pencil at her. "If you leave, I can't promise that there will be a position open for you when you return."

"If I don't move from the curb, I can't experience what is on the other side of the street."

"And what if there is nothing on the other side of the street?"

Edith smiled and shrugged. "Then I suppose I will have to move to another street."

The pencil in her superior's hands snapped in half. "Foolishness!"

THE LETTER

The five weeks spent travelling with Eveline were everything Edith had hoped for. They journeyed throughout France, Italy, and Switzerland. Edith also convinced her friend to visit Belgium, where Edith had spent time as a governess.

"I want to share some of the wonderful sights I experienced when I lived in Brussels. It's a glorious city. The buildings are elaborately carved, and a canal runs through the center."

"I don't speak much French," said Eveline.

"Not to worry. I speak it quite well."

"Since you are so capable, you will have to translate for both of us," Eveline said with a warm smile.

During their stay in Brussels, Edith visited Marguerite, one of the children she had cared for as a governess, and was pleased to see that she had married well into the wealthy Graux family.

The trip ended too quickly, making it difficult for Edith to shift her interest back to England and work. Eveline had met a man in Switzerland and was talking about marrying him. Edith knew their friendship would change after Eveline's marriage.

Having spent most of her money on her holiday, Edith had to return to work. However, when she returned, she was told that her previous teaching position was no longer available and there would be no other positions open for the rest of the school year. Armed with good references, Edith set about applying for other teaching positions. She was sure one could easily be obtained, but none of her applications was accepted.

With each rejection, she grew more despondent. Then the young nurse applied for a position she really didn't want—a position as the Queen's District Nurse in Manchester. Her application was accepted. It was temporary, replacing a supervisor who was having surgery.

Manchester was known for two things: its cold and its coal. As Edith arrived, her carriage drove through the haze of smoke and stopped in front of the District Nursing office. She was greeted by a nurse who had been assigned to be her assistant. The nurse brought Edith to the top floor of the tall, gloomy building where she would be lodging.

Edith looked out the only window in her dark room. It faced a brick wall. Beyond the wall were tall, black piles of coal from the nearby mines. She threw her bags on the dusty wooden floor beside the bed, sat cross-legged on the thin mattress, and surveyed the room. There was a simple washstand with a basin in one corner and a plain wooden table and chair against the far wall. She stared out the window at the brick wall. Leaden gray skies slapped torrents of rain against the window. Wind gusts swooped down and blew waves across the bricks.

She thought of home and how much she missed it. She missed her mother's garden, kitchen, and drawing room. She thought of the skating rink, the bustling Saturday markets, and the common. Her sister was now married and her father was speaking of retiring. *What is Mother doing now?,* Edith wondered. Maybe instructing her servant to bake a wonderful crayfish and bacon savory or a sweet gammon pie? She could taste the nutmeg in the sweet crundle pudding and the blackberry jam made from berries picked along the Swordeston lanes. But Edith knew she couldn't go home. There was nothing here for her now. She had vowed to find her own way, and it had led her to what? To this?

She stared at the wall, watching the rain slide over the rough bricks. Warm tears slid down her cheeks. She wanted to talk to someone, but her friends were married and her dearest friend, Eveline, was busy with her own wedding plans. Even her two sisters and brother were involved with their own lives. She fell asleep without eating supper, fully clothed.

When she woke in the morning, she saw that the sky was clear. The wall had dried in the morning sun and now stood tall and strong, like some ancient ruin that had weathered many storms before. Edith thought, *We have both weathered our share of storms and are still standing. I know now what I have to do. There is only one person I can talk to who can help me find some kind of work.* She sat at the small wooden desk and took out a pen and paper. The table rocked on uneven legs as she began to write: "*My dear Miss Luckes…*"

Edith was interrupted by a loud, staccato rapping on the wooden door of her room. An urgent voice called out, "Miss Cavell! Miss Cavell!"

Maybe someone is hurt and needs my help. Edith put down her ink pen and rushed to the door. She was surprised to see a lad of about thirteen standing there trying to catch his breath. He held a soft cap in his hands.

"Is there a problem?"

He handed her a letter. "This letter just came in special delivery. I was ordered to bring it to you straightaway."

Edith took the letter and saw that it was addressed to "Mlle Edith Cavell." She noticed it was written in the clear and precise handwriting of someone who was educated. *Most likely a woman*, she thought. She noticed the smeared black postmark that read *BELGE*. On the return address was a name she instantly recognized: Marguerite Graux.

She thanked the boy, closed the door, and took the letter over to her desk. Was Marguerite or one of her children ill? They had been well when Edith had visited Belgium just a few months ago.

She put aside the letter she was writing to Miss Luckes, took out her letter opener, and slid it across the top of the envelope. Fearing the worst, she carefully opened it. The envelope held only one sheet of paper. The thick ivory paper crackled in protest at being unfolded. The same penmanship from the envelope was scrawled across the paper. It was in French.

Ma chère Edith..., it began. She read it from beginning to end and then again, to be sure her translation was correct. Then she clutched it to her chest and danced around the room. Her long, flowing hair fell free and flipped around her face. She hadn't swirled and twirled like this since she was a child.

She closed her eyes and a childhood memory flowed in. She was with her brother and sisters in the vicarage wildflower garden. They were holding hands and skipping around in a circle, singing a rhyme well known to Norfolk children. The words tumbled through her head:

> *The Man in the Moon, Came down too soon*
> *And asked the way to Norwich,*
> *He came by the south, And burnt his mouth*
> *Through eating hot plum porridge!*

She opened her eyes and the circle of children disappeared. She prayed. "Thank you, God! This is perfectly wonderful. It is just what I was hoping for."

PART TWO:
TRAINING SCHOOL IN BRUSSELS

— 11 —
THE BELGIAN SURGEON

Doctor Antoine DePage heard the bells of St. Michael chime out seven on Monday morning. He reached into the pocket of his greatcoat, looked down at the watch, and snapped it shut. *Right on time*, he thought. Except for Sundays, which his wife insisted he take off, he saw his patients at the same time every day before going to the operating theater precisely at eight o'clock.

He leaned over his first patient. "Bonjour, Mlle. LeBlanc."

Without waiting for a response, he removed her covers to inspect the suture lines of the hysterectomy he had performed on Friday and drew back. Her dressing was soaked with blood, forming a dark, coagulated puddle around her hips.

"When did they last change your dressing?" he asked as he threw off his coat and flung it on a chair. He shoved up his shirtsleeves and ripped off the bloody dressing.

"I'm not sure, Doctor DePage. I do not think it was changed at all, at least not that I remember," said the pale woman. "My pains are so strong, I can hardly breathe. I beg you, Doctor, do something to help me, *s'il vous plaît*."

"I left orders for pain medication to be administered if you needed it. Did they not give it to you?"

"Once on Friday and once on Saturday, but I have not seen anyone on Sunday. Only the charwoman who empties the chamber pots and the woman who brought my meal."

In a nearby metal cabinet, he found a heavy dressing tied in a cloth wrap. He ripped it open and placed it over the fresh wound. He wrapped it tightly to create pressure on the wound. "That should staunch the bleeding. I will go find someone to clean your bed and give you morphine for pain. Sister!" he shouted over the rows of metal beds filled with patients. "Sister!" He didn't care who heard him.

A young girl, dressed in black robes, rushed down the aisle between the rows of iron beds.

"I am here! Why are you yelling, Doctor DePage? You will disturb all of these patients."

"I will disturb heaven and hell if you do not tell me why Mlle. LeBlanc's dressings have not been changed. Why has no one told me she was bleeding?"

He threw the bloody dressing on the floor in front of the nun. It hit the floor with a splat, covering her shoes with thick, dark, gelatinous blood.

"I expect you to help my patients with their pain after their surgery," he yelled at her. "I wrote an order for morphia if Mlle. LeBlanc was in pain. *Sacré bleu*, why is it that she did not get it?"

He slammed the cabinet door so violently that a ceramic invalid feeder on top of the cabinet crashed to the floor and shattered.

"*Excusez-moi*, Doctor. I have arrived to work this ward just a few minutes ago."

DePage saw her shaking beneath her nun's habit. He felt sorry for yelling at the thin woman. He guessed she was about twenty years old. He knew it was often the poorest and most ignorant women who joined the nunnery who got assigned to ward duty. He also knew they were untrained and not given many instructions.

He relented a bit and asked, "Who was here last night?"

"Sister Teresa, but she left a long while ago. Mother Superior assigns her to the night shifts here. In this way, she can sleep on duty so she can get up early to clean the priest's quarters."

DePage realized the gravity of the problem and could hardly hold back his anger. "Give Mlle. LeBlanc her pain medicine and clean her up—now!" He then walked over to his next patient, who was very much awake after hearing the loud argument.

"Bonjour, Monsier DeBuerger...," DePage began and stopped. The unmistakable odor of feces emanated from the bed.

"I'm so sorry, Doctor. I know it smells awful but there was no one to offer me a chamber pot. I called and called, but no one came. I could not get up with my leg having been cut off," the male patient said quietly.

DePage turned to the nun he had just yelled at. She was on her hands and knees, picking up pieces of the broken ceramic feeder.

"What is your name?" he asked.

She did not look up. "Sister Maria-Marguerite."

"Sister Maria, your next job is to clean up Monsieur DeBuerger. Then I want you to go to each patient on this ward and clean up everyone who is in a mess. If you cannot do it alone, get the cleaning woman to help you. When you have finished here, I want you to find me and I will continue making my rounds. Do you understand?"

"Yes, Doctor. I will try to do as you ask but there are so many patients and I..."

"If you cannot do it, call your Mother Superior and tell her to send you help."

"There is no one else to send. All the nuns have been assigned elsewhere."

It was useless to yell at this poor waif. He turned and headed for the operating theater. Six surgeries had been scheduled for him that day. Maybe that was why he hated Mondays; on Mondays, there was always more to do than the time to do it in—and too many surprises.

The operating theater was the one place where he had total control. He could remove a bleeding uterus and return life to a woman who would otherwise have hemorrhaged to death. He could cut out a colon tumour or a capsule of tuberculosis. He thought of his hands as precise instruments.

DePage strode over and pushed the doors open to the suite of operating rooms and welcomed the familiar odors of carbolic acid, alcohol, and benzoin. He looked around for Sister Catherine. Over the last few months, she had been assigned to be his surgical assistant and had shown more than ordinary ability. She was quick to learn, and he had carefully trained her to his liking. She was now invaluable to him.

He looked over the roster of patients due for surgery: repair rectal-vaginal fistula, debride burns–both arms, remove gall bladder–stones, remove left eye–accident, resect large right colon–tumor.

A woman walked past him as he read. He looked up, but seeing it was not Catherine, he returned to the list: lung resection–TB; remove left breast–cancer. Seven surgeries? He had only authorized six.

Where in hell was Catherine? She always came in earlier to inspect the list and set up the surgical trays with the instruments needed for each case. He pulled out his pocket watch. It was 8:15.

Annoyed at Catherine's lateness, he walked over to the woman who had passed by him. She was standing in front of the desk, looking as if she were waiting for someone. DePage had never seen her before.

"Do you work here?" he asked.

"The Mother Superior just assigned me here. I am Sister Michelina. Are you Doctor DePage?" The woman was shorter than he, about 180 pounds, he estimated. The edge of her skirt was dusty, with flecks of mud clinging to the folds. Her skin was pasty and her eyes a dull brown. A stale and musty odor emanated from her body. She had a noticeable limp when she walked.

He was bewildered. He could feel the muscles of his face twitch. "Where is Sister Catherine?"

"She has been reassigned by the Mother Superior of the Sisters of Mercy to return to the convent."

"The convent! She is a surgical nurse, and her duty is here with me. I must have Sister Catherine here to assist me with these surgeries."

"I am willing to help you, Doctor, if only..."

"You want to help me? Good! Here is your first assignment," he said, throwing the list of surgical patients at the bewildered nun. "Cancel those surgeries! I'll be damned if I will allow an untrained nun, who is too stupid to know what she does not know, to damage my surgery. I refuse to do any further operations until Sister Catherine is reassigned to me! Tell anyone who is looking for me that they can find me with the Mother Superior."

DePage slammed through the hospital doors and rushed to the nearby Saint Augustine's Convent. His black waistcoat fluttered behind him like a flag in a strong wind. Ignoring the receptionist sitting at the entrance, he went up straight to the large office at the back of the first floor. He knew exactly where he was going.

Frustrated with the nurses provided, he often clashed with the Mother Superior, who was in charge of the nurses assigned to many of the hospitals in Brussels. He burst open the carved wooden doors to her office and quickly closed the distance to her desk. Placing both of his hands flat on the surface of the highly polished oak desk, DePage locked his elbows, leaned over, and stared into the eyes of the round-faced nun sitting on the other side. His face was red with anger and urgency.

Reverend Mother Hélène was fully composed. She had been expecting him. She smiled at the irascible little man with the pinched face, who looked more like a bookkeeper than a surgeon. It wasn't a friendly smile. She studied his face. His thin, wire-rimmed glasses had fallen halfway down his nose. He had a full brown moustache and beard, but his thinning hair and premature balding at his forehead made him look older than his thirty-seven years. His face was so close to hers that she could feel his breath as he spoke in rapid-fire staccato sentences.

"Where-is-Sister-Catherine? I-need-her-to-assist-me-in-surgery. Now!"

"And *bonjour* to you, too, Doctor DePage. Nice to have you visit me again. You need not bother about Sister Catherine. I sent her back to the convent."

The Mother Superior had a queenly bearing. Everything about her was solid: her bulky frame, her thick wrists and hands. No hair was visible from under the starched white linens that fitted tightly around her face. Two layers of dark veils fell from her head and curled out into points about her shoulders. A thick wooden cross lay flat against her starched bib. Her hazel eyes fixed on him like an eagle on its prey. Light from a nearby window shone across her face, giving her a saintly glow.

She sat impassively with her characteristic half-smile and glanced down at the book opened on her desk. The tall floor clock slowly ticked off a minute. She looked up, raised one thin eyebrow, and addressed the balding forehead.

"Doctor DePage, we need Sister Catherine at the convent...now." She said the word "now" in the same tone he had used. "The gardens need tending and..."

His eyes flashed with anger as he cut her off. "The gardens! The gardens! For the love of God! She is not a gardener! She is a damned good surgical nurse, and I need her to take care of patients, not plants! And I need her now! Today! Send her back to the operating room."

The Mother Superior loved to poke at his pride. She felt no pity for the blustering physician. "No, I have sent you Sister Michelina. She has worked in hospitals before and knows what to do."

"Well, if she is anything like the one you sent to work on nights in the wards this weekend, the patients would be better off dead! Send that one to tend to your damned plants!"

"I sent you a devoted sister over the weekend. She was quite adequate for the job."

"Is that so? Then explain to me how she damned near left one of my surgical patients to bleed to death and another to wallow in his own excrement! Is that what you call 'adequate?' I work to save these patients. I am one of the best surgeons in Brussels, and you send over your dirty and ignorant Black Hoods..."

"...Sisters of Mercy," corrected the nun.

"...Whatever you call them. I need nuns who are clean and intelligent to care for my patients. I need more nuns like Sister Catherine."

"May I remind you that what you get is totally at my discretion? I will send you whomsoever I choose, whenever I choose, and for now, it will not be Sister Catherine."

She loved torturing this pompous, demanding, hot-headed surgeon. He needed to be taught respect for the church. If just once he came to her with less ego and more courtesy, she might be more cooperative. She had the upper hand, and she knew it. If Sister Catherine was the assistant he wanted, then it would be Sister Catherine she would never give to him. She stood facing the physician.

"Be grateful I sent you Sister Theresa, and that is all I have to say to you. If you do not like her, find your own nurse." She continued to smile. "Now leave my office and do not come back until you have found a few manners!" As a final gesture, she slammed shut the large book that was open on her desk.

DePage stood stunned. He should have known better than to approach this domineering nun. She sat staring at him with her fingers tented and propped under the neck folds of her chin. He knew it was a gesture of defiance that meant he had lost.

He straightened up and stared at the crucifix on the wall behind her, then glanced over to the picture of Pope Pius X on the wall over the fireplace. Inscribed in gold leaf beneath the seated pontiff were the words *Instaurare omnia in Christo,* or "restore all things in Christ."

"I'm not done here! I'll go above you to Cardinal Mercer about this! And I will refuse to do any surgery at St. Jean's until you send Sister Catherine back."

"Then you had better find another profession, Doctor DePage, or you will starve."

She waved her hand as if shooing away an annoying fly. "*Adieu.*"

It took a brief moment for him to regain his composure. "Is that what you think? St. Jean's is not the only hospital in Brussels. I am also Chief of Surgery at the Berkendael Institute, which is not under your control. I will transfer my patients to the Berkendael. I will hardly starve."

He spun around. "Sisters of Mercy—in a pig's eye!" and slammed through the double doors, knocking over the same chair he had when entering. Behind him, he heard the Mother Superior's voice call out, "*Au revoir. Ne revenez pas.*"

Dr. Antoine DePage, Belgian surgeon.

MARIE DePAGE AND THE COMMITTEE

T hat evening, Marie DePage knew, from the slam of the front
door, that her husband had just come home.

"That fool of a woman!" he yelled as he threw off his coat.

"Antoine, please. You will upset the servants. Supper is about to
be served. Could you please get ready to eat before it gets cold? Then we
can talk about what is upsetting you."

Antoine sat at the dinner table. Marie watched him skewer a lamb
chop and attack it with a knife. She listened to the account of the poor
post-operative care given by the nuns and the disappointment of having
Sister Catherine taken from him. He chopped at a piece of potato as he
told her of his meeting with the Mother Superior.

Marie was well aware of her husband's temper. "Did you at least try
to be polite to her, Antoine?"

"Polite? How can I be polite to that…that stubborn warthog who
hides her ignorance under a nun's habit?"

"Calling a Mother Superior a warthog is strong language for a Sister
of Mercy."

Antoine put his wine glass down so hard that it splashed Bordeaux on
his shirt and the white linen tablecloth. He scrubbed at the stain on his
shirt with his napkin.

"Do you know how many patients suffer and even die every year
from infections, hemorrhaging, bed sores—or even from malnutrition
because they are not fed? What good is it if I perform the most difficult
of surgeries and all my work is then ruined because there are no intelligent nurses to care for them afterwards?"

She tried to lighten the conversation. "Maybe it has something to do
with women who are miserable because they wear scratchy black
clothes."

He did not smile.

She went on in her soft, calm voice. "There are other options. When I married you fourteen years ago, you told me that you once considered going into law. Do you ever regret your decision to become a surgeon instead?"

Antoine loved his wife. He knew that he owed a good part of his success to her. In Belgium, class distinctions were very important, and her skill in working with these social layers smoothed over his clumsiness. She was devoted to his work.

"Regret being a surgeon? Never. I love the challenge of being able to do what other surgeons cannot. This is my calling, not the law. I am not only a surgeon; I am one of the best in Brussels. But what use are my skills if the patients die anyway? Is it asking too much that the nurses who take care of my patients be competent and clean?"

Marie's smooth, clear skin, high cheekbones, and arched eyebrows gave her the look of royalty. Her thick brown hair was swept back and piled on her head. Her clothes were never rumpled. She was one of those women who always looked poised. She handed her husband a basket of freshly baked dinner rolls.

Marie DePage,
wife of Dr. Antoine DePage

"It seems to me that every time we have these conversations, they come back to the problem of untrained nurses. There has to be an answer to this, Antoine. I have heard there are schools in England that formally train women to be nurses. Would it help you if I bring a few of my friends and business acquaintances together to discuss if there is merit in forming a committee to consider starting such a school in Brussels?"

Antoine speared a roll with his knife, tore it open, and slathered butter on it.

"A nurse's training school? Here in Brussels?" The butter melted down into the palm of his hand. He licked it before it reached the cuff of his shirt. "Are the British schools run by nuns?"

"No," said Marie, amused at his dinner table antics. She handed him a linen napkin. "I believe they are operated by the public hospitals. It's the funding I don't know much about. Can the public hospitals in Brussels afford such an undertaking? I mean, it's the church that has the money."

DePage railed, "The old bat told me to find my own nurses. I imagine I could do just that if I had a training school based in the hospital, no longer under the control of those damned nuns. Maybe those English have hit on something. We could train our own nurses, as I have trained Sister Catherine. I would never have to depend on Mother Warthog again. Do you have any ideas about who would be willing to be on such a committee?"

"You will have to trust my choices. This is a delicate matter, and not everyone will agree with this idea. We do not want the destination to be lost before the journey is started." Marie smiled at her husband.

The idea of a training school separate from the church now consumed DePage. He envisioned an important change in medical history sweeping toward him, and he was impatient to begin. *Someday, my nurses will replace the nuns in St. Jean's Hospital, and Mother Warthog can find herself another profession.*

* * * * *

Two weeks later, five women and one man gathered in the DePages' home. Antoine explained his frustrations and the disastrous results of not having good nursing care for his patients.

"What does the church think of such an idea?" asked Jeanne Eland, a buxom woman and the wealthy owner of a lace factory.

"It would not involve the church. This school would be based in one of our public surgical hospitals. The nurses can be trained on hospital wards so they will be familiar with the hospital routine by the time they graduate."

"Pardon me for speaking so directly," said Jeanne Eland, "but I believe there are aspects of this idea we are not considering. Do we really want to make an enemy out of the church? Do we have the political ability to start such a project without its blessing?"

"Jeanne is right," said Mme. Charles Graux, twisting the diamond ring on her finger. "My family has done well by cooperating with the church. Maybe if you try to negotiate with the Mother Superior, we could come up with a compromise and not make and enemy of Cardinal Mercier."

Marie shifted in her chair. This was not going as she had hoped. She could see her husband getting impatient.

"I believe we have the credibility to accomplish this," she said. "It does not involve the church, Mother Hélène or their hospitals, so we do not need to challenge Mother Hélène's authority or ask for the cardinal's approval. There are good public hospitals where we can establish our training progamme. The Berkendael Institute, where Antoine is chief of surgery, comes to mind."

A third member of the committee, Mme. Vandervelde, spoke up. She was a heavy woman with curly brown hair and a bulbous nose. She wrapped a small linen and lace handkerchief around one finger and touched it to her nose occasionally as she spoke. "This will not be an easy task. Belgian women believe that nursing is demeaning work. No respectable woman will seek work that will cause her to lose her status in society." She twisted the handkerchief tightly around her finger. "This job was done by charwomen before the church was willing to provide us with nuns from the Sisters of Mercy. That was quite an improvement."

Marie noticed that the handkerchief was so tight that the tip of Mme. Vandervelde's finger lost its color. She said, "I was thinking that we might have to start by bringing in trained nurses from another country to set an example. Then perhaps the local women would see that nursing is quite acceptable."

Mme. Eland watched the other committee members' reactions. Her business relied on the patronage of good Catholics, and she could ill afford to make an enemy of the church, a powerful influence in Brussels. "If you do not mind my asking, where will we get the funds for this?" she asked. "We will need buildings, equipment, supplies, uniforms, and staff.

We do not even have an administrator who knows how to make this work."

"I think I know someone," said Mme. Graux. "My son's wife, Marguerite, had a wonderful English governess a few years ago who now holds a position as a nursing supervisor in England. She speaks fluent French. Maybe we could search her out to see if she would come back to Brussels and help set up this nurses' school."

"And the funding for this?" asked Mme. Eland with a frown.

Hearing no answer to Jeanne's question about funds, Antoine jumped on Mme. Graux's suggestion. "That is an excellent idea, Madame. I have discussed this with other surgeons and physicians, and they have agreed to support it."

"Are these doctors willing to help fund the school?" asked Paul Héger, the only male member of the committee.

"Of course," said Antoine. Marie knew he was lying and shot him a warning look. He avoided her eyes.

Fingering her jeweled ring, Mme. Graux said, "Well, if the physicians will help financially, I am willing to consider a contribution to start the school, but I want a full financial accounting of how the money is used."

Antoine met Marie's eyes. "My wife will keep good financial records and make a report to this committee with full financial disclosure."

Marie picked up the cue. "We all have business connections and wealthy friends we can ask for sponsorships. We could even approach the hospital for funds to establish the training program."

Marie wanted to keep control over the conversation and to move it away from Jeanne Eland. She turned to Mme. Graux.

"Madame Graux, where do you think this British nurse is now?"

"My daughter-in-law recently spoke to her while she was here on holiday. I think she is working in London somewhere. Whitechapel, I believe," said the wealthy matron.

"Mon Dieu, not Whitechapel!" said Mme. Eland. "Can anything good come out of that slum? If she were any good, she would be working at one of London's more decent hospitals."

"As I recall, her father is an Anglican priest, so she probably sees herself as some kind of missionary, by treating the needy and poor and people of that sort."

At that point, Mme. Eland jumped up out her chair. "Anglican! You mean to bring a Protestant here! No one is going to support a Protestant in Brussels! When the newspapers get hold of this, they will sabotage all our efforts. We will be laughed out of Brussels."

Marie looked at Mme. Graux. She knew Mme. Eland had made a powerful argument. She thought quickly. "Consider this," Marie blurted out. "We can ask her to keep her religious persuasion quiet. If she has worked in a place as difficult as Whitechapel, she may well be prepared for what she will experience here. I believe the hospital she trained in teaches in the tradition of Florence Nightingale."

With that, Mme. Eland motioned to the maid to bring her shawl. "I'm sorry, but I cannot agree to this. Are you seriously proposing a project that will defy Cardinal Mercier, challenge the Mother Superior, bring in an Anglo-Saxon Protestant foreigner to start a training school that no decent Belgian woman would dare attend, all to duplicate what the Sisters of Mercy are already doing well enough? Without solid funding and no real assurances of support from any hospital? Do I have this right? Because if I do, I bid you all *adieu*. I have better things to do with my time than to waste it on such nonsense."

As the portly businesswoman took her shawl and swirled it around her shoulders, the edge flipped against her glass, sending it crashing to the floor, where it shattered.

"I'm sorry, Marie. Antoine is a fine surgeon, but he is reaching beyond what he can control." Mme. Eland pointed to the pieces of glass on the floor. "That is what will happen to your husband's career if he attempts this. *Bonsoir*."

When the door closed behind her, everyone shifted uneasily in a momentary silence. Seeing his wife was losing ground, Antoine jumped up and paced about the room as he addressed the group.

"This British woman is exactly what I need. I think we must find her, review her credentials, and send for her. We can interview her as a committee if you like, but if she has even half of the qualifications we need, we will still be better off than we are now. If she cannot help us, we will find someone else."

Paul Héger stuffed some hickory tobacco into his elaborately carved pipe. He lit a match to it and sucked in a few times. The aroma mingled with Mme. Graux's rose-scented perfume. Around the stem of his pipe, he said, "I guess now would be a good time to say something British, like 'it would be a smashing good idea' to begin by making up a list of qualifications." Smiles appeared, and the women eased back in their chairs.

"She had better have a sense of humor," said Mme. Graux, smiling. "She will need it if she is to work with your husband, Marie!"

"And I hope she is vigorous enough to keep up with him," said Paul.

"And has the devotion of a new bride," said Mme. Vandervelde, fingering the cameo on the high white collar of her blouse.

"And is not looking for a husband," added Paul.

"Why is that?" asked Marie.

"Well, we can't have her hoofing about and creating a scandal while she is getting this new school off the ground, can we?" he replied while looking about the room for an ashtray.

"That should not be a problem, since nurses are not allowed to marry," said Marie, handing him a glass one. "We need someone who is also a good administrator and organizer."

"We should start with organizing ourselves," added Mme. Vandervelde. "How about simply calling our group the 'Ladies Committee of the School for Nurses'? That way we can have a letterhead and look more official." She turned to Paul. "That is, if you approve."

"Oh, fine, fine," he said, raising his eyebrows and shifting a bit in his chair. "I'll bring my wife along to make me an official member."

"When we find this English nurse, Antoine, you should be the one who writes to her," said Marie. "And if she agrees to come here, my good husband, you must try very, very hard to be patient with her."

Only the sound of quick puffs on the pipe and the crackling of the burning hickory tobacco could be heard. The church bells of St. Michael's broke the silence.

Antoine smoothed his moustache. *They are giving in*, he thought. He looked at Mme. Graux and peered into the older woman's eyes.

"Madame Graux, if you would be so kind as to find her address, I will write the letter."

— 13 —
A NEW ROLE, 1907

E dith could hardly believe how much Brussels had changed since she had lived there ten years before. The roads were now busy with automobiles and lined with electric street lights. It was so much brighter and cleaner than London. She looked up to the belfry peak of the Hotel de Ville to see the bronze statue of St. Michael balancing himself on one foot. He seemed to welcome her back. The city was bustling with energy, and she felt herself responding to it.

She took a cab and headed south into the suburb of Ixelles, passing lush parks bursting with color from flowers and flowering shrubs. She breathed in the sweetness of the warm August air. God, how she had missed this!

When she entered Dr. DePage's office, a young woman jumped up and threw her arms around her neck.

"Oh, Mademoiselle! You are here!"

"Marguerite!" said Edith, hugging her back and speaking in her flawless French. "I had no idea that I would be seeing you again in so short a time."

Marguerite then introduced Edith to her mother-in-law, Mme. Graux, who extended a gloved hand to the new arrival.

"I am pleased you have accepted our invitation. Marguerite has spoken so highly of you that I feel as if I already know you."

Marie DePage appeared in the doorway of her office.

Marguerite beamed. "Marie, this is Mlle. Cavell."

A male voice blustered from behind them. "How am I supposed to get my work done with all this noise?"

Dr. DePage came in through the office doorway and found himself looking into the most luminous blue-gray eyes he had ever seen. He held out his hand. "Mlle. Cavell, we are so pleased you have come. We have so much to do."

He stood back to look at his new Nursing Director. Her thin frame was dressed from head to toe in a matron's uniform. He thought she was quite attractive. "The school is scheduled to open in four weeks—on October 1st, to be exact. You will have a difficult time getting started, but we have a group of dedicated people here to support you."

He handed her a folded-up piece of paper. "Here is a list of some of the things the Committee thinks you may need."

Marie stepped forward. "As you can see, my husband is so excited about this new idea of his that he can hardly wait to get started. We do want to show you the buildings we have acquired for our new school and where you and the nurses will be staying."

Antoine drove Edith and Marie over to the four adjoining three-story houses. Edith gasped at their condition. They were in total disrepair. DePage hooked the thumb of his left hand in his vest pocket and made a grand gesture toward the buildings with the other. "The Ladies' Committee of the School for Nurses provided funds to buy these four buildings. The official name of the school is *L'Ecole Belge pour les Infirmières Diplômées*, but we will simply call it the *Clinique*."

He looked back at Edith. "Will you be getting married any time soon, Madmoiselle?"

She studied the man's face. What a strange little man to ask such a personal question. "I have no such plans. My work is my life, Dr. DePage."

"Good, because you will not have much time for socializing. I will be honest and tell you that you–or I should say, we–will have a challenge to get this started. Financial support is coming out of the pockets of a few patrons, whom know we will face strong opposition from religious and political quarters. Here in Belgium, there is also a social stigma associated with this type of work."

He studied her more closely. He had expected someone more physically hardy but she barely stood over five feet tall. "Are you sure you are up to all of this? I mean, is your health good?"

Edith's expression was stoic. *Is he always this annoying?* she thought.

"I assure you, Monsieur, that I am quite well. I would not have come here if I thought I could not meet the requirements of this position. I knew it would present a challenge. How many students do you—I should say, we—have right now?"

"Six," said DePage. Marie glared at him. "Uh, well, maybe closer to four. We're working on the other two."

Edith hid her disappointment. *I came all this way for four students?* Marie pointed to a poster fixed to the façade of the building. "We have these posters on buildings all over Brussels."

Edith read the large, square red letters: "Young Girls Wanted."

"Have you sent out announcements to any of the national nursing publications?" Edith asked.

"We thought we would leave that up to you," said Marie. "Let me show you to your quarters."

Antoine stared down at his pocket watch. "I am so sorry I cannot spend more time with you. I must catch up from being away. We will talk about what you need after you settle in."

Marie led Edith to the door marked with the number 179. It scraped against the floor in protest at being opened. Edith entered the building that would be her new home.

They walked onto the first floor. "This will be your room and study. You can put your things here."

Edith put her bags on the floor and looked around. There was a straight chair lying sideways on a table with a small lamp. Hanging above a wooden bureau was a round mirror with a single crack slashed across it. Next to the bureau was a wardrobe with one of the handles loosely dangling on one screw. Two faded pillows were thrown on each side of the two-seat sofa.

When Edith reached to straighten them out, she tripped on the faded, threadbare rug. Grabbing the back of the sofa to catch her balance, she assured Marie, "I am quite all right."

"Good," said Marie. "Tomorrow, you will be presented to the Ladies' Committee, 3 o'clock, in my home. I'll have a carriage pick you up. We are all so excited you are here, Edith. The Committee will love you. I just know it. *Au revoir*." And she was gone.

Edith explored the other buildings. A yellow light forced its way through the dirty windows and played on the swirls of dust kicked up by her footsteps. She breathed in the stale, mouldy air and tried to open some of the windows, but they wouldn't budge. There were draped in ragged and faded curtains. Empty chests with their drawers open were strewn about. She felt the bare wooden floors give under her weight in places. Mouse droppings were evident among the dust and debris.

Edith climbed the narrow stairway that led to the second floor. Across the room was a set of French doors. With a strong pull on the handles, the doors grudgingly opened to reveal a small balcony trimmed with a rusty, serpentine, wrought-iron railing. Not daring to step out onto the balcony, she leaned over and looked down to the cobblestoned rue de la Culture, the street below.

It was quiet and empty except for a woman dressed in black with a scarf over her head, shuffling down the street. She cradled a long, thin, loaf of bread in her arms.

Suddenly, a crow broke the silence with its loud caw. She saw it clinging to a vine that had snaked up the façade of the house. Startled by her presence, it flew off.

"And hello to you too, sir," she addressed the crow.

She retreated back into the room and descended the narrow stairway, keeping her balance by bracing her hands against the dark, peeling walls. Back in her room, she sat on her bed. It was about the same size as the medical stretchers provided during the typhoid epidemic in Maidstone and not much more comfortable.

Feeling the weariness of the long trip, she leaned back and remembered Dr. DePage's words: "We will be opening our school in four weeks. Are you up to it?"

I thought I was. Now I'm not so sure. Only four weeks to turn these four empty buildings into a school, a clinic, and a suitable place for student housing. Nobody told me I would have to perform a miracle, all for four students.

Her thoughts were suddenly interrupted by the melodic sound of church bells. She looked up and noticed a door that led to the back of the building. Opening this door, she smiled for the first time since she had entered the building. A garden! It was a tangle of trees, weeds, flowers, and overgrown vines. *I have a sanctuary,* she thought with delight.

Edith wondered how anything had survived without being tended to. She brushed a few twigs and leaves off a shaded marble garden bench and sat down. The coolness of the stone was a welcome relief from the August heat.

There was a time, in her childhood, when her garden had been her whole world. It had been filled with snowdrops, aconites, primroses, bluebells, and campions in full blossom on tall stalks. She addressed the plants around her. "After the houses are set up, you will be my next duty."

Two crows flew to a branch above her head and squawked down at her. She tried to think of the saying her cousin had taught her about counting crows. He said the number of crows that crossed your path foretold your future. *If I ever needed to know the future, it's now.*

She recited the poem out loud. "Let's see. It's one crow for sorrow. Two for joy. Three for a...girl and four for a boy. Five for gold. No, it's five for silver and six for gold. Seven for...for the secret, never to be told. Eight for a kiss? No, eight for a wish and nine for a kiss. Ten for something you must not miss." The two crows flew off just as she finished. *Two is a good sign,* she thought.

The bells stopped ringing. She looked toward the sky and prayed. "Oh, God, you led me here. Now you must reach down and help me perform a miracle. You turned the water to wine, made the blind to see, and fed a multitude with a few loaves and fishes. Now I call on you to show me how in four weeks, I can turn these four broken-down houses into a successful school and clinic."

Once back in her room, she pulled the chair off the desk, brushed off the dust, and sat down. Miss Luckes had once built a nursing school from almost nothing. *Maybe she will help me if I write to her.* From her traveling bag, she pulled out paper and an envelope and wrote:

September, 1907.
My dear Miss Luckes,

I arrived here and found the four houses, which have been made to communicate. They are only partly furnished and in much confusion. The Committee, who urged that I come, is absent on holiday except for the doctor and his wife, who returned a few days earlier to welcome me. There are no servants and nothing is furnished but my little sitting room.

I am told we have to open October 1st.

There are three Swiss students and one Belgian. They have given me a list of things I will need and there it ends. I will need a full-time school matron who speaks French, if you could please recommend someone to me. The salary will be fifty pounds per annum.

It is pioneer work here and needs much enthusiasm and courage and intelligence, as there are many looking askance at it. It will also require great tact. I hope to pull through this and soon have a model school.

Edith Cavell

Edith Cavell's nursing school.

MEETING THE COMMITTEE

The minute Edith arrived at the DePage house, she knew she was out of place. Her plain blue skirt, puff-sleeved white blouse, and sensible black shoes were in sharp contrast to the shimmering satin, full-skirted dresses worn by the women on the Committee. Expensive necklaces and earbobs glittered in the light from the gold and crystal chandeliers.

The air was thick with a mixture of melted wax from the candelabras, cigar and cigarette smoke, alcohol, and perfume. Mme. Graux welcomed Edith and led her to a seat by the fireplace. There she waited for the meeting to begin, but the discussions remained random and informal. She heard conversations about a trip to Italy, why a Royal Academy of Medicine in Belgium should be established, and where a new brooch cameo had been bought, but nothing about the new school.

Edith looked around for Marguerite and saw she was engaged in a conversation about her children. Edith felt distant from everyone in the room. It was as if she were watching a stage play.

An hour later, Mme. Graux called the Committee to order. "And now, I think it is time we asked our new Directrice, Mlle. Edith Cavell, to tell us something about herself and her plans for our new school."

Edith looked up and saw Marguerite give her a quick wink from the back of the room. She rose from her chair and walked to the front of the room. "I thank you all for bringing me to your wonderful country to undertake this exciting adventure. Some of you know that I previously lived in Brussels. I have since taught nursing and been administratively responsible for various hospitals and nursing schools in England.

She took a deep, calming breath and continued. "I think we all believe a change in the way medical care is delivered is important. Once that change happens in Brussels, it will spread to all of Belgium. We are starting with four students and have plans to recruit more. I assure you that I intend to bring discipline and respect to the nursing profession. I appreciate your donation of four buildings to start this school, but I must tell you, we will need more of your support to fully furnish those buildings. Marie and I will work together to provide you with a list of what will be needed."

She remained standing, waiting for questions, Mme. Graux stood up and said, "Thank you, Mlle. Cavell, for sharing your thoughts with us. This meeting is now adjourned."

Edith was stunned. *How much do they really support this school if there are no questions or discussion? Will I be told at some point that there are no more funds to continue?*

A few committee members shook her hand as they passed by on the way out, but she couldn't read their expressions.

When Marguerite approached her, Edith whispered to her, "This is not at all what I expected."

Marguerite kissed Edith's cheek and whispered back, "They are very impressed with you, and Dr. DePage is enchanted. It will all work out. You will see."

* * * * *

Edith worked twelve to fourteen hours a day to transform the four dilapidated row houses into a nursing school. Every detail had to be decided on: how the clinic would be set up, what equipment would be needed, where the classroom should be placed, where the students would live and eat, and what supplies the kitchen would need. In the evening hours, she wrote out the training curriculum. It seemed like an endless series of decisions that led to other decisions, all of which had to be worked out with Marie DePage, her husband, and the Ladies' Committee.

The classroom was easy enough to set up, but Edith knew that getting approval from the DePages for the progressive curriculum she developed would need some convincing. She sat on the hard wooden chair facing Marie and showed her the curriculum.

Marie looked it over. "Is it really necessary to teach nurses anatomy and physiology? It is best that we leave those subjects to the physicians."

Edith remembered those days as a probationer when she had thought the same thing. She quoted Miss Luckes. "It is important that nurses understand the underlying causes of diseases and why certain treatments are prescribed, and for that they need to understand how the body works."

Marie looked back at the course outlines and read out loud, "*The Principles of Internal Diseases*? Edith, is it your plan to turn them into little doctorettes?"

"No, but they do need to be able to make intelligent decisions about care and treatments. Our trained nurses will be more than simply the physician's handmaidens. They will have the basic knowledge they need to help them make independent decisions. These nurses will be professionals in their own right."

"Well, if we are going to change the role of nurses this much, I think we had better also warn the physicians about what we are doing. Some physicians may feel very threatened by having women make independent informed decisions concerning their patients." Marie thought about Antoine and his temper.

"We had probably leave that task to your husband. Would you also mention to the good doctor that we will need him to teach a class about the elementary knowledge of drugs? If Miss Luckes can't find me another instructor, he may also have to teach the class on microbes of disease."

Marie shifted in the wooden chair. "I don't know. He's very busy, you know. He has just been made the Director of the Pathology Department."

"I'll leave it to you to convince him that it would be in his favor to be directly involved with the training of his students."

"What of their uniforms?" asked Marie. "Shouldn't they also be in black, like the nuns? That would more easily identify them as nurses."

"Absolutely not! I want them to look clean and crisp and not at all like the heavy, stiff, drab apparel of the nuns. A new profession deserves a new look."

Edith opened a notebook and shifted it to Marie's lap. "Here we are. I've drawn the design for our new uniforms. Navy-blue cotton dresses with starched white linen collars, cuffs, and aprons. Their caps will be simple white cotton caps—without strings. I do not want them to look like the nuns, with those flimsy flying wings attached to their heads."

She quickly drew a sketch of the cap. "This style is known as the 'Sister Dora' in England. Both caps and uniforms will provide a stark contrast to the unhygienic past and represent the enlightened present. And besides, nurses can work better if they are comfortable."

By the first of October, the four row houses had been transformed into a nurses' training school, clinic, living quarters, and surgical center. A fifth student, a French woman, enrolled.

On the opening day of her school, Edith stood before her five new nursing students. All sat attentively in their hard wooden chairs, with the exception of the French student, who was busy digging her finger under her starched white collar in an attempt to loosen it. Edith ignored the gesture and addressed her first class in fluent French.

"Up until now, all nursing care in Belgium has been performed by the nuns. Although they were dedicated and hard-working, they had no training. You will be the first nurses to change all of that. Your work will be difficult, but rewarding. We expect you to bring passion, determination, perseverance, and a strong sense of commitment to this profession.

Edith paused and looked at her young charges. "You will be taught about infections, medications, treatments, and even anatomy and physiology. To do this work, you must study hard and enjoy helping the sick. One of Florence Nightingale's requirements is that nurses should do the sick no harm. The days will be long, and you will only have a half-day off each week. You have been chosen for your intelligence and high moral character. We expect you to put both to good use. You will give the physicians the respect they deserve and always address them as 'Docteur.' They in turn will recognize you for the professional you are, and will address you as 'Nurse' when they give you orders."

A plump, blonde Belgian student giggled and held her hand over her mouth in embarrassment. Everyone smiled but Edith.

"Nurse Bohme, could you please share with us what is so amusing?"

"Mme. Cavell, no doctor will address us as 'Nurse.' That is just plain silly. They will not say to us, 'Oh, Nurse Bohme, please do this or that.' If we were nuns, maybe, but this is not England. In Belgium, nurses are treated like servants."

"Nurse Bohme, that is precisely what we intend to change. If you want the physicians to take you seriously, you must first take yourself seriously. The physicians will soon appreciate you as a professional when you act like one. If you or anyone else in this class cannot make this commitment, it's best you leave now."

No one moved.

"And now I will introduce the physician who first had the foresight to start this school, Docteur DePage."

DePage was standing to the side staring at his pocket watch. When he heard his name, he snapped it shut and walked to the center of the room. The students saw a short man with a full chestnut-brown moustache and a neatly trimmed goatee. Thinning hair made his forehead and brow more prominent. A pair of wire-rimmed glasses sat halfway down on his aquiline nose. His quick, dark eyes examined each of them as if they were experiments in a laboratory. He paced and spoke in short, quick sentences, as if he were running out of time.

"Thank you, Directrice Cavell." He walked over to Clara. "I, for one, will be addressing you as 'Nurse Bohme.'"

He looked up. "You and your classmates will soon be part of an important team, helping the physician to deliver the safest and most intelligent care we can offer our patients. While this is a new concept in Belgium, patients will soon notice the difference in their care and request to have trained nurses take care of them instead of the nuns. I and the other physicians look forward to working with you."

A Dutch student, Emilie Vandevelde, raised her hand. "Sir...I mean, Docteur DePage...there are only five of us. How can we possibly make a difference?"

"There will be more of you, I promise. We are interviewing at least fourteen new students this week." He heard Edith clear her throat. "Uh, or something close to that number, but I assure you, this school will grow."

Edith moved beside DePage. "The spread of light and knowledge is bound to follow in years to come. We have made plans to advertise this new training course. In the meanwhile, if you have friends or know of anyone who would like to join us, please submit their names to me."

Clara Bohme's hand shot up. "Mme...Sir...I mean, Directrice Nurse Cavell—when is breakfast?" The girls giggled. Edith stood composed until the classroom grew silent.

"You may address me as Nurse Cavell. Here is your schedule for meals and classes."

She handed each of them a sheet of paper and a notebook. "To answer your question, Nurse Bohme, breakfast is at 7 o'clock. Do not be late. I want you all to keep a daily diary in your notebooks. Once a week, on Tuesday evenings, we will meet in the reception room, where we will chat and have tea together."

She looked over to where the surgeon was standing and saw that he had his hand on the door to leave.

"Docteur DePage," she said in a louder voice, "will be providing us with a piano to enjoy some music during some of these sessions. Isn't that right, Docteur?"

From the other side of the door, she heard: "A piano? Of course. Put it on the list and give it to Marie."

She turned back to the five young women. "I expect you to arrive promptly for classes and to be spotlessly clean when on duty."

The French student, who continued to tug at the neck of her uniform, blurted out, "This collar! It is so stiff it chafes my neck. Do I have to wear it?"

Edith Cavell with her first class of nursing students

"You do. You must not only act like a professional, you must also look like one. If you look and act like a professional, you will be treated like one. I expect nothing less from you. You are all dismissed."

The students filed out past Marie DePage, who was waiting just outside the door. When the last one had left, Marie sat on one of the student chairs and looked up at Edith, who was still standing in front of the classroom. "So, Edith, how was your first day?"

"I believe we have our challenges, but we will persist."

Marie looked somber. "I surely hope so. Our reputations depend on this school's success. Have you read today's newspaper?" She handed the newspaper to Edith. "It seems as if Jeanne was right to warn us of trouble."

Edith's brow furrowed as she read the last line in the article out loud. *"This nursing school is a machine of war against our blessed sisters, who, for a thousand years, have looked after our patients."*

Raising one eyebrow, Edith handed the newspaper back to Marie. "I will make a promise to you and the Committee. If the blessed sisters will leave the work of nursing to trained nurses, I promise that our nurses will leave the work of religion to trained nuns. Tell them to print that."

Marie dropped the newspaper on the floor, jumped up, and threw her arms around Edith.

— 15 —
THE UNSTARCHED COLLAR

A ntoine DePage stood in the center of his surgical amphitheater and looked down at the anaesthetised patient lying on the oblong marble slab before him. A migraine, which caused his temples to throb, was worsening under the bright lights. His eyes began to sting, and his vision blurred from the mist of acrid carbolic acid and the sweetness of the chloroform emanating from the patient's head. He struggled to focus. *Not now,* he thought. He squeezed his eyes shut then opened them again. The blurring cleared. The anesthetist saw DePage struggling and stopped delivering chloroform for a moment, then seeing that the surgeon had regained control, turned back to the patient.

Streams of light filtered through the large, clear windows set high above the two semicircular rows of seats filled with those who came to observe him. Today, observing the surgery was a surgeon from Ghent, six surgical interns, and five nursing students. Everyone focused on DePage. He studied the patient's abdomen.

What he had thought would be a simple obstruction of the large bowel turned out to be complicated by a large tumor that had eroded through the wall of the right ascending colon, spilling caustic contents into the abdomen. With one swift movement, he cut into the man's abdomen and clamped a surgical instrument above and below the tumor. This was his fifth difficult surgery today and he was getting tired. He resected the diseased section of bowel and removed the slippery mass from the open cavity. He held the bloody mass up in the air for all to see, then unceremoniously dropped it, with surgical instruments still attached, into a metal basin, where it landed with a thud.

Suddenly, a spurt of blood splashed across his face, blinding him. He shook his head to clear his vision and yelled at his surgical nurse.

"Wipe my eyes! Clean my glasses!"

His surgical nurse immediately removed his glasses, cleaned them, and wiped his eyes. His vision cleared. He willed his hands to find the bleeding vessel. *Did I nick an artery when I cut into the bowel?*

"Clamp!" He felt the handles of a curved metal clamp being slapped into the palm of his outstretched hand.

"Suction." The suction wand was placed on the edge of the abdomen. When he reached for it, it slid off the covers and onto the floor.

"Damn it! Get another one! Watch what you are doing, for Christ's sake!" He threw a bloody dressing at the woman assisting him. It hit across her chest with a splat.

"Yes, Docteur." She removed the dressing and dropped it into the bucket at their feet, her eyes moistening as she moved to get a clean suction tip.

He felt the bleeding artery pumping between his fingers and pinched it closed.

"Suction. Now!"

The surgical nurse handed him a clean suction tip.

"Took you long enough. Did you go for a toilet break?"

"No, Docteur."

The pain in his head throbbed. He moved the suction wand into the blood-filled abdomen.

Damned school. It's been open for six months now and they still haven't produced a decent surgical nurse. I trained Sister Catherine in three months. All I hear from that obstinate English Cavell is how she needs more equipment or that the students do not want to work the night shifts or how we must attract more students and even what color the goddamned walls should be painted. She called me at ten in the evening to catheterize a male patient! I can train a monkey to do that! I thought we were training professionals. Is my little puritanical matron afraid to put her hands on a man's penis?

He held his hand out to the nurse. "Sponge. Suture. Not that kind, stupid," he said, throwing it on the white-tiled floor. "The catgut suture."

A tan-colored suture was handed to him. *Just one more tie to that bleeder.* He snipped off the ends of the tie. Done. He drew a deep breath. *Now I just have to sew these two ends together and close this abdomen and hope to hell the new nursing students do not kill him before he heals.*

He looked up at the five students lined up along the first row staring back at him. Their navy-blue uniforms were in sharp contrast to the white walls. These five young women represented the hope of a new profession in Belgium. *If they do not make it, my reputation will be ruined and Mother Hélène wins. I would be at her mercy.*

DePage refocused on the bowel he has just repaired; thankfully the two ends were pulling together nicely. He knew the migraine would not let him stand here much longer.

He looked up to his right to find an intern he could trust to perform the final closure, but the intern was not paying attention to him. Instead, he was smiling at someone to his left. DePage followed the young man's gaze to discover a blushing French nursing student smiling back.

"You!" he pointed to the inattentive intern with an outstretched, bloody hand. "Get down here now. You will be closing this patient."

While the surprised intern made his way down onto the surgical floor, DePage looked back up to the attractive nursing student. He pointed a bloody finger at her.

"You," he said pointing up to the startled student. "You are dismissed. Leave now." The student turned pale.

"But Docteur DePage, I have done nothing..."

"Your collar isn't starched," he said, pointing to her soft, wrinkled collar. You know the rules about your uniform. Get out!"

The shocked probationer stammered. "M...my neck is badly chafed and the st...starched collar hurts."

DePage's voice echoed throughout the amphitheater. "Do not argue with me. Get out of my operating theater. Now!"

All movement stopped. The scrubbing hands of the intern froze. The nursing student suddenly bolted up and ran from the amphitheater. Everyone heard the sound of her shoes slapping against the cement floors until they become distant and disappeared.

* * * * *

That afternoon, Edith appeared unannounced in DePage's office. In three strides she was in front of his desk and staring directly into his eyes. She didn't wait for him to greet her.

"You dismissed one of my students today in a most cruel manner. How am I to train nursing students if you treat them like badly behaved maids?"

DePage was annoyed. He was still feeling the effects of the migraine and was desperately trying to work through it. He was much too busy to be confronted by Cavell—again. He removed his wire-rimmed glasses and pinched the bridge of his nose.

"There is nothing to discuss. The girl is out. I will not have her in my school if she refuses to obey orders."

"Your school?"

"That's right. My school." He knew the instant he said those words that it was a mistake.

"Rubbish! When I came here, we agreed I would be in charge of this school and that these students would be under my leadership. It is my responsibility to decide who goes and who stays."

He did not want to have this conversation with Cavell, but he would be damned if he was going to concede to her. "Her behavior was unacceptable."

Edith crossed her arms over her chest. "Frankly, your behavior was far more reprehensible than the student's trifling misdemeanor."

In one swift movement, DePage ripped off his little black skullcap and threw it on the desk. "The girl is out! Dismissed! I never want to see her again! Do you understand?" The cotton cap slid across the polished surface and landed at Edith's feet.

Edith picked up the cap and threw it back on the desk, directly in front of him. She leaned into his face. "Docteur DePage, you are being totally irrational. We will discuss this when you come to your senses. In the meantime, I will keep her out of the surgical theater until we come to an agreement. If we can't agree on this, I may have to reconsider my position here."

He heard the swish of her uniform as she strode out of his office. When the door closed, his shoulders slumped. He reached into the bottom drawer of his desk and took out a bottle of whisky. *Why couldn't she give in just this once? What was one student to her? Tart! That's what this student was! How dare she disrupt my surgical procedure with her flirting? There will be plenty more students to replace her. Someone has to set the standards and make sure they are followed.*

DePage poured out a few fingers of the brown liquid and swallowed it in one gulp. He could never tell Cavell the truth, that this one student infuriated him because she drew the attention away from him. He had no idea how to resolve this matter with Edith.

* * * * *

The next day, Edith crouched beside a mangy terrier-type dog lying under her desk. She ran her hand over his shaggy fur. "Good boy, you are off the streets at last and have a home now. We'll be good friends, you and I. I promise to take care of you."

The dirty brown and white dog looked up at her with sad, liquid brown eyes. His ragged tail thumped against the thin rug.

"You are very sorely in need of a bath. And you need a name. What shall I call you?" She feigned serious contemplation. The dog's ears twitched. "Hmmm. I know, my little furry friend. I shall call you Jack."

The tail thumped again. His tongue was warm as he licked her hand. "Oh, you like that name, do you?" The dog's ears twitched.

"Good, because that's my brother's name. Of course, he might not be so pleased to know I named a stray dog after him, but that's our secret, isn't it, Jack?"

The door opened, letting in a rush of cool spring air. Carefully peering around the edge of the door stood Marie, her head cocked to one side, looking like an inquisitive bird. "I hope you don't mind my dropping in on you like this. May I come in?"

Edith made a quick hand gesture, giving her friend permission to enter.

Marie walked over to the door that was opened to the garden. "Edith, you have accomplished a remarkable miracle with this garden. It is so beautiful now with the lavender, red, and yellow spring flowers and those flowering shrubs. Do you mind if my boy plays out there? I had to bring him with me. He has not been well lately." She opened the back door to the garden to let Pierre out.

"Not at all. I'm so sorry to hear about his illness. Do you think it will soon pass?"

"I think so," said Marie as she removed her hat and shawl and placed it on the back of a stuffed chair. "Antoine will take a closer look at Pierre when he gets home tonight."

They walked into Edith's room, where Marie plumped up a cushion and sat on the small sofa. "You have done so much with this room. I love the personal touches." She pointed to a framed picture. "What church is that?"

"It's the Norwich Cathedral, near where I grew up. My father is a priest and a good friend of the bishop there."

Edith gestured to a simmering teapot. "Fancy some tea? I was about to pour myself a cup."

"That would be lovely, thank you. The English do love their tea. We Belgians tend to be coffee lovers—you can easily put chocolate into coffee, but not into tea." Marie grimaced.

Edith smiled at the comment and poured out two cups of tea. She sat at the desk. After taking a sip, she looked up over her cup at her friend and ventured in.

"Let's be honest, Marie. You didn't come here to talk about the garden, the room, or my country's love of tea, did you?"

Marie gave a doleful smile, took a sip herself, and hesitated, trying to find the right words to start.

"I, uh,…I understand you had a little disagreement with my husband yesterday."

"He dismissed one of my students on the spot for the most trivial of reasons. In doing so, he undermined my authority. I don't consider that a 'little disagreement.'"

"Is there any way we can, maybe, find some agreement between you and Antoine?"

"Not if it means dismissing a student who has worked hard for months to meet the requirements of this training school. If word of this gets out to the public, and I assure you it will, we will be forced to close our doors because we will never convince other women to come here. That is not the way I want to be treated, and it's not the way I treat my nurses. If Antoine cannot behave with decency and respect toward my students, then maybe you chose the wrong person for this position."

"Please, Edith, I know my husband has a foul mouth and is hot-headed. Even though you approach things very differently, you both want this school to succeed. We have come too far to give up on it now. He needs you, and like it or not, you do need him."

"Except he seems to be afflicted with a rare disease that makes him believe he is right all of the time."

"Most of the time he is right, though not always, of course."

Both women sipped their tea in silence. Edith knew that the first person to break the silence of a stalemate loses the argument.

Marie spoke first. "Suppose we reprimand the student in some way of your choice and you keep her away from Antoine until he calms down."

Edith thought for a moment. "All right. Here are my terms. If I am allowed to address this issue with her, I will keep her away from your husband as long it takes for him to get over this incident, but I want it established that I am in charge of this school and these students. If your husband has any further disagreements with my probationers or nurses, he is to come to me first. Are these terms upon which we can agree?"

"If we agree to this, you will stay?"

"I will, unless this agreement is broken."

Marie smiled for the first time. Straining her head sideways, she tried to read a document on Edith's desk. "I hope that's not your resignation."

"No. I'm writing an article for London's *Nursing Mirror* describing our work in Brussels. We need to do more than plaster posters on the walls of Brussels. If we are to survive, we cannot depend on Belgian women alone to keep this school going. They simply are not ready to accept this profession just yet. For now, we must bring in probationers from other countries. To do that, we must let nursing academia know what we are doing here. I want to present our work at the International Council of Nurses, but that will be for another time. This first."

"Edith, that's wonderful! Can you read it to me?"

"I won't read it word for word, but briefly, I have described the school, the daily life of the students, the curriculum, and their qualifications for enrolment. In it I also explain that after they graduate, they will be guaranteed a five-year work contract."

Marie reached out to pick up the paper. "May I show it to Antoine?"

Edith put her hand over the handwritten document. "Only if he agrees to my terms."

"I am sure I can convince Antoine to agree to your terms." She headed toward the door to the garden to pick up her son, when suddenly her hand flew to her throat.

"*Mon Dieu*! What in God's name is that miserable creature?" she cried, pointing to the dog under the desk.

Jack's head was in his crotch and he was making sloshing sounds.

"Oh, that's Jack. He's quite friendly actually," Edith said.

"Edith, he's filthy. You can't have this dog around the clinic and the students. He obviously has fleas or maybe worms. God only knows what else. He may even be vicious."

At the sound of Marie's voice, Jack's head emerged. He gave a few forceful snorts and shifted his gaze between Marie and Edith. Edith bent down and ran her hand over the shaggy head and ears. She felt a fresh wound where the tip of one ear had been torn or bitten off.

"I grant you he is in need of a good bath, but once we clean him up, he will be fine company."

Marie backed away. "I don't know where you got that sorry-looking, mangy mongrel, but I promise not to tell Antoine about him if you promise to get rid of him."

Jack gave a sigh, looked up at Edith, and rested his head on her foot.

"I found him begging at the back door of the clinic. I will not turn him back onto the street to starve to death. If you want me to stay, Jack stays too."

Marie threw her hands up in resignation. "Is that it?"

"Quite."

Marie picked up her son, gathered up her skirts, and carefully side-stepped around Jack.

Edith thought she saw a slight curl in his upper lip as Marie moved past him to leave. When she looked again, his eyes were closed.

— 16 —

ELIZABETH WILKINS

F ive years after the school opened, Edith found herself doing the work of three people. In addition to managing the nursing school and nursing services, she was teaching physicians along side Dr. DePage at the local medical school. What she needed was a competent nurse who could speak French to help her with the clinic and nursing school.

One nurse, Elizabeth Wilkins, answered her advertisement in the *Nursing Mirror*. Desperate for help, Edith hired the applicant without interviewing her because she was in Norwich visiting her mother at the time. One of the first things Edith had done on her return to Brussels was to set up a meeting with the 29-year-old Welsh nurse.

There was a light tap on the door.

"Come in, come in."

Looking up, Edith stared straight at a woman with the most beautiful, cherubic face she had ever seen.

"I'm so pleased to meet you at last," said Elizabeth in French that had the same clipped English accent as her own. She wore a white linen dress with short sleeves and pleats that folded over her chest. A sky-blue sash encircled her narrow waist, accentuating the curves of her figure.

Edith reached out her hand to the young woman and felt a gloved hand give a firm shake. "Please come in and sit down. I am so pleased that you have come, Miss Wilkins. Would you like a cup of tea?"

Elizabeth gathered up her skirt, sat, and crossed her ankles. "That would be lovely." She pulled on the ribbon that held her straw bonnet in place, revealing hair the color of golden silk set up in a pompadour.

Edith inhaled a delicate combined scent of lavender rose. "Let me take your gloves and bonnet." She carefully placed the gloves and bonnet on the desk and called down to the kitchen to have a tray of tea and cakes brought up to her office.

"You wrote that you have been working diligently at the Royal Seamen's Hospital in Cardiff. Did you like working in Wales?" asked Edith.

"It was a good experience that taught me much, but I'm ready to move into a new position, such as the one you described in the *Nursing Mirror*."

"You are Welsh, then, Miss Wilkins?"

"My mother is Welsh, but my father's family is from Wiltshire and stretches way back to Sir Christopher Wren's time."

In contrast to Elizabeth's soft, clear voice, Edith's sounded starchy to her own ears.

"I applied to a hospital in Mumbles, near Swansea once," said Edith.

"And did you like it there?"

"I never got the chance to find out. My application was rejected."

Elizabeth looked startled. "You? The Florence Nightingale of Belgium? Rejected by a hospital in Wales?"

"That was more than fifteen years ago. My reputation was a bit less impressive then."

Elizabeth noticed how the angular features of Edith's face were framed with thick brown hair, pulled up, and with wisps of gray forming on the edges. Webbed creases appeared at the corners of the older woman's thin lips. But it was her eyes that were her most startling feature: steel-blue, quick, intelligent, and filled with a depth of soul. She noticed how Edith's hands, folded on the desk, were red and dry from years of scrubbing in carbolic acid for surgery.

She had been warned that Miss Cavell smiled infrequently and remained emotionally distant, but Edith's smile at this moment was warm and welcoming.

Edith leaned toward her in a conspiratorial pose. "I will confess to you, Miss Wilkins. Great reputations face great obstacles. A sea of success is not without its storms. It's not always easy to navigate."

"But you have to admit, Miss Cavell, that the hospital in Mumbles muddled it up a bit, didn't it?"

They both laughed. Edith heard herself chuckle a little too loudly. There was a knock, the doors opened and tea was brought in on a polished silver tray.

Edith was curious about this young woman, who did not look strong enough to be a nurse. Her hands were like fine porcelain. Edith watched her elegant fingers pick up the teacup, stir in a spoonful of sugar, put the cup to her mouth, and sip with pursed lips. Nothing about Elizabeth seemed ordinary to her.

"So tell me, Miss Wilkins, why would you seek a post in another country? You are at the age when women think of marrying and raising a family."

This was an unexpected question for Elizabeth. She did not want to return to the dirty, crowded port city of Cardiff. She wanted a position in the colorful city of Brussels. Her broader goal was to travel. Other nurses had told stories of Edith Cavell's reputation for being demanding with her students and staff. She had heard that some nurses who applied to her school were not accepted, and of those who were, few finished the course. However, in spite of her reputation for severity, Edith Cavell was also known to be caring and fair. This was what Elizabeth counted on.

Looking at the famous woman, who was now fiddling with a pencil, she was sure she detected an unmistakable kindness in Edith's eyes.

"Miss Cavell, I have no interest in marriage or raising a family. Frankly, I don't believe there is a man worth marrying who would tolerate my ambitions. Just as you and Florence Nightingale have chosen to reject personal gratification for what matters the most in your lives, I too, am married to my work and that is enough for me."

Edith put her pencil down, reached for her teacup, sipped, and then carefully placed it in the middle of the saucer.

"You understand that the work here in Brussels is very arduous. Belgian women still believe nursing is beneath them and tend to be too fond of their own pleasures. It has taken us five years to grow from five students to twenty-five. Until now, only two classes with a total of fourteen students have finished, and most of them have returned to their own countries. Despite the difficulties, we have experienced some successes. We are getting calls from nursing homes and hospitals all over Belgium requesting our nurses. We can hardly meet the demands."

"Miss Cavell, I met with your nursing supervisor, who described my clinical duties, but could you please tell me more of what this position requires?"

"Most certainly. As you know, the position is for a Senior Sister of the Clinique on the rue de la Culture. On a broad canvas, you will help us change how an entire country cares for its people. I will be honest and tell you that you will be working under less than ideal circumstances. The hours will be long and you have little time to yourself. You will be compensated with a small salary and the satisfaction that you are making a difference in the lives to the people who need you. Your meals, uniforms, and housing will be provided."

Edith paused and looked into a face that radiated excitement and promise. "Do you believe you are up to it?"

Sister Elizabeth Wilkins and Jack (Source: *With Edith Cavell* by Jacqueline Van Til, New York, H.W. Bridges, 1922.)

"Very much so. I know I have much to learn, Miss Cavell, but I promise I will be a faithful nurse and loyal to your vision." She pointed to a crack in Edith's teacup. "I'm a bit like that teacup. Even though it is chipped, you can still drink from it. I do believe my usefulness to you will not be impaired by my imperfections."

Elizabeth paused and shifted on her chair, as if she were suddenly uncomfortable. "I thought I would find my calling in Cardiff, but it was not to be. When I read your advertisement for a matron, I believed it would lead me to what I am destined to do. Have you ever reflected, Miss Cavell, that you did not get that position in Mumbles because you were not destined to spend your life in a little village off the coast of Wales? You see? I feel the same way. I strongly believe that my destiny is in Brussels, working under your leadership."

Edith could hardly believe what she was hearing. So many of the nurses who applied for positions were unsuitable because they could not speak the language or could not teach or were not dedicated to the work, but this angelic woman was perfect in every way.

"I think you will suit the position quite well. I have reviewed your resumé and believe you to be well qualified." With that, Edith stood up and held out her hand.

"Welcome to the nursing staff of the rue de Culture Clinique, Sister Wilkins."

— 17 —

TURN OF EVENTS

"**S**omebody help me! Please, God Almighty! Help me or let me die! Get me out of here!" Edith had just arrived on the hospital ward when she heard a woman calling out. She looked around for a nurse or a probationer but saw no one. She walked over to the woman, who was struggling to free herself from a wicker invalid chair.

"Don't worry, I'll find someone to help me get you to bed and give you a sedative." Then under her breath "It's just that I don't know where everyone is right now."

"I think I do," said a priest, coming onto the ward. "There's a crowd at the corner watching a dog fight."

The color drained from Edith's face.

"A dog fight? Oh, no! It might be Jack! Please stay with this woman for just a few minutes? I'll be back."

She heard the woman calling after her as she turned and rushed out the room. "Oh, please come back here. Take me home with you, please. Don't leave me!"

Edith ran down the stairs and out into the street. Turning the corner, she heard the growling and snapping jaws of two animals locked in ferocious combat. She ran towards the crowd of people circled around two dogs. Two men among the crowd yelled out bets to each other.

"Two francs on the pit bull terrier," said a man with a lumpy complexion and purple veins that crossed his flushed cheeks.

"I'll bet you three on the larger dog. He's a street dog and a fighter, he is," said another man, with a toothless, caved-in mouth and hollow red-rimmed eyes.

"If you want to lose three francs that quickly, done!"

Edith recognized the chestnut hair of Millicent White, a newly hired Irish nurse, who was standing in the front of the crowd with the back of her hand pressed against her mouth. Two probationer nurses stood behind her, staring at the horror. Blood oozed from bite marks on the neck of the scruffy larger dog. One of the bull terrier's ears was torn ragged. Open pieces of pink skin formed slashes through the smooth brown coat around his shoulders. Then the muscular pit bull clamped his massive jaws around the throat of the larger thinner, dog and would not let go.

"Get me two buckets of ice-cold water," yelled Edith to two of the probationers in the crowd.

"And you," she said pointing to Millicent. "Get back to the ward and sedate Mme. Dufrene. She's in one of her confused states." Millicent hesitated, looking back at the animals on the ground. "Where is Sister Wilkins?"

"She is off duty today, Miss Cavell," said Millicent.

"Send one of the students to find Elizabeth, and have her wait for me in the clinic."

Millicent nodded her head and hurried away from the crowd.

As Edith waited for the buckets of water to appear, the larger dog was lying on the ground, energy spent, unable to fight back or get free of the thick jaws still clamped around his throat, his breathing now a tight wheeze. The toothless man slapped the other on the shoulder.

"In a few minutes, I'll be three francs richer. Your dog's had it."

The two probationers appeared, each with a bucketful of water, and handed them over to Edith. She pushed in front of the two betting men and threw the cold water from one bucket over the heads of the battling animals.

Water mixed with blood and saliva splashed over her shoes and flowed between the cobblestones. For a moment, the two animals stopped struggling. The bull terrier's coat rippled with shivers, but it would not loosen his grip on the neck of the wheezing dog beneath him. The larger dog desperately tried to twist his head to one side to loosen the jaws, but it was useless. Edith threw the second bucketful of water over them and not waiting for results, she leaned over and beat the bull terrier over the head with the bucket.

"I wouldn't do that, missy," said the lumpy-faced man. "Aside from ruining a good bet, that bull will turn on you. He's in a fighting rage. If he lets go of that dog, he'll turn on you. You best let it be finished."

"I will not stand here and watch that poor animal suffocate in front of me."

She turned back. The metal bucket clanged every time it hit the thick skull of the terrier. Clang! Clang! Finally, the terrier rolled over and lay spent with his tongue lolling out the side of his mouth. Blood and slime drooled out of the mouth of the scruffy-coated larger dog. His eyes were rolled back. Both dogs heaved as they lay on their sides.

"You!" shouted Edith, pointing to the toothless man, who was counting out francs in one hand; her voice mixed with wrath and concern. "Pick up this poor creature and bring him to my clinic."

His lips flapped as he spoke. "Why bother? That dog's a few minutes away from being dead. And when he dies, I win three francs." He gave a gummy grin.

"I'll give you four francs if you pick him up and take him to the clinic."

The lumpy-faced man stepped in. His voice was raspy. "For four francs, I will take him for you, although I do not know why you are bothering. He will be dead before we get there."

He leaned forward and heaved the bloody animal into his arms. The pit bull had recovered somewhat and was standing on weak legs. He shook his head, splattering blood and saliva over anyone who stood near.

A woman in the crowd came forward and pointed to the confused animal. "I know that bull. It belongs to Otto Heindelin on the next street over. Must have crossed behind the buildings and attacked the stray. He's very protective about his territory. That stray must have some fighting spirit to come against Otto's bull. Otto's been training his dog to fight."

"This dog is a stray?" Edith asked the woman, pointing to the dog who lay with vacant eyes across the man's arms.

"He must be. He has been in poor shape for some time now. Occasionally, we throw out a few scraps for him. I think they got into the fight over the scraps."

Edith strode behind the man carrying the dog. Elizabeth, waiting at the clinic, motioned for him to lay the limp dog down on a flat table covered with a sheet. The man then stood to one side, folded his arms over his chest, and watched.

Edith and Elizabeth worked together to clean away the sticky, crusted blood matted into the fur around the dog's neck. Edith was grateful for Elizabeth's help; it made the gruesome task more bearable.

"Come on, my little friend. You are in good hands now," said Edith in soothing tones as she ran her hands over its spine, legs, and boney haunches. Nothing felt broken. She opened the narrow snout, saw that a tooth had been torn out, and placed a piece of gauze over the bleeding gum.

Elizabeth made the same little clucking noises as she would to a crying baby. "Come on now. You can't die now. You have people here to care for you."

The man's raspy voice broke in. "I have to leave. Give me my four francs. You are wasting your time. That animal is dead and does not have the good sense to quit breathing."

Edith shot him a look. "Rubbish! We will even give him a name. He will be called…" She hesitated. "What is your name?"

"It's Don. Why? I did what you asked, and now I want my francs."

"Very well, then. He will be called Don. Come back tomorrow and I will give you your four francs. I am too busy right now trying to save your namesake."

When Marie DePage came to the clinic the following morning, she found Edith out of uniform and slumped in a chair. There were dark patches of fatigue under her eyes. Strands of hair hung loosely about her face and down her neck.

"You did not show up for hospital rounds this morning. I thought I should stop by to see if you are well."

Edith muffled a yawn. "Well enough. Just tired. I have been up all night."

"You have Sister Wilkins and Sister White to help you with night duty."

"Sister White handled the wards. Sister Wilkins and I both did special night duty. We stayed with a confused patient until the sedative calmed her and another patient that needed our immediate attention."

"Is one of Antoine's patient's having problems? Should Antoine be called?

Edith waved one hand in a weak, dismissive motion. "No need to worry. The confused patient finally calmed down, and the other is not Antoine's patient. Given some good nursing care and a few meals, I think he has a good chance of recovery."

"What is his name?"

"Don."

"Don what?"

Edith yawned and looked away. "Just Don."

Just then Don wobbled out of the treatment room and past Marie toward Edith. A bandage, darkened in places, had come loose from his neck and was dragging on the floor. His tail hung limp, and there were open sores where fur was missing. When he got to Edith, he stopped and pressed his head against her leg. His hind legs trembled for a moment; then he dropped.

"Oh, no, Edith. Please tell me you did not take in one of those dogs fighting on the corner yesterday evening. *Mon Dieu*! He looks like he was dead and buried and you dug him up! We have had enough problems with your Jack. Please do not take in a second mongrel. This one is even more mangy than the other."

"Jack could use some company and Don…" She bent down and gently patted the rough coat. "Don needs a home and some decent meals." Marie stood up, grabbed her coat, and in one quick movement, flung her scarf around her neck.

"So, it is settled, then. You will not get rid of that filthy thing." She saw the steel-gray eyes darken and hesitated before adding, "Will you?"

"No, Marie, I will not. If Don recovers, he is here to stay. I will be responsible for him. I don't know why you hate Jack so much. He has the heart of a lion and the soul of an angel."

"He has the mouth of a lion and the soul of the devil. He bit Antoine."

"It was barely a nip on the heels when Antoine raised his voice at me," Edith clarified.

"I said bit, not nipped."

Edith dried her hands with a towel. "Maybe Jack can teach the good doctor to stop yelling. The Lord knows, I can't."

"What do you have to say about his biting the policeman, the postman, my carriage driver, and one of my horses, who, by the way, got an awful infection from it? And let us not forget how he attacked the coal man, the gardener, and…"

A loud banging on the door brought the conversation to a sudden halt.

"Mme. DePage! Mlle. Cavell! Come quickly!" Edith jumped up and ran to open the door. She recognized Antoine's personal secretary.

"What is it? Is there a problem?"

"Dr. DePage ordered me to find you and bring you both to the hospital."

Marie's voice wavered with fear. "Is it Pierre? He has been ill. Is he getting worst?"

"No, Madame. It's not your son. It's the queen!"

"Queen Elizabeth is sick?"

"Injured. She broke her arm after being thrown by a horse. She is at the Berkendael Hospital for treatment and is asking for you by name," the secretary pointed to Edith. "And King Albert is with her. They are in Dr. DePage's examination room. You must come now."

Edith turned to Marie. "Why is the Queen at our public hospital and not at St. Jean's? Whatever is this all about? You go, Marie. I'll get Sister White to watch over the ward. I'll be there as soon as I change into a clean uniform."

Edith had seen the royal couple in parades and ceremonies but had never spoken to them. She knew Queen Elizabeth was from Bavaria and had married the Belgian king just four years ago. Marie and Antoine had a great respect for the royal couple's ability to keep political stability in a country deeply divided between the Dutch, French, Germans, Walloons, and Flemish.

A uniformed driver waited for Edith outside with his motorcar engine idling. He closed the door behind Edith once she was seated. Outside the front door of the hospital, guards in blue uniforms with gold buttons stood at attention. They inspected anyone who tried to enter, but they silently moved aside and gave a quick tilt of their heads when Edith appeared.

She passed through the door and into the examination room, where Dr. DePage stood holding the Queen's right arm. Edith heard the last words of his sentence: "...need to radiograph this to determine if a fracture is present."

Still in her riding clothes, the Queen sat on his examination table. There was a tear in the right sleeve of her silk blouse. Dirt and grass stains were smeared into her riding skirt. Her oval face was crowned with a thick pile of glossy chestnut-brown hair, pulled up and knotted behind her head except for a small section that had fallen loose. There was a scrape over her right cheek.

Before entering the examination room, Edith curtsied. "Your Majesty. You have asked to see me?"

Without waiting for the Queen to answer, DePage jumped in. "Come in. Come in, Nurse Cavell. We both want to see you. Her Highness had the misfortune to be thrown by her horse, and I believe she may have broken her arm. She was doing a training routine, and her horse reared. We want you to accompany her to the radiograph machine. After we treat and stabilize her arm, she wants you to assign one of your trained nurses to her care."

The Queen's voice was so soft that Edith almost didn't hear her when she began to speak. Her French had a distinct German accent. "Nurse Cavell, I hope you object not to my coming to your fine hospital." She pointed with the other hand to a nervous man, dressed in a formal black coat and tie, who was standing by Dr. DePage.

"My physician, Dr. LeBoeuf, implores that I be treated at St. Jean's Hospital. It is where he works, and there is a tradition, of course, that all of royal family in Belgium be treated there. Today, I will change that tradition, because I have heard many wonderful reports of how well your nurses care for our people. So, you will not consider this an intrusion, I hope?"

"Not at all, Your Majesty. We are delighted that you have chosen to come here, but of course, are not delighted that you had the unfortunate accident. We can provide you with the excellent nursing care you require."

"I am a violinist, you see, and it is so important that my arm heal in a most useful way. This has happened just as a most famous violinist and I finished planning for a concert at Brussels Conservatory next month."

"I assure you we will give you excellent treatment."

"I have heard that Dr. DePage is finest surgeon in Belgium. Dr. LeBoeuf is also excellent physician, but he is not surgeon. If bone is displaced, I will need surgery, true?"

"You sound as if you have had some previous medical training, Your Majesty," said Edith.

"Most people knew my father as a military man, but he was also physician. I often assisted him with procedures. So I know how important good surgeon and good nurses are for my most complete recovery."

Between short winces of pain, the Queen still tried to force a smile. It melted any reservation Edith had about the monarch.

"Nurse Cavell," said DePage, "we must take Her Majesty to be radiographed." Edith recognized the authoritative tone Antoine used when he was trying to make an impression.

"How fortunate I am to be accompanied by the Florence Nightingale of Belgium," the Queen replied.

After the radiograph was completed, the Queen turned to Edith.

"I was maybe thinking, should I, the Queen, be treated less well than my own people just to uphold a tradition at St. Jean's? I think, this is not so good. Your school, it is doing well?"

"It is, Your Majesty, but many Belgian women still believe that nursing is a demeaning job. Most of our students are foreign."

DePage held the slick black and white Roentgen sheet up to the light. Letting the developing solution drip into the sink, he turned it one way and then another. Finally, he clipped it to a steel rod over the sink.

"Your Majesty, you do indeed have a compound fracture in the middle of the ulna, or the lower part of your arm. Fortunately, it does not extend into your wrist or up into your elbow, so movement in those areas will not be affected. It is slightly displaced, but the radius—the other bone in the lower arm—is intact. I believe that by using a little chloroform, we can align the fracture. The radius will act as a splint, but we still need to make an additional splint to be sure it heals in the proper position."

"How long will it take to heal?" the Queen asked in a low voice.

"We may be able to remove the splint in six weeks. Then, with Nurse Cavell's excellent nursing care, you may be able to use it properly in eight to ten weeks. I would, however, suggest you avoid any vigorous activity such as riding."

"But the concert, it is so important to our patrons. Other countries will attend. We have worked so hard. What will I tell my patrons?"

"Your Majesty will tell them that the Queen is human and when she breaks bones, she must heal in God's good time, just like everyone else. You will be able to play your violin for the next concert, but I am sorry to say, not for this one. You can also tell them that you are under the care of the best surgeon and nurse in all of Belgium."

Queen Elizabeth and King Albert of Belgium

THE NEW SCHOOL

"Psst! Edith!"

With chalk in hand, Edith was drawing the bones of the arm and hand on the blackboard for her anatomy class. Since word had gotten out about the Queen's choice of hospital, extra chairs had to be brought into the classroom to accommodate the surge of Belgian women who were now applying to the school.

Her students loved this class because "Madame," as Edith was always addressed, drew such beautiful illustrations. Edith turned her head to see who was calling to her and seeing no one, she turned back to the board.

Pointing to the upper arm, she explained, "This is the humerus. You can see how the humerus extends from the shoulder to the elbow, where it joins these two bones in the lower arm, which are called the ulna and the radius. When in use, they pivot off each other like levers."

A hand shot up from the back of the room.

"Nurse VanTil, you have a question."

"Is that where the Queen broke her arm?"

Pointing to the lower end of her illustration. "The Queen broke the ulna right about…"

She was again interrupted. "Psst! Edith! Over here!"

Edith recognized the voice. She looked towards the door and saw Marie standing in the hallway, gesturing wildly for her to come over.

"Excuse me, class. Please study this illustration and be ready to identify the bones in the wrist and hand, as well as the arm, when I return."

She walked out the door to see Marie obviously excited. "What is so important that you need to interrupt my anatomy class?"

Marie's words came in short spurts as she tried to catch her breath. "I ran all the way over here because I wanted to be the first to tell you. It's incredible! The Committee voted for it!"

Edith took Marie's arm and led her to the stairs outside the classroom door. "Come over here and sit down. Catch your breath and tell me again what they did."

"They did it! You are going to get your new school! Since treating the Queen, there has been such an intense interest in what we are doing here, we have run out of room and can no longer accept everyone who is applying. When the Committee said the cost of a new school was too high, Mr. Goldsmith, the banker and the new Chairman of the Committee, agreed to provide the funds. The Committee then gave their approval."

"Splendid! Thank you, God!" said Edith as she looked upward to heaven.

"You had better thank Antoine as well. You should have seen him in front of the Committee. He told them that the extra building we have been using near the clinic could not accommodate all our students. He was unrelenting in his insistence that we needed the new school."

"I can well imagine," said Edith.

"No, truly. He accepted no excuses from the Committee for not approving the new school and challenged every objection and excuse. He also reminded them of the request by the administrator of St. Jean's Hospital to send over our trained nurses to manage their wards after the nuns there went on strike. Can you believe that we now provide all of St Jean's nurses? The Mother Superior is no longer in charge of the nurses there."

Edith's smile widened. "That should make Antoine a very happy man. We have so much to talk over. I need to finish this class and the extra one we added after this one. Can you come back tomorrow evening after my class?"

"Better yet, come to my house tomorrow after class and have supper with us. I'm sure Antoine will want to tell you the details himself. He will love gloating with you over all of this."

Edith turned to go back into her classroom. "And Edith, do not bring your dogs. You know how Antoine feels about both of them. Please?" said Marie with a pleading expression.

"I'll think about it," said Edith as she headed back to the classroom.

The next evening after classes were over, Edith allowed herself to feel the excitement of the news about building a new school. She looked forward to relaxing with Marie and Antoine over a wonderful supper and savouring all the details. The Queen's broken arm had advanced the school and new hospital faster in the last few months than all the efforts made by Edith and the DePages in the last five years.

Arriving at the DePage home, she reached up and rapped the gold lion's head knocker. When Marie opened the door, she rushed to throw her arms around Edith and sobbed into her shoulder. "Edith, it's awful. So many have died."

Edith stood stunned. "Who died? Where?"

Marie's body shook. "Hundreds, maybe more than a thousand, have died. They do not even know how many. It just sank, and they drowned. They said this could never happen."

"What couldn't happen? Who drowned? Marie, what are you talking about?"

"The *Titanic*. It was on its first voyage from Southampton to New York. It hit an iceberg off the coast of Newfoundland in Canada. They said it was unsinkable but it sank anyway in the middle of the night. I cannot imagine, people dropped into freezing water surrounded with icebergs. Some women and children were found shivering in lifeboats with soaking wet clothes. And they were the lucky ones. Most of the men drowned because there were not enough lifeboats. They just went under. I cannot imagine a more horrible way to die."

— 19 —
GRACE JEMMETT

When Edith received the letter, she recognized the handwriting of her sister, Lillian, now the wife of a physician named Longworth Wainwright. Fearful her mother had suffered some illness or died, she tore open the letter.

February 28, 1912
Upton Lodge, Henley-on-Thames, England

My Dear Edith,
We hope this letter finds you well. We continually hear of your courageous work in Brussels, but we do so miss you. Mother always hopes you will soon retire from your work there and return home. She misses you so.

Longworth can find you a position here that is worthy of your experience if you decide to return home. It would be wonderful if we could be together once again.

Of course, the horrid winter weather keeps Mother inside more than she would wish and snaps up her arthritis. Longworth has prescribed liniments for her joints that provide some relief from the pain.

We have not recently heard from our dear sister Florence, who is busy as a nursing superintendent in London.

I am writing to ask a favor of you. We have the tragic case of a young woman aged twenty, who has unfortunately has developed a craving for morphine after being treated for a nervous disorder. Physicians here continue to administer drugs to her without looking into the consequences. She is the daughter of an influential businessman who is too lenient in providing the

*discipline she needs to be treated successfully. He agrees with
us that it would be in her best interest that she be placed with
someone who can help her break this vicious habit.*

*We hoped you might be willing to look after her. Her name is
Grace Jemmett. Her father is quite willing to pay you gener-
ously. We would so appreciate your assistance with her, having
no one else to turn to.*

*If you are willing to assist us in the matter, please write when it
would be a good time for her to travel.*

*Ever affectionately,
Lillian*

Edith reread the letter, folded it, and placed it on the desk. Edith's
position left her with little extra time to take on an additional responsibility, but Lillian and her husband would not have asked this of her if they
were not desperate. There were always new expenses and the fee from
Jemmett's father was sorely needed. If this unfortunate young woman
needed help, Edith would find the time and means to provide it.

*March 21, 1912
149 Rue de la Culture, Ixelles, Belge*

*Dear Lillian,
I am glad to hear Mother is doing so well under your care. I
miss her terribly and count the days I can return home on
holiday to see her.*

*We are now making good progress with our work and have
been approved for a new nursing school. So I am quite busy
and could not permanently leave my work to return home.*

*You may send Grace over to me as soon as you receive this
letter. Please give Mother all of my love and tell her not to
worry so about me. She is always in the circle of my thoughts.
In a few months, we will be together again.*

*Affectionately,
Edith*

* * * * *

When Grace Jemmett stepped off the train, she was met by a slightly built woman with a severe expression and graying hair, wearing gray leather gloves, calfskin shoes, and a blue woolen cape that flipped open in the brisk winter wind, revealing a blue uniform underneath. Grace put her bag down and offered the woman a gloved hand. To her surprise, two arms reached out and gave her a welcoming hug.

"Miss Jemmett, I am so pleased you are willing to live here with me for a while," said Edith. "I hope we can make the stay here pleasant enough for you. Please, get your bag, and we will find a cab to take us back to Ixelles, where I live."

Edith took Grace up the two marble stairs worn down with wear. Grace hesitated at the top stair, staring down at a black grate in the ground next to the stairs.

"It's the grate where coal is loaded into the coal bin down in the basement," explained Edith. "The kitchen, laundry, and service rooms are also on that level. Actually, the basement level is the only place where you can move directly between the four buildings." Edith opened the door and ushered the tall, red-haired woman in. "You will be living with me here at the number 149 house."

Just then, Jack came bounding into the room, tail wagging in circles, expecting a hearty greeting from Edith. Don followed behind, walking stiffly, his tail wagging a bit slower. Grace drew back.

"Don't worry," said Edith. "They are friendly sorts, once they get to know you. If you promise not to bite them, they won't bite you."

"That's one promise I am sure to keep," Grace said softly.

Edith walked Grace though the rooms. "My living quarters, office, and reception area are here at number 149. The house to the left is number 147, where the surgical theater is on the first floor, and classrooms for nursing students are on the second. The house beyond that is…"

"I know," interrupted Grace. "Let me guess. It's number 145."

"Brilliant! And do you know what we do there?"

Grace's voice was flat and uninterested. "I'm sure I'm about to find out."

"It is important that you know where the patient wards are. In general, you are free to move about, but because of your problem, you are not permitted to go into number 145, our Clinique."

Just then, Dr. DePage pushed through the door and with head down, bumped into Grace.

"Sorry. I have been working on a devil of a chest wound, and now I am late for this poor woman's hysterectomy."

He lifted his head and looked at Grace. "Do I know you?"

Then to Edith, "Is this a new nursing student?"

"This is Grace Jemmett. My brother-in-law, who is a physician in England, has asked that she stay with us to, uh, to recover."

"Recover from what?"

"I know you are in a rush, doctor, but may we please step aside for just a moment?"

Edith directed him out of the hallway and into a side room. DePage immediately asked, "Who is this woman?"

"She needs our help. She is addicted to morphia, and we have been asked to help treat her."

DePage whipped off his black cotton skullcap and slapped it against the wall.

"Morphia addict! You are taking a drug addict into this school? Have you gone mad?"

"I assure you, she will not be allowed to be near the ward areas. There are enough of us to keep an eye on her and..." She paused for effect. "... her father is quite wealthy and will pay us a handsome sum to treat her."

DePage shoved the skull cap back onto his head.

"You cannot assure me of anything with an addict. What good are a few extra francs if the reputation we have worked so hard to build is ruined? People will soon find out we are harboring a drug addict. What then? What do we say to them? Tell me."

"We tell them she needs help just like everyone else."

DePage flung open the door. It banged against the wall and snapped back.

"First stray dogs and now stray drug addicts. I swear, Cavell, your penchant for picking up strays will get you in trouble someday. You cannot save everyone and everything."

Edith returned to Grace. "It seems as if you have just met our surgeon, Dr. DePage. He is in charge of all of this and is a bit…"

Grace finished the sentence. "…of a hothead?"

"I agree, he has a temper. But he is truly a genius with the scalpel. It would be best if you stayed away from him for a while."

"I won't have any problem doing that. Are you the matron for all of this, Edith?

"I have responsibilities that involve this school, three hospitals, three private nursing homes, 24 communal schools, 13 private kindergartens, a clinic, private-duty cases, and four lectures a week to doctors and nurses."

"That doesn't leave you much time to watch over me, does it?"

"I assure you, Grace, you will be my priority. Now, let's bring your things to my quarters, where you will be staying. Our manner of living will be quite different from what you are used to, but you are part of my family now. Here we all watch over each other."

— 20 —

Fall 1913, The Challenge

"Keep her there. I'll be right down."

Edith hung up the phone and rushed down to the local pharmacy. The pharmacist held out a prescription to her. "It is for morphia and signed by Dr. DePage." He pointed to Grace, who was standing to one side with a sheepish expression.

The pharmacist explained. "She said she was working for the clinic and that you sent her here to collect this, but it does not look like the doctor's handwriting. It is too legible."

Edith stuffed the prescription into her pocket. "You were right to call me. Grace does work for us, but she has no authority to handle drugs or prescriptions for drugs. If there are any further problems of this kind, please call me."

She glared at Grace who was casually putting a cigarette to her lips. "Come along, Grace."

Once outside the pharmacy, Edith took her elbow. "Put that cigarette out. Did you truly think you would get away with that stupid prank?"

Grace rolled her eyes upward, blew out a cloud of smoke, threw the cigarette on the ground, and crushed it in a circular motion with her foot.

"It was worth a try. Besides, I was bored. I'm tired of preparing vegetables in the kitchen and washing dishes. At home, we have servants who do that."

"You are not at home, and this is not a holiday. Here, we all do what is needed, regardless of rank."

"Oh, is that so?" said Grace, pulling her elbow away from Edith's hand. "I don't see you scrubbing pots in the kitchen or serving porridge."

"I have polished my share of many pots and mopped many floors. There are times now when it would be a relief to do something so simple again. I have been sorely criticised for bringing you here and have suffered repeated embarrassing incidents because of your behavior.

However, I still believe that with compassion and care, you can be cured. Now please try to work with me."

When they reached number 149, Grace tramped begrudgingly up the narrow wooden stairs to her room. Edith sat at her desk for a few minutes to regain her composure. Then she looked over at the clock on her desk and jumped up. Throwing on her cloak, she bolted out the door. If she hurried, she could make the Committee meeting on time. It was important that she attend this meeting because they would be discussing plans for her new school.

She rushed to the conference room on the second floor of the Berkendael Hospital. A highly polished oblong table filled the center of the room. Upholstered leather chairs were carefully placed around it. On one side were windows edged with burgundy velvet curtains, swagged back to let in the light.

Outside, the sulking skies threatened an advancing storm. The black, yellow, and red stripes of the Belgian flag snapped vigorously in the wind. Its ropes slapped noisily against the flagpole. Edith was always amazed at how changeable the weather was in Belgium. A day could start out sunny, as it had this morning, and then suddenly change a shift in the wind would overtake the afternoon sun to bring dark clouds and cold rain.

She looked back into the room. She thought about how the Committee had changed over the last six years. In place of open bodices and ruffled satin dresses were formal dark suits and gold watch chains. Gone from the walls were the rich masterpieces of Dutch art and in their place was a line of sepia-toned black-framed photographs of every past and present member of the Committee. Edith sat at the back of the room next to a polished credenza where tea, coffee, and a plate of cheeses and sliced meats were set out.

The air was filled with a mixture of furniture wax, leather, and cigar smoke. M. Goldsmith sat at the opposite end of the table. He fumbled with a row of buttons that strained to stay closed on his waistcoat, reached for his monocle, and carefully placed it in one eye. Reaching into his vest pocket, he removed an engraved gold watch, studied it for a moment, snapped it shut, and replaced it. Satisfied that everyone was in place, he thumped a polished gavel on a small brass plate, calling the meeting to order. A sudden stillness descended on the room.

"I see Mme. Cavell is here. That is good because we now have a copy of the plans for the new school. I will pass them around for everyone to review. It is truly an exciting time for all of us who have worked so diligently over the last six years to make this happen. However, it is now time to address our concerns with Mme. Cavell."

He motioned for Edith to move into an empty chair at the far end of the table.

"Mme. Cavell, we are all grateful for your hard work. You have made a success of this school, and we are all pleased with what you have accomplished. However, the Committee has been receiving many, shall we say, expressions of dissatisfaction—not of your work, of course—but many Belgians are wondering if it is time to have a Belgian nurse run the school and clinics." He paused and looked around the table.

"In addition, there is some pending political unrest in the Balkans that may make it difficult for an English woman to remain here. We thought that dispute had been settled, but now we hear that Serbian troops are marching into Albania. King Albert was informed that the Kaiser will invade France. If any of this is remotely true, Mme Cavell, we cannot predict what will happen and we may not be able to protect you."

Edith felt her hands go cold and mouth dry.

Goldsmith continued, "I must also be frank with you; having a Belgian nurse in charge of the school and clinics would put us in a better position to raise funds. Belgians would feel more generous if someone from their own country were directing affairs. We have just struggled to raise enough funds for the new hospital and now we seek additional funds for your new school. Prudence must prevail, and we must take the most profitable path. Of course, you could choose your successor and then make a decision to return to home with a pension."

Edith felt a heavy knot in her chest. After all she had done, they couldn't possibly want to dispose of her. How had she not seen it coming? And who would or could possibly replace her? Nurse Wilkins was an excellent supervisor but still much too young, and she wasn't Belgian. Neither was Millicent White. Clara Bohme had graduated and was now married and due to give birth to her first child.

Edith stood and faced the chairman. She paused and slowly reviewed the face of every Committee member. She wondered why Dr. DePage wasn't here. Did he even know about this meeting? The members remained motionless with eyes downcast. She looked directly at the Committee chairman, who managed to maintain eye contact with the slight, resolute figure before him.

Taking a deep breath, Edith said in a calm voice, "M. Goldsmith. Thank you for addressing your concerns with me. I appreciate your regard for my safety. We all live in a troubled world and are all subject to its dangers. I came here under dire circumstances. Your patrons were dying of infection from well-meaning but ignorant bedside caregivers. Against the advice of many Belgians, the church, and politicians, Dr. DePage, his wife, and this Committee had the foresight to start a nurses' training school. In doing so, a new profession was introduced to this country and lowered the rate of infection and needless deaths.

Edith paused and then continued. "I stayed on when there was little money and almost no support from the very Belgians who would now like to see me step aside. Other than Dr. DePage, with whom I assume you have discussed this matter, I am the only person who truly knows how to manage this nursing school, and at the same time can supervise work in three hospitals, run 24 communal schools, and teach four lectures a week to physicians and nurses. I know of no one who can replace me.

"When I can no longer continue, I will train my replacement. It will require more than one person, I assure you. If expense is a consideration, please bear in mind that replacing me will cost you far more than keeping me. No one has complained of my abilities or of my work. Should the time come that I may be in danger in Belgium, I humbly ask that you let me make my own decision as to whether I go or stay."

Goldsmith gave a practiced show of affability, but his smile was not reflected in his eyes.

"Your work is flawless, Mme. Cavell, and we will take your remarks into consideration, but I must add that your habits have also raised some concerns. You allow your dogs to freely roam the buildings and grounds. We feel that a nursing home and a clinic are not suitable places for the filth that comes with dogs. I need not remind you that there have also been problems with your dogs' behavior. It is reported that they are neither properly restrained nor well mannered. One of them has a reputation for biting members of the staff."

Goldsmith saw her lips tighten and cold steel creep into her eyes. He knew he had crossed some forbidden threshold.

"Jack," she emphasized his name, "can be kept under control, and I will make sure that both dogs roam only in my quarters and the garden behind. When walking about, they will be properly restrained. In addition, they are routinely bathed. Does that meet with your satisfaction?"

"That is not all, Mme. Cavell." A vein pulsed at Goldsmith's temple. "There is also the issue of the young woman you have taken in. Many of us do not believe a drug addict, a woman lacking in self-restraint and personal integrity, is a fitting companion for someone in your position."

Why must everything I do now be challenged by a Committee who knows very little about me? "Miss Jemmett was sent here at the request of my sister. She saw that this young woman would soon be destroyed by the treatment of incompetent doctors in England. Had I not taken her in, she would, most probably, be dead by now. In return for the care of Miss Jemmett, we have received a handsome sum from her father. That money helped pay for equipment and part of the salary of a much-needed night supervisor. Miss Jemmett is living in my quarters so I can closely supervise her activities."

"And have you been supervising her activities closely?"

"I have, and so are the other staff."

The Committee members sat transfixed, their heads bobbing from Goldsmith to Edith and back as if they were watching the International Lawn Tennis Challenge.

"When do you expect to return Miss Jemmett to her home?"

"When I have fulfilled my promise to see that she is cured."

"Thank you, Mme. Cavell."

"Will that be all?" Edith asked.

Goldsmith gave a few quick waves with his hand. "You are dismissed."

Outside, the skies opened up in torrents. Edith pulled her cloak around her against the wind that blew cold darts of rain into her face and ran back to her office. Jack greeted her with enthusiastic hand licks and Don with a short staccato of welcoming sneezes. Edith threw off her wet cloak, then turned and saw Elizabeth sitting on the divan.

Seeing her friend, Edith relaxed, "*Bonsoir*, Sister Wilkins. I must let these two out into the garden. They have been shut up most of the day."

"I let them out when I came in an hour ago, but with the rain, they didn't stay out long. I also fed them."

Edith slumped in the chair opposite Elizabeth and sighed. Elizabeth was always a welcome sight. Elizabeth had been everything she needed and wanted, a loyal nurse and friend. She did everything exactly as Edith herself would have done it. Working with her was one of the few pleasures she acknowledged to herself. How had she managed before Elizabeth arrived?

Edith was sure Elizabeth felt the same closeness as her. Otherwise, how could they work so well together, anticipating each other's needs? She knew they shared an invisible understanding that tied them in some special way to each other. She was anxious to share the proceedings of the Committee meeting with her; Elizabeth would help her put it into perspective.

Elizabeth shifted in her seat, her foot twitching nervously as she tugged on one ear lobe. She was first to speak, but didn't look at Edith. "I hope you don't mind my dropping in on you like this, but something has come up. There is no easy way to say this, so I'll just say it straight out. I will be tendering my notice in a few weeks. I have a chance to travel, and I'm keen to make a future for myself in a hospital in Switzerland."

Suddenly, Edith felt as if all the links that held her life together were coming apart. This couldn't be. The idea of losing Elizabeth gripped her like an illness. A slight nausea settled in the pit of her stomach. After a minute of uncomfortable silence, Elizabeth stood, picked up her cloak, and turned to leave.

"Please, Elizabeth, don't leave. At least not just yet."

Elizabeth could barely hear her. She turned to look directly at Edith, who looked back at her with eyes that were beginning to well up with tears.

"Please sit down. We need to talk about this. Today has been filled with unexpected surprises, but I must confess your resignation was the most unexpected. Could you tell me how you came to this decision? Did I or someone else offend you, or is the work too hard, or the pay…?"

"No, it's none of those reasons."

Elizabeth sat back down on the divan, picked up the crimson velvet cushion , and hugged it. "It's not you or the staff or the work or even the pay. Not at all. It's me and what I planned for myself. When I was working in the Royal Seamen's Hospital in Cardiff, the sailors told me wonderful stories of their travels to other countries. My family was so poor they gave me to my grandmother to raise. I knew I could never afford to travel, so I thought the best way to do so would be to secure positions at hospitals in countries I would like to see. I have always wanted to go to Switzerland, so when I saw an advertisement from a hospital there seeking a nurse, it seemed like the opportunity I was looking for. I applied for the position, and they have accepted me."

"Sister Wilkins...Elizabeth...do you see what we, not just me, but you and I, have accomplished here? I could have never done this without your help. Plans have been approved for our new nursing school. As we grow, your experience and skill will be invaluable, and your position and influence will increase. This is an opportunity for you, and I confess that I truly do need you, now more than ever."

Elizabeth's eyes fixed on Edith's fingers slowly caressing Jack's head, then she forced her gaze back to Edith's face. When she had decided on this plan two years ago, it seemed so simple. Work in Brussels, get experience, and after a year so, move on to another place. She was too young to stay in one place very long and had already stayed here longer than she planned. Maybe later she could think about staying in one place for awhile, but not now.

She looked at Edith and saw how tired the older woman looked–or was it sadness? She couldn't tell. All of the matron's physical strength seemed to have drifted away except for those piercing eyes that held Elizabeth transfixed. She felt a sense of doubt creeping in. "Mme. Cavell..."

Edith interrupted her. "Please, Elizabeth. We have gone through too much together not to be calling each other by our first names. When in private, please call me Edith."

"Edith, you make a strong argument, but I have been thinking about Switzerland for so long. If I stay here, there will be the new school to attend to and more to do at the Clinique, more students and more demands for our graduates. When will there ever be time for me to go to Switzerland if I don't go now?"

It's all beginning to unravel. If I hold on too tight and become too intent on my own goal, I will lose Elizabeth. Edith stood up. "Could you excuse me for a moment?"

Her shoes made wet patches as she walked over to her desk. She pulled out a gray, hard-covered book, opened it, ran her finger down a list and turned a few pages, studying them. Then she shut it and returned to sit opposite Elizabeth. She could not let Elizabeth walk out of her life and her work. Elizabeth had become too important to both.

"Would you be willing to accept a fully-paid trip to Switzerland in return for continuing your work here with a promise of a promotion when you return? I would be very much in your debt if you accepted such a proposal."

Elizabeth rubbed her earlobe. "How long would I be allowed to have on holiday in Switzerland?"

"How long would you like, and when would you like to go?"

"In the spring, for a month perhaps?"

Edith placed her palms down on the table. "It is settled, then. Is April to your liking, say, for four weeks?"

Elizabeth sprang out of her chair and flung her arms around Edith.

"You would do that for me? Edith, I promise I will write to the hospital in Switzerland straightaway thanking them for their consideration and regretfully for withdrawing my application."

Edith slipped her arms around Elizabeth and held her until she felt Elizabeth's hold loosen.

Edith stepped back and looked at Elizabeth's guileless face. "Thank you for doing this. I know this is a sacrifice for you. I pray this holiday will make up for some of what you have given up and show my appreciation for all you have done here. But I also must tell you that there were serious concerns expressed at the Committee meeting today about the unrest in the Balkans. They think fighting might break out between Germany and France. You must promise to keep me posted of your whereabouts should this unrest become more serious. I am concerned for your safety."

"And what of you? When will you take some holiday time for yourself?" Elizabeth asked.

"I will return home in July next year for my mother's birthday and our family holiday by the sea in North Norfolk. I will be able to rest there during our time together. I don't expect anything much will come of the situation in the Balkans; those countries always seem to be in some sort of disagreement with each other. So make your plans. Know that I will miss you so very much while you are gone."

Newspapers declaring the beginning of The Great War
Source: (Photo by author, taken at the WWI museum in Ypres, Belgium.)

— 21 —

THE THREAT OF UNREST

E dith opened the note slipped under her door.

Please come to Antoine's office for an 11:00 a.m. meeting. Cancel afternoon meetings. Important. Marie.

As soon as Edith walked into DePage's office, she knew something was wrong. Marie caught her eye, held it for a moment, and then looked away. Edith slowly placed her cape on the coat rack by the door and unpinned her white cotton nursing cap.

"Come in, Edith. Sit down," said DePage. "We have a serious situation to discuss."

She slid into the chair in front of his desk and held her cap in her lap. *He's following up the Committee's decision and is going to sack me. I've given up everything to change the delivery of healthcare in Belgium, and now it will all be taken away*, she thought. Church bells chimed in the distance. Before now, they had been a confirmation that she was doing God's work, but now they felt like a mockery.

"Edith? Did you hear what I said?"

Her lips trembled slightly. "The Committee wants my resignation so they can put a Belgian in my place. They believe this will improve the image of the school by not having a foreigner in charge of nursing in their country, and all of this will bring in more donations for the school that I, or rather we, started."

"Are you and I in the same room? I never said anything of the sort."

"But isn't that why we are here? You want me to resign and leave, or take some sort of consulting or teaching position, remove my dogs, get rid of Grace, who is…"

"Nurse Cavell, I'm not sure who is using drugs, you or that troublesome addict whom you molly-coddle. Do you think I would let a committee of rich stuffed shirts remove the most important person in this entire hospital system? Over my dead body!" said Antoine, banging his fists on the table for emphasis.

"But how can you refuse what the Committee requires?"

"Simple," said Marie. "When M. Goldsmith told Antoine what they intended to do, Antoine simply informed him that if you go, he goes."

"You would put your entire reputation and position at risk for me?"

Marie gave her husband an admiring look. "You should have seen Goldsmith's expression when Antoine gave him that choice."

"And he didn't challenge you?"

Antoine removed his little black cap and rubbed his receding hairline. "Of course he did. But he didn't get anywhere with it. I walked out. You gave up your country and position to work for me. You didn't know me, or what I would ask of you. Do you think that after all these years, and all we have built here together, and all that we have ahead of us, that I would do less for you? What kind of man do you think I am? I cannot do this without you, Edith, and neither can Marie. If I let them remove you, this woman over here—" he gestured toward Marie. "—would make my life so miserable, I would have wished it were me being given the boot instead of you."

He removed his glasses, pinched the bridge of his nose, and looked straight at Edith.

"I've never told you this, but a few years ago, when I was in Cologne representing you at the International Council of Nurses, I had no idea how well you were known internationally. People—important people like Lavinia Dock and even the President of the Council, Ethel Fenwalk or Fenwick or some such name—came up to me to extend their good wishes to you and congratulate me on what we had accomplished in Brussels."

"We knew you were writing about our progress in the *Nursing Mirror*, but we had no idea of the international reputation you had garnered. Separating you from this work is absolutely unthinkable," said Marie.

Antoine added, "Marie is right. Like it or not, it looks like the three of us will just have to put up with each other for a very long time. The Committee will have to come up with some other plan to raise money."

DePage replaced his wire-rimmed glasses, cleared his throat, and stood up with a worried expression. "All that aside, I brought you both here to tell you that our job has just gotten more difficult. King Albert had a private conversation with me yesterday. He is worried about the upheaval in the Balkans. There seems to be no way to settle the tension between Serbia and Austria. He is very concerned that Germany will declare war on France and that Belgium will be in the line of fire."

"I don't understand," said Marie, a puzzled look on her face. "What does the one have to do with the other?"

"I admit, it's a bit difficult to understand, but it follows like this. Russia is an ally of Serbia. Germany is an ally of Austria. An incident between Serbia and Austria would bring both Germany and Russia into a war with each other. Any countries that have agreements, alliances, or treaties with Germany or with Russia could mobilize. Theoretically, there is a chance of this conflict igniting all of Europe."

Edith tried to understand what Antoine was saying. "So where does France fit in, and why would Germany invade France?"

"There has never been a good relationship between France and Germany. France is an ally of Russia. Germany would welcome the excuse to invade France to stop France from aiding Russia."

"And England is an ally of France, so an invasion of France would draw in the British," Marie added, looking at Edith.

"Correct," said Antoine. "England has also pledged to maintain Belgium's neutrality, and the route Germany would most likely take to conquer France would…"

"… be through Belgium," interrupted Edith. "But this is all so speculative."

"But not impossible. The King and Queen have made me president of the Red Cross in Belgium. The King asked that I send a few ambulances over to the Balkans. So, I need you both to stock those ambulances with medical equipment and provide staff, including nurses."

He sat on the edge of his desk and faced the women. "As a precautionary measure, King Albert also asked that we set up Red Cross field tents and ambulances around Brussels."

Marie spoke up first. "But won't this alarm the people and cause a panic?"

"People read the news. They know we may be in the path of trouble. God knows, we have been invaded often enough over the years. King

Albert thinks that taking these actions will demonstrate that he is looking ahead.

DePage looked at Marie, then at Edith.

"There's more. The King is concerned about Kaiser Wilhelm's mounting imperialism and talk of world power. He ordered me to set up medical tents along the French border in anticipation of casualties should Germany attack France. We know that if the Kaiser should be so foolish as to do this, England, an ally with France, would put quickly stop his invasion. And as the head of a neutral country, King Albert anticipates that King George V will appeal to him for medical assistance."

A chant Edith had heard from English soldiers floated into her mind.

We don't want to fight;
But by jingo if we do,
We've got the ships, we've got the men,
We've got the money too!

Antoine stood up and fitted his black cap on his head. The muscles in his face tensed. "I'm afraid this will require that I be away from Brussels for a while. We must all be prepared for the worst."

— 22 —

SUMMER HOLIDAY

Louisa Cavell waited anxiously for her daughter to arrive. The year that had passed since they had last been together seemed far too long. After her husband had died four years ago, Louisa spent much of her time keeping in touch with her four children.

Florence was a nursing superintendent in a London hospital, Lilian had married Dr. Wainright, and Jack was now the editor of the *Norwich Union Magazine*. Louisa was able to communicate with Edith through letters, but she always worried about her daughter being in a foreign country.

Louisa had known from the beginning that Edith was different from other girls. Her husband had interpreted Edith's independent nature and boundless energy as being a "tomboy." Against Louisa's advice, he sent Edith to three different schools so she could "learn to act like other women." He thought he had found the right place at Laurel Court in Peterborough. It was attached to a cathedral and the two women who ran it enforced strict rules. Louisa argued that her husband was too harsh with Edith.

"That independent nature will serve her well," she would tell him.

"That independent nature will never win her a husband," he would answer back. "And if she doesn't get married, she may well have to struggle financially all her life."

When Edith arrived home, Louisa felt whole again. She hugged her oldest daughter until her arthritic arms ached. She was shocked to feel how light her Edith felt in her arms.

"Edith, you are too thin. You need lots of good home-cooked food in you. Aren't they feeding you properly over there?"

Edith noticed the silver streaks that lined her mother's silky brown hair. The skin on her mother's face seemed to have lost its lustre.

"Mother, you say that every time I come home. I assure you they are feeding me quite well. We have a very devoted cook although admittedly her cooking is not as wonderful as it is at home."

Louisa motioned her daughter to come over to the kitchen table. She smoothed out a white tablecloth embroidered around the edge with a pattern of red, yellow and orange fruit.

"Sit with me and have some cool lemonade and some lovely raspberry scones with jam and butter. You know I still go to that farm in Swardeston to get fresh berries. It's Lilian's favorite, you may remember. Oh, of course you do." She poured lemonade into two glasses.

"We have so much to talk about, my dear. I want to know all about what you are doing. I read in your last letter something about a new school. You also wrote something about sending out ambulances all over the place. Whatever is going on?"

Looking at the plump scones, Edith felt the hollowness of not having eaten much during the long trip. She wondered how many scones she could eat before her mother would accuse her of starvation. She casually reached over, picked up a scone from a gold-rimmed china plate and buttered it.

"Do you remember when Queen Elizabeth broke her arm?"

"The Queen broke her arm? I didn't hear about that."

"The Queen of Belgium is also named Elizabeth. After the Queen came to us for treatment and care from our nurses, our school suddenly became popular and the enrolment picked up so much that we needed a new school."

Louisa loved watching her daughter sit at her table eating her food. "And did you get it? Your new school?"

"It is being built right now."

Louisa thought for a moment. "And what of the ambulances you are sending hither and yon? Does it have anything to do with that incident I read about a few weeks ago in the *Eastern Daily Press*? You know the one about that Austrian archduke, or whatever he was, who was shot by someone or other in Serbia."

"It was a Slav who did the shooting, not a Serb. No one believes it will be of any consequence but King Albert has asked us to provide medical support in case the Germans use it as an excuse to invade France.

If that should happen, England has promised to protect Belgian neutrality, and then, no doubt, we will be pulled into the conflict."

Louisa saw that Edith had quickly finished her scone, so she put a second one on her plate.

"Eat up, my dear. Someone is always killing someone else over there. It's as bad as trying to figure out which part of Ireland is fighting about what. It's all so confusing to me. Why can't people just get along with each other?"

Edith buttered up the second scone. "Don't worry, Mother. No one thinks much of it right now. I have asked Sister White to send a telegram to me if there are any problems that involve our work."

"And who is watching over the school while you are here?"

Edith squeezed a lemon wedge and plopped it in her glass.

"Marie DePage will keep things running at the school, and Sister Wilkins, who is back from her trip to Switzerland, is supervising the Clinique. She is taking care of Jack and Don and keeping watch over Grace."

"And how is Grace doing? With her problem, I mean?"

Edith looked around the tiny kitchen. It was so different from the one in the vicarage, where the kitchen window overlooked the flower garden. As a child, she had sketched those flowers on cards to raise funds for the new parish hall. Sometimes, in the middle of concentrating on the details of a petal or pistil, she would look up through that window and see her mother smiling back at her.

"Grace? Oh, I admit that there are times I would like to throttle some sense into her, but on the whole, I believe she is doing much better. Unfortunately, she is quite clever at securing medications to sustain her habit. I am often getting told off for her behavior, but her progress, however small, convinces me that it was a good move for her."

Louisa picked up a stray crumb with her finger, studied it, and carefully removed it from her finger to the edge of her plate. Her tone was nonchalant. "Sister Wilkins–that's Elizabeth Wilkins, isn't it? She's the nurse you frequently write about in your letters to me. As I recall, she is the English nurse who speaks good French. You seem to depend quite a bit on her. You must think very highly of her."

Edith spoke while running her finger in the moistness that had formed on the outside of her lemonade glass. "I depend on both Elizabeth Wilkins and Millicent White. Elizabeth is English, and Millicent is the daughter of an Irish doctor. While Elizabeth tends to compromise, Millicent is a strict disciplinarian. I think highly of them both and of all of my staff." She watched the design drip down the glass and disappear into a small puddle at its base. "Now, Mother, let's talk about when we will be going down to the sea. For months I have been looking forward to walking on the beach in the sun."

Louisa reached over and brushed a crumb from the corner of Edith's mouth with her napkin. She let her hand rest on Edith's hand. It felt so good to be able to reach out and touch her daughter. *Why did Edith stay in Belgium,* she wondered, *when there were so many good hospitals in England?* She hoped that they could discuss later.

"I've reserved a cottage for us in West Runton. Lilian will be joining us with her children, as will Florence. I don't know about your brother Jack. He is always so busy, but you will see him in due time. And your cousin Edward, who always asks about you, will also join us."

Louisa placed one hand on the back of her chair and the other on the table and slowly lifted herself up. Edith saw her mother hesitate a moment before straightening herself. Her gait was stiff as she walked to the sink. Edith felt her mother's lips barely brush the top of her head and looked up into her mother's gray eyes. "Let me help you with those dishes."

"Nonsense, dear. You've had a long day. Go unpack and change while I clean up here and start preparing for supper."

* * * * *

Edith felt the warmth seep through her shoes as she walked down the path to the beach at West Runton. She spread out a blanket close to the cliffs to prevent the wind from blowing sand at her and prepared to read a book she had found at the cottage. Removing the beach robe that covered her one-piece bathing dress, she slipped on a crinkled bonnet and laid down her towel.

As she looked out over the water, the sun seemed to cradle her in its warm arms. White boats with wind-bloated sails glided around the coast line. The wind carried the sounds of children's delighted squeals as they splashed each other in the waves.

Edith settled comfortably on her towel. It felt so freeing to be out of her starched and confining uniform and away from the odor of disinfectant. She inhaled the fresh ocean air and the fragrant smell of summer. This was exactly what she needed.

She thought back over the birthday party the family had held for her mother the day before. It had been a successful reunion; even her cousin Edward had come. Edward's father, Edmond, had imposed the same strict rules on his family as her father had. Edith and Edward had often confided their childhoods to each other. She reflected on their relationship.

Edward had always shown a keen interest in her, and she returned his interest by answering all of his letters. In many ways, he was like a brother to her—though he wished he was something more. Everyone knew he was different from other men in the family. It was a family understanding that he would probably never be able to marry because of a nervous disorder he had inherited from his mother.

"Edith," he would say, "if we weren't cousins, would you have married me?"

She would always answer, "Edward, even if I could marry you, I love you too much to do so. I need you as a good friend more than as a husband. My life is much too confusing to mix you up in it."

"I remember you once writing to me that you wanted to do something useful for people who were helpless, hurt, and unhappy. Do you think you have done that?"

Edith looked into the angular face that was typical of the Cavell family.

"I think I am doing a good deal of that now."

"Then, Edith, why don't you come home now and spend the rest of your time with us? We miss you so much. I miss you. Don't you want to be with me and the rest of the family?"

"Edward, you are so dear to me, but I must finish the work I started. I will continue to keep in touch with you. You know that."

The night before she was to return to Norwich, she had trouble sleeping. The time spent with her family and Edward had awakened repressed emotions. She had been a bit of a loner all her life, but at least here in Norfolk, she wasn't the Anglo-Saxon Protestant foreigner. Her roots were here. She was a member of a family, speaking her own language and eating familiar food.

Maybe I should have left as the Committee requested, she thought. But then what of her desire to accomplish something extraordinary, to follow in the footsteps of Florence Nightingale? She turned these considerations around in her mind like a child with a toy kaleidoscope, looking at it from all angles. Maybe Edward was right.

At the age of 48, hadn't she already accomplished enough? She had created an entire new profession in another country. But what of her responsibility as a daughter? She had taken care of her father. Shouldn't she now be taking care of her mother, who was obviously failing in her old age? After tossing and turning in her bed for hours, sleep mercifully claimed her.

After the sea holiday and back in Norwich, Edith was anxious to spend some time at the cathedral. She walked through the Gothic archway that was the entrance to the cobblestoned courtyard. She remembered how as a child, she had run through this courtyard and into the cloisters. She recalled the slapping sound her feet had made against the blocks of stone, the sound reverberating down the archways and back to her.

Edith walked through the large carved oak doors and under the immense stone archways that seemed to stretch straight up into heaven. She inhaled the musty air and the odor of burning candle wax. She moved to the side into St. Andrew's chapel and knelt down at the front altar. "Lord," she prayed. "I beg Thee to guide me, for there is no sacrifice too great for me to make for Thy sake. Lead me into Thine own understanding. Guide me into the path Thou hast chosen for me. In Thy Holy name. Amen."

She walked through to the back of the cathedral and out into the gardens behind and sat on the same bench she had sat on when she was sixteen and prayed for forgiveness for being caught smoking. Her thoughts were now clouded with the threats of war. If war did come, was it her duty to go back to Belgium or join a Royal Forces field hospital in England? Shouldn't she be caring for her own countrymen? What if she were killed in Belgium? She stood up. *Enough of these morbid thoughts. God has a lot more for me to do still.*

She walked back towards the city center and passed a shop with a newsstand out on the street. She stopped and looked down at the bold headline. *AUSTRIA DECLARES WAR!*

Her mind raced. What did this mean? She remembered Antoine's discussion about larger countries supporting smaller countries in the event of war. She bought the newspaper and read the history of the pent-up hatred and conflicts between Serbia and Austria. She read how the Austrians were already fighting back by shelling the Balkan city of Belgrade. She rushed home to tell her mother the news.

When she burst through the front door, her brother Jack greeted her. "And hello to you, my dear sister. I thought I'd drop by to have a chat you before you leave."

"I'm so glad to see you, Jack. I've just read the headlines. What do you think of them?"

"It's all nonsense. They're always fighting about something over there. They're like two old ladies having a squabble over a loaf of bread."

"I'm not so sure this time. It looks serious enough to me."

Despite Jack's lack of concern, doubt began to cloud Edith's thoughts. Was she English or Belgian? After Jack left, she saw the flowerbeds around her mother's house were in desperate need of trimming and weeding, and she decided the garden was a good place to gather her thoughts.

While working on a patch of heartsease, Edith heard the church clock pealing out the time. It made her stop for a moment. Looking up, she noticed a boy standing just outside the red brick wall, straining to look at the number on the cottage door.

"Are you looking for something, lad?

"Is this 24 College Road?"

"It is."

"I'm looking for a Miss Edith Cavell. I am instructed to give her this telegram directly."

Edith stood up, wiped the dirt from her hands on her skirt, then reached over the wall for the telegram.

"I am Edith Cavell."

He placed an oblong yellow envelope in her hand. "They said it is important that you read it straightaway."

Edith ripped through the envelope and read the neatly typed letters.

Telegramme
August 2, 1914
For: Madame Edith Cavell, 24 College Road, Norwich, UK

Germany declared war. Hospital and Clinique taken over by Red Cross. Imperative that you return immediately.

Millicent White

Map of Belgium with major cities.

PART THREE:
GERMANY INVADES BELGIUM

— 23 —
RETURN TO BRUSSELS

Louisa Cavell's neighbor leaned over the adjoining fence and held up the front page of the *Eastern Daily Press*. Edith read the bold headlines, "GERMANY DECLARES WAR ON FRANCE, August 2, 1914."

"What do you make of all this?" the neighbor asked.

Edith folded Millicent's telegram, stuffed it in her pocket, and took the newspaper in her dirt-smudged hands. She quickly scanned the article: Germany had invaded Luxemburg. All of Europe was mobilizing –Austria, Serbia, Russia, France, and now England. The declaration of war by each country was now merely a formality. Belgium's ability to maintain its neutrality was in question.

The neighbor kept on talking as she read. "Don't you hate this horrid heat?" he asked, plucking his shirt away from his chest. "I'm a volunteer constable, you know. This war means I may have to join up."

Edith handed the paper back to him. Her mouth went dry, but her response was calm. "It seems as though events are unfolding faster than we can possibly comprehend. Could you please excuse me?"

She went into the house and handed her garden tools to her mother. "Could you please put these away? I must wash and pack."

"But your holiday isn't over. Must you rush back?"

"War has been declared. Belgium will soon be invaded. We were afraid this would happen. We set up Red Cross stations along the border, but we now know they won't be nearly enough. I have to return straight-away. I can't leave my nurses to face this alone."

Bits of leaves and dirt fell to the floor as she pulled off the flowered dress she had worn for gardening. She removed the telegram from her dress pocket and reread it. She felt her eyes burn but refused to let her mother see her in tears. Her mother stood aside, watching her rush about preparing to leave.

"But isn't your first duty to your own country? England will need every one of its trained nurses."

"England has many trained and brilliant nurses, and Belgium has too few. At a time like this, my nurses need me more than ever."

Louisa watched her daughter disappear to wash. She had lived through the Boer War, the Irish rebellions, and had read about the Crimean War, but this terrified her. Her children would soon be swallowed up in it. Oh God! This can't be happening!

Edith placed her suitcase on the bed and began to pack her things into it. Louisa lowered her voice.

"To be honest, Edith dear, I need you. Jack is a voluntary constable and may be called for duty at any time. Lillian and her husband will be busy at the hospital down in Henley. I don't think I can manage alone."

Edith saw her mother's shoulders slump. There were yellow half-moon areas under her mother's eyes. Why hadn't she noticed them before now? She stopped packing and put her arms around her mother. "I love you more than anyone. I promise to write to you as often as I can and return as soon as possible. I would take you with me, but it would not be safe for you."

"How is it safe for you, then?"

Edith let the question hang in the air. There was no time for discussion. The trip back to Brussels would be arduous, and civilian travel would soon be curtailed.

"Let me pack you a lunch before you leave."

"That would be lovely, but you must be quick about it."

At the railway station in Norwich, Edith hugged her mother and then turned to her brother.

"Take care of her for both of us," she told Jack.

He did not return her embrace. "I hope you will soon come to your senses, Edith."

Edith remembered how thrilled she was when she had found out she had a baby brother. She remembered how, when he was older, he would chase her, teasing her with his pinches, and when he caught her, he would give her a hug. *When had the chasm between us develop?* She smiled, showing him that the bond between them still mattered, but the smile died on her lips when he didn't return it.

Edith disappeared into the crowded train. Peering out of the dusty window, her eyes blurred. She saw her mother searching the train windows for her and tapped on the window to get her attention. Her mother tried to hide her true feelings behind a forced smile. Edith smiled back. The understanding between them needed no words. Edith felt torn between the responsibilities she was leaving and those pulling her forward. She had decided a long time ago that her calling was not only to England, but to all people, especially those who needed her help the most. Right now, that was the Belgians.

With a hiss of steam, the train slowly pulled away, lengthening the distance between her and her family. She watched her mother wipe her eyes with the back of one hand and wave a white hanky with the other. Then the train turned on southwards and both mother and brother disappeared.

Louisa felt a creeping dread as she watched the train disappear. She remembered when she and Frederick looked up the meaning of their daughter's name: "Happy in war." At the time, she had thought the explanation ludicrous, but now it gave her a chill. She felt strongly that if her daughter got back to Brussels, she might never see her again.

* * * * *

When Edith's train arrived in London, everything at the station was in a state of confusion. Germans trying to leave England pressed together, as if for security.

The ticket agent at the window told her, "You can buy a ticket but we don't know what train you will be able to board or when it will leave."

With ticket in hand, she ran from conductor to conductor for information. "There's a war on, Miss. We're transporting troops," they told her. She anxiously watched a few trains arrive, fill up with soldiers, and depart without room for her. Finally, when all the troops on the platform disappeared, she was allowed to board. After walking through crowded carriages, she squeezed into a seat.

When the train arrived at the Dover dock, she found frenzied tides of people rushing about. An angry Italian in front of her argued with the ticket agent that he had been waiting for hours and should be taken first. With ticket in hand, Edith stood in line. The wooden boards of the dock reflected back the sun's heat, making it feel hotter than it was. Fighting back light-headedness, she dared not move from her place to try to get aboard.

Edith breathed a sigh of relief when she saw the channel steamer *Malle* loom up on the horizon and pull up to the dock. Streams of people pushed their way off, while others, impatient to board, pushed to get on. She felt the crowds press in on her and shove her up the gangplank.

Once her eyes adjusted to the dimmer light inside the steamer, the scene reminded her of the streets of Whitechapel. There were no empty seats. The air was musky with sweat, unwashed clothing, and rotting food. Groups of people huddled on the floor, leaning against their hastily packed bags and suitcases. They stared at each other with desperation and fear in their eyes. She was moved by the sun-burnt faces of those who had come to England to relax on holiday but were now leaving hurriedly, anxious about the uncertainty of the future. As she passed a Japanese couple searching a map stretched out between them, the steamer lurched forward, throwing her off her feet and onto the lap of a man who was sitting opposite them.

"G'day, miss." A man with a wide grin greeted her.

She pulled herself off his lap. "I'm so sorry. I was looking for a seat when the boat threw me off balance."

He slid over on the wooden bench. "There just happens to be enough space here for a little lady such as yourself."

"Thank you for being so kind. It's been a very long and tiring day." She pushed in on the bench and placed her bag under her feet.

"You look a bit worked out. Where are you coming from, if you don't mind my asking?"

"I've come from Norwich to London and then down here to Dover."

"If you like, you can put your bag over by me. There's more room on the other side under the bench."

"Thank you, again, sir." His hand reached over, plucked the heavy bag from her, and shoved it under the seat.

He was curious about her. He liked her face; it was plain but full of intensity. She reminded him of his aunt, who was an Australian cattle rancher down in Wonthaggi. "You must have family on the other side to be traveling there with a war coming on." It was half statement and half question.

"My family is in England. I'm in charge of a nursing school in Belgium and manage nurses at a few of the hospitals there."

She took a closer look at her new traveling companion. His face was angular with deep-set lines. His skin was the color of richly steeped tea and contrasted with a lighter-colored scar on the side of his face. The top buttons of his shirt were open, revealing wiry, blond chest hair. She guessed him to be in his thirties.

"My name is Edith. And yours?"

"Rob. Rob MacFarlane." He held out a large hand. "Pleased to be at your service." Edith gave it a light shake, feeling the roughness of his palm against hers.

"Are you traveling to meet family?"

"My family is in Australia, up in the Tablelands, except for one tough old aunt who runs a sheep farm further south. There's a war brewing, and I mean to be a part of it. Did you hear the talk that we might be in danger?" he asked.

"You mean once we land?"

"I mean now. Right here, on this boat. There's talk we might be target practice for a German torpedo." He looked around the steamer cabin. "One hole in this old hull and we're all fish food. Hope you can swim."

"I can, but I prefer not to. Why on earth would the Germans torpedo a harmless passenger steamer?"

He removed a worn bush hat, its leather band decorated with crocodile teeth. The inside rim was darkened with sweat. He ran his hand through a ruff of sandy hair.

"Cuz it's war, miss. The Huns have declared war on France and will march through Belgium to get there, and this old rust bucket is heading straight to Belgium. He plopped his hat back on his head and cocked it at a slight angle over one eye. "Last year, your First Lord of the Admiralty..." He searched the ceiling for the name. "... a fellow named Winston Churchill, I believe, ordered ship owners to arm themselves for protection from pirates. Now that passenger ships are armed, the Germans say they are justified in shooting them down because they say any ship that carries guns has hostile intentions."

"But Belgium is a neutral country. France, England, and even Germany have agreed to honor that neutrality."

The corner of his mouth lifted in a wry smile. "Do ya really think that anyone who wears a spike on his bloody 'ead is going to honor anything that stands in his way? Belgian neutrality means nothing to them. They have already attacked a province on the eastern border of Belgium at a place called...I can never remember all those foreign names, but I have it here." He pulled out a pocket-sized notepad and turned a few pages. "Here it is, Liège. That's what the Tommies on the train told me. I wrote it down. See?" He held the notebook page up to Edith. She squinted at the crudely written words. Then he flipped it shut and placed it back in his jacket pocket.

"Liège! They couldn't possibly destroy Liège. It's a fortress surrounded by steel and cement walls. It's also a major industrial center. King Albert would do everything he could to protect it."

"That he will, but it won't be enough. His army is outnumbered and will be cut down like so much wheat at the harvest. The Huns have howitzers that will be blast those walls apart and crush 'em flat. Being a nurse, you will sure have your work cut out for you. You're English, eh? If I were you, I'd turn around and head straight back to London. There'll be plenty for you to do at home and more than you can handle in Belgium. War changes everything."

Edith looked over at the Japanese couple. They had stopped arguing over the map. The woman curled up in her seat and nestled into her husband's shoulder. Her body rocked back and forth with the movement of the boat. His head had fallen forward as if the string that held it up had been cut. They looked so peaceful together. She wondered how they could sleep so easily while the world was falling apart. She turned back to Rob. "I told you why I am going to Belgium. Why are you?"

"Me? I've been through it all before. Been a Bush Ranger and hauled a stint in the Aussie army 'til I got wounded." He held up his disfigured hand. "I tried to enlist in the Australian Imperial Force but they wouldn't take a wounded bloke like me. Truth is, I'm still a soldier and in full feather now. I'd like a fair go at those Huns. I figure I'll throw my lot in with the Frenchies or the Tommies, if they'll have me. Then maybe, after we've whipped those Hun arses and if I'm still in my boots, I'll write about it."

"I'm sure you will see your way through. Once the English and French mobilize, all of this will be over in short order."

"I always find it hard to believe that the same country that composes such beautiful music and produces some mighty fine art can also butcher women and children, don't you?"

"Butcher women and children? Germans are doing that? To what purpose would they kill innocent civilians? Their Kaiser is related to the Belgian's King Albert, for goodness sake," Edith said with dismay.

"The Huns are brutal. They will kill and torture anyone who gets in their way. No one is spared. Relative or no, not even women and children. If one person gives them any trouble, they'll burn down the entire village and slaughter the whole lot of them. I'm ready to have at 'em."

"You seem very sure of all of this, Mr. MacFarland," Edith said.

"Don't mean to be cruel, but you being a nurse, I'll tell you the truth of it. I'm told they have already destroyed a few of the villages that lead to Liège. In one of those villages, they tied one old gent to a cartwheel and drove off with 'im. They made children dance and sing nursery rhymes over a pile of corpses that was their parents and older brothers and sisters."

He pulled out binoculars from a leather satchel, turned toward the window, and searched the waters. He saw the foam boiling along the sides of the ship and the reflection of the steamer lights glistening on the water, but beyond that, the sea was black as oil.

"Don't see any enemy ships out there but we'll never see those stinking, sneaky U-boats. It will be a while before we see any lights off the Belgian coast. Might as well just settle in."

A feeling of dread crept up into her throat. She felt the beginnings of nausea as the boat rolled and pitched. Rob looked at her and pulled out a flask from his pocket. The silver cover had been worn to a dull gray. He handed it to Edith.

"Looks like you could use a nip, too. This pitching will even out when we change direction."

"No, thank you. It will make things worse."

He withdrew the rejected flask, took a swig, and replaced it in a breast pocket. He stretched out his legs and shifted his hat down over his eyes. Edith was grateful that he stopped talking and left her to sort out her own thoughts. She reached into her purse, pulled out the *Book of Common Prayer*, and turned the worn pages to a prayer entitled, "In the Time of War and Tumults":

Almighty God. Save and deliver us, we humbly beseech thee,
from the hands of our enemies; abate their pride, assuage their
malice, and confound their devices; that we, being armed with
thy defense, may be preserved evermore from all perils, to
glorify thee, who art the only giver of all victory; through the
merits of thy Son, Jesus Christ, our Lord. Amen.

Edith slumped back and closed her eyes. She was tired and would be traveling through the night and into the next day. She found comfort in holding the small leather-bound book when sleep overtook her thoughts.

Hours later, a sudden jarring woke her up. She heard the dock pilings creak and groan under the weight of the steamer as it bumped against them. They had arrived at Ostend, Belgium. People were standing and pushing against each other to get off. The smokestacks belched black smoke over them as they spilled out onto the landing.

Edith saw the tall Aussie stride through the crowd, his worn leather satchel slung over his shoulder. Suddenly, he stopped, turned, and tipped his hat to her. "G'day, Miss Edith," he called out and disappeared into the melee.

As Edith left the boat, the on-coming crowd cannoned into her. Pushing through the crowds off the boat and away from the surge of people moving about the dock, she rushed over to the nearby railway station. There she found masses of blue-uniformed Belgian troops flooding the station docks. She approached a conductor who was in charge of boarding. "Pardon, monsieur. I am a nurse and must get to Brussels immediately to organize my hospital staff in preparation for casualties. Could you direct me to the train that goes to Mechelen?"

The official looked at the little woman who spoke French with an English accent. He shook his head and shrugged. "I could, but it won't help you. No one knows when these trains will arrive or depart. It may be a few minutes or it may be a few hours. He pointed to the regiment of soldiers who were filing into the train. "Soldiers first. Then civilians. *C'est la guerre*, Madame. It's the war," he translated and walked away.

Channel Steamer Belgium Ostende Sortie de la Malle (vintage postcard)

— 24 —

THE INVASION

It was Sunday when Edith finally was able to catch a train to Brussels. She looked out the window of her compartment. The neatly squared patchwork of planted fields looked too perfect to be real, but here they were, in shades of green and gold, soon to be harvested. Her eyes watered and burned from the sun's brightness, but sleep was out of the question.

To ease the pain in her eyes, she turned away and focused on the dark interior of the train. She looked around and saw fear and uncertainty in the eyes of those seated near her. An elderly couple gripped each other's hands. A younger woman spoke French to her female companion while hugging a bundle on her lap.

Gradually, the metal wheels slowed down and screeched to a stop at the central station in Brussels. A wave of people shoved her along with them from the train onto the platform. They pushed through groups of Germans trying to catch a train back to Germany. Set back from the tracks, a crowd gathered around a soup kitchen set up by the Red Cross. Others, too sick, old, or frail to walk, were tended to by family and volunteers.

Once outside the station, she was starting to look for a taxi when she heard shouts coming from the Grande Place, a short distance away. Curious, she walked down to the square. The closer she got, the more the noise sounded like a festival. Stepping out from a narrow street leading to the square, she stopped and stared.

The Grand Place looked as though it was hosting a festival in its open market place, with black, red, and yellow flags fluttering from balconies, multi-colored umbrellas set over café tables, and carts brimming with flowers. High up on the spire of the main building, the Hotel de Ville, the ever-present red and green flag of Brussels waved to the crowd below.

A youngster ran past her chasing a small brown and white dog. "Frances, be careful! Stop running!" called out the mother, who sat at an open café with a drink in her hand. In the middle of the plaza, men and women gathered around a band and sang the national anthem. In front of the *Hôtel de Ville*, the stately Town Hall of Brussels, small units of untrained soldiers dressed in makeshift uniforms and carrying obsolete guns, resembled a comic opera as they marched in uneven rows.

People lifted their glasses in salute to them and cheered as they passed. When one soldier saw Edith watching his clownish regiment, he snapped to attention and gave her a salute. Suddenly he was knocked off balance by the brown and white dog running between his legs and little Frances chasing it. As he struggled to regain his stance, his hat flew off, skittered across the smooth stones, and landed at Edith's feet. She picked it up and handed it back to him. He plopped the soft cap back on a head of tangled brown hair and called out "*Vive la Belgique!*" and gave another salute.

"*Vive la Belgique*," she replied.

Edith purchased a cold lemonade at one of the cafés and after finishing it, she walked back to the station to hail a taxi back to Ixelles. The driver took her down Avenue Louise, a main road leading from Brussels into Ixelles. At the head of the avenue, Edith noticed a strip of paving stones torn up and heaped in a pile along the edge of the road. Next to the stone pile, men were digging a trench and stringing the barest of barbed wire along its edge. Some of the men stood in the trench holding guns across their chests. They looked as unreal as the regiment marching in the Grand Place.

Edith tapped the driver on the shoulder. "Who are those men?"

"They are a group of volunteers who joined the Civic Guard. They mostly dress up and march in parades."

"But how could they ever hope to fend off the German army?"

The taxi driver shrugged. "They know they cannot and are likely to die."

* * * * *

"**N**o need to wait for her; she isn't coming back. Why should she? She is a Brit after all and knows she will be better off staying in England. Why do you think she left when she did? I'll tell you why. Because she knew there would be a war. She doesn't care about us. Even if she does return, so what? There will be no school for her to manage. Not now. And who will help her? You two English nurses?"

"Yes," said Edith as she came up behind the German probationer who stood with her hands on her hips in front of Elizabeth and Millicent. "And whoever will join us, but I can assure you, it won't be you. Pack your bags straightaway and prepare to return to Germany, immediately."

Elizabeth ran to Edith and threw her arms around her. "You've come back! We knew you would."

Edith inhaled the familiar scent of lavender rose. Millicent reached out and took Edith's hands in hers. She held on for a moment, needing to touch her to believe she really was back. "You got my telegram."

"I left within the hour after I received it. Thank you for sending it."

"I never doubted you would return. Please excuse me, Madame. There is much to do. Nurse Wilkins will tell you all that has happened. Also, I don't mean to press you but we have a problem with our German maid, Maria."

"What problem?" asked Edith. "She is German. She must return home."

"That's the problem. She says she knows no one in Germany. She says her home is here. She is begging us not to turn her out."

"I was thinking that since she speaks fluent German, she may be of some help to us," said Millicent.

"Then we will do our best to keep her, but do warn her that we may not be able to protect her from those who do not feel kindly toward Germans right now. To keep her safe, I will retain her as my personal maid."

Elizabeth picked up Edith's bags. Together they walked into Edith's living quarters. "Thank heavens you're safe. We've been hearing rumors about the possibility of the Germans blowing up passenger ships."

"I heard those rumors too," said Edith, sitting on the divan and kicking off her shoes. Jack came bounding in from the back garden. He sprang up and down on his hind feet, trying to lick Edith's face. His tail twirled in circles, sending pieces of leaves and dust flying into the air.

She bent over and hugged the excited dog. His whiskery muzzle was wet against her cheek. "I missed you, too, my little friend."

Then she stopped and looked around. "Where's Don?"

Elizabeth sat next to her on the divan and touched her shoulder.

"I'm so sorry to tell you this. Don...well, he disappeared a few weeks ago. We don't know if he jumped over the garden fence, ran off, or was stolen. We've looked everywhere. No one has seen him. Don was a wanderer before you picked him up. Millicent thinks he might have gone looking for you. He may very well wander back."

Edith's eyes brimmed with tears. "Perhaps you are right. I'm sure you did your best." She leaned over and ran her fingers through Jack's fur. "How are the patients doing?"

"They have all left. We have only one patient who fell off a bicycle, but he is only slightly injured and will soon be gone. It is just as well because we have been busy preparing to move all of our nurses and probationers who are not Belgian out of the country. Traveling is difficult and transportation is unreliable. The biggest problem is moving the German nurses and probationers out, because there are thousands of other Germans who are leaving at the same time."

Edith leaned back into the divan cushions. "Once we have the exact numbers, I will go to the American legation and appeal for help. I'll ride with our nurses to the border if that's what I have to do to assure that they get safely back home. I am responsible for these nurses, and my responsibility won't end until I know they are safe."

Edith gently slid Jack off her feet and wiggled her toes. The cooler air from the garden felt good on her swollen feet. "How many nurses will be left after everyone is gone?"

"Six."

"Six? How can we staff the hospital and the clinic and care for the patients in their homes with only six nurses?"

"Many women have volunteered. Our biggest problem will be finding enough people and time to train them."

"What do Marie and Antoine think of this?"

"Since it is believed that many of the wounded will be spread about, Marie and Antoine have turned larger public buildings and homes into Red Cross hospitals. We placed Red Cross flags on all hospital buildings, hoping it would prevent the Germans from damaging them."

Elizabeth noticed Edith massaging her feet. She jumped up. "I'm so sorry. I've carried on without asking you how you are. You must be hungry. I'll get you something to eat."

"It would be lovely if you got me something from the kitchen, but I need to freshen up first. Then we can continue making plans."

Edith looked directly at Elizabeth, touched her hand, and then let it go. "You have done splendid work here. I couldn't have done better. I must ask you, though, are you sure you want to stay? No one would blame you for returning home. The British Red Cross has put a call out for nurses. No one knows what will happen here. When the Germans arrive, we will all be at risk."

"When you took me on, I promised I would be faithful and loyal to your vision, Edith. Your vision is now mine. I told you I believed my destiny was here, working under your leadership. Nothing has changed."

"There is one difference between then and now, my friend. You have learned all I can teach you. You no longer work for me, but rather at my side as an equal in every sense of the word."

The corners of Edith's lips turned up slightly to form a wry grin. "You were never, ever, a cracked teacup."

After Edith had washed and eaten, she asked about Marie DePage.

"The King and Queen have turned their palace into a hospital and have asked Marie DePage to be superintendent. She said when you got back, she would call you to tell you about it."

"And the King and Queen, where will they stay?"

"The Queen lives in a small portion of the palace hospital; the King left Brussels to help the people in Louvain. I heard the entire government, including the King and Queen, will soon move to the fortress in Antwerp. The only governmental official left in Brussels will be *Bourgomaster* Max. The mayor will remain at the *Hôtel de Ville* to try to negotiate the city's safety with the German military."

The next day, Edith received a call from Marie. "Thank God you're back. Things will go so much better now that you are here."

"Have you heard when the English troops will arrive?" asked Edith.

"I heard an announcement was imminent declaring England's entry into the war. Antoine was called to the French border to set up field hospitals where the French armies are mobilizing. It is probably best he will be out of the city when the Huns take it over. His temper might just put him in prison—or worse."

"I'm told the palace is now a hospital."

"Yes. All the beautiful furnishings have been removed and replaced with rows of camp beds. The Queen has furnished white coverlets for each and allowed visiting children to fasten little Belgian flags on them. One room has been turned into an operating room by using the tables with glass tops for surgery.

Marie rushed on. "With Antoine gone, we have been depending on Dr. LeBoeuf. He has been immensely helpful here and also at St. Jean's."

Marie's voice became muffled for a minute and then came back. "Sorry. The radiograph machine has just arrived and they wanted to know where to put it. Did you know that Mme. Graux has turned her home into a hospital?"

"I haven't spoken to Marguerite for a while, but I heard she will be doing the same. Once the English army arrives, won't they stop the Germans before they reach Brussels?"

"I don't know. Who knows? Maybe. We cannot afford to count on that happening and not be fully prepared," said Marie.

"Of course not," said Edith.

Jack trotted happily behind his mistress as she made her rounds between the St. Giles, St. Jean, and St. Pierre hospitals. On the way back to the nurses' quarters, she noticed two Belgian army officers in a motorcar driving up and down the streets looking for recruits to join the army.

"It is your duty to protect your homeland," they called out. "Come out and join us to fight the enemy. Save your women and children from the murdering Huns."

Edith pondered how a country on the brink of devastation could so quickly put aside old factions and find a united voice in patriotism. She was beginning to understand how this little country, set at the crossroads of former conquerors over the past centuries, still managed to face its enemies and survive. She remembered the last words of King Albert before he left for Antwerp: "A country that defends itself can never die." I hope that is still true today.

Edith passed a doorway where a mother was hugging her son. The young man kissed her, then turned to his wife and held her tightly. "I'll be back. I promise." He reached down and tousled the hair of his two young boys. One boy clung to his leg, the other looked up and cried, "I don't want you to go. Please, Daddy, stay."

An older man stood behind the little group, his eyes downcast. His hands were shoved into the pockets of his baggy trousers. When the farewells were done, he pulled one hand out of his pocket and held it out to his son. His voice was raspy. "From my father to you, my son. You make me proud."

The silver pocket watch glinted in the sun. His lower lip trembled as he hugged his son. He picked up his tearful grandson and held him in his arms. "We must let your father go. He has his duty to do. Once he has done it, he will come back. You must be brave like your father."

Edith recalled her own farewell with her mother just a few days earlier and felt the sadness return. She walked past the officials in the motorcar, who impatiently waited for their new recruit. In the back seat, an elderly gent, wearing a threadbare military cap and a blue-gray military jacket decorated with faded ribbons, sat rigid, staring straight ahead, ready to serve once again.

A tug on the leash made her look at Jack. He was lifting his leg against the motorcar's tire. She snapped the leash back. "Oh, no, you don't."

She turned to the officer. "So sorry. His manners are horrid."

The officer leaned against the idling motorcar with his arms folded. He looked at her and then over at the dog and smiled. "Tell him to save it for the Huns."

* * * * *

On August 7th, Edith heard the news that the walls around the fortress of Liège had fallen under the powerful German guns.

Millicent had just come back from buying supplies in Brussels, when she saw Edith. She set the bag down on the granite stairs.

"I heard." she told Edith. "People in town are very angry about Liège. They are roaming the streets and breaking the windows of German businesses."

A loud engine noise interrupted her. Both looked up into the sky as did everyone else on the street. A man with a rifle unshouldered it and shot at the object overhead. Edith and Millicent had never seen anything like it. Flying serenely over the city was a monoplane with a fanned-out tail and the German flag painted on the side. It was heading south toward Liège.

Within a day, lines of refugees from Liège streamed into the city. Some pulled their own carts, piled high with a few possessions. A dark-haired girl clasped a scrawny hen. Another grasped a rope tied around the neck of a dusty goat protesting against being in the procession.

Edith felt particularly sorry for one Belgian soldier who limped along, dragging his rifle on the road. Tied to his knapsack, which hung loosely around his shoulders, was a tin cup and an extra pair of boots, gray with dust. Edith ran out and invited him in to rest. "Please come in for something to drink."

The soldier agreed and followed Edith into the Clinique. He grimaced as he shifted off his knapsack. The tin cup rattled as it hit the wooden floor. Edith and Elizabeth watched him guzzle down a cup of water and hold it out to them for more. After the second cup, he looked up at the women standing over him and saw their Red Cross armlets with the words *La Croix Rouge de Belgique* written on them.

"Liège has been captured. Destroyed. Burned to the ground." He coughed, wiped his face with the back of one sleeve, and looked up at them. "They killed women—thrust bayonets through their breasts."

He held his cup out to them. "More water, please." He gulped it down. "*Merci.* They shot children, innocent children." Tears made lines in the dust on his cheeks. "They hung one of our soldiers up by his thumbs and used him for target practice."

His voice grew louder. "They are soulless beasts who kill for pleasure."

Edith took a cold cloth and wiped the dirt off his face. "Do you think they will invade Brussels?"

"Louvain will be next. Then Brussels."

"But the British and French soldiers should be here any time now," said Elizabeth, who, hearing voices, had come downstairs.

He stood and grimaced as he hoisted his knapsack back up to his shoulder. "Not fast enough, *Madame*."

Edith told him he could stay as long as he needed.

"*Merci*. I must find my regiment, or what is left of it." Just as he got to the door, he turned around. "You both are English. The Germans—they hate the English. It will not matter that you are women—or nurses. Leave before it is too late. That is, if it isn't already."

He disappeared into the steady parade of ragged and dispirited refugees.

A Belgian nurse probationer had overheard the soldier describing the massacre in Liège. "If you think I will care for any German soldier brought to this or any other hospital, you are greatly mistaken. I will not save one hair on their miserable heads just to have them return to kill more women and children." She pointed to Jack, who was doubled in half, vigorously chewing on his hindquarters, his nails scratching against the floor boards. "I'd treat this disgusting thing before I'd ever touch a Hun."

Edith put her hands on the girl's shoulders and looked into her face. "You will do your duty to any human that needs your care. You are in training to be a professional nurse. You must learn to rise above your prejudices and treat whoever God puts in your care."

The probationer turned and ran out the room sobbing.

Once war was declared, the *Nursing Mirror* asked Edith to be its war correspondent, which Edith agreed to. Worried that communications might soon be cut off, she wrote a report on August 13, 1914.

Nursing in War Time: The Preparations in Brussels
There are two sides to war — the glory and the misery. We begin to see both. We shall see the latter more clearly as time goes on. Liège has resisted beyond all hope, and the soldiers who defend her are the heroes of the day. The Belgian army has paid for its glory, and the hospital keeps a record of the cost.

Here in Brussels, we are away from the fighting. God alone knows for how long. Distant guns were heard last night and today, a great battle is taking place we know not where.

Everyone who can work is doing what he can for his country, and England herself cannot be busier or more self-denying. The Red Cross reports 15,000 beds ready for the wounded. The wounded sent here are few, but are arriving as doctors can be found to treat them. Those that are here cannot wait to be patched up before they are off again to join their regiments. We have a few trained nurses at present. We hear many are being diverted to the London hospitals. Those we have, are doing excellent work and are in great demand.

Yesterday I went to inspect a little factory from which every-thing had been removed. The walls were whitewashed. Here and there on the ground floor are beds with white linen sheets and blankets neatly tucked in. Small tables are covered with clean towels on which bowls and jugs are ready for use. There is a fresh smell of creosote from the newly scrubbed floor. The cellar has been transformed into a store-room for arms and uniforms. The little kitchen is supplied with utensils.

We just heard there has been a great battle–over 700 wounded. Some have arrived; others will come in during the night or tomorrow. Crowds assemble at the railways to see the wounded carried into the waiting ambulances; the men with bowed heads and the women with wet eyes. War is terrible in this little country, where everyone has a relative or friend in the army. The young men, gone so short a time and so short a distance and in such brave spirits, are brought back—one dare not think how.

From your war correspondent in Brussels, Edith Cavell

Worried that her mother might see the article published in the *Nursing Mirror*, Edith wrote her a short note.

149 rue de la Culture, Bruxelles   *17 Aug. 1914*
Telephone 9559

My darling mother,
Just a line—and please let me know at once if you get it—as I am
afraid my letters do not always arrive. All is quiet at present.
We live under martial law, and it is strange to be stopped in
the street and have our papers and identity examined.

If you should hear that the Germans are in Brussels, don't be
alarmed. They will only walk through, as it is not a fortified
town, and no fighting will take place in it. Besides, we are quite
prepared and living under the flags of the Red Cross. I should
be glad to receive some English papers as none have reached
us since I left England. Two of our nurses arrived on Tuesday.
They had a great deal of trouble getting through. My dearest
love and Grace's to her family. She is well and has been given
the choice of returning home but has declined.

I will write whenever I can.

Affectionately yours,
Edith

Having written the article and the letter, Edith now had to find a way to
post them and thought of an American merchant and his wife who came
to Brussels every year. Over the years, they had become friends. She
folded the letter, sealed it, and then noticed a small cedar box on her
bureau. She tucked it under her arm and rushed to the apartment of the
couple, knocking several times before the door opened. The couple was
stunned to see Edith standing there.

"Come in, Edith. You caught us at a difficult time. We have just
finished packing and are about to leave for New York."

Edith moved into the room and saw that it was bare of personal
items. "I'm sorry to intrude like this, but I need to ask you to do something very important for me." She handed him the two letters and the
cedar box. "The post between America and England is still operating.
Would you please post these when you arrive home?"

The man took the box and opened it. Inside were some folded letters and what looked like very old jewelry. His wife peered over his arm into the box. "We will do our best to get it past the border guards," he said as he picked up a suitcase. "Sorry to rush you, but we must be going."

* * * * *

For days, the streets in Brussels continued to be flooded with refugees coming into the city and Germans trying to leave it. Longing for some reliable news, Edith called over to Marie.

"The Clinique is quiet, except for emergencies. The hospitals are also quiet, which is a good thing since we haven't many doctors or nurses. The wounded are not coming to us, so where do you think they are going?"

Marie's replied with a muffled voice. "I hope you do not mind my eating lunch while we talk. It is surprising we are so quiet. I thought we would be seeing wounded soldiers and people coming in from Liège. The Germans must either be killing them or taking them prisoners."

"That's horrible!" said Edith. "One more thing. Our wealthier patients have left without paying their bills, which means our funds are low. I hope you don't mind, but I wrote to the *London Times* appealing for funds. It looks like our financial situation will only get worse."

"I'm sure Antoine would approve. He did leave us in charge. He called yesterday to say Louvain is now occupied. The people there were told that if they put away all weapons and did not resist, the Germans would not shoot them. Most of the shopkeepers have closed their businesses and left. It's a religious town—mostly priests and scholars. There is no one to provoke the Germans there. Hopefully they will just pass through."

"After Louvain, what next? Brussels?"

"It looks that way. Antoine said the British will be sending their regiments to protect the French border before they come here."

"And leave us unprotected?" Edith said in a startled voice.

"The plan is that we do not show any opposition. The Germans want France, not Belgium. Unfortunately, we are the pathway that leads to

France, but they only want to march through. The real fighting will be along the French border."

Suddenly, Edith's cook ran into her office, flapping her apron up and down. "Poisoned! We are all being poisoned!"

"I must ring off. My cook is in a bit of a stew." Edith hung up the phone And turned to the cook. "Please stop running around and tell me who is being poisoned."

"All of us! The boy who delivered my food said that all of the wells have been poisoned. We must leave immediately or die."

"That would be difficult to do. Let's wait until we know for sure if it is true."

"It is true! I know it is! The delivery boy heard it from the baker, who heard it from..."

Edith interrupted her. "Until we find out what the real truth is, let's boil everything we use for drinking. We should know if there is poison in the water by the end of the day."

"Yes, *Madame*," said the cook, slamming the door as she left. Then, from the other side of the door Edith heard, "But if we all die, it will be your fault."

Edith collapsed back into her chair. *If the Germans don't kill us, we will all die of fear and anxiety.* Knowing she had to stop the rumor from circulating, she got up and walked around the Clinique and then over to the hospital. She was relieved to be told the story of the poisoned water was not true.

That evening, Edith saw red flashes light up the darkened sky. A shell exploded, rattling the windows. A glass fell off the shelf and shattered to the floor. She ran up to the roof. Other nurses were already standing at the roof's edge looking toward the east.

"*Mon Dieu,*" said one nurse as she pointed to enormous clouds of thick, black smoke billowing towards them. Jacqueline Van Til ran to the other side of the roof. "Over here! Look over here!" The entire northeast horizon was bright with flames. A rocket burst into the sky and exploded. They stood staring, their faces slack with fear, frozen in place at the sight. Suddenly, they heard a blast and glass shattering out onto the streets below. They rushed down to inspect the damage. Edith gathered her nurses together. She could feel one nurse trembling near her and put a hand around her shoulder to steady her.

"We must all remember that we have dedicated our lives to do our duty. Our lives no longer belong to us but to those we vowed to serve. We are to keep our heads high and trust that God will care for us as we care for His children. We must stay strong."

Another rocket whistled across the sky and burst somewhere in the blackness, spewing up a fountain of fire. The building shook with every blast. One nurse whimpered quietly to herself.

"There is nothing for us to do now," Edith continued. "Tomorrow will be a difficult day. We should try to get what rest we can so we will have our wits about us. The Germans will be entering our city tomorrow. We must be brave."

Two nurses walked out of the room holding onto one another's arm for courage, leaving Edith and Elizabeth alone in the Clinique.

Elizabeth looked over to see Jack cowering under Edith's desk. "God help us," said Elizabeth.

"I believe He will," said Edith. Another burst: the lights flickered, went off for a few seconds, and then came back on. Jack raised his head, gave a primal howl, and crawled over to Edith. Elizabeth crouched down and smoothed the hair over his head and back.

Edith moved to the sink, filled a kettle with water, and lit the burner on her gas stove.

"Will you be able to sleep tonight?" asked Elizabeth.

"Probably not. I think I'll stay up, have some tea, read, try to calm my little friend here and be alert for problems. And you?"

"I confess that I am a bit rattled. Would it be all right if I sat here a bit longer?"

A blast of bugles shattered the silence of the streets. It was followed by someone shouting, "Lay down your arms! We will shoot anyone who has a gun! We mean you no harm! Put away your artillery!"

"To be honest," said Edith as she took down two teacups, "I could use the company, and I couldn't ask for better company than yours. The enemy is at our gates. I won't be able to rest tonight. I'm thinking of going to the trenches down in the street and bringing the Civic Guard some coffee and a bite of food to fortify them through the night. Would you like to come with me?"

"Shouldn't those men have left by now? They will never hold back the entire German army. Bringing them food will be like serving them their last supper."

"It's true, but some have chosen to stay. Only the English army can save them now."

Edith raised her cup but hesitated before it reached her lips. "Elizabeth, you have been a true and loyal friend. I must beg you to make me a promise."

"You know I would do anything I can for you."

"If things go badly here, promise me you will contact my mother."

"I don't foresee that will be necessary, but I will do as you ask."

"One more thing. Should anything happen to me, I want you to take over the school and keep our mission alive."

"I can't promise you that. It is out of my control. You know the Committee wants a Belgian to run this school. Of course, they'll soon learn it would take four Belgians to do all that you do."

"Or one good English woman. This work will flounder without you or me as the Directrice."

"And what makes you think I will be around if you are not?"

"God did not lead me here to do His work to have it destroyed. He sent you to me for a purpose. I don't believe that purpose has yet been fully realized."

"Maybe or maybe not. All I know is that if God sent you here to do this work, He surely wants you to complete it. You were the one who told me that God never changes His mind."

Elizabeth reached across to touch her cup to Edith's. "Would that He could change our tea into wine."

"We don't need a miracle for that." Edith jumped up and headed for her cabinet. Elizabeth heard the pop of a wine cork and saw Edith return with two glasses in one hand and a bottle of Bordeaux in the other. With an exaggerated gesture of triumph, she placed them on the table in front of Elizabeth.

Another rocket blasted in the distance. The ceiling light flickered and the two glasses quivered. Elizabeth poured the wine and handed a glass to Edith. Edith noticed the tremor in her hand.

"I'll hear no more of either of our impending demises. To England," said Elizabeth raising her glass.

Edith touched her glass to Elizabeth's. "We wait for England. May she soon arrive."

— 25 —

A GRAY UNDULATING MASS
OF SOLDIERS

E dith woke up with a start. Although she had had only a few hours of sleep, not knowing what the day would bring, she could not stay in bed. She shuffled over to the window. Looking up and down the street, she noticed that all the window shutters were closed. The streets were silent. It was a strange silence. No, it was more than a silence. It was an absence, the absence of everything. People. Automobiles. Bicycles.

She looked over at the thick ivy vines that snaked up the brick wall of the building across the street. Every morning, crows gathered among those vines and woke her up with their raucous cawing. Now, not a bird was in sight. The air was swollen with anticipation. It was as if the entire city had inhaled and dared not exhale.

She walked to the washbasin and looked in the mirror. The face that stared back at her had gray streaks streaming down her mountain of brown hair and tiny fissures scratched in around her mouth and eyes. She wondered how the woman who stared back at her could only be forty-eight. This woman looked a decade older. She turned away from the image, washed, and changed into a clean uniform.

Elizabeth, Millicent, and Grace were eating breakfast when Edith and a few of the staff joined them. Some had puffy red eyes. Others walked with heads down, eyes shifting up to look at their Directrice and then down again. A few mumbled "*bonjour*" under their breaths.

Millicent was first to break the silence. "I heard the Huns are just outside the city gates and will be marching into Brussels today. Is that true?"

Edith addressed the solemn faces around the table. "This may well be the day we have all dreaded. If the Germans march into Brussels today,

---

161

they may well march through Ixelles to get there. I implore you to stay silent, support each other, and do what is expected of you. As difficult as it is for all of us to face this, we must stay strong."

"Sorry, *Madame*," protested José, the house boy, "but if I get a chance to kill the murdering Huns, I'll…"

Edith put her hand up to stop him. "We must never resort to returning evil with evil, because that makes us equal with them. There is no victory in violence. It only leads to more violence. We must leave justice to God."

José threw his spoon down, pushed his chair back, and stood to leave. Edith's voice came across like the crack of a whip. "Sit, José. We have details to discuss."

For the next few minutes, the only sound was of clinking utensils against porcelain dishes. Grace broke the silence. "What will our duties be today? The Clinique is empty. We've scrubbed everything twice. What more is there for us to do? Scrub everything three times?"

"Twice is quite enough, Grace. Today, there will be no duties unless you are already assigned to them. If you are to be at a certain hospital, home, or school, please go there and stay there for your scheduled time. If you have no assignment, you are free to do as you wish, but I caution you to be careful. Stay together. I want everyone to gather in the meeting room after supper at six. Do not be late. Since all communication and travel will be taken over by the Germans, we must arrange a time and a way to stay informed and organized. That's it, then. You may leave when you are done."

"Do you mind if we go down to the streets to see what is taking place?" asked Grace.

"You may do as you wish. Personally, it gives me no pleasure to watch them humiliate our proud city, so I will remain here and be available if anyone needs me."

As she lingered to speak to some of her staff, the cleaning lady burst into the room. Her face was flushed, and her eyes moved wildly around the room. In a breathless and hoarse voice she yelled, "*Les Boches sont là! Les Boches sont là!*" She tripped over a chair and fell against José. They tumbled to the floor with arms and legs entangled. Edith and her nurses helped the cleaning lady up off the stunned boy and brought them both to their feet.

"Where are they now?"

"Coming through the Triumphal Arches at the Rue de la Loi. Oh, *mon Dieu*! That leads right past the palace. They will take over the palace! There are thousands of Germans! With horses pulling huge guns. And they have spikes on their helmets. We will all die! I should have escaped to the seaside with the others when I had a chance."

Edith saw the grip of fear behind the woman's eyes.

"Listen to me. You stayed because you have a job to do. We all do. Yours is as important as mine, José's, and everyone else you see here. Now sit down and calm yourself. It won't help if we all lose control."

The cleaning woman sat down, then lifted her apron to her face and sobbed into it. Elizabeth moved to her side to comfort her.

* * * * *

Back in her study, Edith thought about the invasion. What she dreaded most was the thought that she might never see her mother again so she sat down to write her a letter,

> *My Darling Mother and Family,*
>
> *If you open this, it will be because that which we feared has now has happened. Brussels has fallen into the hands of the enemy. They are very near now and it is doubtful if the Allied armies can stop them. We are prepared for the worst.*
>
> *I have given dear Gracie and the Sisters a chance to go home, but none of them will leave. I appreciate their courage, and I want now to let the Jemmetts know that I did my best to send Gracie home, but she refused firmly to leave me—she is very quiet and brave.*
>
> *I have nothing to leave but £160 in the Pension Fund, which has never been touched and is mine to leave. I wish Mother to have it with my dearest love. It will supply the place of my little quarterly allowance to her.*
>
> *If I can send my few jewels over, will you divide them between Flor and Lil? I shall think of you to the last, and you may be sure we shall do our duty here and die as women of our race should die.*
>
> *My dear, dear love to Mother and Flor, Lil, Jack...*

A knock on the door interrupted her. She quickly blotted the letter, put it under some papers, and opened the door. A man stood facing her, holding a greasy leather cap in one hand and something she didn't recognize at first in the other. She detected a residue of smoke on his clothes. He made a little bow.

"Are you Mme. Edith Cavell, the nurse?"

"I am."

He leaned back a little. His eyes shifted up one street and down the other. Then he stepped forward. He had a curiously sad gaze. "I was asked to return something to you." He held out his hand and Edith recognized the cedar box she had entrusted to the American couple to post to her mother.

"The American couple to whose care you entrusted this send you their regrets."

Edith took the box and cradled it in her hands. "What happened? Are they safe?"

"They are safely out of the country, but they were afraid they could not get this box past the border guards. We struck up a conversation at the train station. When they found out I was going to Brussels, they asked me to return this to you. I'm sorry I have taken so long returning it to you. Transportation has been difficult, and the telephones have been cut off. I hope you understand."

"Of course. Thank you for returning it. Would you like to come in and sit for a moment while I get you something to drink?"

"*Non, merci, Madame.* This is not a good day to linger on the streets. The Huns will be marching into the city today. I assume you already know they will be coming up from the southeast, which puts Ixelles and Uccle directly in their path." He made a little bow. "*Bonjour, Madame. Je vous souhaite bien.*"

"I wish you well, too."

Edith put the box on the desk and looked inside. Everything was there. The jewelry was untouched, but the letter was gone. She hoped that meant it would be mailed to her mother. She picked up the picture of her mother that sat on the desk. She smiled, running the tip of her finger over the glass, and her mother seemed to smile back.

How will my mother know if anything has happened to me, and how will I know if anything has happened to her? Is she aware of what is happening in Belgium?

She folded her letter and was about to place it in the top drawer of her desk when she noticed the glass of water on her desk tremble a bit. Then she heard a distant rumble that made the earth shake. She ran to the roof. Elizabeth followed behind her. They looked to the south and saw them—a gray undulating mass of soldiers marching eight in a row up the avenue just off the street where they stood. As the soldiers came closer, Edith saw that the sound came from thousands of hobnailed, goose-stepping boots pounding against the cobblestones. They stomped with mechanized precision to the rhythmical beating of mammoth brass cymbals and kettledrums large enough to entirely fill the horse-drawn cart ahead of them.

Edith and Elizabeth stood with eyes fixed on the scene, then simultaneously turned to each other to confirm what they saw. Elizabeth tried to grapple with the enormity. "How ...how many of them do you think there are?"

"I don't know. Thousands, hundreds of thousands, maybe. There seems to be no end to them."

Elizabeth lifted her hand to her eyes to shield them from the sun and strained to look down the avenue. "There are the other three major avenues, including Avenue Louise. They could be using any of them as well."

"Or all of them," said Edith.

The dark gray uniforms slithered like a serpent, up the wide avenue in a continuous forward movement. Row on endless row, the soldiers held their heads high in patriotic pride, smartly uniformed, rosy-faced, and healthy. Heavy guns rolled by, their openings like vicious mouths of steel. Elizabeth squinted from the sun glinting off steel bayonets that spiked up like thousands of glass shards.

Edith looked for some humanity in the soldiers' expressions but found none. The visors of their pointed helmets hid their eyes. Their heads never turned to one side or the other but stared straight ahead. The soldiers responded *en masse* like mindless puppets, not to verbal orders but to shrill whistles that hung from the lips of regiment officers. Behind them bumped along gray caissons carrying heavy artillery. They were heading straight to the center of Brussels. Edith turned away. "We'll find out more about this when we meet together this evening."

Then something that broke the order of the line caught her eye. She turned back to take a second look. A German soldier had broken rank. He stooped down in front of a small Belgian boy, who gripped the hand of his mother. The mother pulled the frightened boy to her until the soldier held out his open hand. In it was a piece of chocolate. When the boy took the chocolate, the soldier stood up, smiled, and tousled the child's hair. Edith could hardly believe what she had seen. A turmoil of emotions flooded through her. Good men fight and die on both sides, all for the same reasons.

That evening, her meager staff sat around the table in the center of the meeting room. When Edith entered the room, the murmur of conversation abruptly stopped.

"As you already know, our city is now under siege. I am expecting we will soon be treating wounded soldiers from Liège and wherever there has been fighting. I know how distasteful this is to all of you, but I expect you each to act like professionals. Before we start further discussion, I ask that you share your experiences today."

Millicent White was the first to speak up. "I was assigned to help Mme. DePage. There are a few *Boche*, uh, I mean German patients, on her ward. After we cared for their wounds, Mme. DePage asked me to walk over to St. Michael's Cathedral. When I got to the church, hundreds of people were already standing on the stairs. Everyone was silent, as if they were watching their own funeral."

"Did the army pass by you?" asked José.

"Oh, yes. There were thousands of them on horses. At the front of each squadron, black and white pennants hung from the lances of the squadron leaders. I was puzzled to hear the tune of *God Save the King*.

"They were singing a British anthem?" asked Edith, one eyebrow cocked.

"I thought so at first, but as they rode closer, I heard the words *Heil Dir im Siegeskranz*, like it was a terrible chant."

"Can someone here tell us what that means?" asked Edith, looking around the table.

"I can," said Marie, the German maid. "It means they are thanking God for their victory. I guess that means over us."

Millicent continued. "They rode their horses over the steps of the church and right into the crowd."

"Was anyone hurt?" asked Jacqueline.

"Not that I could see, but they did scatter people all over the place. Then they stopped on the top step and simply stood there like conquerors looking over their victory. Their horses defecated on the church steps."

There was a collective gasp and murmur in the room.

Millicent continued. "I was close enough to see the looks of arrogance on their faces. Some had scars slashed across their cheeks. Some smiled and others were indifferent. A few wore monocles and flicked riding crops against their horses. One officer had a head that looked like a boiled potato. He was smoking and sweating under his collar, which was hidden under rolls of fat."

"Oh, my! I hope we never have to feed that hog," said the cook. Everyone but Edith smiled.

"I saw the fat one look at us as if we were vermin. He flicked his lighted cigarette at us, kicked his spurs, and rode past the church to join his squadron, which was riding down into the *Grande Place*."

"Did they remove the flags from the cathedral towers?" asked Elizabeth.

"Not that I saw, but I couldn't watch any longer and thought I should get back to Mme. DePage. I reported everything I saw to her," said Millicent in a subdued tone.

"Thank you," said Edith. "I know that was difficult for you. Can anyone else tell us what they saw?"

Jacqueline spoke up. "I saw some of what happened at the *Grande Place*."

"And what was that?"

"I saw them march in from all sides. The officers Millicent saw rode directly up to the *Hôtel de Ville*. All of the surrounding guild houses were closed. No one could be seen in the windows or on the balconies. There were no Belgian flags anywhere except the one on the spire of the *Hôtel de Ville*."

Edith's voice rose. "They surely didn't touch that flag. No foreign power has ever dared to remove it."

"I'm sorry, *Madame*, but they promptly removed that flag and hoisted up their own."

"Ah, *mon Dieu*! We are doomed!" cried the cleaning lady again and buried her face in her hands.

Edith put her hand on the woman's shoulder. "We are not doomed if we keep our wits about us."

Jacqueline continued. "I don't know everything that happened, but I saw soldiers setting up camp all over the marketplace. When I left, an officer with a bushy mustache and goatee beard was standing on the stairs talking to a city official."

After a few moments of silence, Edith took control of the meeting.

"If no one has anything to add, I've made out schedules and duties for everyone. Those working during the day will meet here every evening at six. Those of you who will be working in the evening, we'll meet at ten in the morning. Should there be any problems or questions, either I, Nurse White, or Nurse Wilkins will be immediately available. I will let you know if the telephones and posts are restored. If you find a newspaper, do not let anyone see you with it and please bring it to me."

To everyone's amazement, Edith then sat at the piano and began to play.

"It might help morale if we sing a few songs together." She waved for them to gather around the piano. "Come on. Join in." They stood looking at her and then at each other. Grace went over and began to sing and Elizabeth voiced a few weak strains. The rest left.

The cook filed out with the cleaning lady. "I dropped a saucepan onto the pavement right behind them. You should have seen those Huns jump! Before they could find where the crash came from, quick as you please, I hoisted the pan back up into the window by a string."

* * * * *

That evening, Edith went back up to the roof. The fading sunlight filtered through a haze of gray dust. Everything was gray. The ivy leaves snaking up the wall were gray. A layer of gray dust settled over the cobbled streets. Even the waves of soldiers who continued to pour into the city looked like hordes of gray ghosts.

"Frightening, isn't it?"

Edith turned quickly to see Marie DePage standing behind her. Edith reached out her arms in greeting. "So good to see you, Marie. Let's go downstairs to talk."

The two women gathered their skirts and descended the stairs and moved into the empty Clinique. "How were you able to get away?"

"Millicent relieved me at the palace hospital. They have doubled their guard around the palace and the parliament building and God only knows where else. They have the palace all roped off. We will not be seeing any patients there unless they are German. I am sure of it."

"What have you heard from Antoine?"

"Not much since the telephone lines have been seized. He is still working in the medical tents on the French border. He really wanted to take you with him, but I told him I desperately needed you here. The fighting out on the French border is fierce."

"Have the Brits landed?" Edith asked.

"I heard rumors that they have and are fighting along with the French out there."

"Finally! The English have arrived! Thank God! If the English army is in Belgium, then this nightmare should all be over soon."

"Mind you, Edith, I'm not sure. It's all rumor. There are no newspapers printed or mailed to us, so I can only be sure of one thing; if something is not done soon, there will be terrible consequences. Mr. Whitlock, the American consul, visited with me yesterday evening. He was looking in to see if Antoine had given us any news about the French border. Did you know that Mr. Whitlock is now representing the English, as well as the Americans?"

"No, I didn't," said Edith, moving her chair closer to Marie. "What did he say?" Marie reached for one of the clean, loose bandages from the pile of bandages between them on the desk and began rolling it up on her lap.

"He told me he was invited to be at the *Grand Place* to witness the meeting between General Thaddeus von Jarotsky, who is *Kommandant* of the brigade now encamped on the plaza there, and *Burgomaster* Adolphe

Max. He said Max met the *Kommandant* on the stairs of the *Hôtel de Ville* and ceremoniously handed over the keys of Brussels to him. He said the *Grande Place* is set up like a military camp, with tents, outdoor cooking stoves, horses, and mounted sentinels at every entrance. Whitlock said between the smell of horse manure, a few thousand sweaty men, some with their shoes off, and the smoke from cigarettes and cooking stoves, the odor reminded him of a slaughterhouse. But that's the least of it."

"I heard the Belgian flag was removed. What else, Marie?"

Marie plopped the finished bandage on top of the pyramid of rolled bandages and looked up at her. "He said General von Jarotsky, who wants to be addressed as 'His Excellency,' demanded that Max hand over twenty high-ranking Belgians, members of the Municipal Council, to be used as hostages."

"But that's impossible!" said Edith, jumping up and sending the bandage rolls over the table and onto the floor. She picked the bandages off the floor and threw them onto the table. "They want us to turn over those men as hostages to be jailed and possibly tortured and killed?"

"And that's not all. He also demanded a war contribution of twenty million francs," Marie's dismay was tangible.

"That's even more insane! Who can afford to pay a twenty million franc levy? Most of these people are poor and live simply. Many make their own clothes and grow their own food."

"And the *Kommandant* demands that we feed his troops."

"We barely have enough food to feed ourselves. Did the *Burgomaster* agree to this?"

"Mr. Whitlock said Max refused to turn over any hostages, but could not convince 'His Highness' or 'His Excellency,'" –Marie rolled her eyes to the ceiling– "the *Kommandant*, to lower the levy or decrease the amount of food demanded."

Marie gathered the bandages thrown on the table and began to pile them up again. Have you seen the proclamations they posted on buildings and walls, listing new regulations and punishments if anyone disobeys?"

"No. What kind of regulations?" Edith's voice sounded weary.

"Things like curfew times, no one is to have a gun, no one is to aid an enemy soldier, no one can harm any German soldiers, no reading of newspapers unless they are printed or approved by the *Kommandant*, no removal of German flags–that sort of thing."

Marie finished piling up the bandages once again. "But you have to love our Max. Underneath their posters, he wrote in red that we are to remember that we are still Belgians and owe our allegiance to our king."

The two friends smiled at the bit of bravado shown by the only official person left in the city who could speak for the Belgian people.

"Mr. Whitlock said the German soldiers did not know they were in Brussels."

"Where did they think they were?"

"They thought they were in Paris because everyone spoke French."

Marie put her hand to her mouth and yawned. "Do you mind if I stay overnight at the Clinique? It's getting late, and I think it is now past the curfew time so I should not be on the streets."

Edith got up, being careful not to spill the newly piled bandages again.

"Don't worry. There's no shortage of empty beds here. Stay for breakfast before you return. *Bon nuit, Marie*." She hugged her friend and started to walk away. Then Edith stopped and turned around.

"I can't help but remember how eight years ago, I sat in the *Grande Place* with a friend of mine. We were on holiday together. It was during the Festival of Flowers in August. The flowers were all so brilliant. During lunch, my friend asked me if I had ever considered leaving nursing."

Marie raised her eyebrows in interest. "How did you answer her?"

"I told her that nursing was my life and soul and that I would never leave it."

"And if I were to ask you that same question today, how would you answer?"

There was a pause, the length of which surprised Marie.

"Sometimes I look back on the days when I was young. Life was so fresh and beautiful. The countryside in Norwich was a wonderful place to raise a family. A very fine young man named Edward asked me to marry him. At times, I wonder what my life would have been like had I accepted. I could have continued my painting."

Edith stopped and tilted her head. "Did I ever tell you that I used to draw and paint? I was actually quite good at it."

Marie smiled at this new personal revelation. "I remember your anatomical drawings in class as being quite good."

"Those were easy to do. I drew flowers and animals. Even landscapes. When I was in Mumbles, I loved sitting on the beach painting seascapes while listening to the seagulls and the power of the surf pounding against the shore."

Edith's voice drifted off, paused, and then abruptly changed. "We, that is Edward and I, continue to be very good friends. We post letters every few months. He never married. He says he is waiting for me. Can you imagine? Waiting for a 48-year-old spinster like me? There are other loves in my life now that are stronger. My devoted staff and friends like you have become my family. The deepest, longest lasting, and most meaningful parts of my life have been the hardest earned."

Edith went on almost wistfully. "I made a vow years ago to follow the example of Florence Nightingale and devote my life to the sick. Since then, my course has been set either by myself or God, I'm never sure which. There is no turning back now, Marie."

Once again, Edith started to walk away, then paused and said with a wry smile, "Besides, I am inclined to strongly believe I would have not done well tied to the harness of marriage."

* * * * *

The next morning, Edith finished breakfast and whistled for Jack to accompany her on her rounds to the hospitals. When she got to the corner of her street, she saw a small group of people gathered and talking excitedly among themselves. She heard snippets of their conversation.

"Unthinkable!"

"What will we do now?"

"Poor fellow. Brave as a bulldog."

"Miserable bastards!"

Edith stopped and asked if there was a problem.

"Haven't you heard?" asked one woman with a black shawl draped around her shoulders. The corner of her mouth twitched as she spoke.

"Heard what?" asked Edith, pulling back on Jack's leash. "Stay. Sit." Jack did neither. He strained at the leash and sniffed at the feet of the people gathered. Edith pulled him away and turned to an elderly man who held a yellowed handkerchief to his nose.

"Heard what?" she repeated.

"You do not know?" said the man. His voice was muffled by his handkerchief as he talked. Then he blew his nose. He wiped his unshaven face with the handkerchief and then stuffed it into his back pocket. "They arrested our Burgomaster Max. They are deporting him to a prison in Germany."

Adolphe Eugène Jean Henri Max,
Mayor of Brussels, Belgium 1869-1939.

26

DETAILS OF THINGS HERE

L ouisa was beside herself. She hadn't heard from her daughter in weeks. The words, "She is fine and can take care of herself," twirled around like a prayer wheel in her mind but gave her little comfort. She scoured newspaper articles looking for information about the invasion in Belgium and read about the atrocities in Liège and Louvain with horror. At night, her mind was flooded with frightening images. She tried sending a telegram, but to no avail. Not knowing what else to do, she decided to post a letter and prayed it would reach her daughter.

21 August, 1914
My Darling Edith,

It is almost against hope that I am writing for news of you and Gracie—if at all possible let me have a line or wire—no news is intolerable, one conjectures all sorts of things—my anxiety is terrible but I am afraid yours must be much worse. If you are both safe and well in the midst of all the horrors of war and in-vasion I shall be truly thankful—I pray for you constantly that God will grant you His loving protection—I go to stay with Lilian next Monday to spend a few days or a week, so if you could possibly send a line, address me at Erpingham House, Cliff Road, Sheringham.

I cannot write on any other topic. My heart is filled with one thing.

My dearest love to you, dear child.
                              Your loving Mother

Edith had not received anything from her mother and worried that none of her previous letters had reached her. Sick with the thought that her mother would read about the devastation and worry for her safety, she quickly wrote another letter and gave it to a friend who would be traveling west to Ninove, a city that had not yet been invaded and could still post mail.

30 August, 1914
My Darling Mother,

I know you must be in a state of great anxiety about us here in Brussels, but I hope you will receive the letter I sent through Antwerp a day or two ago and that it will relieve your mind—A friend is going west of the city to the town of Ninove tomorrow, where he hears it is possible to wire and post. I hope you will get it shortly. If you do, please send me news of Flo & Lil, also Mrs. Jemmett. I hope news of Brussels has been published in the newspapers. I cannot give you details of things here, as this letter might fall into the wrong hands.

We are almost without news of what is going on around us & tho' some filters thru' it is very unreliable. We would give anything for an English newspaper, but of course none are allowed. The mail arrived for the 19th & since then we are in the dark, the wildest rumors are current.— We know for certain that there is fighting near at hand for we can hear the cannon & see the smoke with field glasses. We have a few German wounded in our hospital but no allies. There has been a terrible loss of life on both sides and destruction of towns and beautiful buildings that can never be rebuilt. I am keeping a record for more peaceful times which will interest you later.

We are still able to get food tho' prices are higher and we have reduced the scale of living a little. We go on quietly with our usual work and hope for the best. Gracie is not very well—one of her cold attacks, brought on perhaps by the unsettled state of things—but please do not tell the Jemmetts. The days are very

*fine and warm and mornings are misty, looking over the plain
this peaceful Sunday. One cannot imagine how near are the
terrible dogs of war nor how ruthlessly that peace may be
broken. Do not fear for us. We are well out of the town, as you
know, and are not afraid.*

> *With my dearest love to you all,*
> *Ever your loving daughter, Edith*

Along with this letter, she sent an editorial she had written a week earlier
for the *Nursing Mirror*. As their war correspondent, she felt it was
important that the nursing community know the circumstances in
Belgium. So much had changed in her life, which was totally out of her
control, that she clung to the few things that gave her some sense of
familiarity and order. Submitting articles to this newspaper, as she had
for the last eight years, was one of them.

21 August, 1914
To the Nursing Mirror

*It is many months since I wrote to the Nursing Mirror the first
of what was to have been a series of articles on the nursing of
the wounded. On August 13, we had no conception that soon,
we were to be virtual prisoners in the gay city of Brussels. We
were full of enthusiasm for the war and full of confidence in the
Allies. Crowds assembled everywhere to talk over the prospects
of a speedy peace.*

*We prepared 18,000 beds for the wounded; all sorts and
conditions of people were offering to help, giving mattresses
and blankets, rolling bandages, and making shirts. Our chief
thought was how to care for those who were sacrificing so
much and facing death so bravely at Liège and elsewhere. After
Liège had fallen, we heard that the enemy was coming on as
an irresistible force. There were sinister tales of burnt and
battered houses, of villages razed to the ground, of women and
children murdered, of drunken soldiers and raping, looting and
mutilation. And still we hoped against hope. "We wait for
England," was on the lips of everyone, and till the very last, we
thought the English troops were between us and the invading*

army. In the evening came the news that the enemy was at the gates.

In the afternoon, with much pomp and circumstance of war, the German troops marched into Brussels, and to the Town Hall, where the brave tricolor came down and the German stripes of black and white and red took its place. The Belgian crowd watched this desecration in silence and with profound sadness; some wept. The city was handed over to the enemy by our beloved Burgomaster Adolphe Max, who was then arrested and is now a prisoner in Germany.

There were at least 20,000 soldiers who entered the city and camped for the night. Some were so terribly stiff that they could scarcely walk, and many had their feet sore and blistered with the long marching in heavy boots. On August 21, many more troops came through. From our building we could see the long procession. We were divided between pity for those poor fellows and hate of a cruel and vindictive foe bringing ruin and desolation. I saw several of the men pick up little children and give them chocolate or seat them on their horses, and some had tears in their eyes at the recollection of the little ones at home.

From that day until now, we have been cut off from the world outside–newspapers were first censored, then suppressed, and are now printed under German auspices. None are allowed in from England. The telephone service has been taken over by the enemy. The post too was stopped. All letters must remain left open and contain no news of the war. The few trains are in German hands and whenever you go, you must have, and pay for, a passport. No bicycles are allowed and practically no motors.

I am but a looker-on after all, for it is not my country whose soil is desecrated and whose sacred places are laid waste. I can only feel the deep and tender pity as a friend within the gates, and observe with sympathy and admiration the high courage and self-control of a people enduring a long, terrible agony. They have grown thin and silent with the strain. They walk about the city shoulder to shoulder with the foe and never see them, or make a sign."

Edith had encouraged her nurses to keep diaries of their nursing experiences, just as she had done when she was a probationer. After war had been declared, many of them put their diaries aside to give their full attention to their new duties, but Jacqueline Van Til found that writing in her diary eased her anxiety and helped her to focus her thoughts. The military activity was in the center of the city, not in the southern neighborhood where the school and Clinique were situated. She used the quiet times to continue writing her entries.

On her way to work one day, she passed a group of Belgians staring up at a piece of paper tacked to the side of a building. None of them were tall enough to read this latest of the German Proclamations, so a shopkeeper came out with a ladder. The shopkeeper set it against the building, gathered her skirts and climbed up. The dour woman read out it loud to the audience below her:

Proclamation   Brussels, August, 1914.

German troops will pass through Brussels today and the following days, and will be obliged by circumstances to call upon the city for lodging, food, and supplies. All these require-ments will be settled for regularly through the communal authorities. I expect the population to meet these necessities of war without resistance, and especially that there shall be no aggression against our troops, and that the supplies required shall be promptly furnished. In this case, I give every guarantee for the preservation of the city and the safety of its inhabitants. If, however, as has unfortunately happened in other places, there are attacks upon our troops, firing upon our soldiers, fires or explosions of any sort, I shall be obliged to take the severest measures.

The General Commanding the Army Corps

When the woman finished, one hand holding onto the ladder and the other held up in the air, she addressed the crowd below her. "With this and a few francs, you can get a glass of beer in any bar in Brussels."

The expressions of those below turned into smiles and then sneers. It seemed to Jacqueline that the only time she saw Belgians smiling now was when they were making fun of their captors. When a woman walked up to the gathering begging for food, their smiles flattened and they turned and walked away.

27

BOGER AND MEACHIN

"Colonel Boger, sir. Are you awake?"

Boger's eyes flew open and saw a man's unshaven face hovering over him, with a wound across his forehead. Every time the man spoke, waves of stale breath blew into Boger's face. He grimaced, lifted his head, and looked around.

"Where the bloody hell am I? Who are you?"

"Sergeant Fred Meachin, sir. I'm in the 1st Cheshire Regiment. Your regiment. Don't you recognize me?"

Boger shook his head and lifted his hand to wipe his eyes.

"Of course. Sorry, I didn't recognize you." He noticed the bandage on his hand with surprise and curiosity. "I remember we fought at Mons. What happened?

"We were forced to retreat from Mons, sir. You were wounded. Don't you remember?"

Boger let his head fall back onto the pillow and winced with pain from the jolt.

"I remember being hit and then moved off the field by..." He coughed and gripped his side with pain. "...by a few of our men." His eyes flew open as he gripped Meachin's arm. "Did you see them?"

"See what, sir?"

"In the sky—angels riding silver stallions." Boger stopped when he saw a questioning look on Meachin's face, and his voice flattened. "Of course you didn't. You think I've gone daft."

"No, sir. They were there all right. Many of us saw them. In the night sky, they were. They were throwing down some kind of spears of silver light. At first, each man thought he was the only one to see them, but after a few of us opened up about it, we realized many of us saw the same thing. So if you're daft, we all are." He leaned closer and whispered into Boger's ear. "We have to keep our voices down or the *Boche* will hear us."

"*Boche*? Are we prisoners?"

"Well, not exactly, sir, but we are being closely watched. We're in a convent hospital at Wiheries outside of Mons. The *Boche* think we are too badly wounded to make a run for it so they are a bit lax in their guarding."

"How many of us are there here?"

"About forty. Corporals Chapman and Lewis are among them. Not all the wounded are Brits. Some are French and Belgian."

"And when we are better? What then?"

"Then, I think, sir, they mean to take us to prison camps in Germany."

"Rubbish! We need to escape straightaway and that's an order." Boger swung his legs over the edge of the bed to stand. A searing pain ripped through his ankle. He fell back, gripping the edge of his bed. Meachin picked up his legs and gently brought them back onto the thin mattress.

"Right. Sir, neither of us are in any shape to go anywhere right now, but if we keep our powder dry, we can plan our escape while we heal up a bit."

Boger was silent for a moment, then looked more carefully at Meachin. "The wound on your head looks nasty."

"Oh, I'm all right. It's not too bad, really. Got my head grazed with a bullet and got hit by a piece of shrapnel. I lost consciousness for a while. When I woke up, I found a Belgian Red Cross station. Crawled to it and asked about you. They told me you had just been brought here, so I asked them to bring me here too."

"How long have I been here?"

"They said you came in late yesterday evening. I came in before dawn this morning. I couldn't rouse you up until now."

A deep voice boomed behind Meachin.

"Ah, I see you are awake, Colonel Boger. I am Dr. Valentin van Hassel, the convent physician. May I look to your wounds, sir?"

Boger flipped the covers off and leaned up on one elbow. "My ankle has been shot up." He held up the bandaged hand. "My hand took one to it." Then he lifted up his uniform jacket. "Got one in my side, but the ankle is the worst. Can't walk on it."

The physician carefully inspected Boger's hand and side. "We can dress up your hand and side. With some medical care, they will heal."

When the doctor tried to remove the shoe on the wounded foot, however, Boger stifled a cry of pain and gripped the sides of his bed. The physician drew back and stood thoughtfully running his fingers over his mustache.

"I must tell you, your ankle looks serious. After we cut your shoe off, I will be able to get a better look. You should also know the only surgical instruments I have are a knife and scissors. If your ankle requires surgery, I will not be able to help you. We have very few medical supplies now. Much of what we had was used up, and we haven't been able to replace anything. We do have some antiseptics and clean bandages. I'm sorry to have to tell you this but if it heals badly, you may be a cripple for the rest of your life. If it doesn't heal, you may develop gas gangrene and die of infection."

Refugees fleeing from Louvain, Belgium (vintage postcard.)

"And if it heals? What then?" Boger chucked his chin in the direction of the guard standing at the door. "Do they haul us away as prisoners?"

The physician stroked his mustache in a slow, methodical way. "That is their plan, but we shall see. Be assured that while you are here, you will have a clean bed and be fed. The nuns will see to your wounds."

Weeks went by, but Boger still could not stand for very long. His ankle was swollen and red, signs that an infection was still festering. One morning, Boger was approached by the cleaning woman. Leaning close to him, she pulled out a bundle of clothes from under her skirt. "Here, take these and hide them." She quickly shoved them under his blankets.

"There is no time to talk. Listen closely. I will get more of these to you. Give them to your friends. On September 25, you must all put them on. When you see the guard is having his breakfast, leave one at a time. Climb over the east convent wall. Someone will be waiting for you there."

"Who is helping us?" whispered Boger.

She looked up and saw the German guard staring in her direction. "I must go." She gripped her water pail and rags and scurried away.

The Belgian Civic Guards were totally unprepared to fight
the German army (vintage postcard)

— 28 —

THERE ARE NO WOUNDED

As the days grew shorter and the shadow of German occupation grew longer, Edith felt a growing frustration. She had made the decision to stay in Belgium to help the wounded, but there were very few wounded coming to the Clinique. Casualties were treated in Brussels by German nurses or sent by rail to Germany.

Longing for news from home, Edith paid five pounds, almost a month's salary, for an issue of *The Times* that was two weeks old. It gave the news for October 13, 1914, the 71st day of the war. She studied the map showing German battle lines that crossed Lille, Ghent, Malines, and Antwerp. She read how the forts in Antwerp were still holding out, but Ostend, the port where she had entered Belgium, had been bombed.

On the western border, Ypres in Flanders was under siege. A thousand British soldiers, the remains of five battered battalions, had held off thirteen German Battalions until French reinforcements arrived. While in Brussels food and commodities such as coal and oil continued to be scarce, Edith read the advertisements for Mackintosh's toffee deluxe and refined oil for lamps all available back home. She also read a column describing an Englishwoman who had left Belgium to go to the London Hospital to lecture about the medical and nursing services in occupied Belgium. She flung it across the table.

Millicent entered the room and saw the paper slide across the table and stop, half hanging over the side. "Are you all right now?"

"Quite," came the terse reply.

Millicent picked up the newspaper, folded it, and tucked it under her arm. "We can't let anyone see this lying around, now can we?"

"What are we doing here, Milli? No, really. Our staff are almost all gone. We are down to only six probationers and the new school building is only half finished with no completion date in sight. There are only a few patients in the hospitals, and our ward staff at the Red Cross hospitals have been replaced with German nurses."

Edith continued. "Dr. DePage is somewhere out on the battlefield, and Marie is in Brussels trying to maintain some decorum while working with German nurses at her palace hospital. We have almost no finances, food, or fuel. Winter will be soon be here and we will be freezing under our blankets. The Germans are advancing through Belgium, destroying everything and everyone in their path. And I just read about some woman who went back to The London to discuss our work here. Our work, not hers."

Millicent walked over to Edith and gently placed a hand on the older woman's arm. "'Tis upsetting for all of us, to be sure. I know sitting around is not your cup of tea, and making clothes for refugees is not what we came here for, but there's something to be said for waiting this miserable war out a bit. 'Tis best not to lean heavy on what you can't do and think instead about what you can."

Edith looked like a chastised dog, and Millicent softened her tone. "All of this will pass, you'll see. Then you will continue what you set out to do. No need concern yourself with what anyone else says of your work here. Everyone knows who you are and what you are doing here, and that's the truth of it."

Millicent tapped the folded paper. "Do you mind if I take this back with me to read?"

"Take it, I've already read it. Thank you, Millicent. You are a loyal friend, and I appreciate all you have done."

"Em, one more thing. I overheard some talk that Marie DePage may leave Brussels to work in the field hospitals with her husband. Is it true?"

Edith gripped the arm of the divan. "Are you sure? When is she planning to leave?"

"I haven't heard exactly when. Maybe it's just another rumor."

"I will have to ask her about it."

When the door closed behind Millicent, Edith looked for solace. She had already lost the guidance of Antoine. What would she do if Marie left as well? She prayed. "I will wait for You to show me the next step. Thy will be done. Amen."

— 29 —

LAST HOPE

On the morning of September 25, Boger and his soldiers put on the civilian clothes secretly brought in to them by the cleaning lady. When the guard left for breakfast, they slipped out of the ward and climbed over the convent wall. Boger leaned on Meachin to walk. Two soldiers lifted Boger over the wall and eased him to the ground.

Just as the cleaning lady had promised, on the other side, a Belgian man waited for them. His small, quick eyes darted around as he spoke to them. "I am Albert Libiez, Dr. Van Hassel's son-in-law. Welcome to freedom, my friends. There is no time to talk. You must split up in groups of twos and threes." He motioned to Boger and Meachin. "You two, come with me. The rest of you can hide in the forest or the village. Many of your regiment have regrouped in the forest. If you decide to stay in the village, you will find the villagers to be most willing to help you escape, but it will be more dangerous."

The men hugged each other and wished each other well. Then they divided up and disappeared.

Libiez brought Boger and Meachin to his house in the village of Wihries and hid them in the loft of his garden shed. He dressed them to look like the local villagers. Boger, wearing a floppy tie and black hat, easily passed as a Belgian civilian.

Meachin wore the overalls of a common laborer. Pads were placed between the shoulders of his jacket to give him the appearance of a hunchback. This would also be a silent answer to the question as to why, as a younger man, he was not in the army.

The two British soldiers were allowed to spend some time during the day in Albert's house. Boger had a French language manual and practiced speaking French. Meachin thought it a waste of time and preferred to play cards.

During breakfast, Albert Libiez often told them of recent news of the war. "You should be very proud of your men," he said one morning. "Your soldiers have rallied from their defeat in Mons and joined forces with the French and Belgians. They formed a counter-attack across the Marne and drove the Germans back."

Meachin slapped Boger on the shoulder. "By golly, we've done it! It's the beginning of the end for those slimy bastards. We'll be home by Christmas. Maybe earlier."

They were interrupted by Libiez's wife, who ran into the kitchen out of breath. "Quick! You must run and hide!" She said waving her hands away from her as if she were shooing a fly off the table. "I just heard that over a hundred German cyclists have entered the village and are searching the houses one at a time. They are the same German *Landsturms* who destroyed Liège and tortured people there. They are looking for enemy soldiers."

"They are also looking for wine and things to loot," said Albert. He brought out a few bottles of wine and set them on the kitchen table. "You two, stay here and pretend you are villagers. I have a plan."

Boger sat in Albert's kitchen drinking tea, while Meachin nervously watched the troops move from house to house. When they reached the neighbor's house, Albert said, "They are coming here next." Boger and Meachin stood up. When the Germans reached the fence in front of their house, Boger and Meachin walked past them, handed each soldier a bottle of wine, and walked to the gate. One soldier took the bottle and held the gate open for them.

Boger tipped his hat to them. "*Merci, vous êtes si aimable,*" he muttered. Meachin smiled and nodded as he limped past, shuffling and hunched to one side to exaggerate his faked deformity. The two German soldiers made fun of him as he passed by.

It was after dark when they returned. Alpert explained that it was too dangerous for them to stay. He handed them a small bundle and gestured to two Belgian nuns. "Here is some food. I have asked Sisters Marie and Madeline, who are from the convent at Wasmes, to come here and take you back with them. They will care for you until we can find a way to get you both out of the country."

Once they settled for the night in the convent, Boger removed the oversized boot he was wearing to accommodate the dressings. Walking had increased the swelling, and his dressings were saturated with a yellow ooze. *The infection is spreading up my leg. Soon it will infect the rest of my body. If that happens, I'm a goner. I'll never see my wife and daughters again.* The nuns dressed his ankle but could do nothing more. He slept fully clothed, not knowing what the next day would bring him.

During breakfast, a short, stocky, balding man with a thin goatee greeted them. "Bonjour, my good soldiers. I am Herman Capiau, a friend of Albert Libiez. I understand you are in need of some assistance. I am a mining official in a nearby village. I may be able to help you. I have three suggestions. I can help you to hide out in one of my coal mines, although I fear the winter cold will be uncomfortable there. I can bring you to the forest, where many of your soldiers are already hiding or..." He hesitated and looked at Boger's foot that was propped up on a chair. "I can take you to a hiding place in Brussels, where we will try to find medical help for your foot."

Both men agreed that the last choice was the best.

Herman Capiau held up his hands. "I must warn you. Brussels is an occupied city. Thousands of German soldiers are encamped there. You will be shot on sight if any of them become suspicious of you."

"We've fooled them before and we can do it again," said Meachin.

"I will accompany you on a train to Brussels, but before you leave, we will provide you with passports and identification papers. You can go nowhere without them."

After Herman obtained the faked papers, he gave each of them a train ticket, a package of food, and a bottle of wine. Then he brought them to the train station. Once on the train, the three men sat in the same coach, but occupied separate seats.

At their first stop, a group of young German soldiers pushed through the train doors into their coach. They were in high spirits and good naturedly pushed and shoved each other, arguing over which seat to take. When the train lurched forward, one of the soldiers fell onto Meachin.

"Look at Rimmel," teased one of the Germans. "He'd rather hug a cripple than a woman."

"That's because a cripple cannot run away from him like the woman in the village did," joked a tall blond soldier.

Rimmel pushed himself off Meachin. "Stupid cripple. You deliberately tripped me."

Meachin looked down at the floor and didn't answer.

"Look at me. I'm speaking to you. Admit that you tripped me." Meachin felt the pulse pounding at his throat. He gritted his teeth and shook his head no. Rimmel pulled at Meachin's hair, twisting his head up. "Tell them you deliberately tripped me up, you disgusting imbecile."

Meachin pulled his head away, which made the other soldiers laugh. He glanced up to see Boger poised on the edge of his seat as if to spring. Capiau caught Boger's eye and shook his head.

Imitating a hunchback, the blond soldier bent his back over, twisted his head to the right, and dragged one leg.

"Come and get me," he teased Rimmel. In one swift movement, Rimmel turned to grab him just as the train jerked around a corner, throwing them both off balance. They fell to the floor. When they got up, the blond soldier shoved Rimmel back. "Clumsy ox."

Rimmel was reaching for his pistol when a third soldier stepped between them. "Save your bullets for the British swine."

Rimmel moved his hand away from the gun and spat at Meachin. "*Dummer Krüppel!*" He snatched up Meachin's bottle of wine and held it in one hand as he brushed off his gray tunic with the other. Then he followed his group out to another coach.

* * * * *

When they arrived in Brussels, the three waited until the German soldiers left the train before they exited. Once they were on the train platform, Boger spoke with a smirk. "I think he fancied you."

"Bugger off–," shot back Meachin, "–sir."

"You did well back there," said Herman. "That is the kind of performance that will keep you alive."

Capiau took them to the house of someone he was sure would take them in. "Sorry. If British soldiers are found here, we will be arrested," he was told.

Another place was suggested but when they arrived, they were again turned away. By the end of the day, Boger could no longer stand on his throbbing foot and leaned heavily on Meachin to walk. At the last place, Capiau was told to try the palace hospital, run by a woman named Marie DePage. "She will take in anyone who needs medical help."

It was dark by the time they reached Marie's hospital. A cold drizzle pushed the night's chill through their clothes. They stood there shivering. When Marie came to the door, Herman confessed that the two men with him were British soldiers.

"I am so sorry, but I cannot help you. It would be too dangerous for them to be here. Too many Germans." she told them.

"I know I am asking much of you, but perhaps you can please help them in some way. One is badly wounded and needs medical attention. We have been everywhere we know to go, and there is nowhere left. He cannot hold up much longer."

Marie looked over at Boger, who was leaning on one leg, hanging onto Meachin's shoulder, and grimacing in pain. He looked up at her. "Please, sister. I have fought for your country, and now I need your help so I can come back and fight again."

Marie motioned for Herman to come closer and lowered her voice. "I cannot take them in. The nurses here are German and will recognize them. There is one more place you could try. It is a small hospital in Ixelles run by a British matron. I cannot guarantee she will help, but it's all I have to offer."

She went to the desk, hurriedly wrote a note, and handed it to Capiau. "Her name is Edith Cavell. Mention my name and give her this note." On a separate piece of paper she wrote out the address and pressed it into his hand. "You have to go now."

It was late in the evening when they arrived at the Clinique of the rue de la Culture. Boger clung to Meachin, trying to get a solid footing on the slippery, uneven cobblestones. Both men stumbled and splashed their way to the entrance. Capiau moved in front of them and up the granite stairs to the door. He heard Boger's voice behind him say, "Let's pray this nurse takes us in. She's our last hope, isn't she?"

Capiau turned to face the dark green door with its brass number, 149. Hesitating a moment, he straightened his posture, pulled at his cuffs, and shrugged himself up an inch taller. He reached out to knock on the door. "Yes," he said, "I am afraid she is."

Col. Dudley Boger, Edith Cavell's first "guest."
When she saw his wounds, she took him in without hesitation.

— 30 —
DECISION

By late evening, the sagging gray sky had long since turned black. Edith usually spent the evening with her staff, but tonight, she was in no mood to talk. Spies and paranoia were so prevalent that she found it best to say very little to anybody. It was comforting to simply spend the evenings with a blanket over her shoulders, writing letters to her mother, sisters, and Edward. She dipped her pen into the ink and started writing.

> *It has turned wet now & chilly & I am very anxious about our small supply of coal as none is coming in with the trains.—I hope we may be able to get a good supply before the winter sets in.*

A man's voice carried up from the floor below. Jack's head shot up, his ears erect. He jumped up. A ridge of prickly hair stood up along his back. Edith put her hand out to calm him and felt his body vibrate from a low growl. The voice was unfamiliar to her. The man spoke in short, crackling phrases, like twigs that snapped when stepped on.

"*S'il vous plaît.* Forgive me. It is late, I know. It is important. I must speak to Mme Cavell."

With head down and eyes fixed on the door, Jack slowly moved over to it. Edith heard Marie's German accent. "Not to disturb Mme. Cavell. Too late now. Tomorrow, you come back."

"No, please. It is of the utmost urgency. I must see her tonight. I will wait."

Millicent was in the nursing office reading *The Times* while waiting for the shift duty report from the day nurse. She was riveted to the headlines: *German Proclamation Against Russia, German Armies over the French Border.* She looked up when she heard the man's voice. It was urgent and authoritative. She saw Marie trying to close the door on a well-dressed man who held it open and stepped inside. Her thoughts raced. German police were in the area, searching for hidden Allied soldiers. She strained to look past the man and saw two others standing in the shadows. In one swift movement, she crushed the forbidden newspaper into a ball and stuffed it behind her.

"Mme. White," called Marie, "please for you to come here and talk to this man. He will not leave."

Millicent walked over to face a man with fine features, a high brow, and deep-set brown eyes. She guessed he was Belgian, but these days no one could be trusted. Prisms of light flashed off the drops of water on his spectacles. He held his hand out to her.

"I am Herman Capiau, an engineer from the town of Mons. I have come a long way to speak to Mme. Cavell. I have a letter from Mme DePage explaining why I am here."

"I will take your note to Mme. Cavell. Wait here."

Just then, the door at the top of the stairs opened, and a snarling Jack sprang down the stairs and lunged for the man. Marie caught his collar just as his jaws snapped a few inches from Herman's leg. The muscles in her arms strained to hold him back.

"Jack! Come here!"

In one swift movement, the dog twisted his head away from Marie's grip and bounded back up the stairs to his mistress.

Herman's hands trembled as he took out a handkerchief, removed his spectacles, and wiped them. When he replaced his spectacles, he stood face to face with a pair of blazing blue-gray eyes the likes of which he had never seen before.

"I am Mme. Cavell. Why do you wish to see me?"

Marie handed her Herman's note. Edith thought it might be a fake until she saw the familiar letter head and Marie's elegant script.

I am sending Mr. Herman Capiau to you because I cannot help him here. Please listen to his story and use your better judgment. I hope you will act in good faith.
—Marie DePage

"Come with me where we can have some privacy and where my dog will not have a piece of your leg," said Edith. Elizabeth put Jack back in Edith's quarters while Edith motioned Herman into the nursing office. "Would you like to remove your coat?"

"Thank you, but no. I cannot stay long. I will come straight to the point. There has been a terrible battle at Mons. Many of your countrymen have been separated from each other and have scattered in retreat. Most are wounded and living in the woods with no food. The lucky ones have been found by villagers who are risking their lives to help them. With the help of the Prince and Princess deCroÿ and many others, we have been able to rescue some of the men. Unfortunately, the Germans found thirteen of them hiding in a haystack and shot them."

"Thank God for the work you and the deCroÿ's are doing, but why are you here to see me?" Edith asked.

"I have two such English soldiers with me now. They desperately need medical treatment and have nowhere else to go. One is a colonel who will most assuredly die if his ankle wound is not treated. The other has a head wound. They are disguised as Belgian workmen. Please, if you do not take them in, I fear they will..."

"English soldiers here? Where are they?"

"Outside on your doorstep. They are very weak."

Edith jumped up and went to the door. When she opened it, she stood staring into the tortured faces of the two men who could barely stand.

"Marie, come here and help those poor chaps inside."

"But, Madame, they are filthy and wet and we do not know who they are."

"I know who they are. Do as I ask."

As soon as the two men were helped in, Herman Capiau rushed to the door and pushed past them. "I must go. There is much to tell you but not now. I must avoid the curfew. I will return to you later." Edith heard his shoes tapping in a full run against the stones until his footsteps gradually faded away.

The two Englishmen stood as if they were balancing themselves on a boat in rolling waves. Their faces were lined with fatigue and pain. Water dripped off their soaked clothes and onto the floor.

"What are your names?"

Boger wobbled on one foot but straightened up a little and saluted with the hand that wasn't gripping Meachin's shoulder, said, "Colonel Dudley Boger of the 1st Cheshire Regiment of the British Expeditionary Force."

Meachin grimaced under the weight of his friend. "Sergeant Fred Meachin, 1st Cheshire Regiment, BEF. Glad to make your acquaintance, Miss."

"Please come in and sit down before you both fall down," said Edith.

Once the two men had gratefully occupied the sturdy chairs, Edith crouched in front of Boger, gently removed his shoe and saw that his bloody sock had dried into the wound. She detected the distinct odor of infection and necrotic skin.

Edith carefully removed the sock and examined his foot and ankle. "We will attend to this as best we can until we can find a surgeon to clean out the deceased skin."

She smiled at the disguise of Meachin's hunchback. "Very clever," she said, with one raised eyebrow, as she removed the bandage on his forehead. "You will have a fine scar to brag about to your children."

"Right. I've two of them. Both girls. The older is Violet. Me and the wife hope she becomes a nurse, like yourself. I can tell you're a real nurse and a true Englishwoman, although what you are doing in this bloody hell-hole, I don't understand."

"Sometimes, Sergeant, I don't either. I'll have Elizabeth prepare two beds for you downstairs near the boiler, where it is warm. You will be hidden well enough. Marie will find some food for you."

Once the men had eaten, Edith brought in dressings, a bottle of cleansing solution and tincture of iodine. She put a clean towel on the bed and helped lift Boger's foot on to it. Boger's head jerked back when she opened the bottle of clear liquid.

"Good Lord!" he rasped. "What is that foul stuff?"

"This, my friend, is an antiseptic known as Dakin's solution, named after the physician who invented it, I suppose. It smells so bad, even the germs can't stand it, but it cleans up wounds quite nicely."

He winced as the wound foamed when she poured it on. When she finished cleaning and dressing his ankle, the two men told her all that had happened to them.

"God must surely be looking after you," she said as she gathered up the bottles and soiled towels, "and so will we."

After Edith finished treating the men, Millicent joined her. Edith sat on the chair with the scrumpled-up newspaper. She pulled it out from under her and stared at the headlines.

Millicent broke the silence. "You know, we'll be in more trouble than a hat full of trolls if these lads are found here."

"What would you have me do? Send them back out into the street, where they will be shot, die of infection, or starve? If we want this war to end, we had better do our part to help. People are putting their lives in danger every day, and what are we doing? Sitting here sewing and knitting garments."

"I don't mean a'toll that we send them back out into the street. I'm just wonderin' how long are we to keep them? What are you planning to do with them?" Millicent asked.

"Mr. Capiau said there were many people working to help guide these soldiers out of the country. He said they plan to move them into Holland and that he would get back to me with the details."

"Can we trust him?"

"I trust Marie DePage. She wouldn't have sent him to us if she thought he would put us in danger."

"'Tis certain we must be prudent about this. The Huns will be wastin' no time in shootin' us if they find we have broken their rules by takin' in the likes of those lads downstairs. We won't be any good to anyone except the good Lord if we be shot."

"In times like these, there is a higher duty than prudence." Edith headed for the door.

"Did you hear that Marie DePage will be settin' out in a few days to be with her husband at the front?" asked Millicent.

Edith stopped. "I heard she was thinking about it but that it wasn't certain."

"She asked me to take over at the Palace Hospital. Since it is quiet here, I told her I would, with your approval, of course."

Edith's face tightened. "Of course. I will have your duties reassigned. I have been thinking of asking Elizabeth to be my Assistant Matron. Maybe this is the time to do so."

Millicent continued. "It's all happened quicker than Mme. DePage thought. She just got a note from her husband askin' her to join him. I think their son is fightin' out there, too. She said she wants to see you before she leaves."

"I will see her tomorrow morning." When Edith's hand touched the cold metal of the door handle, she stiffened for a moment. "I promise you this: I hear what you are saying, and I will do my best not to involve my staff with the matter of these English soldiers. Now there is much to do and I'd best get on with it."

"Just remember," said Millicent, "you are working under the flag of the international Red Cross, who put their trust in you to honor their neutrality. If you get caught, I doubt they will be able to help you."

— 31 —
THE UNDERGROUND

Probationer Paula van Bockstaele was glad to finally be caring for patients, even if they were Germans. She was tired of the mundane work of rolling bandages and re-sterilizing unused surgical instruments. In the middle of her night shift, her eyelids felt like lead. She thought a cup of tea and a slice of toast might help her stay awake and headed for the kitchen. She struck a match and touched it to the gas ring and watched the circle of blue flame burst into life.

Suddenly, her eyes caught a shadow moving across the wall. *It is only the reflection of light from the burner against the dark wall,* she told herself. Then the disembodied shadow moved again. Was it an intruder lurking around to steal food or a German soldier spying on the staff? Her pulse burst into a faster beat, and she dropped the match. The maid had said that this place was haunted. The shadows took on a form and came towards her.

"It is a ghost!" she gasped and was about to scream when the shadow spoke in English. "Hallo, Nursie!"

"You're not a ghost. You're an English soldier! What in heaven's name are you doing here? Does Madame know you are here?"

"She certainly does. She's the one who took me and my friend in. His foot is awful bad. Shot up. He will need surgery tomorrow. Poor chap. I hope they can save his leg."

"But how did you get here?"

"Tell you what, Nursie. Old Fred here sure fancies sharing a cup of tea with you. You make us one and I'll tell you straightaway everything that has happened."

* * * * *

Several days later, Herman Capiau returned to the Clinique to discuss plans for the two soldiers with Edith. "I cannot thank you enough. There is so much to do and little time to get it done."

"Exactly who is helping you?" Edith queried.

"What I tell you is of the utmost secrecy. You can tell no one. Absolutely no one. Do you understand?"

"Of course, but it is important that I know what and with whom I am now involved."

Capiau spoke to her as if he were teaching a class. He illustrated everything with his hands. "We are developing an underground system to move soldiers separated from their battalions out of the country and over the Dutch border. Many of them are wounded, some badly. All are hungry and very tired. There is a young schoolteacher, a Louise Thuliez, who goes out into the fields and forests at night. She has a young friend who helps her. They find these wretched souls hidden in shell holes, barns, deserted houses, and in the woods. Some are taken in by sympathetic villagers or farmers; others are taken to join the men who live in the woods. The worst are brought to the ancient castle of Prince Reginald and his sister, Princess Marie de Croÿ. On the face of it, they function just like you, under the Red Cross, where they also treat injured Germans. But they hide wounded Allied soldiers and treat them."

"How do they hide these men from the Germans?" Edith truly wanted to know.

"Good question." He put a cigarette to his pursed lips. Smoke poured out of his mouth and nose as he spoke. "Their castle stands in the middle of the forest of Mormal. It has been the de Croÿ ancestral home for centuries and includes as many as thirty rooms and various other buildings on the grounds. They secretly move soldiers in and out at night. Should the Germans get suspicious of their activities, they shift the soldiers to another room or another building."

"Is there a doctor to treat them?"

"Just as they have in the Palace Hospital, the Germans brought in their own doctor."

"I suppose they brought in German nurses as well?"

"They have, but the Princess de Croÿ was previously trained by the Red Cross and is quite capable. If they are too badly wounded, we try to find them a better place to be treated until they are well enough to be moved out of Belgium."

"I heard there were people who helped our lads escape, but I had no idea it was so involved. About the two English soldiers I am caring for, how will you get them out of here?"

"That might be a problem. Unfortunately, we have not yet worked out how to move them to the border." He saw the color drain from Edith's face. "But, Madame, do not worry. We will have the answer to your question very soon. There is a man in Brussels, a Belgian architect named Philippe Baucq. He is very smart and a devoted patriot. He is helping us produce the identification papers we need—passports, travel and work papers."

Herman leaned over conspiratorially and lowered his voice. "He is also producing an Underground newspaper called *La Libre Belgique*. I shall sneak a copy to you. It is the only newspaper that will tell you the truth of what is happening in Belgium. Everything the Germans print is lies. Whatever they say, they do the opposite. You can believe nothing and trust them for nothing."

He stubbed out his cigarette and smiled. "Do not worry, my friend. I will soon learn where in Brussels there are guides who can take your men to the border. You will see; it will all be fine. A thousand thick-headed Huns are not as smart as one dedicated Belgian. Your two English soldiers are doing well, yes?"

"Colonel Boger had surgery to clean out his wound. Fortunately, he did not have gas gangrene. With daily dressings and a good disinfectant, I believe his infection will clear up. His leg will be a problem for him for some time, but he could possibly be well enough to be moved in another week."

Edith continued, "Sergeant Meachin is doing very well. Although he frightened one of my probationers almost to death in the middle of the night, my staff likes him. They all want to feed him as if he were a pet. He did protest rather loudly when they wanted to disguise him in women's clothes. He said being a hunchback serves him well enough. It allows him to move about. I must say, the staff who know about these soldiers are quite amused that the Germans walk by the Clinique not knowing who is inside."

* * * * *

"**S**he is perfect," said Herman to Reginald. "She was suspicious and cautious at first, but that is good, is it not? Very smart and dedicated. As soon as she saw the wounded men, she did not hesitate to take them in. I think she is exactly the contact we have been looking for in Brussels."

"It is perfect that her Clinique is situated outside of central Brussels and away from the main German encampments," said Prince Reginald de Croÿ. "But is she reliable? Can she keep quiet about this? Any break in the chain, a stray comment, or a whispered confidence to the wrong person, and we will be facing the wrong end of a German revolver."

"She is not like other women, who giggle and gossip. She has a quiet way about her and does not show her emotions easily. Being the matron of a nurses' training school, she is not liable to arouse suspicion."

"The Huns regard everyone with suspicion, and they especially hate the English. That may be a problem."

"The Huns are not likely to harm someone who cares for their own."

"And as a woman, she will draw less attention. If she could simply receive the men we send her until we can guide them over the border, we will have the link we need to move them out of the castle, through Brussels, and into Holland. The Huns are close to discovering our route to the French border."

"Maybe you should meet her yourself. I was thinking of having Louise speak to her next, but it might be best if you made the next contact."

THE PRINCE

P rince Reginald de Croÿ shifted his position on the wooden chair opposite Edith's desk. He pointed to a picture on her wall. "That is a magnificent church. Where is it?"

Edith made note of his concise way of speaking. "It is Nor'ich Cathedral, which my father often visited. I worshipped there as a child. It is indeed magnificent. But you didn't come here to discuss an Anglican church with me."

"No, Madame, I came here to ask if you will help us save your countrymen." He looked up at the picture. "Some of them have probably attended that very cathedral."

"By help, I assume you mean you want me to medically treat the wounded soldiers you bring to me," Edith said in her straightforward manner.

"Correct. And also provide a safe place, a respite, if you will, where I can place soldiers until we can guide them to the Dutch border. A link in the Underground chain, you might say. I believe we can keep the exposure to danger at a minimum to yourself and your staff."

Edith peered at the tall, thin, scholarly-looking prince. He didn't look like someone who ran an underground operation. He had a patrician face with a high forehead and sloped, narrow eyes. His thick, black mustache ran across the middle of both cheeks. There was a cleft in his narrow chin.

Edith had heard rumors about shadowy patriots who had formed an association to help fallen soldiers separated from their comrades. Now, the very head of that group was sitting in front of her. *Maybe this is the way I can do the most good. If there are others in the same desperate situation as the colonel, maybe I am the perfect person to help. But if I do this, I will have to be deceitful and dishonest—both traits I detest. But aren't they justified when it means saving lives from murderers?*

She remembered Millicent's comment, "We won't be any good to anyone except to the good Lord if we get shot." Her eyes fixed on the prince. "How can you assure me that none of us will be in danger?"

"You are an intelligent woman. I would be foolish to try to convince you there is no danger, but we have been in operation since the start of the war, and so far, no one has been caught. Besides, they will hardly suspect a nurse who is running a clinic that has a German doctor and is treating German soldiers. I hope you understand the gravity of our situation and will join us. We most desperately need your help."

Reginald saw Edith stare at a place on the wall behind him.

Yea, though I walk through the valley of the shadow of death, I will fear no evil: for Thou art with me; Thy rod and Thy staff they comfort me.

"Madame?"

"I will do whatever I can to help, but I do not want all of my staff involved."

He stood and grasped her hand with both of his. "Your country will be proud of you. Those who survive because of your help will bless and thank you. There are just a few more important details.

Reginald de Croÿ went on. "To protect the identity of those who work with us, we have given them false names. Louise Thuliez is called Madame Martin and Philippe Baucq is Monsieur Fromage. Yes, that is 'cheese' in English, but it is Philippe's little sense of humor. Also, to ensure the trustworthiness of those who come to you, they must give you the password. It is 'Yorc' which is my last name spelled backwards. When they come to you, they must ask for Monsieur Yorc."

— 33 —
ADA BODART

A da Bodart was cooking supper when she heard a man yelling in
the street.

"I have done nothing! Let me go!" She ran to the window to
see her middle-aged neighbor being dragged out of his house by two
German soldiers. Ada's heart raced. There was nothing she could do to
help the man. If she went outside, they might also arrest her.

"You refuse to work at the munitions factory. You are stupid and
lazy," said one of the soldiers, shoving the man head first into a motorcar
with the word *Geheimpolizei,* Secret Police, painted in white letters on
the door.

"No, please! My wife is sick. I wanted to work, but I had to care for
her."

"More lies! You will either work here or in Berlin."

"Please, I beg you, do not deport me. My wife needs me," the man
was in tears.

"Germany needs you first."

The words fell like hammer blows. The soldier motioned with his
hand to the driver. "Take him to the Tir National Prison. The *Kommandant* will decide what to do with him."

Two soldiers pushed in on either side of the man. A third soldier,
Kapitän Mayer, who had ordered the arrest, did not go with them. He
stood on the sidewalk and looked up and down the rue de la Culture. He
was tall and had razor-clean cheeks. A white collar hid his muscled neck.
His broad shoulders narrowed down to a tight waist, which was encircled
with a highly polished black leather belt.

Mayer studied every house on the narrow street. Regarding them
with suspicion, he looked for any sign of resistance—a Belgian or
American flag hanging from a window, the playing of the *Marseillaise,*
or the use of the English language. He reached into his tunic, took out a

cigarette, placed it between his thin lips with tobacco-stained fingers, and lit it. He inhaled slowly, turned, and focused his eyes back up the other side the street. He saw nothing but brick row-houses. The only break in the silence was a crow screaming down at him from the ivy that snaked up the side of one house.

The *Kapitän*'s eyes fell on a small Red Cross flag waving from a wrought-iron balcony on the second story of one house. He wondered about it. The building did not look much like a hospital, but he knew many of the homes had been turned into small hospitals. *All the better for our wounded men*, he thought.

He put the cigarette to his lips and inhaled deeply. He could never understand these wretched people. Why do they not behave properly? *We have burned their villages, shot thousands of them, sent them to prisons, and forced them to work in the factories in the Fatherland. What more can we do to make them comply? Their stupid little rebellious acts will accomplish nothing. Force is the only thing they understand. They think they can make fools out of us, but they are wrong.*

He saw two German soldiers standing on the street corner. One was cleaning his boot on a boot scraper set into the wall. The other was blowing warmth into his cupped hands. Mayer walked over to them. The soldier warming his hands snapped to attention. The other couldn't pull his foot out of the boot scraper quite fast enough and stumbled. Once he steadied himself, he clicked his heels.

"Is it your duty to watch the activity on this street?" asked Mayer.

"Yes, *Herr Kapitän*. We were assigned to this area a few days ago."

"What have you seen?"

"Nothing much, except a few nurses and patients coming and going at the Red Cross hospital over there." He pointed to the Clinique.

"How did it become a hospital?"

"We do not know. We think it is a school of some kind where they treat patients who are not badly hurt."

The second soldier interrupted. "I think it is a school to train nurses, *Herr Kapitän*."

The officer put the cigarette to his lips, inhaled, flipped it onto the ground, and crushed it with a grinding motion under his hobnailed boot.

"I want you to watch it carefully. If you see anything suspicious, you are to notify me immediately. Do you understand?"

Both men straightened, clicked their heels together, and saluted. "Yes, *Herr Kapitän*."

The officer saluted back. "For the Fatherland."

"For the Fatherland," they repeated in unison.

* * * * *

Ada gripped the windowsill as she watched her neighbor being dragged into the car. Her first thought was to rush to aid his wife. Then she saw the German captain scrutinizing the street. She untied her apron, shut off the gas stove, and covered the bowl of potatoes. She would visit her neighbor's wife later. Right now she had something more important to do. As soon as the captain was gone, she threw on her coat and hat. Grabbing a small piece of paper, she hurriedly scribbled on it and buried it in her knitting basket.

Edith and Elizabeth were planning their staff assignments for next week's duty shifts when they heard a hurried tap on the door. Elizabeth opened it to see a woman standing there fidgeting with her knitting basket. "May I please see Mme. Cavell?"

Elizabeth opened the door wider and Ada quickly stepped in. Her eyes darted around the room and landed on Edith. "May I see you alone?" she asked.

"You can say anything in front of Nurse Wilkins. She is my assistant matron."

She watched Ada fidget with the yarn in her knitting basket. After an awkward silence, Edith looked down at Ada's basket. A bit of paper was turned face-up to Edith. It had a single word scrawled across it: *Yorc*. Ada gave Edith a colluding wink.

"I have much to do," said Elizabeth. "They brought in three soldiers today, and I must check the assignments." As she passed out the door, she gave Ada a quick nod. Ada nodded back and then turned to Edith.

Edith led the stocky woman up to the nursing office and motioned for her to sit. Ada removed her coat, folded it on her lap, and placed her hat on top of it. A feather on the hat reached to just below her chin. There was an awkward silence between them for a moment. When Ada finally spoke, she kept her voice so low that Edith had to lean closer to hear. The feather poked up between them.

"Thank you for receiving me, Mme. Cavell. Everyone on this street knows you, of course, but you probably do not know me. I am Ada Bodart. I live down at the end of this street with my husband and seven children. Actually, only two now. Five of my precious boys are fighting in the Belgian army, God help them."

Edith detected a slight Irish lilt. The woman had quick, watchful eyes, a solid build, and glossy brown hair. Ada lowered her head. "I came here to warn you."

"Warn me of what?"

"We work for the same organization, you and me. We are on the same side. There is trouble. My neighbor has just been arrested for refusing to work in the munitions factory. He told me he could not work there knowing the weapon he made might be the one that would kill his son. His wife is not well and cannot work. She needs him to care for her.

"I can look in on her. Is that the reason you came here?"

"No, Madame. The *Boche* police are watching the neighborhood. Two guards are stationed at the corner. We must move your two English soldiers away from here."

Edith pulled back with a start. "How did you know…"

Ada leaned so close that the feather almost touched both of their chins.

"I have been helping Messieurs Baucq and Capiau to form an escape route into Holland. M. Baucq is helping us forge papers for these soldiers. I have been finding safe places for them to stay. There is a house just off Avenue Louise where we can place your two Brits until we complete the plans to guide them out."

"I had no idea anyone around here was involved with these… uh…activities."

"Madame, there is so much you do not know and it is best kept that way. You must prepare the men to leave at 4 o'clock tomorrow morning. They are well enough to travel?"

"Colonel Boger's ankle is better but not fully healed. He can bear some weight on it but he cannot walk long distances."

"We will find a different way to move him to the border. The other man walks, yes?"

"Yes."

"Good. We will send someone over tonight to guide them to the safe house. Prepare some food for them to take. Do this yourself so your cook does not become suspicious. It may be some time before we can bring more food to them. We do not want to draw attention by visiting an unoccupied building too often."

Ada stood up, put on her coat, adjusted her hat with a hatpin and picked up her knitting basket. "Someone will be here tonight. *Adieu.*"

Walking down the stairs, Ada called out to anyone who might hear, "I think I know a plumber who can fix those leaky pipes for you."

At four in the morning, Edith gave the two British soldiers a set of Belgian work clothes. She leaned in front of Boger and patted her knee, directing him where to place his foot.

"You will have to change this dressing least once a day," she instructed him as she put on a clean dressing and bound it in place with a porous rubber bandage for support. She avoided his eyes. "Try not to get your fingers in it, and keep it clean."

Fred Meachin saw her eyes were welling up with tears. "Will we ever see you again?" he asked.

"A few of us, including myself, will take turns bringing you food until we can safely move you out. I'm new at this business of caring for soldiers such as yourselves. But I'm pleased to be able to serve you and my country."

Dudley Boger took her hand. "Miss Cavell, we would not be alive if you had not taken us in. How can we ever repay what you have done?"

"You can make it back to England alive."

"I'll do my best, and when this is over, we'll share a pint and talk about old war wounds."

She handed each a postcard. "When you get to in Holland, sign this with a fictitious name and mail it back to me so we will know you have arrived safely."

The men took the postcards and tucked them in their shirt pockets.

"One more thing: It will be best if you don't speak of what I have done for you when you get home."

"Mum's the word."

That night, Ada and Edith brought the men to their new hiding place on Louise Avenue.

— 34 —
MILLICENT

A morning frost glistened over the cobblestones. Edith was attaching a lead to Jack's collar in preparation for making her rounds when Millicent walked through the door.

"I must talk to you, Edith."

"Can it wait until I return? The doctors are waiting for me at the hospital."

Millicent rubbed her hands together. Edith wasn't sure if it was because she was cold or nervous. "No, it can't wait," she told Edith. "It's very important."

"What is it?"

"I'm in trouble. Serious trouble." Edith stood up and pulled back on Jack's lead as the dog strained to leave. She waited for Millicent to explain. "The German guard at the Royal Palace Hospital is suspicious of me and threatened to arrest me if I don't leave the ward."

"Impossible! For what reason?"

"He is suspicious of my nursing documents. He believes I am taking notes on German soldiers and passing them on to… I don't know who. He has threatened to charge me with espionage if I don't stop writing."

"That's foolishness. Just show him the notes."

"He can't read English, and he doesn't trust what anyone else says. He threatens to have me deported. As he put it to me, 'I'll have you sweeping the streets of Cologne.'"

"That's rubbish. I can transfer you and let the German nurses deal with their own wounded over there. You can work at the surgical ward at St. Jean's."

"It's no use. I mean to petition the military governor to return to England."

"Millicent, we have had our disagreements, but I truly appreciate all you do and depend on you. Please, let's see if there is some way you can stay. The war will be over soon. Then we can continue our work."

"I can't do anyone any good if I am deported or shot. At least at home, I can work in the Royal Forces field hospital caring for British soldiers. Maybe after the war, I can return. 'Tis a very dangerous place here right now. You never know when you'll be dragged away for no reason, and the good Lord knows right well we've given them enough reasons. I can help you around the Clinique and with your...special project, until I get my interview with the military governor."

Millicent worked with Edith and Elizabeth to reassign her duties. By the end of the week, she had managed to stuff all her belongings into a single large bag. One evening, when everyone was working, she agreed to bring supper to the two men hidden away on Louise Avenue.

Dudley Boger greeted her with outstretched arms. "You are an angel, my dear. What have you brought us?"

"We were fortunate to have been able to buy some mutton and were given potatoes by a neighbor who has a garden. There's a wee bit o' beans."

"Splendid," said Boger as he took the basket of food from her and lifted the lid to peek under it.

"But before you eat, 'tis best I change your dressing."

Boger sat down, removed his boot, and offered her his foot.

"How's it looking?"

"So much better. You have taken good care of it."

When Millicent was finished, the soldiers dug into the basket of food. She told them of her experience at the Royal Palace Hospital. "I'm petitioning the military governor for permission to return home."

Boger waved his laden fork in the air. "You would be perfect."

"Perfect for what?"

"Perfect to take these dispatches to the War Office." He put his fork down and handed her a manila envelope.

"You could do it yourself," said Millicent. "They will soon have you over the border. You may even get home before I do."

"These are important papers. If I get caught with them on me, I will be shot straightaway and they will never reach the War Office. They will never suspect a woman, especially a nurse as pretty as yourself."

"What if they search me?"

"I've got it! Brilliant, I must say. That elastic bandage you placed over my dressing? Why not wrap it around the dispatch against your leg? Surely they wouldn't fancy tearing a dressing off on a leg wound."

* * * * *

The next day, Edith found Millicent sitting with a cup of tea and holding a handkerchief to her nose.

"Whatever's the matter?" asked Edith, removing her coat and shaking off a few snowflakes from the shoulders.

"I've just come back from my interview with the German military general. He refused to permit me to leave. He says I am needed in the hospital wards to take care of 'these heroic men who are suffering for the sake of the Fatherland.' Why is it always the Fatherland? Whatever happened to the Motherland?"

Edith smiled at her friend's attempt at humor.

"If you are still convinced you must leave, I believe we can find you a way out. I have a few connections."

By the end of the week, Millicent possessed a false passport and a ticket to board a barge to Antwerp. She hugged Edith and promised to write when she arrived home. She gave the bandage around her leg a tug to make sure it was secure and jumped onto the barge. As the barge slowly moved away, the snowflakes became thicker and heavier, blurring out the figure of Edith standing on the dock.

After a day of moving along the canal, Millicent felt the barge stop. Shouting and harsh voices were heard from the dock. She looked out the window and saw the barge being pulled to one side.

"Out! Everyone out!"

Through the swirl of snow, she saw German uniforms. A German guard entered the cabin and shoved a bayonet into her ribs. "You. Leave. Now."

"Where are you taking me?"

He shoved her towards the stairs to go up and to the outside. "Questions *verboten*. Out!"

Millicent left her suitcase and walked up the ladder and out to the dock. Another bayonet was pushed at her.

"Remove your coat!"

"But it's freezing."

"Remove it or I will rip it off."

Millicent slowly removed her coat. The soldier grabbed it from her hands and threw it on the ground.

"Scarf and hat—off!" She removed them and they were grabbed away and searched.

A soldier ran his hands roughly through her hair. He pulled at her braids until they fell loose; her hair blew about her face and neck. Then he ran his hands roughly over her body. He started at her neck and shoulders. She felt his hands move around her back. When he reached her chest, he groped her breasts and leered.

The odor of sweat, cigarettes, onions, sausage, and beer made her stomach lurch with a wave of nausea. Her cheeks burned and she glared at him. A nearby soldier gave an amused smirk at the gesture of the soldier. The rest of the soldiers were busy searching other passengers. His hands continued to move down her body. They slid around her hips and lingered for a moment on her buttocks, then moved along the outside of her legs. His hands stopped at the bandage.

"I have an infected leg wound. I am going to see a doctor in Antwerp."

She felt his hands quickly release her leg. He picked up her coat and shuffled through its pockets. He pulled out a brown envelope and held it up to her face.

"Papers?" He didn't wait for an answer. Opening the envelope, he inspected her false passport and barge ticket. Millicent remained expressionless. "You are going to Antwerp?" he asked.

"Yes."

He threw the coat and papers at her. "Then go."

She picked up the hat and scarf off the mixture of snow and mud and put her coat back on. She stumbled over the slippery plank back to the barge. Once inside, she saw that her bag had been opened and the contents strewn around the floor. Particularly obvious were her undergarments. Her body shivered uncontrollably. She stuffed everything back into her bag without any thought of neatness and fought back tears.

She imagined what Miss Cavell would say about all of this. She could hear her saying, "Nurse Millicent, you have seen sickness at its worst and even death. As long as you are not harmed, you can do whatever you set your mind to do."

The boat lurched as it pulled away from the dockside. A stench of diesel mixed with exhaust fumes floated through decks below. She rubbed off a patch of condensation from the grime-streaked porthole and looked out.

"What you become a part of becomes a part of you," Edith once told her. All of a sudden it hit her. She was no longer a part of the nursing community that meant so much to her. Millicent had never felt so vulnerable and alone.

Barges similar to the one used by Millicent White
to escape from Belgium.

— 35 —

BETWEEN SIXES AND NINES

When Elizabeth arrived to give Edith the day's report, she found the older woman leaning on her elbows staring at a spider that was weaving a gauzy web between her mother's picture and the desk lamp.

Elizabeth shifted her cloak off her shoulders and removed her linen nurse's cap, placing both on the divan. "You look between sixes and sevens, today," she said to Edith. "Fancy a cup of tea to cheer you up?"

Edith stared at the spider sitting in the middle of the web and did not look up. "I remember once, during my first class here, telling a probationer who was about to step on a spider that all life was precious, even that of a spider. I told her it was our duty to save life and not to do harm. Do you believe that, Elizabeth?"

"I think so, to a reasonable extent."

"Don't you sometimes feel as if we should be doing something more here—something more meaningful?"

Edith watched as the spider closed in on a moth and spun a shroud around its helpless prey. "I feel trapped in a terrible battle that destroys life, and powerless to change any of it."

She sighed. "We now have only a few brave probationers, and even fewer patients for them to gain experience with—except for the German soldiers, who lie in their beds pointing their pistols at us. The hospitals are nearly empty and they're struggling to make ends meet because no one can afford to be treated."

Elizabeth put her hand on Edith's. "You should be proud of this school, which exists because of you, and of the new one that's now being built. Things will get better in due course."

Edith felt the comforting warmth of Elizabeth's hand. She noticed the fine, delicate fingers, the light blue veins that ran beneath porcelain skin. Elizabeth never seemed to succumb to the changes of age. Edith looked at her own hand, the creases about her knuckles and the dried skin that was dotted with small, dark circles.

Raising her head, Edith said, "The new school is just sitting there, looking like the skeleton in Dr. DePage's office. The work on it is abysmally slow because there is no room on the trains for building supplies. The workmen have all enlisted."

Her eyes searched Elizabeth's face. "It makes me feel old and useless. Do you ever despair?"

"Not when I am with you. I trust your judgment." Elizabeth moved to the little kitchen, filled up the kettle, and lit the gas ring. "Even in the matter of taking in those two English soldiers."

"We moved them out last night, you know. At four in the morning, actually. We gave them some bread and coffee before they left."

"What of the colonel's ankle?"

"They arranged for him to travel down the canals on a coal barge to the Dutch border."

"And the sergeant? Is he traveling with him?"

"No. He was disguised as a fishmonger and paired up with a guide to take him over to Ghent and then out of the country."

"How will we know if they made it?"

"They were each given a postcard to send back when they arrive." She watched the spider sucking the life out of the trapped moth.

"And what if they don't make it?"

"Then at least we gave them a fighting chance. At some point, dear Elizabeth, we will have to decide if it is worth continuing to put ourselves at risk."

The screeching tea kettle interrupted their conversation. Elizabeth took down two teacups and placed them next to the stove.

"Edith, I remember you once quoting Florence Nightingale in one of your classes. I believe it was something like, 'Feelings waste themselves in words; they ought to be distilled into actions, and into actions which bring results.' You turned your feelings of helplessness into action by saving those two men. Only God can help them now."

Edith turned away from the lethal spider and placed a tea cosy over the ceramic teapot in front of her. Elizabeth sat facing her.

"Do you know how many people are putting their lives in danger to help poor fellows like those two soldiers?"

Edith didn't wait for an answer. "There's a prince and his sister, a princess, who is also a nurse. There's a miner and his wife, who put their lives at risk to guard and shelter soldiers who are separated from their regiments. There's an engineer, who rescues them from the German hospital in the Wiheries. Right here in Brussels, there's an architect named Phillip Baucq, who makes fake papers for them and prints an Underground newspaper. Ada Bodart, the seamstress who lives down the street, has not one, but five, sons fighting for this country. She hides soldiers and then arranges guides for them.

Taking a deep breath, Edith continued. "Out in Mons, there's a young schoolmistress, Louise Thuliez, who guides the wounded between Mons and the Wiheries, sometimes walking miles each day. There's a chemist who helps forge papers, a market stallholder, a dentist, and an innkeeper, who puts them up and moves mail out of the country. There are two young women who go out into the fields at night to find these wretched souls, and a whole group of guides who lead them to safety. Those are only the ones I know about. All of this is done right under the noses of the Germans."

She poured tea for both of them and raised her cup to her lips. Looking through the wisps of steam, she said, "I shouldn't be telling you this because I would never forgive myself if I put you or anyone else in danger."

Elizabeth searched Edith's face. "Have you agreed to be a part of this group?"

"I have, but I can change my mind. Millicent took me to task, warning me that I might put us all in danger. I miss Millicent so much. Do you agree with her and think me reckless for doing this?"

"I am quite capable of making up my own mind about matters such as these. It is my choice to be involved. Truly, you cannot do this alone. I understand your reluctance to include the staff, but the truth is, that will be almost impossible. What about Gracie? How are you going to keep her out of this?"

"She's staying with friends for a month until I figure this all out. I promised her parents I would look after her. It's too late to send her back to England, and frankly, I don't think she would go even if she had the chance," Edith said, taking a sip of the hot, refreshing tea.

After they had finished their tea, Edith's tone brightened. "It will soon be the first Sunday of Advent. I've been thinking of Christmas."

Elizabeth was always surprised at how quickly Edith could shift from melancholy to merriment. "I think we can find a tree. The Germans haven't chopped everything up yet for firewood. We can have the staff bring whatever decorations they choose. I'd like to invite some children, especially those who have so little. I have been collecting dolls for such an occasion, and I think we have clothes we can give to them. My family did this very same thing years ago. I miss the laughter of children."

Elizabeth stifled a yawn. "I'm so sorry. I think your plans are brilliant, but it's getting late and I haven't given you my report yet." She pulled out a folded paper from her uniform pocket. "The report from the Palace Hospital is that they are full and would like to have another nurse for evening care to replace one of the German nurses who left."

"After the way they treated Millicent? I'll not send another nurse until I speak to the officer in charge. And the Clinique?"

"There are eight new German soldiers in the Clinique. One has a head wound—not too serious. Three have shrapnel wounds. One fell from a wall and broke his leg. From the smell of him, he spent more time in the local brasserie than fighting on the front. There's a soldier who came off the worst in a fight with another German soldier; both eyes are swollen and blackened. Another got kicked by a horse and has a nasty wound on his shin. He shot the horse."

Edith grimaced and shook her head.

Turning the sheet of paper over, Elizabeth went on. "Also, there is a British private named McDonald who fought at Ypres. He was brought in by a German Red Cross stretcher attendant. He is suffering from shivering fits and intense headaches. The German officer told the nurses to remove him from the bed to make room for one of the German soldiers."

"Do we know what is wrong with him?"

"Not yet. The German doctor said it was only a trifling ailment and that he need not be taking up a bed there. He's been vomiting, so he may be dehydrated. We moved him to Berkendael Hospital. He'll get better treatment there."

Edith nodded in acknowledgement of Elizabeth's report. "I'll check on him when Jack and I make our rounds tomorrow. For now, we should both get some rest." She picked up Elizabeth's cloak and carefully placed it around the younger woman's thin shoulders.

"Thank you, Elizabeth, for being here with me. I could not manage without you." She picked off a piece of lint from the shoulder of Elizabeth's dark blue cloak and inhaled the familiar scent of lavender rose. "You are the closest companion I have ever had." They stood face to face, quietly looking at each other.

"Mme. Cavell." It was the maid's voice from the other side of the door. "A woman is here to see you. She says her name is Mme Martin. Should I let her in?"

"I will be right down."

Elizabeth buttoned up her cloak to leave.

"Will you please wait for me a few moments until I see this woman?" asked Edith.

"Do you know who she is?"

"I have heard of her, but we have never met. It won't take long."

Downstairs, Edith found a woman about thirty, short, dark-haired, and with small, active eyes. The woman extended her hand to Edith. "Mr. Yorc sent me. May we speak privately?"

Edith brought her to her office and closed the door.

"My name is Louise. I—well, not just myself, but all of us who are working for the freedom of Belgium and defeat of the oppressors—thank you for your help. There are too few of us and so much to be done."

"You came here for help. What is it you need?"

"I will be brief. We have ten soldiers who need refuge. Nine are English and one is French. I am told you have enough beds for them until we can arrange for guides."

"I can do that. When will they arrive?"

"Tomorrow, sometime about midday."

"Midday? But there are German soldiers monitoring the street activity."

"They will be disguised as Belgians. No one will notice." The visitor looked up at the clock on the wall. "I must leave before the curfew starts. You have come to us from God." Louise reached for the doorknob, hesitated, turned around, and motioned for Edith to come close.

"Your maid, she is German?"

"She is, but there is no question about her loyalty."

"I hope your faith in her is not misplaced."

"We offered to send her back to Germany, but she knows no one there and begged to stay. She helps us with the language."

"She is still German, and I have come not to trust any of them. When it means choosing between friends and the Fatherland, friends do not fare so well. Please be careful. *Au revoir*."

"I heard what she said," said Elizabeth.

"About Marie?"

"No, about the ten soldiers. What about Marie?"

"She's concerned about Marie's loyalty because of her German heritage. Do you believe her mistrust is justified?"

"I don't know. She would make the perfect spy, but I can't imagine her working against us. She is so much a part of our family. Maybe it would be wise to keep her away from our patriotic activities. I will watch her more closely as well."

"I know it is late, but would you please prepare ten places for our guests tomorrow?" Edith gave Elisabeth's hand a quick squeeze.

"You know I will do whatever you ask, my friend."

— 36 —

BRAND WHITLOCK AND
MORITZ VON BISSING

When the Germans invaded Belgium, the hallways of Brand Whitlock's office became crowded with frightened refugees. As the American ambassador, he had the daunting task of helping thousands of American, Dutch, French, and English to get out of the country. It had not always been like this.

Two years before, when President Wilson appointed him this post, he had been delighted. Tired of politics at home, he yearned for a quiet, but civilized place, where he could enjoy the culture, relax, and write. Brussels gave all of this to him and more. He and his wife were treated like royalty.

When war was declared, the English ambassador handed him the keys to his office saying, "It's all yours, old boy. Call me if you have any questions." The French ambassador turned his responsibilities over to the Marquis de Villalobar, the Spanish ambassador. The day the Germans marched into Brussels, Whitlock and Villalobar stood at the window in his office and watched the streams of German soldiers in their greenish-gray uniforms march down the boulevard straight to the governmental center.

The two men had listened to the drumming of thousands of heavy-heeled boots against the cobblestones.

"We will never forget this," said Villalobar. "These Belgians have seen it all, haven't they? Over the centuries they have suffered through invasions from France, Austria, Spain, and now this. I don't know how they endure except through sheer will."

Whitlock gestured toward the relentlessly advancing troops. "Not exactly the picture of the good-natured Germans slugging down steins of beer and puffing away on tasseled pipes, is it?"

Mr. Brand Whitlock, appointed American Ambassador to Belgium in 1913.

By the next day, every governmental building had been occupied. Whitlock, his secretary, Hugh Gibson, his legal advisor, Gaston de Leval, and the Marquis de Villalobar from Spain were the only diplomatic staff left behind. The Belgians declared they would fight, but everyone knew it was mere bravado. They could never stop this massive German invasion.

The next day, the German ambassador came to Whitlock's office. "These poor, stupid Belgians," he said to Whitlock. "Why do they not just get out of the way? They have no power to stop us. It will be like placing an infant on the tracks as the train approaches."

* * * * *

W hitlock now stared at the announcement he had been handed and then read it to Villalobar. "It says that His Majesty, the emperor and king, (I assume that's the Kaiser), has set up a new government in Belgium and taken over the leadership of the executive department of Belgium. It's signed by a Baron von Bissing, Général de Cavalerie."

He handed the letter to Villalobar. "Looks like the cavalry has arrived. We now have a new German governor general."

"What happened to General von Luttwitz?"

"Sacked, I suppose. I think we had better go meet our new general."

It was in the early twilight of a winter day when they stood outside the iron gates facing the sign that read: ACHTUNG! They waited while the guards inspected their identification papers.

Once their identities had been confirmed, the two diplomats were escorted to the staircase leading to the office of the former Belgian Minister of Arts and Sciences, where a second escort approached them. He gave them a stiff nod and introduced himself as the Baron von der

Lancken. They were led up the grand staircase to von Bissing's new office.

Whitlock's eyes swept over the room. Two German flags stood like sentinels on either side of the highly polished desk. There was a sideboard against the side wall where a pitcher of water and glasses had been placed, and four high-backed, tapestry-covered chairs. In the corner, a fireplace blazed behind a gilded grate. The walls were of dark, polished wood. The German flags with their red, white, and black stripes and the coat of arms were the only bright colors in the room.

Von der Lancken formally announced their presence to the new German *Kommandant*. Whitlock was stunned at his appearance.

Von Bissing was a man of about seventy years, thin, with graying black hair combed straight back and plastered down. His face was narrow, hard, and weather-beaten. A thick black moustache covered his thin upper lip and stretched across his cheeks; the ends curled up towards his ears. There was an air of elegance about him.

As the *Kommandant* moved out from behind the desk, his heavy sabre clanked against his leg. With barely a smile, he shook their hands and motioned for the two diplomats to sit. His dark eyes were without warmth and noticed everything. He had the look of someone who had seen it all and had renounced pity and compassion a long time ago. He held out his hand to Whitlock first. Whitlock felt the calloused roughness of his palms and was surprised at the strength of the old general's grip. Von der Lancken stood to his right and translated everything he said into French.

Von Bissing had the tobacco-scorched voice of a smoker. "Thank you on behalf of the Kaiser for responding to my invitation." Silver spurs jingled from the heels of his knee-high black-leather boots as he moved. Whitlock noticed his movements were stiff, making his gait appear automated.

The tall windows on the side of his office cast a rectangle of light across half of the general's face and desk. Whitlock was surprised to see that in this light, von Bissing's eyes were blue, not black. Von Bissing settled in his seat and carefully moved a clean marble ashtray to one side.

"I called you both here to formally announce I am now in control of Belgium. It is a country that has been governed badly. The democratic communal system has not worked and will be abolished. These changes will be good for the country. I will reorganize Belgium and make it more civilized."

Whitlock spoke first. "With all respect, General von Bissing, are you aware that the people you rule are out of work and starving? They cannot plough their fields because their horses have been taken. Their cattle and oxen have been killed for food. It serves no useful purpose for you to treat the people of the country you are temporarily occupying so poorly."

"Temporary? Who told you our presence here is temporary? We have not occupied Belgium. We conquered it. It now belongs to Germany."

"General, Belgium is a neutral country," protested Whitlock.

"Belgium's neutrality was a sham. The Kaiser was aware of its ...shall we call it...its 'little arrangement' with France."

"You are aware, General, that the world will demand an explanation for this. The Hague Convention was formed to protect the rights of neutral countries and to prevent the invasion of countries like Belgium. Heavy reparations will be demanded from Germany if it does not abandon its occupation of Belgium."

The general's face was impassive. "It means nothing to me what the world thinks. Your Hague Convention is not worth the paper it is printed on. It was masterminded by the United States, England, France, and, I might add, the Russian Czar. There was nothing in it for Germany. It will not stop us from achieving our destiny of imperial unity. Your Hague Convention is an old woman with no teeth."

Whitlock felt himself break out in a cold sweat. He worked to keep his voice calm. "Sir, I think you underestimate what the Hague Convention means and the seriousness of those who have written it. It isn't just a set of clauses thrown together when people had nothing else to do. I can assure you, the countries that have agreed to it will not take your invasion lightly."

General Moritz Ferdinand Freiherr von Bissing, Governor-General in occupied Brussels.

Von Bissing crossed his arms across his chest and leaned back in the chair. The corner of his mouth quivered for an instant and then turned up slightly.

Whitlock thought it was the first show of anything that looked like a smile–or was it a sneer?

"You have been placed here by your President Wilson, true?" the General asked.

"That's right," Whitlock responded.

"We know that America is in no condition to fight the war, which your newspapers refer to as 'over there.' That is why your weak president declared your country as neutral."

Whitlock felt the back of his neck flush.

"I assure you, President Wilson is not weak. He chose not to enter this war, but do not test his patience. You are already at war with Russia and France and are now fighting Britain. Do you think you will win if America allies with Britain?"

"The Americans are soft and the British are lazy. British officers sit in their trenches drinking tea while we slaughter their troops. They have been in this war for months and have won nothing. They could not even win their own war against ignorant savages in Africa who fought with sticks and knives. I assure you, England will be defeated."

"They prevented your troops from marching into France," said Villalobar, speaking for the first time. "I am curious, General. What gives Germany the right to take over this or any other country? Belgium is no threat to you."

"If the Belgians have made a pact with France, they are a threat. Taking over this country is simply a means to an end."

"And the end being?"

"The end being the spread of German *Kultur* throughout the world. Ours is the way all people should live."

Villalobar stared at the cravat fastened by a metal star that dangled from von Bissing's wrinkled throat. He recognized it as the emblem of the Order of the Black Eagle, the highest order of chivalry in Prussia.

"*Kultur*, meaning German culture, such as Wagner, Strauss, and Goethe?" Villalobar continued his questioning.

"*Kultur*, meaning the German way of life. The government rules how people must act and think. It is a bitter struggle, gentlemen, but whoever wins this war will deserve to rule. Victory will prove superiority. German superiority."

The thought came to Villalobar that von Bissing's wedged-shaped face closely resembled the eagle on the medallion. "Is it part of German *Kultur* to starve the people you rule?" he asked.

"The feeding of my army always comes first. The strongest will survive."

"You must know you can never own the minds and spirits of an entire country, General. Especially this one," said Villalobar. "The Belgians will never stop resisting."

Von Bissing's voice was filled with menace. "Two spirits dominate the world: the mind and the sword. The Belgians may possess the first, but Germany holds the second." His weathered hand gripped the hilt of his sabre. "It matters very little to me if they agree to cooperate with our government or not. If they end up as slaves, it is of no consequence to me. As long as I am able to make them work for the Fatherland, I need no more."

Van Bissing's voice took on an almost snake-like quality as he hissed, "Sometimes smaller countries must be made to sacrifice their independence and even their language to ensure imperial unity. In Belgium, there are too many languages. They fight among themselves over who should control their country, the French or the Flemish. They will find unity in speaking one language—German. We will bring peace and contentment to Belgium."

Whitlock still tried to reason with the old military man. "In deference to your philosophy, General, the United States is planning to bring food to the people you are starving. Mr. Herbert Hoover, who is chairman of the Commission for the Relief Fund for the Belgians, is in London even as we speak. He has asked me to help him organize his volunteer service and has sent a college professor, Mr. Vernon Kellogg, who speaks German and French, to help organize the distribution. Can I tell Mr. Hoover you will cooperate with him?"

"I do not know this Mr. Hoover. I am not pleased to learn he is working out of our enemy's country. It will be your duty to inform him and Mr. Kellogg that nothing can be organized or distributed in this country without our oversight and control. All of these activities are to be coordinated and approved by Baron von der Lancken."

Whitlock studied the younger blond officer standing in front of them for a moment and then turned back to von Bissing. "Of course, General. I will arrange a meeting between the Baron, Mr. Kellogg, and myself to discuss further details."

Both ambassadors sat in silence knowing any further protest would be useless. They glanced at each other and then back at the general in his worn gray uniform.

Von der Lancken broke the silence with a cough. Whitlock took this as a signal to mean the meeting was over and began to rise. "Well, this meeting has been most..."

"Sit down."

The words felt like two knife stabs. Von Bissing leaned toward Whitlock. "I have not dismissed you."

Whitlock dropped back into his chair, silently cursing the general's power. The general smoothed out the curled end of his moustache with the tip of two fingers as he spoke.

"There is a small matter of—how shall I put it?—a contribution by the Belgian people to the war effort."

There was a moment of silence as the two ambassadors realized the implication.

"Contribution? You mean a levy?" asked Whitlock incredulously.

The general tented his hands and put his yellowed fingertips to his chin. "I prefer to call it a contribution for all that we are doing for Belgium. I am issuing a decree that I expect to receive the sum of 480,000,000 francs."

Whitlock felt himself involuntarily rise from his seat. Von der Lancken saw the gesture and put his hand on the butt of his holstered pistol. Villalobar's arm shot out in front of Whitlock and the American dropped back into his chair.

Whitlock tried to keep his voice from shaking.

"That's an impossible amount for these people. How can you expect to put a levy of that size on people who already have nothing to give?" said Villalobar.

The old general smoothed out the other side of his waxed mustache. "Since you have invoked the Hague Convention, I will remind you that based on its article 49, we have the right to collect taxes to pay for the costs of governing the country which we occupy. I will be meeting with the Provincial Councils of Belgium to discuss the method of payment."

"You will never get a quorum of the councils. Half of their members have left the country," said Villalobar. "And those remaining will never agree to this outrageous amount."

"No matter," said the general, flicking dust off his sleeve. "I have decreed that a quorum will not be necessary for their deliberations. They will give me their approval. One more thing. Any further communication with this office will be directed through Baron von der Lancken." The translator stiffened and stood a bit taller at the sound of his name. "I have made him the head of our Department of Policy."

"What is the jurisdiction of that department?" asked Whitlock.

"It is whatever I please it to be."

* * * * *

It was a bleak afternoon when Whitlock and Villalobar left the building. They drove back to their office to report this meeting to their staff. The clouds hung low, and gusts of wind blew against the side of their motorcar.

"Do you understand that this claptrap about *Kultur* is really an excuse to destroy democracy?" asked Whitlock.

"I know. It's nothing but another term for Prussian imperialism. They always thought they were superior to everyone else and had the right to rule the world, the damned fools."

"Did you notice he seemed upset about our efforts to feed the people he is starving?" asked Whitlock.

"Of course he is," said Villalobar. "The only way the people can get food is to work. The only work they can get is in the Huns' bomb factories. The Belgians obviously don't want to work in those factories because they might be making the bomb that will kill one of their own. If they are fed, they will not work in the factories unless they are forced to do so."

"The problem is that there has been so much uncertainty. Belgian officials, like our poor Burgomaster Max, suddenly disappears and just when we have established a working relationship with someone, he gets dismissed and someone new appears. I have barely learned how to spell their names before they are replaced."

Whitlock shifted his long legs. "Did you see that mustache? I'll bet it takes him longer to wax that thing every morning than it does for my wife to get ready for the opera. Speaking of which, she wants me to leave my post. She says it will only get worse."

"Are you taking her advice?"Villalobar asked.

"I told her not to worry. Now that the Brits are here, this war should be over soon."

The vehicle stopped at a crossroads to let an ambulance go by. Villalobar looked out the window to see a pair of soldiers pushing an old man behind the back of a café. As their car started to move again, they heard a shot. Villalobar looked out the back window and saw a woman coming out of the café screaming.

"Oh God, this nightmare can't end fast enough." he muttered.

Whitlock looked back at the café as it disappeared from view. "Soon, I hope. Our governments expect us to keep them informed when we hardly know ourselves what's going on. Getting reliable information is impossible because the German communiqués and newspapers are so filled with lies, we have to rely on rumors and word of mouth."

The motorcar stopped in front of the gray stone building in which their offices were housed. The driver jumped out, ran around, and opened the door for the two ambassadors. The wind had picked up and the sky threatened to bring rain. Whitlock felt the bleak, cold December air rush at his face. A chill ran through him.

"I'll tell you one thing I'm sure of. This new Hun isn't like the others. I don't think we will forget how to spell his name. The Kaiser sent over his top gun..."

"Or top sword," interrupted Villalobar. "We do not know how long this will last, but as I see it, they think they are here to stay."

— 37 —

THE REGISTER

I t was two days before Christmas when Edith put a leash on Jack and
headed for the hospital to make her morning rounds. Once inside the
hospital foyer, she threw off her cloak, straightened her muslin cap,
and handed Jack's leash over to the secretary. She first went to the men's
ward, where Jacqueline Van Til was busy picking up breakfast trays.

"How is Private McDonald, the Tommy we brought over from the
Clinique yesterday? What did the doctor say about his symptoms?" asked
Edith.

Jacqueline pointed to the far end of the room, where a screen of
curtains surrounded the last bed.

"He's over there. The doctor thought it was liver trouble yesterday
and ordered sour milk to clean out his system, but he vomited it up. His
temperature this morning was over 140°F before I bathed him with cool
cloths. He complains about the brightness of the morning light so we
moved him away from the window and put a curtain around him. He
overreacts to any noise."

Edith walked over to the patient, who held a pillow over his head,
gripping the sides. She noticed that his skin was red and that beads of
sweat pooled in the center of his chest. Edith leaned close to him and
lifted a corner of the pillow. The man jumped. "Don't touch me!"

"It's all right, Private McDonald. I'm here to help you. May I please
take a look at you? I promise to be careful."

The man squinted at her from under the pillow corner. He gave a
slow nod of approval. Once the pillow and covers were removed, Edith
saw that his bed linens were drenched in sweat.

"Nurse Van Til, please pass me the rectal thermometer and some
Vaseline." Edith snapped her wrist, shaking down the mercury marker.
"Help me turn him on his side."

A few minutes later, she held the thermometer up to the light. "It's 106°F. We need to cool him down immediately!"

"I have already tried wet cloths, but they aren't cold enough because there is no ice."

"Then move him to a room where we can open the window. Bring as many towels as you can find and water to soak them in."

MacDonald was placed on a gurney and moved to an unused treatment room, where they threw the window wide open. The cold morning air rushed in, causing him to shiver violently.

"Are you trying to f...f...freeze me to death? It was warmer in the b...b...bloody trenches," he stuttered.

"You are over-heated, and we must get you cooled down," said Nurse Van Til.

"Put a sheet over him to calm his shivering. It will work against us," said Edith. "Where is the doctor?"

"He has not made his rounds yet this morning. He has been doing double duty between here and St. Jean's. All the other doctors are out in field hospitals. This patient was seen by the German doctor only yesterday, and he thought it was just a..."

"Trifling ailment. He was wrong. This man is seriously ill." Edith saw the distraught look on Van Til's face. "It's not your fault. Go take care of the other patients. I'll stay here and work to get his fever down. I'll call you if I need help. If you see the doctor come in, send him here immediately."

An hour later, Edith had gotten McDonald's temperature closer to normal. "How do you feel?"

"Like I fell off a horse and was marched over by an entire Boche regiment, but I'm a little better now. I'll tell your nursing supervisor how kind you were to help me through this."

"I'm sure she will be pleased to hear it."

McDonald struggled to get up on one elbow. "Nurse, what's wrong with me? I mean really? I just ain't right."

"I'm not sure. The doctor will be around soon. Maybe then we can get some answers." Edith was re-soaking the wet cloths when she realized someone was standing behind her.

"What brings the good Matron Cavell to this patient's bedside?"

McDonald jumped at the male voice and put his hands over his ears. Edith stood and faced the physician.

He had a pencil-thin moustache and thinning hair slicked over his nearly bald skull. A too-large suit hung loosely on his short frame and bagged around his ankles, making him look like a child wearing his father's clothes. His head stuck out above a large collar, reminding Edith of a turtle. She thought him to be about sixty.

"This British soldier was moved over from the Clinique with an ailment the German doctor called 'trifling,' but there is more to it, I'm sure," Edith explained.

The physician looked over glasses perched halfway down his nose.

"He looks fine to me," he said in a tired voice, pulling out his pocket watch. He snapped it open and stared at it. "Except for being soaking wet and not wanting to go back to the trenches."

"He's not fine. He had a fever of 106°F before I brought it down."

The doctor leaned over to inspect the patient. "And how are we today, Monsieur..." He pulled a piece of paper out of his pocket, and stared at it, "...McDonald?"

"It's Private Douglas McDonald. Got me a blistering headache for two days. Stomach's upset. Hate to mention this in front of a lady, but me bowels have been acting up."

"We can take care of that easily enough. Nurse Cavell, give him nine grains of salicylic acid now and ten grains of bismuth subgallate every three hours if he needs it."

"I will, Doctor, but I think we need to consider what is causing this. Maybe we should consider examining his blood."

"If the salicylate does not work, we can switch to bromides. Now, if you'll excuse me, I have more important things to attend to than a young soldier who is looking for an excuse to avoid the front lines."

Edith gave McDonald the salicylate and bismuth and changed his bed linens and gown. She closed the window down to a crack and placed a glass of water at his bedside.

"Try sipping on this. Take in any fluid you can tolerate, except sour milk. It is important you keep hydrated."

The man's hand trembled as he took the glass and raised it to his lips. "Thank you, ma'am. I don't mean to cause you trouble. Tell the doctor I'm no coward. I want to go back and fight."

"I know. No worries. Try to rest." Edith held up a small bell. "If you need help, just ring. I'll tell Nurse Van Til to check on you frequently. I'm not going to move you back into the ward until I know what's wrong with you."

"Could you please pull the curtains over the window before you leave? The light still hurts me eyes."

After she finished her rounds, she stopped at the desk and picked up Jack's leash. "Let's go, old boy. We have big plans for Christmas." She turned to the secretary. "What are your plans for Christmas?"

"Nothing special, Matron. Since my husband has joined the Civic Guard, we have not been able to afford anything extra. I'll be working here part of the day while my mother takes care of my little girl."

"I would be pleased if you came and spent the rest of your Christmas at the nursing quarters with us. We have been able to gather enough food for a wonderful meal, and there will be a present for your little girl. What is her name?"

"Regine."

"That's a beautiful name. Will you come? I would love to meet Regine. There will be many other children there as well. We'll have a jolly good Christmas, you'll see."

"Thank you, Madame. I accept your gracious offer."

Edith left with Jack to go back to the nursing quarters at the school. "It will almost be like old times, Jack. You'll be getting lots of leftovers tomorrow." The dog suddenly sat down, violently scratching at his neck. "And a bath tonight."

* * * * *

After Edith bathed Jack, she sat at her desk and started to write in her new diary, which she called the "Hotel Register."

To herself, she thought, *I can't keep track of everyone who has passed through but it's important that I keep some sort of record of those we've treated. When this war is over, I may want to look them up.*

No.	RANK	NAME	REGIMENT	ARRIVAL	DEPARTURE	WHETHER WOUNDED
1	Col.	Boger, Dudley	Cheshires	Nov.1, 1914	Nov. 18, 1914	3 times, including severe foot wound
2.	CQMS	Meachin, Fred	Cheshires	Nov. 1, 1914	Nov. 18, 1914	Shrapnel wound

Edith wondered what had happened to these men. She missed them. Life had been so boring before they arrived. Now it had a new purpose. She recalled the verse from the book of Ephesians she had read the night they arrived.

> *"For we are God's workmanship, created in Christ Jesus to do good works, which God prepared in advance for us to do".*

She added one more heading to the register: "Further overseas service." *I will try to keep track of these men after they have passed through.*

Since she had not received a postcard from either Boger or Meachin, she decided she would go to the American consulate after Christmas and ask if the men had made it home. In the meantime, there were more soldiers hidden in the Clinique whose lives depended on her. She would surprise them with a wonderful Christmas. She was thinking of how she would decorate the Christmas tree, when she heard a knock on her door.

"Madame, you have visitors. May I let them in?"

"I'll be right down, Marie."

At the door stood two men dressed in Belgian clothes. One held out his hand to her while holding on to a soft cap with the other. "Sergeant Jesse Tunmore. At your service."

The other man followed suit. "Private Lewis. Glad to make your acquaintance, Miss."

Edith shook their hands, but didn't let them in. She stood at the open door and gave them a questioning look.

"You sound British but how do I know who you really are? You don't look wounded."

Tunmore answered first. "Mr. Joly sent us to you. He said you would understand."

Edith opened the door and let them into the entrance. Tunmore kept talking about the people who helped them get there, but Edith's doubts were not completely allayed. They hadn't mentioned the password. She had been warned to be very careful of soldiers who might be sent as spies posing as Allied soldiers. "Can you prove to me you are English?"

Tunmore looked into Edith's steel blue-gray eyes and knew he had better come up with something convincing.

"I recognize that picture on your wall. It's Nor'ich Cathedral."

"You know Norwich?"

"Grew up there. Been going to that cathedral since I was a lad. I loved playing on that old pile of ruins out on the green, until my father hauled me away by the collar."

"Well, Sergeant, it was one of my favorite places to play, too. I'd do anything to help a Norfolk man. Can you vouch for your friend?"

"We've been fighting together. Every inch of him is a true-blue Brit."

"Are either of you wounded?" Edith asked.

"I'm still fit, but my private here is in a bad way. Shell-shocked. He doesn't say much and has violent nightmares. Sometimes he just stares and shakes. He needs to get away from it all for a while."

"The accommodations here are simple but adequate. I'll set you up with clean beds downstairs, where it is warm. You'll not have much privacy, but you will have company—a few other Tommies waiting to be guided out of the country. The Germans can't see you down there, but you must not wander about. They are watching all the activity on this street."

"We won't be any trouble, miss," mumbled Lewis.

"Of course you won't. Come with me, then. Once you're settled, I'll get you something to eat."

— 38 —

CHRISTMAS HERE AND THERE

T he tall, handsome Sergeant Tunmore soon became a favorite among the staff. "Brilliant idea! Me and the other chaps will trim the Christmas tree," he said when he heard of Edith's holiday plans.

On Christmas day, almost fifty children arrived. Their eyes widened when they saw the gifts under the tree. After everyone was seated, the doors to the dining room were flung open. Tunmore and his crew carried in platters heaped high with roast beef, carrots, potatoes, and brown bread.

"Eat first," he said. "Then you can open your gifts."

He took his place at the head of the table next to Edith. "I think I can speak for the others as well as myself, Miss Edith. You have performed a miracle today. Makes me feel like I'm home."

"This reminds me so of my Christmases at home in the parish. We used to invite all the children in Swardeston to come and celebrate," said Edith. She felt happier than she had since the beginning of the war.

"This group is much too quiet," said a booming voice from the doorway. Edith turned to see the Reverend Stirling Gahan handing over his coat to José.

"My dear, this is lovely. No, it's more than lovely. It's marvelous."

He reached for Edith's hands and held them in his. "I'm sorry I'm late. Muriel couldn't come. She is at home with a bad cold. She sends you her kind regards."

He looked over the guests, who sat waiting for permission to start eating. "Where is Elizabeth?"

"She volunteered for duty at the hospital. We have a very sick patient there. We will take a plate over to her and the rest of the staff later. Now that you are here, would you be so kind as to lead us in a prayer before the meal?"

"Absolutely." Gahan walked to the middle of the room.

"Who is he?" Tunmore whispered to Edith.

"He is the only English Anglican minister left in Belgium," she whispered back and stood up to address the group.

"My staff and I all welcome you to our Christmas table and thank you for coming to share this special occasion, the day God sent His Son to walk among us. It was His supreme sacrifice. Many of you here know what sacrifice means because many of you have also sent your sons, brothers, and fathers to save us from an enemy that has come to destroy our country, but cannot destroy our souls. I hope you all enjoy the food and gifts that God has given us today. Now I want to introduce my dear friend, Reverend Stirling Gahan, and ask him to bless this meal."

The children squirmed and fidgeted. A mother slapped the hand of a boy who reached for a slice of bread. "Wait," the mother whispered.

Reverend Gahan stood facing the group with lifted hands. "Let us pray. We thank Thee, Lord, for this wonderful meal. Bless these people who have endured so much. Bless the hands of Thy servants who work to serve and all of those who come for help. Protect and give them strength in these difficult times. We thank Thee for this food; bless the hands that have prepared it. Surround us with Thy love. In Thy precious name, amen."

"Amen," chorused the crowd, and the clatter of silverware against dishes began.

When the meal was over, plum pudding was served. Tunmore spooned into his dessert. "Best Christmas meal I've ever had, by far," he said. "Who made this plum pudding?"

"I did," said Edith. "It was my mother's favorite recipe. Do you like it?"

"Why, it's simply brilliant. When I get home, I shall call this day Operation Plum Pudding."

After dessert, Edith rose from the table and said, "Now then, who wants a Christmas gift?"

There were shouts of "I do!" and "Me!" and "Me too!" from the children. Edith took them over to the tree in the middle of the room where she, Reverend Gahan, and Sergeant Tunmore gave out gifts of mittens and scarves, knitted socks, sweaters and hats, dolls and toy soldiers. Edith looked over her family of British soldiers and staff. She listened to the children playing and chattering. It was a rare moment when she allowed herself to feel the joy of being proud for what she had accomplished.

"Now for a few good Christmas carols," said Gahan. "Who wants to pick the first one?"

"*Silent Night!*" called out Regine.

"Good one, my little friend. Come up here and help me lead this fine group in *Silent Night.*

The girl, who just reached the height of Gahan's belt, started to sing, "*Silent night, holy night; All is calm, all is bright.*"

Tunmore leaned over to Edith. "We are so fortunate to be here with friends. There are Tommies spending this Christmas huddled in trenches eating rations."

* * * * *

Private Frank Sumpter heard it first. He eased his head up closer to the edge of the trench to listen.

"*Stille Nacht, heilige Nacht: Alles schläft, einsam wacht...*"

The familiar Christmas carol was coming from the German trenches.

"*Nur das traute hochheilige Paar; Holder Knabe im lockigen Haar.*"

He peered between two sandbags piled on the edge of his trench and stared across the 300 yards between the British and the German lines. A metallic-gray evening twilight gave a ghostly glow to the frozen ground.

There was a stench of decomposing flesh from fallen soldiers and horses. Flies buzzed around the rotting corpses, eating at what the rats had left. Sumpter looked back to the men in his trench. On one side of it, a few soldiers were huddled around a makeshift stove waiting for a pan of water to boil. Two soldiers sat opposite each other, playing cards on wooden boxes with "AMMUNITION" stenciled across their sides. A similar box set between them served as a table. When they shifted to place or pick up a card, the duckboards beneath their feet slapped against the murky water below.

"If you have to get killed in this bloody war," said one man as he picked up his cards, "how would you prefer to go? By gun, explosives, or bayonet?"

"You forgot the fourth choice," said his card-playing partner.

"Eh? What's that?"

"Being shot in the back after shagging all night."

"After shagging all night?"

"Well, certainly not before." His face opened up into a wide grin as he studied his cards.

Sumpter looked to the other side of the trench where a medic, with a large red cross sewn onto the mesh of his helmet, was setting a sling on a soldier's bandaged arm. The soldier's head was wrapped in a circle of gauze that draped over one eye.

"Sorry, old chap. You'll be off when the ambulance makes the rounds at midnight."

"*Schlaf in himmlischer Ruh; Schlaf in himmlischer Ruh.*"

Private Archibald Stanley was smoking a cigarette while reading a letter from home.

"Did you hear that?" asked Frank.

"Hear what?" asked Archibald with apparent indifference.

Frank again raised his head over the ridge of sandbags.

"Keep doing that and you won't be hearing anything but the angels singing," said Archibald.

"Listen. I swear, the bloody Boche are singing Christmas carols."

He began to softly hum along with the melody. "*Sleep in heavenly peace; Sleep in heavenly peace.*"

Archibald heard him humming. "Have you gone bonkers?"

"Shhh," whispered Frank. "Listen." He pointed to the other side. Archibald listened.

"*Stille Nacht, heilige Nacht: Hirten erst kundgemacht...*"

"They aren't shooting," whispered Frank. "Even the bastard Huns recognize Christmas."

He sang a little louder. "*Glory streams from heaven afar; Heav'nly hosts sing alleluia.*"

Then his eye caught some movement. A hand appeared over the German trench holding a miniature Christmas tree. The hand placed the tree on the edge facing the English trench. It was decorated with shiny metal pieces that reflected light from the trench.

"*Durch der Engel Halleluja, Tönt es laut von fern und nah.*"

"It's a trick," warned Archibald. "These slimy bastards will do anything to kill us."

"I don't think so. Look, they put out a Christmas tree. I think it's a peace offering."

"Peace offering, my foot. It's a Trojan horse, that's what it is. How stupid do they think we are?"

A voice called out from the German trench. "If you no shoot, we no shoot. We will share our beer with you. Agree?"

A trumpet from the German trench picked up the tune of *Silent Night*. The two British soldiers huddled over the boiling pot of water, lifted their heads, and began to join in. "*Glory streams from heaven afar: Heav'nly hosts sing alleluia.*"

An English soldier picked up his trumpet and took up the melody. Another put his cards down, pulled out his harmonica, and played along.

Frank turned to Archibald. "Let's play it out a bit and see where it goes. Don't shoot unless they do." He put his head up a little higher and yelled out, "Agreed!"

"Let them be the first to step out in the open," warned Archibald.

"You come out first!" called Frank.

A gray uniform slowly rose from the trench. He had a second miniature Christmas tree in one hand. "For you," he said, holding it out to Frank.

Frank saw no gun on him, so he raised his body a little higher and held out a brown square. "Chocolate?"

"*Ja! Gut!*"

Now both sides were singing together.

"*Christ, in deiner Geburt; Christ, in deiner Geburt.*"

"*Jesus, Lord, at Thy birth; Jesus, Lord, at Thy birth.*"

Another gray uniform climbed out of the trench. "Cigarettes." He held out an unopened pack to Frank, who was taking the Christmas tree from the first German soldier.

"Plum pudding?" said a second English soldier, rising out of his trench and looking warily at the German trench. He held out the tin.

The German soldier took it and exchanged the cigarettes for the tin and gave a slight bow. *"Danke."*

A few of the English soldiers began to sing, *"Oh come all ye faithful, joyful and triumphant."* Some of the German soldiers knew the words and joined them. A drum sounded, but Frank couldn't tell from which side. Other German soldiers climbed out of their trenches. None of them were armed. Archibald stood watching as the khaki and gray uniforms slowly emerged from their trenches and mingled in the space between the trenches called "No Man's Land." His eyes darted among the soldiers, waiting for some sign of treachery. His rifle pointed outward between a space in the sandbags. "You can't trust the Boche," he muttered to the soldier with the arm sling.

Men from both sides were emerging in the moonlight. One English soldier exchanged a tin of bully beef with a German named Wilhelm for a tin of jam. Wilhelm went back to his trench and handed the tin of beef to a friend who was lying there. "Here, Karl, you look like you could use a little more to eat."

"Not now. My stomach hurts, and I am too tired. Tomorrow, you will be killing the man who gave you that tin."

"It's Christmas. Maybe just for one night, we can stop killing, yes?"

"For one night, I would prefer to have a naughty blond with big breasts in my trench. Not a bunch of British pigs."

A British soldier tossed a round football between them and the two sides challenged each other to a game of soccer.

"Let's see if your balls are as big as ours," joked a Brit.

"You would be jealous if you knew how big our balls are. Your women would all leave you for us," said Wilhelm.

Both sides scrambled to find wooden posts and pounded them in the frozen ground as goals. A tall German soldier rolled a large keg of beer into the crowd and poured beer into waiting tin cups. "This gut beer. Not that piss you Brits drink."

A gray-uniformed soldier held up a decorated German stein filled with beer. "Winner gets this special Winner's Cup."

Their breaths clouded up in the frosty air as they played. Others stood watching and cheering their teams and sipping beer. A tall German standing next to a British soldier, held out a woman's photo and pointed to his chest. *"Mein Fräulein."*

"She's a looker," said the Brit. He reached in his pocket, pulled out a picture, and handed it to the German. "My wife and son. He's four."

"*Ein stattlicher Junge*," said the German.

"What?"

The German slowly formed the words, "A handsome boy."

"Oh, yeah, he is a handsome tyke, all right. Takes after his ol' man, eh?"

* * * * *

E dith tried to imagine how her family was celebrating Christmas. Maybe friends from the vicarage had joined them. Most certainly her uncle and cousin Edward would be there. She wondered if Edward ever got the letters she wrote to him. Maybe Sergeant Tunmore will carry a letter or two out for me when he goes over the border.

At eight o'clock, the children began to tire. Edith thanked them all for coming. Reverend Gahan gave the benediction, ending with, "Lord, we ask that You look after our soldiers who are fighting and dying to keep us safe and free from the enemy. Although they are away from their loved ones, they are never far from You. We pray that on this holy day, they will be free of cold, pain, and misery, and find comfort that Thou art with them. Amen."

Tunmore and Lewis's eyes filled with tears. "Amen," they said in unison.

* * * * *

A t 0800 the next day, Captain Stockwell climbed out of his trench and faced the German officer with whom he had shared a beer the evening before. They saluted, bowed to each other, then raised their pistols in the air and fired three shots. Brits and Germans scrambled back to their respective trenches. The shadows of the football and beer barrel stood out like single sentinels on the barren "No Man's Land."

Stockwell walked back to his trench and announced, "The war is back on again." The informal Christmas truce was over.

Within minutes, a bright red German biplane flew over and dropped a bomb on the British trench. After the smoke cleared, Frank looked down the trench and quickly counted two dead and three wounded. Archibald reached for a round steel hand grenade and pulled the pin. "Slimy Boche bastards! This one's for you!" he cried and heaved it toward the German trenches.

Private Karl Rimmel was still lying in the bottom of his trench fighting off a queasy stomach. He heard a thud at the edge of his trench and cringed, with his eyes closed and hands over his ears, just as it exploded. He spat out the dust and wiped his eyes before opening them. Ahead of him, he saw Wilhelm sliding down the side of the trench. A ragged hole gaped open in his chest. Pink froth bubbled from his exposed lungs. Three other lifeless bodies lay further down the trench.

Rimmel vomited, then looked up, unable to take his eyes off the horror. Suddenly, his hand flew to a sting in his right thigh. He stared at his hand. Warm, sticky blood oozed from between his fingers. A circle of blood widened from a ragged hole in his trousers and pooled onto the mud beneath him.

"Help me!" he called out to anyone who could hear him above the shooting. With his fingers stiff and cold, he fumbled to remove his belt and tighten it around his upper thigh.

"Medic!" he screamed.

His voice was lost in the thunderous bursts of artillery. No one came. He felt a cold panic and fell back staring at Wilhelm's body. The last thing he remembered was seeing the tin of British bully beef roll out from his friend's open hand.

An article in the *Daily Express*, April 28, 2009, shows a diary documenting the 1914 Christmas truce between the Germans and the Allies.

— 39 —

PRIVATE McDONALD'S ILLNESS

In the quiet of the night, Edith's worries churned around in her mind, especially over the building of the new school. Progress was painfully slow. Would it be finished by the time the war ended when she would need it to continue her work?

She thought of her work with the Allied soldiers, desperate for help, who continued to seek asylum with her. She didn't know where to stop, nor did she want to. But food was becoming more and more scarce; she wondered if she could continue to feed them. It was also becoming more difficult to find guides for them all. Her fears lingered until she thought of the postcards from "Cousin Lucy," which were the code words meaning those soldiers had made it safety to Holland and on to home.

In the Red Cross hospitals, the Germans demanded that soldiers well enough to be moved report to the German authorities. Elizabeth circumvented that by telling them, "To the left is the German *Kommandant*, to whom you are required to report. To the right is the house of Mme. Bodart, where you will find a friendly cup of tea. The choice is yours."

No one ever turned left. Mme. Bodart's house became another Underground safe haven for soldiers waiting to be escorted out of the country.

Edith got up and walked over to her desk. In the corner of the drawer was a "Cousin Lucy" postcard which she read, smiled over, and put back. She took out the register of her clandestine visitors. Dipping her pen into the black ink, she carefully wrote in two more names.

No.	Rank	Name	Regiment	Arrival	Departure	Whether wounded
4.	Sgt.	Tunmore	Norfolks	Dec. 23		Shrapnel wound
5.	Pte.	Lewis	Cheshires	Dec. 23		Severe shell shock

In just a few days, Tunmore and Lewis had come to feel like family, but soon, they would also be leaving. Tomorrow, she would take their pictures for false passports and arrange for guides to take them to the border.

Edith thought about the poor health of Private McDonald. *We are missing something, but what?* She went to the book shelf and ran her finger across the spines of her nursing textbooks, found The *Nurses' Complete Medical Dictionary*, and heaved it on to her desk. Flipping through the pages, she came to "Headaches." She read a few pages and then turned to "Neurological Disorders." Suddenly she stopped. Her eyes were fixed on a particular paragraph.

> *Early clinical manifestations include non-specific malaise, apprehension, or irritability, followed by fever, headache, photophobia, and sometimes vomiting. Almost all adults present with at least two of the classic symptoms of headache, fever, and neck stiffness. Disturbance of consciousness usually develops later. If the patient's head is moved in various directions, these movements will be difficult and painful."*

That's it! She slammed the book shut, got dressed, and threw her cloak over her shoulders. It was long past curfew. *If I'm stopped, I will tell them there is an emergency at the hospital.*

She dashed into the men's ward. Not seeing the nurse who was on night duty, she walked directly to over to McDonald.

"So glad to see you, ma'am. Stomach's a bit queasy. I've rung the bell, but no one comes. Anyway, not yet. I think I'm going to throw up."

She held a basin to his chin as he gave a stomach-churning retch and threw up. "I will get you some bismuth. That should calm your stomach." She went to the medicine cabinet and pulled out a bottle of the chalky liquid. "Here, drink this and lie back."

McDonald drank back the liquid and screwed up his face. "Tastes worse than our bully beef. Me and the chaps always wondered how they could take a very fine cow and turn it into something so vile. Maybe that's what has made me ill."

"Well, now, it didn't do much for the cow either, did it? I need you to lie very still. I want to try a test on you." She put her hands on either side of his head and gently rocked it side to side. McDonald's hands shot up to hers and held them in a grip.

"Stop! It hurts my neck! No more, please."

"Private, did you notice anyone else in your regiment feeling as badly as you?"

"Don't know, ma'am. We were all separated and went out on our own."

"Were you injured in any way?"

"Yes. I fell into a shell hole just before a bomb exploded behind me. That hole saved my life. I was lucky to only get a small cut on the back of my head where a piece of metal stuck in. The medic pulled it out straightaway. Didn't bleed much."

Edith heard the doors to the ward swing open and saw Probationer Von Blockendaele and the doctor pushing a gurney into the ward.

"Just got this German soldier in a few hours ago with a serious thigh wound," said Von Blockendaele. "He needed surgery immediately or he would have bled to death. There was no one else but myself to assist the doctor. Everyone was sleeping when I left."

The three of them moved the German off the gurney and onto a bed.

"They brought him in from Ypres," said the physician, holding the chart closer to his face. "A Private Karl Rimmel. Extensive thigh damage from shrapnel. I was able to remove pieces of metal that might have hit a nerve, and tied off the damaged vessel. Lucky it missed his femoral artery, but not by much."

The doctor looked at the blood-soaked dressing on Rimmel's thigh. "He will bleed some more—might be a good thing. It will clean out the wound. I have instructed your nurse to reinforce the dressing as needed. Keep a close eye on him."

"About the Brit, Doctor–Private McDonald?"

"Yes, he is doing better on the salicylates and bismuth," the wiry physician answered in an almost dismissive tone.

"Doctor, just a moment, please. I've examined him again and I believe his symptoms are suggestive of meningitis."

"Meningitis? Impossible."

"He has a stiff neck, headaches, and intolerance of light. He is nauseated, vomiting, and irritable. He said that he fell into a shell hole and suffered a small head wound. I believe that caused the infection."

The physician pulled off his linen surgical cap and shoved it into the pocket of his white coat. He strode over to McDonald's bed.

"He did not mention a head wound before."

"That's because the shrapnel was removed by a medic before he arrived."

The doctor was about to place his hands on either side of the soldier's head when McDonald cried out, "Get your bloody hands off of me! That nurse already did that and damn near killed me with pain. I need something stronger for the headaches."

"Give him morphia, a half grain now and every three hours if necessary. You can move him back into the men's ward away from the other beds. Since his meningitis is not viral, there's no reason to keep him in total isolation. Be sure to instruct your nurses to sterilize everything that touches him, and tell them to wash their hands."

The stooped doctor walked away, wiping his hands on a handkerchief and shaking his head. "Poor bastard."

Typical World War I hospital ward (vintage postcard.)

— 40 —

THE INSPECTION

Elizabeth heard a motor idling outside the nurses' quarters. She tried to peer down through the wrought-iron railing of the balcony but a dead plant, left out for the winter, blocked her view. She shifted to look beyond the plant pot and saw a young soldier emerge from the driver's seat of a gray motorcar and close its door, on which was written the word *Polizei*. He reached in and brought out a rifle. A tall blond man in an officer's uniform stepped out of the back seat and adjusted the gun holstered on his side. The first soldier stood at attention behind the blond officer and held his rifle across his chest.

Edith was dressing the wounds on the back of Lance-Corporal Jack Doman.

"Got my horse blown clear out from under me," he explained to Edith. "Lucky the shrapnel hit my back and not my front. Blew one of my horse's legs clean off. I loved that horse, but there was nothing I could do."

"So what did you do?"

"I shot him. It tore my heart out to do it. Really it did."

"Edith! Quick! Come here!" Elizabeth called out. "German officers are at our front door—with guns."

Edith shoved Doman into a patient's bed. "The Germans are here! Quick! Into bed with you!" She threw the covers over him. Turning to leave, she saw his army boots sticking out at the end. "Oh, dear, that won't do." She pulled the covers back over his boots. "Stay still. Do not speak."

Before Elizabeth opened the door, she tucked in a loose strand of hair and fixed a pleasant smile on her face. When she opened the door, a clean-shaven official stood there. A soldier holding a rifle stood behind him.

"I am Herr Kapitän Bergan and this is Private Kessler. We are inspecting every building in this area. You are in charge of these four houses, yes?"

"No, Captain. I am Elizabeth Wilkins, the nursing supervisor. Mme. Cavell is the Directrice in charge. I'll get her for you."

He put his hand out. "Step aside. Our inspection has been ordered by Governor General von Bissing. I need no approval from your Directrice."

Edith came through the back of the room and strode beside Elizabeth.

"I am the Directrice here. Has there been a problem or complaint?"

"No complaint. We have been ordered to make a routine inspection of every house in this area."

"May I make it easier for you by showing you around?"

"I will go with you. My private will also make his own search. Understood?"

"Certainly. Come this way," said Edith, leading him into the Clinique.

The officer made a sweep on his hand to the soldier. "*Suche überall, search everywhere.*"

Elizabeth quietly walked into Edith's office and stepped on a button underneath the rug in front of the sofa. It signaled the men in the coal cellar below to immediately hide themselves and any evidence of their presence.

The captain strode from bed to bed, carefully inspecting each patient. One bed had a little German flag stuck in the metal frame. Another had a picture of a young woman with braided hair, smiling. There were cigarettes, combs, books, and leftover food on their side tables. When he came to Doman, he stopped and looked down at him. The area around his bed was bare.

"This man, who is he?"

"He is a poor Belgian peasant suffering from a chronic rheumatic condition. He was just brought in today. Poor fellow, he is in so much pain."

"*Wie heist du?* What is your name? " the German officer asked, leaning over his bed.

"I'm sorry. He is French and does not understand German. We gave him a very large dose of morphia, which left him unconscious."

Keeping his rifle ready, the private descended the stairs into the coal cellar. There was a dim, yellow light glowing through a window high up on the wall. Confronted with a pile of coal, he picked up a shovel and jabbed at it. A cloud of coal dust billowed up and coal cascaded down onto his polished boots. He backed away, stamping off the dust from his boots.

He pulled a handkerchief from his pocket, and leaning down to wipe them clean, he noticed two mattresses leaning against the wall. He looked behind the mattresses but saw nothing. Next to them was a small table turned upside down with two chairs thrown on top. He kicked them out of the way and inspected the stone floor. *Nothing.* He thought he heard something–a cough or sneeze. He turned, hesitated, looked back once again, and listened. *Nothing.* He inspected the walls. *Nothing.* He hated this work. He signed up to kill the enemies of the Fatherland, not to inspect filthy coal cellars. He walked back up the narrow stairs, glad to be in the daylight.

Edith led the captain into her office.

"You, stand there," he said, pointing just inside the door. He walked around the room overturning pillows, looking in cabinets, and shuffling through books on her shelves. He saw a Bible on a small table and picked it up. "Do you believe in God?"

"Very much so."

"*Gut.* Me, too. I pray every night for God to protect me."

"As do I," said Edith.

He put the Bible down, walked over to her desk, and inspected the neatly piled papers. Moving to the front of the desk, he pulled the drawer open. Seeing nothing but pens, ink, and blank paper, he was about to close the drawer when he spotted something. He reached in the corner and picked up the postcard from the Netherlands. "Who is this Cousin Lucy?"

"She is my niece who lives in Amsterdam. She stayed with me for a while, but moved to Amsterdam when the war started. She worries so about me and wants me to join her, but I can't leave my work here."

He gave her a hard look for a long moment. She held his gaze until he flung the card onto the desk and walked away.

The private inspected the kitchen, where he was met by the cook and Marie, the maid. Marie engaged him in a short conversation in German, which made him smile. After he left, the cook turned to Marie. "What did you say to him?"

"I told him how nice it was to see such a fine young man from the Fatherland, doing his duty. I said I missed my family and offered to give him something to eat."

"You are not giving a Hun any of my food! I thought you had no family in Germany."

"I do not," said Marie with a grin.

When the captain approached the door, the private was already waiting for him. "Nothing here, *Herr Kapitan.*"

"*Gut!* Good!" said Bergen. He turned to Elizabeth and Edith. "We will go now. You should know that we have orders to inspect here without warning–day or night. Be prepared."

"That will be fine, Captain. But remember this is a Red Cross hospital. We are caring for your own men, and we are protected by international law."

"That may be true, but you are a civilian and not an army nurse. Do not stray from the rules of my government. Governor General von Bissing will not tolerate those who break the law."

"Of course, Captain. I understand," said Edith as she held out her hand. The captain looked at it and walked out of the room.

Edith and Elizabeth sank down onto the couch as one. Elizabeth felt her stomach churn with anxiety.

"That was close," she said. "We need to be very careful. Maybe we should stop taking in soldiers for a while to deflect any suspicion. We are obviously being watched."

"Nonsense. They aren't particularly suspicious of us; they are generally suspicious of everybody. It was just a routine inspection. Besides, how can we turn soldiers away knowing we are their last hope? What do we say to the others in the Underground who are taking greater risks than we are? When the war is over, we can return to the work we came here to do."

"It's not our lives after the war I am worried about. It's our lives during the war," said Elizabeth.

"I can't live a life of regret and fear. I always wondered what I would do if I were in the situation of Miss Nightingale when she cared for those wounded soldiers in the Crimean War. I thought I would shy away from my duty, but I haven't. And I won't. Do you understand what I am saying?"

Elizabeth took Edith's hands between hers and held them. "Of course I do. We will do this together."

— 41 —

CHAPMAN AND DOMAN

The day after the surprise inspection, Edith called Lance-Corporal Doman and Corporal Chapman together. "It's time to discuss our plans for matching you up with your guides. You must be ready to leave tomorrow afternoon. Our first step will be to go to the house of a priest I know, who has made the arrangements. You must follow me and keep your wits about you at all times. Understood?"

"Yes, Sir, er..Ma'am," said Doman snapping out a smart salute.

"A priest will be our guide?" asked Chapman with eyebrows raised.

"Why not?" said Doman. "Isn't God on our side? You heard the chaps talk about the angels over Mons, didn't you?"

"You believe that story?"

"I know some of the men who saw it. They are good chaps."

"Probably with too much French wine in them."

"I really believe they saw what they said they saw. God sent His angels to look over us."

"Well, He's done a hell of a job. There's thousands of our Tommies rotting out there in muddy fields who ain't ever going to see another sunrise."

Edith cut into the conversation. "Lance-Corporal Doman, are you going to be able to make it with your wounds?"

"I'll make it even if I have to crawl out of this bloody country."

"Good, because you may very well have to do that. The Germans are tightening up security around the borders, making it harder for us to move across. We used to be able to bribe most of the guards, but the older ones have been replaced by younger ones who are not so easily bought with a few francs or a bottle of cognac."

"Colonel Boger told us you were the only person he knew who could help us," said Doman, reaching into his pocket for a cigarette.

"I do what I can, but there are many of us working to keep the likes of you two safe from the enemy. Unfortunately, your Colonel Boger did not make it over the border. I recently found out that he was captured in a raid on a café and sent to a POW camp in Ruhleban, Germany."

Doman let the unlit cigarette dangle from his lips. "He was captured by the Boche? He's in prison? I can't believe it!"

"He had a very bad ankle wound. It may have slowed him down. This is why we must be so very careful," said Edith.

Chapman fished in his pockets for a match. He pulled one out, struck it, and held it out for Doman to use. "And Meachin?" he asked. "Do you know if he got away?"

"I don't know the details but I did hear from some of the other soldiers that he had a hard time of it but that he did get out in the end. They said once he made it to England, he was arrested as a deserter until he explained everything. He sent me a postcard just like the ones I am giving to you both. Mail them back to me when you reach safety. You are to say they are from Cousin Lucy."

"Cousin Lucy?" said Doman, looking at the card while letting the cigarette dangle from the corner of his mouth.

"That's the code name for soldiers like yourselves who have made it beyond the Belgian border."

"Then Cousin Lucy it is."

* * * * *

The next morning, Edith made her rounds at the hospital. She went to McDonald and found him asleep. "We have been giving him morphia every two hours," said the nurse on duty.

"Every two hours? I thought it was every three hours," said Edith looking at his chart.

"The doctor increased it to every two to keep him comfortable. He has eaten very little. I fear for his life."

"You have a good reason to fear, but if we can keep his temperature down and some nourishment in his system, he may just pull through. Has the nausea stopped?"

"Yes, Madame. He has had some diarrhea. The bismuth helps but doesn't totally stop it."

"Keep working on him. Try to get him to drink salted broth. I haven't given up on him, and neither should you."

"How is Private Rimmel, the German with the thigh wound?"

"His thigh is healing, but he also has a fever. I don't know if it is from the wound or from something else. He also complains of abdominal pain and is having some diarrhea. The doctor thinks it is just from all he has been through." She hesitated. "That German is not very pleased to be here."

Edith walked over to the young soldier's bed. All she could see was his close-cropped blond hair sticking out from the covers. She peeled the covers back a few inches. "Private Rimmel, my name is Nurse Cavell. May I please examine…?"

He yanked the covers out of her hand and pulled them back over his head. "No, you cannot. I want a German nurse. No English nurse is to come near me."

"I'm sorry, sir, but I only have English nurses available to care for you right now."

"I feel like a beaten dog, so how well are you English caring for me? I trust none of you. You all mean to punish me. I am not better. I am worse. You are trying to poison me."

"I assure you, sir, we are not. We have cared for many German soldiers."

"And they lived?"

"Most of them."

Rimmel turned away from her and curled up on his side.

"Can you tell me what you are feeling so I can help you?"

"You want to help me? Get me a German doctor and nurse. If you cannot do that, then go away and let me die."

"What can we do for him?" asked the ward nurse. He won't let us clean him unless he has diarrhea, and he refuses our food, saying it is poisoned. He will only let us redress his thigh wound when the dressing gets bloody."

"Keep trying. He is too sick to be moved back to the Clinique, where there are German nurses. But maybe I can convince one of them to come here to stay with him. In the meanwhile, try to get him to drink some broth and give him salicylates for his temperature and bismuth for his bowels."

* * * * *

That afternoon Edith met with Chapman and Doman. They were dressed in Belgian work clothes. Chapman was wearing a gray jacket, and Doman had on a long black coat with a brown scarf. One carried a sack and the other a black shoulder bag containing their food, a change of clothing, and a passport. Edith inspected them and approved. "They will never think you are English if you don't speak. When the situation requires you to speak, do not try to communicate with them. Simply look as if you don't understand German."

"That shouldn't be hard."

Edith smiled. "Follow me. Don't' walk together, and don't swagger when you walk. Englishmen have a characteristic walk that draws attention to themselves. Doman, walk as if you have a bad back. And Chapman, walk a little more stiffly."

Both men awkwardly practiced their new walks. "You look like you have a pile of shit in your pants," laughed Doman.

"And you look like you're constipated," retorted Chapman.

In the early evening, they followed Edith through the streets to their new hiding place. The priest welcomed them in. He had a pleasant face and appeared to be in his forties. "You will be staying here until I find guides to take you further," he said. "It may take a few days, but you will be safe in the meantime. Please do not leave the house. There are German sentinels posted on every street. They will recognize two male strangers, especially two who walk like you both."

Doman and Chapman looked at each other and then at Edith. The priest turned to Edith and gave her a hug. "You have been sent by the angels, my dear."

The priest reached into his pocket and held out a torn visiting card to her. "I will send word to you when we are able to take these fine gentlemen to meet their guides. You will then take them to the local estaminet where you will order four beers and place this torn card on the table. When our guide sees it, he will produce the other half so you will know he is your contact."

Edith put the torn card in her pocket and gave the English soldiers a solid handshake. "You will be safe here and will have a few more days to heal from your wounds." She turned to leave.

"Nurse Cavell," said Chapman, "I was just wondering." He looked down at his shoes and then back again. "I don't mean any disrespect, but I have to ask you, have you done this before? I mean, shouldn't a man be doing this?"

Edith arched an eyebrow and turned around to face him. "You mean have I taken soldiers to their guides?"

"Yes, ma'am. That's what I mean."

"Yes, I have, corporal. Men aren't the only ones fighting this war. There are no medals for what women do." She turned back to the door and stopped. "But if you mean buying two chaps a beer in an estaminet while waiting for a stranger to find us from a torn visiting card, no, I've never done that before." She slipped through the door and gave a quick wave back to them over her shoulder. *"Au revoir."*

RIMMEL'S SICKNESS

Edith had now established a new routine–breakfast with her staff, feed the soldiers she was hiding, dress and care for their wounds, visit the Clinique, then walk over to the Berkendael Hospital to make her morning rounds. The wind whistled and whipped at her cloak as she hastened her step to the hospital. Dried leaves scratched across the ground, lifted in swirls, and flung themselves against her legs. She pulled her cloak tighter around her and made it to the hospital just as freezing rain began to pelt down.

Leaving Jack with the receptionist, Michelle, she headed straight for the male wards. She found the ward nurse, a Belgian named Angélique, collecting breakfast trays and stacking them on a metal cart. Upon seeing her matron, the nurse came to a stiff halt, and gave a small bow. "Mme. Cavell."

"*Bonjour*, Nurse Angélique." Edith walked over to the metal cart. "Is this Private McDonald's tray?"

"Yes, Madame. He is able to eat his porridge and is taking in fluids better. We must still medicate him for his headaches, but he is no longer vomiting. This morning his temperature is 99.6°F."

"Excellent," said Edith.

When she walked over to the private's bed, he immediately recognized her and sat up.

"Good morning, Miss Cavell. You're looking quite fit this morning."

Edith sat in a chair beside his bed and reached for his hand. "The nurse tells me you are now able to keep down food and drink."

"'Tis true, although I can't say the food is much better than my army rations." He leaned closer to Edith and said quietly, "Any chance someone could pinch me a fag?"

"I see you are feeling better, but no cigarettes just yet. Maybe in a few days."

McDonald rolled his eyes to the ceiling and assumed an exaggerated look of disappointment. Edith noticed his eyes looked tired. "Are you getting enough sleep?"

"No bloody way. Nobody gets to sleep here with the likes of that Hun over there. He has been up all night ordering his nurse around. It must be another German nurse because I heard them arguing in German with each other. I heard him complain because he was in the same room as a Brit. Cheeky little bastard, I'd say."

Edith released his hand. "Excuse me for a minute."

"Angélique, is there a German nurse with Private Rimmel?"

"Yes, Madame. The doctor arranged to have one sent over from the Clinique. I am glad to have her help, because I do not think I could care for him by myself. He wants a pistol so he can force us to do whatever he wishes."

"I hope no one gave him one."

"No, Madame. I told him it is forbidden to have one in the hospital."

Just as she approached Rimmel's bed, the porridge bowl flew past her head, and crashed against the metal cart.

"It is all swill! Garbage! Fit only for the pigs you all are."

Edith strode over to his bed. "Private Rimmel, we will not tolerate having dishes thrown at the staff. If you do not like the food, you can blame your own government for depriving us of the food we need to take care of soldiers like you. The food you have now has been supplied by an American organization. Were it up to your government, we would all starve."

"Maybe you would starve, but not me." Suddenly his face turned white and he broke out in a sweat. He raised his head and vomited over the bed covers. At the same time, his gut gave a rumbling gurgle. A fetid brown ooze seeped through the sides of the sheet. "Bertilda! Bertilda! Where the hell is my nurse?" he yelled.

"She left for a few minutes to care for a personal need," said Angélique to Edith. "I agreed to watch the private until she got back."

"Has he been vomiting and having diarrohea before now?" asked Edith.

"Yes, and he has abdominal pain and a fever. It seems to be getting worse."

As they spoke, a young blond, squarely-built nurse appeared at the bedside. "I see he has vomited again. All night this has been going on—diarrohea, too. I will clean him."

Suddenly she made a face and began to retch at the foul odor. "Excuse me," she said and ran to the nearest bucket, leaned over, and vomited. She wiped her mouth, walked away for a moment, and then returned. "I am so sorry but I could not help myself; the odor is so foul, but I am better now."

Edith could feel her own stomach reacting to the fetid odor, but willed herself not react. She thoughtfully stared at Rimmel; then spoke in a carefully modulated tone. "Bertilda, take down the covers and lift up his bed shirt. I want to see his abdomen."

"Hey! Stop staring at me and clean me up," the German ordered.

The German nurse removed the covers and lifted up the front of his cotton gown.

"What do you think you are doing?" He struggled to pull his gown out of the hands of the German nurse. "Go find someone else to play with and leave me alone."

"Karl," said Edith, "stop struggling and be still for just a moment. Let me examine you and then we will clean you up." She pulled his gown up again and felt an icy chill come over her. She wanted to deny what she saw, but the signs were unmistakable: rose-colored spots covered his abdomen.

"This man has typhoid," she said simply. "We must isolate him from the others straightaway."

The eyes of the German nurse widened. "Typhoid? Are you sure? How do you know this? You are not a doctor. I wish to have the doctor come here and confirm this."

"When the doctor sees him, I assure you he will say the same thing. I know what typhoid looks like. Years ago, I worked in a typhoid epidemic that affected a whole town of people. Those red spots on his abdomen are signs of hemorrhagic bleeding under the skin, caused by toxins. They're a true sign of typhoid fever."

Nurse Bertilda backed away from the bed and ran to where her coat hung. "I am sorry, I cannot stay. I am needed at the Clinique. I must go." She ran out the door and down the stairs; the door of the hospital slammed shut behind her.

"Well, Private Rimmel, it looks as though you will have to put up with us from now on. Your German nurse just left," said Edith.

"I did not like her anyway. She missed her calling. She should have been a tank driver." He searched Edith's face. "Is it true that I have typhoid?"

"I'm sorry to have to tell you this, but I am sure of it."

"Where did I get this typhoid? From another sick man?" He struggled to get up on one elbow and pointed to McDonald. "Maybe from that man over there."

"No, you did not get it from anyone here. You contracted it from the stagnant water in your trench that was contaminated with the feces of flies and rats. It may also have been spread by contaminated soldiers who urinated or defecated in the stagnant water at the bottom of your trench."

"But you can cure me, yes? I will not die from this?" Rimmel asked, a tremour in his voice.

"I can do for you what I have done for many before you and treat your symptoms. The best treatment will be good nursing care. You will have to cooperate with my nurses. If you don't, then all we can offer you is prayer that the good Lord will help you get through this. I will not lie to you; even with good care and treatment, many still do not recover."

Rimmel's stomach went into spasms as he heaved and retched again. He coughed up blood-streaked sputum into a nearby basin. "Look, I am bleeding now."

Edith took the basin from him. "That is from the irritation of the lining of your throat caused by retching. We will try to keep your fever down, and slow down the vomiting and diarrohea."

"You will do this for me?"

"We would do it for any soldier who came here for help."

Edith turned to Angélique. "I think we've seen the last of Bertilda. Once she reaches the Clinique, we can be sure none of the other German nurses will come over here to work."

"We could send him back to the Clinique to be cared for there," suggested Angélique.

"He's too sick for that, and the beds are too close there. Here, we can partition him away from the others."

"But he is so sick. He will need someone to stay with him."

"I will talk to Nurse Wilkins to arrange a schedule of nurses to be with him. I will stay with him this evening, and will take turns with the other nurses. Be careful to wash your hands and uniform between wearings. I will send over a rubberized apron to keep his fluids off your uniform. Everything must be disinfected with a solution of one part carbolic acid to twenty parts of water. Place a rubber sheet under his bed linens. I will talk to the kitchen staff to liquidize his foods–strained soups, boiled eggs, gruel–that type of nourishment. He's a very sick man who is also recovering from an extensive thigh wound. We will need to be vigilant. The last thing we need is an epidemic of typhoid among the patients and staff."

— 43 —
THE VISITING CARD

Several days after Edith had discovered typhoid fever in the ward, Edith arrived at the priest's parish house to escort Doman and Chapman to their guide. She found the priest with his head buried in the Underground newspaper, *La Libre Belgique*. Startled, he quickly folded up the paper until he saw who his visitor was.

"It says here that we are hopelessly deadlocked out on the Western front," he told her. "Two hundred and forty thousand French casualties at what they call 'Hill 180.' Can you imagine? It says we need more heavy artillery. Do you think the Americans will ever join in and help us?"

"I don't know. I hope so. They sent over Herbert Hoover to provide food and clothing through his Fund for the Belgians."

"And who do you think gets that food?"

"We have been able to secure some of it at our Clinique and hospital."

"Nothing gets into Belgium unless it first goes through the hands of the Huns, who use it to feed their troops, so only some of it feeds the enemy." Just then, Doman and Chapman entered the room. "We had best save that discussion for another time," said the priest.

Doman reached out his hands to greet Edith. "Hallo, Miss Edith. We've been waitin' for you. Food's good. Company couldn't be better... your company exceptin' of course. But we're ready to leave this fine establishment and head back home."

Chapman stubbed out a half-spent cigarette and carefully picked a piece of tobacco off his tongue. "This Belgian tobacco is vile. It gives me a sore throat. Good to see you, Miss Cavell. Glad you didn't forget your old pals here."

"I'm true to my word," said Cavell with a smile. "Let's hope you'll soon be smoking English tobacco."

Like a general inspecting her troops, Edith looked over the bags of the two men to be sure they had a day's worth of food, forged passports, and travel papers. Satisfied all was in place, she handed the bags back to them. "They should have made you inspector-general of the BEF," laughed Chapman. "When this war is over, we will personally see to it that you get recognized for your work saving our Tommies. Ain't that right, Doman?"

Edith didn't wait for an answer. "Just get home safe, both of you, and that will be reward enough." She turned to the priest and thanked him. "The arrangement to meet our guide hasn't changed and is still as we planned?"

"It is. Do you still have your half of the visiting card?"

She held it up. "I do."

He gave Edith a pat on the shoulder. "Good woman. Then you are all set. I pray that God will look over you and these soldiers."

"Thank you, Father. I hope you include yourself in that prayer."

He turned to the two soldiers, "Well, off with the both of you. You can't be hanging around here forever. Remember all I've told you—keep your eyes to the ground, and for the love of God, do not speak."

Edith gave last minute instructions. "Stay a few feet behind me. When we get to the tram, I will pay for your tickets. Sit separately, but where you can see me. I will nod when it is time for us to get off. We will all get off at the same time, but through different doors. Once we arrive at the estaminet, you, Lance Corporal Doman, will walk in first and pick a table in a far corner. Corporal Chapman, you follow and sit next to him. I will be behind you both and join you. I will order three beers, but Lance Corporal Doman, you will pay for them." She reached in her purse and pressed a few coins into Doman's hand. "We will sit and wait for your guide to find us. He will give us further directions."

"And if he doesn't find us? What then?"

"Then we will drink our beer and reverse our course."

They heaved their bags over their shoulders and turned to leave.

"And one more thing," said Edith. "When you get home, please could you contact my mother in Norwich and give her this note. I haven't heard from her in a while, and I never know if my letters get through. Please assure her I am quite well."

"I'll see to it," said Chapman, taking the note from her.

They entered the tram and sat a few seats apart from each other and opposite Edith. A middle-aged Belgian woman sat next to Edith. Across from them sat a German soldier. He shifted his glance between Edith and the woman, then fixed his eyes on the woman's lapel, where there was a flower made with the colors of the Belgian flag. His voice was like steel. "*Entferne die Blume.* Remove the flower."

"I cannot," the woman replied. "It is sewed onto the coat."

The soldier scowled, reached over, and tore it free. He looked at it again and noticed it was still attached to the woman's coat by a long thread. He pulled at the string until his hands held a wad of yarn. When another man on the tram laughed, the soldier stood up and pulled out his pistol and pointed it in the direction of the laughter. Everyone put their heads down or looked away. Unable to determine who laughed at him, the soldier re-holstered his pistol and sat back down.

Typical Belgian café l'estaminet

Edith was relieved to see the next stop come into view. She stood up and gave the English soldiers a slight nod. They stepped off from separate doors and fell in behind her.

Edith led them to a small estaminet. The low ceiling made the café feel crowded when in fact, it was not very busy. In the far corner to the left, Doman found an empty table that was surrounded by four chairs. Chapman followed, and then Edith. The air was uncomfortably warm with the odor of stale beer, spent cigarettes, and food.

Edith squinted through the dim light and saw that there were German soldiers mingling with the local patrons. Clouds of smoke hovered over small groups of people sitting at the tables. One group of people was playing cards. Light glinted off coins in the center of the table. Another group laughed as they watched a woman dance to a tune played on a harmonica. They pounded out the rhythm with their feet, while their eyes were riveted on the open-laced bodice, revealing an ample cleavage.

To the right was a highly polished wooden bar with brass foot-bars. On the floor stood a tarnished spittoon, its mouth covered with a brown, encrusted slime. A waiter standing behind the bar wiped glasses and placed them on a shelf backed by a mirror, in which he watched the room's reflection.

Edith motioned for the waiter to come over, *"Garçon. Trois bières, s'il vous plaît."*

"Oui, madame." He returned with three mugs of beer; foam spilling over the sides and onto his hands. He plunked them down onto the wooden table. *"Trois francs, s'il vous plaît."* Doman handed him the money. *"Merci, monsieur."*

They quietly sat sipping their beers for a few minutes, then Edith slid the visiting card to the center of the table and waited. Edith chatted with them in French. The men moved their heads looking as if they understood what she was saying, but their eyes darted around the room, waiting for someone to come forward and claim the card. Chapman drummed his fingers. His head jerked to the door every time someone entered it. Doman's foot tapped nervously against the wooden floorboards. He leaned close to Edith and said out the side of this mouth, "What if no one comes? Maybe something happened to him. Maybe he got arrested."

Chapman joined in. "The longer we sit here, the more chance those Huns will figure out who we are."

Edith shot them a scolding look. "Shhh, both of you. Be patient. Smile and look as if you enjoy being here. Our guide is as nervous about the danger of meeting us here, as we are about him."

From the bar, a short, ruddy-cheeked Belgian approached them. He had deep-set, dark eyes, and a bushy dark-brown mustache. He placed his beer mug on the table next to Edith's card, then placed the missing half of his card next to hers. Their eyes met in recognition, and a flicker of relief passed over the soldiers' faces. Edith nodded for the guide to sit down. She greeted him in feigned recognition, then lowered her voice to introduce Doman and Chapman.

"I cannot tell you my name," said the guide. "I must make this brief. German soldiers may hear. We must find another place to meet in the future." He whispered to the men. "Listen closely. I will guide you by boat to a small village south of Antwerp. Other guides will meet you there, and take you individually to the Dutch border. Always be vigilant. You may recognize the Germans, but you will not recognize the spies. Do not speak. Most Germans do not speak French, and many Belgians in this area do not speak German, so silence will not put you under suspicion. Talking will."

Edith and the men raised their glasses in a toast to each other.

"Here's mud in your eye," whispered Chapman. They threw back their mugs, gulped down their beer, gave Edith a hug, and followed the guide out the door. Edith unconsciously held her breath as she watched them leave. She did not exhale until they walked past the German soldiers loitering outside, then they were gone.

She lingered a few minutes, stared into the amber liquid, and drifted into her own thoughts. This was the hard part—seeing these men leave and not knowing whether they would make it out or not. She lowered her face into her hands. Tears formed in the corners of her eyes. She felt unprepared for the web of deceit and lies into which she was now entangled. It was a curious place for the daughter of a vicar to find herself. She wiped her eyes and shouldered her coat. It was time to return. There will be more British soldiers waiting for her help.

When she arrived back at the Clinique, she took out her register and was writing in two more names when Elizabeth knocked at the door. "Come in, come in."

"Welcome back, Edith. It went well, then?"

"Yes, it was quite a bit of intrigue, actually, but it all worked out. Were you able to gather enough nurses to take care of Private Rimmel?"

"The doctor agrees with your diagnosis. He has ordered hydrotherapy to keep his fever down. In addition to the salicylic acid, we are to give him a gram of calcium lactate every four hours. We are trying to keep him hydrated, but it is difficult. His fluid loss is greater than what he can take in. She looked over the staffing schedule. "I see you put yourself on night duty to care for him. You look tired. Why don't you take tonight off and rest up?"

"I am perfectly fine. That young man needs around-the-clock care until his condition stabilises, and we don't have the nurses to cover that."

Elizabeth sat on the sofa, took off her left shoe, and rubbed her foot. "I know you too well, my friend. You will do what you set your mind to. Any time you change your mind, please tell me, and I will cover your shift for you." She put her left shoe back on and took off her right one. "Actually, Edith, I didn't come here to only discuss Rimmel. We have another British soldier, a Private Arthur Wood. He is waiting in the cellar to meet you. He fought in the Audregnies and managed to survive by living in a turnip patch. The Belgian workers who protected him were nearly shot when they refused to betray his whereabouts to the Germans."

Edith pushed herself up out of her chair. No matter how tired she was, she could never turn any of them away. "Thank you, for getting Private Wood settled in." She ruffled Jack's fur. "Come on, old boy. Let's go meet our new guest."

— 44 —
RIMMEL'S MOTHER

Before Edith reached Rimmel's bed, she knew from the look of the nurse attending to him that something was very wrong. Nurse Janette Lebaire stood to face her. She was a thin waif of a woman. More girl than woman, thought Edith, when she first saw her. Her skin was pale and she had light brown hair with the consistency of wheat that stuck out in wild strands out from under her muslin nurse's cap. Janette wiped her forehead with the back of her arm. A heavy rubber apron hung loosely from her thin shoulders. Thick rubber gloves, too big for her hands, were covered with feces. A stench of vomit and diarrhea emanated from the two buckets placed by the bed, and soiled linen lay in a heap on the floor next to a mop.

Janette had the look of a scolded schoolgirl. "Mme. Cavell, please forgive me for such a mess. No matter how hard I try, there is too much cleaning up to do with his sickness."

"You have done what you could. I'll put on an apron and gloves, and together we will clean this up straightaway. While we are cleaning up, you can give me a report on his condition. Then I will take over."

After everything had been cleaned up, Edith lifted Rimmel's head and shoulders and placed another pillow beneath them. She put the open end of an invalid feeder to his lips. "You need to drink something." Rimmel barely opened his mouth, took in some of the broth, and choked, spraying it over the clean sheets. He pushed her hand away. "No more … pain...stomach."

He grimaced and tightened his hands over his stomach. There was a deep growling sound, followed by gurgling, and then the familiar stench. Edith went to the cabinet and brought back clean linen and bedclothes.

She rolled Rimmel to one side to clean beneath him. His voice was weak. "Who are you? What are you doing to me?"

She noticed the redness around his buttocks and reached for some cream. "I am your nurse and am here to take care of you. I will clean you up; then you must rest."

Rimmel's red-rimmed eyes were glazed over. The woman's voice was soft, but full of authority. The image of a short woman with gray-streaked brown hair tied back flickered before him. Then it was replaced by another image—that of his mother. His thoughts drifted back to a time in his childhood when he remembered his throat burning from a hacking cough that made bird-like sounds, his stomach churned, and he vomited over the bedclothes.

"I am so sorry, Mother."

He heard his mother's voice say, "I will clean you up; then you must rest."

Cool cloths were placed on his forehead and neck. "This will cool down your fever." Humming—she was softly humming. His head was lifted; the pillow was fluffed up and placed beneath him. The coolness to his head and neck felt good. He inhaled the familiar scent of soap. His mother always smelled of soap.

"Mother? Is that you?"

"You will be better if you try to rest," said the soft voice.

It is my mother. She is here to care for me once again. He wanted to see her better, but against his will, his lids fell shut. He felt her moving him about in the bed—washing his back and buttocks, soothing cream being rubbed onto him. The hands felt strong.

He reached out, "Please, Mother. Hold my hand."

Edith removed the rubber glove, took his hand in hers, and held it. He felt the thin fingers and prominent knuckles. *These hands are the rough, working hands of my mother. She must have just come home after cooking and cleaning for that wealthy couple.* He tried to open his eyes again, but the lids were leaden. He tried again. The hazy image cleared a little. He saw a blue uniform with starched white cuffs and collar. *It's Mother's maid uniform. She is home now and has brought me something good–a cookie or an apple.*

She leaned over him and wiped his lips. He gripped his stomach and was about to vomit when he felt a cool cloth being placed over his neck and forehead. The nausea eased. His lips flickered in an attempt to smile and then relaxed. He felt secure now. His mother would look after him.

His dreams took him back to the time when he told his mother he had volunteered for the war. She immediately protested, "You are only nineteen. Your father left me, and now you are leaving me, too. Please do not go. There is work for you here in Berlin. Karl, please, you are all I have left."

"There is no work here except in the munitions factories. I appreciate all you have done for me, Mother, but I am a man now. You taught me about honor and courage. You pushed me to be physically strong. It is my duty to protect you and my country from our enemies. It is time for me to do my part to bring back peace to the Fatherland."

"Is there is nothing I can say to convince you to stay?" Karl could no longer look into his mother's blue eyes. In a gesture of resolution, his mother dropped her hands to her side. "I understand you must go, but before you leave..." She ran into her bedroom and returned with a small Bible, "...please take this with you. God will watch over you. He has anointed the imperial Kaiser to do His will. He will protect those who serve the Kaiser."

She slipped a small picture between the tissue-thin pages, kissed it, and handed it back to him. Her eyes began to well up. "God bless you, my son. Return home safe to me. I will pray every day for your safety." Her hand was trembled as she gave him the worn, leather-covered book.

He stuffed it inside his jacket pocket. "I will keep it with me always." She reached up and pulled him to her. Her tears formed a wet spot on his shoulder. She kissed his cheek. "Remember, no matter how old you are, or where you go, I will always love you."

He waited until her arms around him eased. "I love you too, Mother. Be comforted that I am in God's hands. I must go now."

"Is this your Bible?" asked the woman's voice.

His heavy-lidded eyes half-opened. He stared up into his mother's piercing blue eyes. "Do you remember? You gave it to me. I keep it with me just as I promised you."

"May I read it out loud to you? I don't know very much German, but I can read it. I know you will understand." He heard the pages being turned. "I see a passage in Psalms that is underlined, so it must be important to you." He heard the voice read:

"Bless the Lord, O my soul, and forget not all His benefits: who forgiveth all thine iniquities; who healeth all thy diseases; who redemeth thy life from destruction; who crowneth thee with loving kindness and tender mercies; Who satisfieth thy mouth with good things; so that thy youth is renewed like the eagles. The Lord..."

* * * * *

"Nurse Cavell. How is our young private doing today?" Edith jumped up at the unexpected voice and turned to find the doctor standing behind her.

"He is gravely ill, Doctor. He is hallucinating, probably from dehydration from the frequent vomiting and diarrhea. He's taken very little in."

She moved aside as the doctor pinched the skin on the soldier's inner arm, and forced his eyelids open with two fingers. He took a tongue depressor out of his breast pocket, opened Rimmel's mouth with it, and looked in. He placed the tongue blade back into his pocket.

"You are quite right, Nurse Cavell. His skin is loose, and his tongue is fissured. His eyes are sunken. He is dangerously dehydrated."

Rimmel lifted his shoulders off the pillow. "Is that you, Father?"

Edith gripped his hand. "No, Private Rimmel. It is the doctor's voice you are hearing. You are very sick and in the hospital."

Rimmel coughed and retched, gripping the basin Edith held under his chin. He stared up at the physician. "Am I going to die? Please, do not let me die. I promised my mother I would return and take care of her. She is alone."

The physician methodically ran his fingers over his mustache. He motioned for Edith to move away from the bed. "Keep up the hydrotherapy and sips of broth. Only good nursing care and God can bring him through this." He turned to leave and then hesitated. "Are you sure you want to stay the night?"

"Quite," said Edith, as she reached over and pulled the used tongue depressor out of his breast pocket with her gloved hand.

8

— 45 —
TREATMENT

An hour later, the physician approached Edith, who was attempting to administer bismuth to Rimmel to ease the nausea. The doctor hesitated, "Do you think we should be going through so much trouble for a Hun? If he comes out of this, he will go out and kill more of our people."

"We all have a purpose in life. Both of us have vowed to care for the sick and to do no harm to anyone under our care. Let God be the judge as to who should live or die."

"But we have precious few supplies. Maybe we should save them for our men and allies."

"You write the orders for what he needs to get well, and I'll find the supplies."

"Give him a half a grain of morphia intramuscular."

"I'm shot! Slimy, bastard Frenchies got me!" yelled Rimmel as he felt the needle of morphine prick his arm.

"Karl, the doctor ordered this to help you," said Edith as she injected the morphia. "Try to be still."

Rimmel looked up at Edith and fell back. "The doctor is here? I will be good, Mother, I promise."

"You must promise me you will stop resisting us. Can you do that?"

"Yes, Mother. Please do not leave me."

When the doctor left, Edith sat back on a wooden chair beside the bed. Everything was quiet now. That was one advantage of working nights. She hummed quietly to herself. At the sound of her voice, Rimmel's lips twitched into a faint smile and his body relaxed.

She picked up his Bible again and was about to read more passages when a small picture fell out from between the pages onto her lap. She picked it up and saw a sepia-toned picture of a woman about her own age, with brown hair pulled up over her angular face. The woman wore a laced blouse with an oval cabochon at the neck. Her thin lips were set in a serious look, but her light-colored eyes were clear and piercing. Edith guessed they were blue. She slipped the picture back between the pages.

After a few hours, Edith made a quick round to the other patients. McDonald was asleep. She went back to Rimmel and lit an oil lamp next to his bed. She found a pen and paper and drew a beautifully detailed rose. She labored over the intricate details of the petals, stem, and leaves. She remembered once doing the same thing for a patient when she was a probationer. Beneath the flower she wrote: *I pray you will blossom like a rose, –Edith Cavell.* When she finished, she put it on top of his Bible. When he wakes up tomorrow, it will be there for him to see—if he wakes up tomorrow.

Throughout the night, she soothed him with damp cloths and moistened his mouth. She cleaned him every few hours, an activity she almost welcomed because it kept her awake. As the end of the night crept into early dawn, she felt her own fatigue creep in. She checked the clock on the wall. It was five in the morning. She knew from having worked nights in the past that this was the worst time to try to stay awake.

In the yellow glow of the lamp, she stared at Rimmel. His features seemed familiar to her. Then it came to her. He looks like my brother when he was the same age. She realized how much she missed Jack and hoped her mother had shared her letters with him. *That is, if she gets my letters.*

Rimmel stirred and tried to sit up. He grabbed at her hand. "It is so dark in here. I am afraid of the dark, Mother. Hold my hand." Edith held his hand. A feeble smile crossed his lips and then disappeared. Edith reached for a clean towel with the free hand and placed it on the floor beside Rimmel's bed. She knelt on it, and while she prayed, a deep weariness came over her and her eyelids became too heavy to keep open.

In the glow of the dawn, Elizabeth came by with the morning duty nurse. When she walked into the male ward, light was streaming through the windows. Some of the men were beginning to stir. She walked over to where the little lamp glowed, to find her matron on her knees asleep with one hand holding Rimmel's hand. She touched Edith on the shoulder.

"Edith? Are you all right?"

Edith awoke and blinked the sleep out of her eyes. She squinted in the bright light. "Oh, yes, of course, quite. We needed a miracle to save this young man, so I decided to pray for one."

She eased her hand from Rimmel's loose grip and leaned on the chair to help her stand, then straightened her back. "I need to get some breakfast and take a nap. If the day nurse has any questions about his care, wake me up."

"Edith, did you forget you were scheduled to bring Private Wood to meet his guide this morning?"

"I guess I did forget, but a little nap will refresh me in time to meet him."

"You can barely stand. I'll ask José to do it for you."

"You'll do nothing of the sort, Elizabeth. I'll take a nap when I get back from bringing him to his guide."

"How is the German soldier?"

"I think he is stabilizing, but he's so dehydrated that he is hallucinating. He thinks I'm his mother."

"He could think worse things. Do you still plan on taking the shift with him tonight?"

"I do. If he is going to get better, we should see changes by this afternoon. If nothing helps, you may not need me or anyone else to work another shift for him. He is in danger of either perforating his bowel or dying of dehydration. He can't be left alone."

Edith looked over at McDonald's bed and saw that it was empty. "Where is Private McDonald? I saw him sleeping there last night."

"I think he is up stretching his legs and probably found someone to give him a fag. By tomorrow, he will be well enough to leave."

"Of course, you've told him that when he is released from the hospital, he is required to report to the authorities, haven't you?" asked Edith.

Elizabeth placed her right hand over her heart. "Absolutely, as a good representative of the Red Cross and working under the protection of its flag, I tell all of the men what the law requires them to do." She dropped her hand and gave that wonderful, beguiling grin that Edith loved. "And then I give them the directions to Ada Bodart's house. I can't help it if they refuse to follow the law, and prefer tea with Ada Bodart to imprisonment." Elizabeth's smile then disappeared into a look of seriousness. "There is one more thing you should know. Yesterday evening, I noticed German soldiers carrying boxes of supplies, desks, and chairs into the house across the street from our school. I'm afraid they are setting up a local command post over there."

Her words hit Edith like a blow to her chest. She understood what this meant.

— 46 —
"It's a Long Way..."

"*I*t's a long way to Tipperary. It's a long way to go! It's a long way to Tipperary, to the sweetest girl I know..."

Six drunken Irish soldiers were staggering down rue de la Culture when one of them saw Elizabeth standing at the door with her hands firmly planted on her hips.

"Steady, lads," one voice slurred. "Sergeant at thirteen hundred about to make an announcement."

"What announcement?" said another. "Do we push forward or retreat?"

Another voice said, "Retreat? Irishmen never retreat."

When they got to where Elizabeth stood, a young, red-haired soldier with a splatter of freckles across his cheeks said, "Lassie, ye be lookin' mighty sweet! Come on and have a pint with us." He leaned on one of the other soldiers for balance. Elizabeth glowered at the young man. "Are you old enough to drink?"

"Yes, ma'am. If I'm old enough to fight, I'm old enough to drink." He elbowed the ribs of a tall, splinter-thin man next to him. "Ain't that right?"

The tall man stumbled into Elizabeth, almost knocking her down. "Pardon, miss. Me foot won't go where me head wants it to go. Ever had that happen to you?"

Elizabeth glared at the stumbling, weaving group in front of her. "For God's sake! What do you all think you are doing?"

The tall soldier flipped off his cap and made a sweeping bow to Elizabeth. "My dear, sweet lady, we were just having a wee bit o' fun down at the pub. Ye can't blame a few hard-fighting soldiers for a moment or two of frivolity, now can ye?"

"Yes, I can. There are German soldiers billeted right across the street and spies everywhere. You can't be so careless as to put yourselves and all the rest of us in danger of being arrested. You were told to be quiet, not swagger down the street singing at the top of your bloody lungs!"

The soldier in the back gave three wide, exaggerated steps that brought him out in front. "Pardon, miss. We met up with some fine French lads who told us the *Chez Jules*, or *Jules Chez*, whatever the Frenchies call it ..." —he turned and grinned to the men behind him— "... just down the street there, was a safe place to relax. We only had a pint or two."

"That is a local pub in a small neighborhood. Everyone knows everyone else. You are all strangers, and it won't be long before one person tells another, who will pass it on to someone else, until it gets to the ears of the Germans that there are Brits here. Soon they'll be at our door looking to arrest the bunch of you." She held the door open and gestured toward it. "Get inside, all of you, and be quiet. I'll discuss this with Mme. Cavell as soon as she returns."

That evening, when Elizabeth met Edith at the door, Edith could tell by the flush on Elizabeth's cheeks that something was wrong. Elizabeth paced around as she told her about the incident with the Irish soldiers. "They were walking down the middle of the street singing in English. They have no idea of the danger they are in. Jacqueline is convinced that the people farming that little potato lot across the street are not farmers but spies sent to watch us. Their irresponsible behavior will put all of us in danger."

Edith's eyes followed her distraught friend. "Perhaps Jacqueline's imagination is getting the better of her." She hesitated, then said, "What would you have me do? They are not prisoners. We can't watch them every minute. There are too many of them now. They have been through so much, Elizabeth; it's hard to deprive them of a little liberty."

"A little liberty! Do you call their strutting down the middle of the street in front of the German headquarters 'a little liberty?' Listen to me, Edith, you have to talk to them, and I mean now, before they go back out there again."

"I'll talk to them tonight and have them locked in for now."

"Will you call Ada Bodart and ask her to remove them in the morning and place them in one of the other safe houses until guides can be found to escort them out of the country?"

"I'll call her tonight. In the meantime, we'll have to figure out how to keep anyone else brought here quiet to prevent a similar incident."

The next morning, the Irish soldiers were moved out of the nurse's quarters and into individual houses. Once they were gone, Edith went back to the hospital ward to check on McDonald and Rimmel. She found McDonald sitting on the side of the bed eating breakfast.

He looked up from his porridge. "Mornin', Miss Cavell."

"I see you are doing better today."

He took a bite of dry toast and washed it down with a drink of black coffee. "Just a bit of a headache, but not enough to knock me off my trolley like before."

"Do you think you are well enough to travel?"

"I think I'm feelin' fit enough. My legs are still a bit wobbly. By tomorrow, I'll be steady enough."

"Good. Walk about the wards to gain your strength. I'll stop by tomorrow to talk to you about what happens next."

McDonald lifted the bowl to his lips and let the last bit of porridge slide into his mouth. "Cheers."

"Cheers. I need to go see how our German private is doing."

"The one who was yelling something about God punishing the English? He was quiet last night."

While waiting for the Belgian nurse on duty to finish handing out breakfast trays, she leaned over to inspect Rimmel.

Startled by her presence, he sat up, "Who are you? What do you want?" Then he stopped and stared at her for a moment, gave a faint look of recognition and sat back.

"I am one of the nurses who has been caring for you. I'm the one who left you the picture of the rose on your Bible. Do you remember any of that?"

"I think so. You look so much like..." He blinked hard and stared at her. "That is impossible, because I am here, and she is there. And you are here, so you can't be there."

Edith smiled at his confusion. "You seem to be somewhat better. How do you feel?"

Rimmel took a moment to absorb the question. "My stomach feels like it's been run over by an enemy tank." He smacked his lips. "My mouth tastes like the inside of my boot." He shook his head. "My head—it hurts...throbs." Then he gripped his wounded thigh. "My leg still hurts. Will I be able to walk again?"

"Your thigh muscle has been quite damaged. It will take some time to heal, but you will walk again. However, I don't think you will be fit enough to go back to the trenches," Edith said in a calm voice.

"No fighting? But I am a soldier. That is what I do."

"I'm sure they will find other work for you when you are well enough. Have you been drinking enough?"

"The nurses have been giving me sips of water, tea, and broth. I asked them for a beer but they refused."

"So, you are feeling better." She saw the ward nurse approach.

"Mme. Cavell, I see you have already been making the rounds. The doctor said Private Rimmel is doing better. His temperature is down. He has stopped vomiting, and had only one bout of diarrhea in the last shift." She saw an approaching figure and nodded in that direction. "Here comes the doctor now."

The physician seemed disturbed. He ran his fingers over his head several times, folded his arms across his chest and then unfolded them again. He gave a slight nod of recognition to Rimmel and asked that Edith step away from the bed with him.

"I am sorry to have to tell you this. The German command will be taking over this hospital tomorrow. We are to move all the Belgian patients to St. Jean's. All Allied soldiers who are patients here are to remain until they are well enough to transfer to prison. All of your nurses will be replaced with German nurses, and I will be replaced with a German doctor. By the end of the day, my office will be cleaned out, and I will be transferred to St. Jean's."

He reached up, removed his spectacles, and rubbed his eyes. "You, Marie, and Dr. DePage have worked so hard to build the reputation of this hospital. I have never worked with finer nurses. I am so sorry. I know what this means to you and your staff."

"It means my staff will no longer have nursing positions, which means they will not have a salary. It also means the few nursing students we have at the school may have to leave." Edith paused, looked away and then back. "I'm sorry, Doctor. I don't mean to lash out at you. I was not prepared for this. None of this is your fault. Thank you for all you have done. Dr. DePage was fortunate to find you to cover here for him. St. Jean's will be just as fortunate to have you on their staff. Look how well you treated Rimmel. He was close to death, and now it seems he will most likely survive."

"Yes, well, we will see if that was such a good idea or not. I hope to see you at St. Jean's. Now I must finish my rounds and pack up." His thin fingers grasped hers. "And one more thing; I cleared Private McDonald for discharge. Today."

Edith gave his hand a firm shake. "I will personally take care of it, Doctor. Thank you."

She walked back to McDonald. In a low voice, she said, "We cannot keep you another day. I just found out that things have changed. Tomorrow, the Germans will be taking over this hospital. Since you are officially discharged, I am required to tell you that the present law says you must report to the Kommandant as soon as you leave here. However, I know the address of a Mme. Bodart who lives nearby. If you choose to break the law by not reporting to the Germans, and decide to go to her house instead, I can assure you will get a lovely cup of tea." She waited for his response.

"I would love a cup of tea," he said, smiling back at her.

"Then we had better gather up your belongings and leave now. I will take you to her house to enjoy that cup of tea."

While McDonald collected his few items and stuffed them into his pillowcase, Edith returned to Rimmel's bedside.

"I want to inform you that as of tomorrow, I and my staff will no longer be taking care of you. You will be pleased to know that General von Bissing has announced that his physicians and nurses will be taking over this hospital tomorrow. I wish you well, and hope someday we can meet under better circumstances."

Rimmel took her hand. "I remember you now. You sat with me and read to me out of my mother's Bible. I kept the rose you drew. It was kind of you. You did so much for me. You could have let me die."

"We never know where the pathway of our lives will lead us, do we? We are all God's children, no matter what uniform we wear. It's not for me to judge who lives and who dies. That is up to God. I hope you continue to get better, Private Rimmel. Farewell."

"Auf Wiedersehen."

− 47 −
MARIE DEPAGE

With the exception of helping out on the wards, all responsibilities for the Clinique and the hospital had been taken from Edith. It did not take her long before she totally shifted her focus to working with the Belgian Underground. It was late afternoon when she flipped open her register to write in more names of rescued soldiers. It was impossible to add the names of every person who passed though her house. Many came in groups and left so quickly that she didn't have enough time even to learn their names. She felt especially close to the English soldiers.

She gave many of the British soldiers letters to mail to her mother and other family members, never knowing if they were delivered. Edith gave the Norfolk soldier, Private Arthur Wood, her personal Bible with a letter to give to her mother. It had been many months since she had received any word from England. Her mother's health was always a concern. *I ache for the day I can see you again. We'll enjoy a dinner together of your steak and onion pie and ginger upside-down pudding and talk about how I treated hundreds of soldiers right under the noses of the enemy.*

She dipped her pen in the inkbottle and wrote:

No.	Rank	Name	Regiment	Arrival	Departure	Whether wounded
16.	L/Cpl.	Dorman, J.	9/Lancers	Jan. 27	Feb. 11	Severe shrapnel wounds in back
17.	Cpl.	Chapman, R.	Cheshires	Jan. 27	Feb. 11	Not known
18.	L/Cpl.	Holmes, F.	Norfolks	Feb.	March	Severely wounded
19.	Pte.	Wood, A.	Cheshires	Feb. 23	Feb. 28	No wounds

A slow shadow crept over the register. She looked up and jumped out of her chair, spilling ink over the blotter. Snatching the register away from the black pool of ink, she heard a familiar voice.

"You had better clean that mess up. You know what Antoine would say about a messy desk."

Edith threw her arms around her old friend. "Marie, is it really you? How have you been? I've missed you so much." Holding Marie's shoulders, she stepped back and gave the doctor's wife a long look. "Let me see you. You look well. Have you lost weight? You look a little thinner."

"As do you. The war does has a way of keeping us slim," said Marie, sliding off her coat.

Edith walked her over to the divan and moved the crimson pillow to one side. "Please, sit and let me make you some tea with some biscuits."

Marie sat on the divan, fluffed up the pillow, put it behind her shoulder, and leaned back.

"It has been much too long," she said.

"Yes, much too long," Edith called out from the kitchen. "How is your work going at the LePanne hospital?"

"It is difficult. Hundreds of ambulances and stretcher-bearers bring in the wounded daily. Everything is in short supply—beds, linens, instruments, sterilizers, medicines, and even ambulances."

Edith set a few biscuits on a small dish. "We have similar problems."

Marie continued. "Have you seen any of the men who have been gassed? They are coming to us from Neuve Chapelle. It causes vomiting and sneezing fits so violent that they can hardly breathe or eat."

"Sounds horrid. I have heard of this but haven't seen any of them myself."

A shrill whistle from the kettle interrupted their conversation. Edith prepared the tea and set the tray before Marie, then sat next to her.

"The Germans have taken over our Berkendael Hospital. The physician there was transferred to St. Jean's. I sent some of my nurses with him, but many of the others are out of work. I have agreed to work with the Belgian Underground to rescue soldiers, but I'm having difficulty finding enough food to feed both us and them."

Just then, the door opened and Jack came bounding into the room with José behind him. Seeing Edith, the dog wagged his tail furiously and jumped up to lick her face.

"I am sorry to bother you," said José, "but Jack was scratching at the garden door to be let in and…" His voice trailed off when she saw Marie. He gripped her hands and pumped them. "You are back! You are here to help us? Yes?"

"Sorry, José. This is just a short visit. Actually, I came to say good-bye. I will be leaving the country for a while."

"Good-bye?" said Edith and José in unison.

"I came here to tell you I will be leaving for America in a few days to raise funds from business people who will contribute to the cause. We cannot win this war without additional funds."

Edith nodded to José. "Thank you for bringing in Jack. I'll talk to you later about all of this." He nodded in understanding and backed out of the room.

"I don't know what I would have done without José," said Edith. "He's invaluable in helping me care for these soldiers and move them out to their guides."

"Do you worry about the Huns finding out about your secret activities?"

"If I worried too much about it, I couldn't do it, but I try to be careful and not involve my staff. Of course, Elizabeth, knows everything as do José and the cook, but not Grace and most of the others." She put the teacup to her lips, sipped, and reached for a biscuit. "How much money do you expect to raise?"

"As much as possible, of course, but our goal is $100,000."

"That's brilliant! Do you know who you'll approach?"

"It has all been arranged by Cardinal Gibbons and the Surgeon General. A few American military officers will also be helping me. I am scheduled to visit Chicago, Pittsburgh, and some cities as far west as San Francisco, where I hope to meet Mr. Hoover. A bank account has been set up to handle the donations by a man named J. P. Morgan, who is the president of two banks, one in New York and the other in London. It is all pretty exciting."

"While we are on the subject of money, I must tell you I have been forced to use some of the school's funds to continue our work. Everyone is so impoverished, it is impossible to get anything done unless you give them at least a few francs."

"Do not worry. Antoine will understand. Use whatever funds you need, Edith."

"I keep a detailed account of how the money is spent."

"What about Hoover's Fund for the Belgians?" asked Marie. "I thought that would help with food supplies."

"The fund? We get some of it, but it is rumored that German officials are taking a lot of it for themselves and their troops."

Marie's jaw dropped. "Are you telling me we are supplying food to our enemy?"

"That's what I am told."

"I will have to discuss this with Mr. Hoover when I see him."

"What about things up at battlefront?"

"They are slaughtering thousands of our men with artillery we cannot match. I must raise enough money to pay for military and medical supplies. We will never win this war unless we have more supplies."

At that moment, the skies opened and the rain began to pelt against the windows. Edith felt a strange fear creep over her. "Are you sure you want to do this? Crossing the Atlantic is dangerous right now. The weather is unpredictable, and the Germans are firing torpedoes at ships without warning, including hospital and passenger ships."

"I will be traveling on a Belgian liner. Even though we are an occupied country, Belgium is still considered neutral. I have to do this, Edith; we are desperate. It is the only way we can supply our field hospitals. The hospital in LaPanne was built for two hundred beds. Do you know how many we were treating before I left? Two thousand, and the worst fighting is yet to come. We are not sufficiently prepared to treat such numbers. My oldest son is fighting on the western front and Lucien turns seventeen next month, when he plans to join his brother. I have to do this, Edith. The next wounded soldier could be one of my sons. How can I stand to see them lying there wounded and not be able to help?"

"Is there anything I can do to help, Marie?"

Marie fingered her spoon. "Actually, yes. Maybe you can send some of your unemployed nurses out to the field hospitals. We just have to figure out how to get them there without being captured."

"If my nurses agree to go, I can make arrangements to get them there. We have a good deal of experience in providing papers and guides."

"Good. We will have to work out the details."

"What are you doing for doctors? Antoine can't do it all himself."

"He is very tired, but you know how he is. He will not stop to rest. When I return from my trip, I hope to bring a few physicians with me. In fact, Dr. James Houghton from New York has already agreed to come back with me."

"How long will you be gone?"

"About two months. I have reservations at the end of April to return on the *Lapland*. I want to be home before Lucien leaves for the front."

"I will miss you so much, dear friend. I keep hoping for the time when the three of us will be together again to complete the work we started. Once we have things underway, maybe you could take a holiday with me to Norwich. I so want you to meet my mother. We can tour around the countryside. I'll show you the beautiful cliffs that stand above the beach at West Runton. We'll travel into London, visit the theaters in Leicester Square, and walk about Westminster Abbey. It will be wonderful."

Marie reached for her coat and flipped it around her shoulders. "That all sounds wonderful, but I have to go. There is still so much to do before I leave. I will return as soon as I can. I recently heard there is a much faster British ship that can make the crossing in only four days. It is called the *Lusitania*. Maybe I can catch it for the return trip."

A thunderous rumble shook the skies. A blast of wind rattled the windows. Edith stood up and tried to blink away her tears. Tears formed in the corners of Marie's eyes as well. Edith wanted to tell her not to go but had no good reason to do so.

Marie hugged Edith and was surprised at how fragile Edith felt. "For now, we must all try to come through this alive. I guess that is as much as we can hope for."

When the door closed behind Marie, Edith turned and leaned against it. She wished she could create a haven where all the people she loved would be safe.

A feeling of utter loneliness and grief crept over her. She thought of talking with Elizabeth about it. Elizabeth always knew how to dissipate the fog of fear and uncertainty in her. But what would she say? That she hated to see yet one more friend leave? Elizabeth might think her weak. Marie would only be gone for a few months, and the war might be over by then. Marie and Antoine will return, and the nursing school will thrive once more.

She lowered herself to the floor beside Jack. He stretched himself out, gave a long sigh, and laid his head on her lap. She ran her hand over his rough fur. "I was hoping for so much more than just staying alive."

— 48 —
April, 1915
"Crush the Underground"

Lieutenant Bergan rode south of the Grande Place to the lower end of the city, passed a few lace and tapestry shops, then headed down a narrow alley. He held an anonymous note that gave directions to the home of a key conspirator, active in the Underground. He read it again. "He lives at the corner of rue de l'Étuve and rue du Chêne."

"Stop here," he ordered his driver. The motorcar stopped in the middle of a small cobblestone circle. Lieutenant Bergan got out and inspected his surroundings. He stared up at the street sign and then back down at his directions. He was sure this was the place, but since he could not speak French, he handed the note over to his interpreter.

"This is the written address," his interpreter assured him.

Bergan looked around. There was no house, only a statue of a male child, dressed in a Belgian military uniform, with one hand on his hip and the other holding his penis while relieving himself into the fountain below. The locals called the small bronze statue *Manneken Pis*, and dressed it in costume during festivals. This was not the Underground traitor he expected to find; it was meant to humiliate him. He had received many such notes, but there was no way of knowing which leads were authentic, until he investigated them.

The famous Mannekin Pis or "Wee Boy" fountain in Brussels (vintage postcard)

A note he received last week described in detail where English soldiers were hiding. When he followed the directions, the lieutenant had discovered they led him to the toilet of an abandoned building. Yet another childish trick of these deceitful Belgians. He crushed the note in his hand, tossed it into the fountain, and vowed, "Someday, I will piss on you."

Bergan hated this city. It was filled with lying, treacherous Belgians, who refused to acknowledge they had been conquered by a nation superior to them. It was not his choice to be here. Orders had come directly from Berlin, that he transfer immediately to Brussels to head the Secret Police. He missed his home and his wife. He hoped the war would end soon so he could return to them and advance his career. His assigned task was to set up a criminal investigation office to destroy the Underground. He was ordered to arrest and punish the traitors harshly enough to be a warning to others who worked against the Imperial Army.

Although Bergan was resentful of the assignment, he was also confident he could complete it. He had joined the police force when he was twenty and was one of the privileged few to learn the art of espionage from Berlin's most experienced spy, Colonel Walther Nicolai. Nicolai was a master of deception and knew every trick of espionage. Bergan was now as good as his mentor and had earned the reputation of succeeding in whatever he set out to do. He had thought he would soon be promoted to the chief of the Secret Police in Berlin. Instead, he was assigned to this miserable garbage heap of a city.

When he arrived in front of the gray granite building that housed his office, he was met at the curb by one of his staff. "We have a message from General von Bissing. You are to go immediately to his office and report on your progress."

Bergan felt his throat tighten. What would he say? That he had spent most of the winter tracking down false leads and had accomplished nothing? He felt an uneasy dread. He knew von Bissing had the power to destroy the career of anyone who displeased him. He had to think of something to tell him that would sound like progress was being made.

His driver pulled up in front of the black iron gates that surrounded the building of the former Ministry of Arts and Sciences, where an escort waited for him. They exchanged a stiff salute, and Bergan was led up the grand staircase to von Bissing's office. Just before entering, he hesitated, straightened his shoulders, tugged the wrinkles out of his jacket, smoothed back his blond hair, and after fixing a determined look, knocked on the ornately carved oak door.

"*Kommen*," ordered the precise voice on the other side of the door.

Bergan opened the door and walked into a large, spacious room with ornate rugs, dark, carved furniture, and walls covered with richly colored tapestries. He stood at attention and clicked his heels in salute. "Herr Baron von Bissing, I came immediately at your request."

"Sit," commanded von Bissing as he pointed to the seat across from his desk. "I appreciate your promptness. Please, relax. Join me in a glass of fine vodka."

Bergan looked into the weathered face of his superior and noticed how his eyes inspected him in one glance.

"Thank you, General," said Bergan as he eased into the high-backed chair. Von Bissing picked up a carved glass carafe and carefully poured out two glasses. He handed one to Bergan. Holding up his glass, he said, "*Ein Prosit zum Kaiser!*"

"Victory to the Fatherland," countered Bergan. They touched glasses and gulped back the liquor. There was an awkward moment of silence. Bergan had learned a long time ago that when on the defensive, it was best to let the other person lead the conversation. He tried to gauge the general's mood. From years of interrogating, he had become an expert at reading people's expressions, but the general's dark, penetrating eyes, wedged-shaped face, and thin lips betrayed nothing. Bergan had learned from past meetings with von Bissing that his best clues to the general's mood came from the tone of his voice.

Von Bissing had the sandpaper voice of a smoker, but his words were clear and precise. "I am most interested, Lieutenant, in the progress of your investigations into the Underground. They are going well, yes?"

Bergan kept one hand on the glass and the other in his lap. He wanted to appear in control, but felt the muscles in his face involuntarily tense. "We have investigated many leads from Underground informants."

Von Bissing placed his hands under his chin, the tips of his fingers touching his bottom lip. His eyes stayed fixed on Bergan and held him there like two gun sights.

"How many have you arrested?"

"They are clever, these Belgian fools. They waste our time with false leads."

"So you have not arrested anyone?"

"I am sorry to say, no one of any real importance. I have put spies in various parts of the city, but they have not come up with much. My time is wasted following up on false leads. I need more people to help."

Bergan heard the spurs jingle from under the general's desk as he shifted his feet. It reminded him that von Bissing was an old cavalry officer. *I'm sure he would rather be riding his horse than sitting at this desk. He does not want to be here any more than I do.*

"How many more do you need?" asked von Bissing.

Bergan heard no anger in his tone, so he dared to venture further. "As many as you can approve. I could do better with a more diverse staff—young, old, men and women, laborers, and professionals. They would look more like Belgians and I could put them around the city to report suspicious activities. I would also be more successful if I had additional police to follow up on these reports. We could then infiltrate and destroy these rat's nests."

Bergan could feel the pulse pounding in his neck but his worries eased a bit. *Is it possible that this meeting could be turned around to my advantage?* He tried to measure the effect of his request. The general smoothed out the curled end of his left mustache with the tips of his fingers.

"It is of immediate importance that this Underground be crushed."

"I understand, General."

"You have, no doubt, already heard of what happened at Neuve Chapelle a few weeks ago?"

"I heard there was a battle there with the enemy, but I thought we were victorious."

"We were, but it took us three days to recapture the front line after they broke through. We paid a very high price for that victory. They are now setting up blockades on all of our ports. We must defeat them on all fronts."

"I am hearing rumors that the Underground is housing the enemy right here in Brussels."

Von Bissing slammed his fist on the desk, making the glasses and carafe jump. "This must stop! Force is all they understand. You will have what you need. Discuss your needs with Baron von der Lancken. He will transfer the amount you request to your budget immediately."

Bergan could hardly believe his good luck. He had arrived expecting to be chastised and was leaving with all the additional resources he could ask for. Von Bissing had the power to make things happen.

"There is one more thing, General," Bergan dared to add. "There is a German detective who works out of another office. His name is Otto Mayer. He is fluent in English, French, and even Hindi, having lived in London and India. He came to Brussels because his wife is working here. He is now working undercover as a waiter in a popular local restaurant. I kindly request that he be transferred to my office to work directly under me. I can use a man with his abilities."

"I will discuss this with his captain and order his transfer to your office."

The general stood, adjusted the sword that hung from his belt, picked up the carafe of vodka, and filled both glasses again. He raised his glass. "To your great success."

Bergan stood, picked up his glass, and raised it to the general. "And to yours and that of the Fatherland."

They saluted each other and Bergan headed for the door. His hand had just touched the doorknob when he heard von Bissing say, "One more thing, Lieutenant. If you succeed in destroying this Underground, I will recommend to the Kaiser that you be rewarded with a handsome promotion when you return to Berlin."

"Thank you, General."

Bergan was delighted in what he had achieved at this meeting. He slid onto the leather back seat of his waiting motorcar. As the car lurched forward and bumped along the streets, the driver handed Bergan a newspaper. "I thought you might like to see this. One of our guards took it from a Belgian merchant who was arrested today. That guard gave it to me." Bergan took and unfolded it. It was the *Geneva Tribune*. His eyes fell on an article on the front page.

"On April 1, a French aviator flying over a German camp dropped what appeared to be a huge bomb. German soldiers immediately scattered in all directions, but no explosion followed. After some time, the soldiers crept back and carefully approached the bomb. They discovered it was actually a large football with a note tied to it that read, April Fool!"

"French idiots," spat Bergan. He crushed the newspaper and threw it on the floor.

— 49 —
THE NET TIGHTENS

As the April rain dissolved into a cool mist, Otto Mayer walked up the stone stairway of the gray granite building where the sign *Geheimpolizei* was posted in black letters at eye level. He could feel the fingers of suspense dance along his spine as he wondered why he was asked to report to Lieutenant Bergan of the Secret Police for a new assignment.

Mayer proceeded down the drab tan hallway, dimly lit every ten feet by glass lamps hanging from ceiling wires, until he came to the plain oak door of Bergan's office. He took one last pull of his cigarette, forcibly blew the smoke through his nose, threw the remaining half to the floor, and crushed it with his shoe. He wondered if this new assignment would remove him from his undercover position as a waiter. Whatever it was, as long as he remained in Brussels with his wife, it really didn't matter to him. He knocked on the marbled glass panel of the door.

"Enter," commanded the voice on the other side. Maintaining a straight bearing, Mayer entered Bergan's office and stood in front of the officer's desk. Bergan was on the telephone and motioned for him to sit in the wooden chair on the opposite side of his desk. Mayer lifted the chair away from the oak desk, dropped it down, and sat with his right leg crossed over the left at the knee.

Seeing an ashtray filled with spent cigarettes and ashes strewn around it, he motioned for permission to light a cigarette and got a nod of approval. He flipped a cigarette out of the pack directly to his lips, lit a match on the sole of his upturned shoe, put it to the tip of his cigarette, took a deep drag, and blew out the match with his exhaled smoke. Noticing a smudge of dirt on the top of his right shoe, he took out a neatly folded white handkerchief and wiped it clean. Carefully folding the soiled spot inside the handkerchief, he placed it back in his pocket. After taking two slow puffs, he saw Bergan hang up the telephone.

Bergan rose halfway out of his chair, awkwardly avoiding the papers piled on his desk to reach his hand in greeting to Mayer. Bergan noticed that Mayer was broad-shouldered and at least a head taller than himself. Bergan figured Mayer to be about ten years younger than himself. Mayer's red hair was neatly parted in the middle and his cheeks shaved so close that they shone under the light from the ceiling.

He is so clean, thought Bergan, *and so very German*. After a moment of close scrutiny, Bergan began. "I wish to thank you for transferring to my department. You were highly recommended by your superior. Your reputation is excellent."

Mayer pulled the ashtray closer to him, carefully tapped the ash from his cigarette, and with a slight tilt of his head, looked up. His voice was calm and even. "I appreciate the opportunity to work with you, Lieutenant. I will do what I can to prove your trust has not been misplaced."

Mayer's words were so evenly measured that Bergan wasn't sure if it showed a strong confidence, or maybe even arrogance.

"From what I am told," continued Bergan, "you are exactly the person I am looking for. My purpose in requesting that you be assigned to my staff is that you are fluent in French and English and, I am told, you are also very intelligent." Mayer's gaze so openly assessed him that Bergan felt as if there were a stain on his shirt. Suppressing the urge not to look down, he continued. "The Underground is wasting our time and hindering our work here. I want you to work closely with me to find out all we can to stop it."

"That will be difficult unless you have many people infiltrating different areas of the city."

"General von Bissing has given me his approval to hire more people, average-looking working people—factory laborers, farmers, merchants, and even waiters such as yourself. They will work among the Belgians and report back to me."

Mayer's chair creaked under his weight as he leaned closer to the desk. He raised his bushy red eyebrows in interest. "Do you have any specific place where you want me to start?"

"I keep hearing rumors that enemy soldiers are being billeted south of the city and are assisted to rejoin their regiments or to cross the Dutch border. We have posted warnings against this treasonous activity and the serious consequences for anyone who is caught participating in it."

Bergan opened up a file on his desk, removed a sheet of paper, and handed it to Mayer. "There are vague rumors about some type of Underground activity in Ixelles. I placed informants to work in the potato fields there. They tell me they have seen suspicious-looking men around rue de la Culture who speak neither French, Flemish, nor German. My informants think these men are English. There is a local café they sometimes go. I inspected the area myself, but saw nothing unusual. Although I have reason to be suspicious, I have no proof to that would warrant an arrest. I want you to investigate these rumors so we can act or put them to rest."

Bergan took out a map and spread it between them. He ran his finger over a thin line labeled rue de la Culture. "There is a group of houses on this street. One contains a Red Cross clinic, and the other three are used as a nurses' training school, run by an English matron whose name is…" He ran his finger down the list until it stopped near the bottom. "…an Edith Cavell. We think she is hiding soldiers in some way—maybe even working with the Underground."

He put the paper back in the folder and handed it to Mayer. "Use any means necessary to find us enough proof to expose this operation. A military post has been set up across the street. I will see that they allow you to work from there. Make no mistake. If this English woman is found to be responsible, we will not hesitate to treat her like anyone else who commits treason."

"You would put a woman before the firing squad? It says here she is a nurse who cares for German soldiers and that she works under the Red Cross."

"No matter, she is English. What better way to show our enemy that we will spare no one who defies our rule? I am willing to put all of them in front of the firing squad if I find they are committing seditious acts. We will show them what will happen if they defy us."

Mayer saw Lieutenant Bergan about to stand and knew it was a signal that this meeting was over. He spoke in a calm, almost casual voice, but with an unmistakably strong tone of purpose. "I will not disappoint you. If there is any illegal activity going on, I will find it. We will show them who is in control here."

"Please arrange weekly meetings with my secretary to report on your progress."

Mayer punched out his cigarette, tucked the file under his arm, and turned to leave. "As you wish, Lieutenant Bergan."

Just as his hand touched the metal doorknob, he heard Bergan say, "One more thing." Mayer's hand froze. "This operation is of the highest priority for the governor-general. If you succeed, I am certain I can arrange for a handsome reward and a promotion for you."

"I assure you, we will succeed. Von Bissing will be pleased with both of us."

CLINIQUE.

Sketch of the Clinique on rue de la culture where Edith Cavell worked.

— 50 —

THE INSPECTION

Elizabeth Wilkins approached a tall stranger standing in the hallway at the bottom of the stairs near the nursing office. "Is there something I can do for you?" she asked.

The red-haired man spoke in perfect English, "Have you any more left?"

"Any more nurses? I'm sorry, I'm afraid our staffing numbers are depleted. May I ask why you inquire?"

Otto Mayer unfolded his arms and riveted his eyes on Elizabeth, noticing everything about her—her posture, hands, expression—any telltale sign of lying. In a mock-conspiratorial tone, he leaned closer to her and asked, "What, no more Tommies?"

Elizabeth blinked twice and let out a breath she hadn't realized she was holding. "There are no Tommies here. Who are you, and why are you asking?"

Mayer noticed her unease as she answered him. "I am Lieutenant Otto Mayer, a member of the German Secret Police. There are rumors of Allied soldiers hiding in these buildings. Are you Mme. Cavell?"

"Mme. Cavell is the Directrice of this school but she is not here at the moment. I am Elizabeth Wilkins, the Chief Nursing Supervisor. I am in charge during her absence and can answer your questions."

He looked around the room and up the stairs. "Well, then, Supervisor Wilkins, have you any knowledge of hidden enemy soldiers?"

Elizabeth felt as if he could look through to her brain and read her thoughts. This was one of the worst times for an inspection. Edith was at the construction site of the new school and four Allied soldiers were in hiding in the basement, totally unaware that they were moments away from being captured.

"Of course not. Hiding Allied soldiers is illegal. This is a Red Cross facility. We train nurses and treat wounded soldiers—all soldiers, including Germans. That's all we do. I'll escort you around so you can see for yourself. You can start your search in my room." She brought him out of the hallway and into her own room.

Mayer went immediately to her desk and examined the papers lying on top. He opened drawers and pulled out more papers, carefully studying each one. Elizabeth fought not to show fear. *How can I get word to someone to remove the soldiers?* Outwardly, she remained calm and in perfect control.

"Here, I'll help you," she said, as she handed him paper after paper. "Here are the records of our nurses in training—and here are the food bills. We hardly have enough to feed ourselves, let alone additional soldiers."

Mayer scrutinised each sheet of paper as Elizabeth continued, "And here are our oil and coal bills, although as you can see, we haven't been able to get much of either." Elizabeth handed him every possible unimportant paper she could find. "Oh, yes and this one is the plumbing bill for fixing a leaky pipe on the kitchen sink. It made quite a mess."

Finally Mayer threw the handful of papers onto her desk. "Enough of this. Take me to your wards."

Elizabeth guided him out into the street and over into the clinic section of the row houses. All the while, her mind was racing as to how to alert the hidden soldiers. Once on the ward, Mayer inspected patient after patient, occasionally moving a bed cover for a closer look. He spoke to a few in German and others in French and seemed satisfied with their answers.

While he was talking to the patients, Elizabeth saw her chance. With Mayer no more than a few feet away, she motioned to one of her nurses on duty to come closer and managed to whisper one word: "German." The nurse immediately understood, quietly left the room, and found José, the houseboy. They had rehearsed this before.

José knew the planned escape route and where to place the men for such an emergency.

"But I must put on my shoes," protested one English soldier.

"No time, move! If you wait to put on your shoes, we will all be arrested. Now go!" A second man scrambled to get his shirt on. "No time!" urged José. The three men hurriedly gathered what they could in their arms and ran after José, who took them out the back door into the garden, and over the fence to another house used by the Underground network.

While Mayer was inspecting the soldiers in the ward, another thought jolted Elizabeth. *Edith's room! The register of soldiers she is keeping—I have to get it away from her desk before Mayer finds it. In just a few moments, Mayer will reach the end of the beds and be done here. What then?* She watched as he finished inspecting the last patient. Approving what he saw, he turned to Elizabeth. "Take me to your nurses' quarters."

"There are papers you missed here. I assume you want to be thorough." She guided him over to the ward desk. "Here are the records of our current patients and those we treated in the past. You may want to inspect them to be sure they are all in order."

She saw Mayer flip through the folder of names and carefully run his finger down the list. If there was ever going to be a chance to slip away, this was it. Moving behind a curtain, she inched over to the door. Just as she was about to leave, she heard him call out, "This patient's name here, a Private Karl Rimmel? Is he still here?"

Elizabeth slipped back behind a table piled high with bandages and started to straighten up the pile. "I remember him quite well. He had a thigh wound that needed surgery and was very sick with typhoid, so we moved him over to the main hospital. He is doing better and has been discharged. I was told he was not well enough to return to the field and was assigned to guard duty." Mayer grunted and returned to the folder.

It has to be now, before he reaches the nurses' quarters. "If you'll excuse me for a moment. I must assign my nurse to her next shift."

"Do not take long. I will be finished in a few moments."

"I'll be back straightaway."

She rushed to Edith's quarters and snatched the register, newspapers, and documents off Edith's desk. Her eyes darted around the room. *Where to put them? Under the mattress—no, too obvious. On top of the book shelf—he's too tall; he's sure to see them there. Under the sink basin—he would see them if he moved the curtain. The water closet—that's it! He won't look there for papers.* She shut the water off to the toilet and flushed it. Then she reached up to the tank, raised the lid, shoved the papers and register into the empty space, and replaced the lid. Praying that she had found and hidden everything that might be suspicious, she rushed back to the clinic.

When she got to the door, she stopped, shoved a loose hair back in place, and calmly walked into the clinic. Inside, Mayer was talking with the German physician. She walked up to him. "Do you want to inspect the nurses' school next, Lieutenant Mayer?"

"I have changed my mind. I want next to inspect Mme. Cavell's office."

"Certainly."

Once in Edith's office, he went immediately to her desk. Elizabeth stood quietly and watched Mayer riffle through every paper. Every time he held a document up and demanded, "Explain," she felt the hair on her neck rise and her pulse quicken. Satisfied with her explanations, he opened the top drawer of her desk. In the back, he pulled out a postcard and read it. "Who is this Cousin Lucy?"

"It is Mme Cavell's niece who moved to Amsterdam during the war Mme. Cavell has no children of her own, so they are very close." Mayer threw it on the desk. Elizabeth watched as he examined Edith's books, pulled aside the curtain under the sink basin, opened her bureau drawers, and shoved her clothes about. He even removed the pillows from the sofa and ran his hand along the inside seam of the sofa. He pointed to a closed door. "What is in there?"

"The water closet."

He motioned for her to open the door and walked in. Standing in place, he turned in a circle, his eyes taking in every detail. He gave a wry smile at a pair of stockings drying on a rail on each side of a dressing gown. Noticing a small cabinet next to the sink, he pulled the drawer open and shuffled through the items—a toothbrush, powder, hairpins, a comb, bottles of lotions.

Finding nothing of interest, Mayer asked to be taken to the nurses' training section in the row houses. Since the enrollment of new nurses had all but come to a halt, the school section was almost empty. He only gave a quick scan of the empty classroom and then left.

Out in the street, Mayer pulled himself up to his full height and stared down at Elizabeth. "I advise you to have nothing to do with assisting the enemy to escape. There are severe penalties for those who engage in such business." She felt the heat of his breath as he hissed out his warning.

She stared back hard into his cold eyes. "I assure you. You will find nothing of the sort on these premises."

* * * * *

E dith was in a buoyant mood as she walked back to the nurses' quarters from the new construction for the new nursing school. It was going slowly, to be sure, but she was elated that her dream of a new school would someday be realized. Just ahead of her, the clouds opened up, and a beam of sunlight shone down. It felt warm and nourishing on her skin. She inhaled the fresh air and looked up at the trees that lined the street. They were laden with green buds, pregnant with the promise of a lush spring.

When she opened the door of the nurses' quarters, she saw Elizabeth crying. Elizabeth blew her nose and spoke through the handkerchief. "Edith, it was awful. The German Secret Police were here. They know. I'm telling you, they know we are hiding soldiers here." She burst into tears. "Please, Edith. We have to stop. I hid your papers and register in the tank of the water closet only minutes before he went through your desk."

Edith removed her cloak and carefully hung it on a nearby coat rack. "The soldiers–were you able to move them out?"

"I was able to get word to José just minutes before they would have been found. You have to destroy everything that could raise suspicion." She reached out and took Edith's hand. "We have done a great work here. We have saved many who would have died, but it's time to stop--even if it's for a little while. They know, Edith. They are watching us. Please listen to me. This has to end."

Edith patted Elizabeth's hand as she would a child's and walked over to the water closet. She returned with the register, newspapers, and documents in her hands, placed them on her desk, and stared at them. "I can get rid of most of these…"

"No, all of them! There can be nothing left as evidence. Trust me, they will come back, and when they do, I may not be able to protect you when you are not here. Destroy everything. Burn it all. They may already be looking through our garbage."

Edith got up and put her arms around Elizabeth. "Thank you for all you have done. I'll consider everything you said, but I can't just simply stop. We are an important link in the Underground now. If we close down, everything else shuts down. I don't know if I can morally do that. I just can't look into the eyes of men who have been wounded to save this country and France and turn them away. I know what you are saying is true. We are at risk. I need to think about how to proceed more carefully."

"And you will destroy the papers and documents?"

Edith looked over at the pile of scrambled papers on her desk. "If I destroy all of these documents, how can I account to Marie and Antoine for what I have done with the money?"

"I think they will believe whatever you tell them. If these documents are found by the Germans, you may not get a chance to explain anything to them. I don't want them to take you away. What would I do if you were gone?"

Edith brushed aside a lock of hair that dangled over Elizabeth's eyes. "If anything happens to me, you will take over. Maybe it's time to train a Belgian nurse to learn some of your duties. It's a lot to think about, but not now." She stepped back from Elizabeth. "It's getting late. We'll feel better after supper."

After their meagre meal, Edith went to her quarters. When she opened the door, she saw that the pillows on the divan were ripped open and bits of stuffing were strewn about the floor. Alarmed that someone had rifled though her desk, she opened the drawer to find nothing missing.

When she leaned over to pick up the pillows, she glanced over at Jack and saw the sheepish look on his face. "Did you do this?"

The dog's eyebrows shifted between Edith and the pillows. "You did, didn't you?" She raised her finger in admonishment. "Bad boy!" She grabbed his collar and pushed him out the back door into the garden. "Bad boy! Out you go until I clean this mess up."

She picked up the pillows and placed them back on the couch. The crimson velvet pillow, however, was torn at the seam and much of the stuffing was strewn about. She went around picking it up from the sofa and floor and stuffed it back into the torn seam, making a note to sew it up later. Then she gathered up the newspapers and documents and stuffed them in a bag to give to José to burn. The register of soldiers' names fell open on her desk. She looked down at it, staring at the names.

No.	Rank	Name	Regiment	Arrival	Departure	Whether wounded
38.	Pte.	Stanton, E.	Middlesex	April	About 7 days	Shell shock
39.	CSM	Catty, J.	Connaught Rangers	April	Several days	Not known

Edith knew Elizabeth was right. Maybe she would talk to Philippe Baucq and the de Croÿs about backing out for a while. She would, of course, give them time to find another place to hide the soldiers. Maybe the inspections would stop then.

She looked back at the names on her list. Every man had a face and every face loomed up in her mind. She could see these men, hear them, feel their relief when she gave them a place of refuge—a safe house where they would get medical treatment. Many thought they would die, and some kissed her hands when they found out she was a nurse. She gave them a reprieve from death. Isn't that what nurses were meant to do? Restore life? Heal the wounded? What kind of nurse was she if she abandoned the very people she took vows to care for? She was nothing. A coward. Not a nurse at all. She stared at the names—Dudley Boger, Fred Meachin, Jessie Tunmore, Private Lewis, and Fred Holmes from Norfolk.

She held the register between her hands and prayed that the God who controlled the fates of men would reveal to her what He wanted her to do. When she opened her eyes, she knew she couldn't stop rescuing soldiers. If it saved just one more life, she had to keep going, even if she got arrested.

Straightening her shoulders, Edith decided to destroy all the documents but the register. It represented the lives of many she saved. She held it with both hands to her chest. *Where can I hide it so I can easily retrieve it but the Germans will not find it?* She looked around her room.

Not the water closet again; it would get wet, the ink would run, and the entire document would be lost. Not behind the books on the bookshelves; if just a few books were removed, it would be found. Maybe in the sofa—but then she remembered how Elizabeth said the police searched inside the sofa seams. She picked up the torn pillow. This might be just the right place. The stiff horsehair in the pillow would hide the shape of the little book. It could be easily removed and put back. Even if the police shuffled the pillows about, they weren't likely to look inside them. She shoved the register deep inside the crimson pillow. She sewed the opening, so it was just large enough to fit the small register, then placed it, torn side in, back on the sofa.

The next day, Edith rose early to return to the new construction. There had been a question about where to put the plumbing for the sinks and she didn't want to have them installed in the wrong place. Money for construction was always tenuous; she could not afford to do the job twice. *When Marie gets back from America with additional funds, we might have just enough to finish this,* she thought.

When she returned to the rue se la Culture nursing office, she was met at the door by a nurse. It was obvious the young woman had been crying. Her voice wavered as she spoke. "They came back."

"Who came back?" Edith demanded.

"The tall man who was here yesterday came back with two other policemen. They took her."

"Took who?"

"They took Sister Wilkins for questioning."

"Is she arrested?"

"I don't know, I don't know," the nurse said, twisting a handkerchief between her hands. "They just pushed the door open, grabbed her arms, and shoved her in a car."

"How long ago?"

"A few hours ago. They didn't even give her time to put her cloak on."

Edith lifted the distraught nurse's head up to meet her eyes. "Look at me. Tell me. Where did they take her?"

"I do not know. They just took her away. They did not say where."

— 51 —

MAPES AND MARIE

E dith rushed to the nurses' quarters to ask one of her Belgian nurses where Elizabeth might have been taken. "If it was the German police, I think they would have taken her to their headquarters at the police station," said the nurse. "I can give you directions." Edith grabbed a pen and paper from the nearby desk. "Tell me where it is. I must go to her."

"That may not be a wise thing to do. You cannot help her now. She is strong and will say nothing, but if you go down there, they may arrest you as well. Then they could use you against each other."

Edith slowly lowered her pen. The shock of what the Belgian nurse said washed over her like iced water. She remembered Elizabeth's words. *Trust me, they will come back, and when they do, I may not be able to protect you.* She felt her knees weaken and leaned against the desk to steady herself.

"Are you all right, *Madame*? May I fix you something to drink?"

Edith shook her head. With tear-stained cheeks, she walked back to her office. When she opened the door, she saw Elizabeth standing there. Edith ran to her, threw her arms around her friend, and held her tightly as if to convince herself that it was really Elizabeth. "One of the nurses just told me they took you away. What happened?"

"They came back and without warning, took me to the police station and interrogated me. They asked me about you and the work we are doing here. They tried to make me confess to hiding enemy soldiers, but I denied everything. They made me give them a list of our staff, but they couldn't find a reason to arrest me, so they brought me back. You did destroy those records, didn't you? This is not over. There will be more raids when we least expect it. There is no way we can continue to hide these soldiers. If they find just one, or a trace of one, we will all be arrested."

Edith saw Elizabeth's hands trembling and put a steadying hand on them. "I will discuss with Princess Marie de Croÿ, how we can divert these men for a while. She may be able to take in a few extra men herself, until…"

Princess Marie de Croÿ,

"….until what? Until we decide to take more in ourselves and the German police find them here, and kill them? They'll be safer trying to make their own way than they will be here."

"We will sort this out later. If they actually had evidence, they would have arrested us by now. I promised Marie I would try to find ten nurses who are willing to go work in the Red Cross field hospital in Antwerp and escort them there. She said they are desperate for more nursing help. Once I have enough volunteers who are willing to be transferred, I will return to deal with this matter."

Elizabeth folded her arms across her chest. "I need more than that. Before you leave for Antwerp, I need to be assured that you will stop hiding soldiers here."

Edith knew she could not continue to harbor soldiers without Elizabeth's help. In a tone of resignation she said, "Philippe told me there is a large house in Brussels that is taking in soldiers. I'll divert our men there."

Elizabeth unfolded her arms and put her hand on Edith's arm. "I know this is hard for you. It is for me, too. I fully believe in what we are doing, but the time has come to stop before we are all arrested. Who knows what they would do to us and those we are trying to save?"

Edith patted her hand. "Of course, you are right, Elizabeth."

"There is one wounded soldier here, but he was treated by the de Croÿ and is healing quite nicely. We will move him out as soon as possible."

"You have had enough for today. Go and have a rest. I will guide him to the new safe house before I leave," promised Edith.

* * * * *

The next day, Edith contacted Philippe Baucq and explained what had happened to Elizabeth.

"They are closing in on us," said Philippe. "We have lost many of our guides. I have been thinking of doing some of the guide work myself. We have to keep these men moving, or we will not have enough room."

"It's too much of a risk. You have two small children and a wife who need you. For their sakes don't do this. Is it possible that the de Croÿs could hold on to them a little longer until we find and train more guides?"

"Not possible. The Germans are highly suspicious of them too. The de Croÿs are trying to lower their risk and cut back on how many soldiers they take in."

He pulled a slip of paper out of his pocket and handed it to Edith. "Here is the address of another safe house in Brussels. It is not far from your new school. I will tell them to expect you."

"It is getting very hard to continue, my friend. There are so many more men than we have places to put them, or guides to take them out to Holland. I'm afraid we may have to let many of them fend for themselves."

When Edith arrived at the house of the address Philippe had given her, she was greeted warmly. After introductions, Edith asked if she could visit with the soldiers who were there. She was told that an English soldier named Private William Mapes was in an attic room and then shown the stairs leading up to it. At the top, she peered around the open door and called out. "May I come in?"

A British voice answered, "I'd love the company, Miss."

When she entered the room, she saw a young man with a dark mustache, stretched out on the bed holding the Underground's newspaper *La Libre Belgique*. A white bandage was wrapped around his ankle.

Mapes bolted up. "Sorry, sister. Didn't mean anything by that."

"Are you Private William Mapes?"

He pulled his braces over his shoulders. "At your service."

"My name is Edith Cavell. I'm a nurse who is working with the kind people here."

"Call me Billy," he said, stretching his hand out to her. "Everyone else does. Wouldn't recognize myself if you called me anything else."

Edith broke into a broad smile. "Why, you're a Norfolk man. I recognize your accent."

"Do you now?" said Billy smiling back. "Got a bullet through my ankle. It's on the mend, though. Guess it wasn't my turn to pop my clogs."

"I'm also from Norwich–Swardeston actually. My father was the vicar at St. Mary's."

"You're a long way from St. Mary's and in no good place for a fine Englishwoman such as yourself."

Edith pulled up a chair, leaned over, and stared at his ankle while she spoke. "We are working with the Red Cross over at the Clinique, or clinic, as we say in English. It has been turned into a hospital of sorts, although it is mostly staffed by German doctors and nurses now. Do you mind?"

Without waiting for an answer, she picked up his foot and began to unwrap the ankle. "We've taken care of quite a few of the Tommies from your regiment over the last few months." She examined the wound. "It is healing quite nicely."

"Yes, there's a fine group of lads in my regiment, but we all got separated when the Huns went at us. Just too many of 'em."

"Yes, I've heard the stories. All of them horrid." She rewrapped the ankle. "The wound is closed. I suspect you are out of danger for infection."

"It still pains me a bit when I walk on it."

Edith stood up. "I would have put you up at my training school, but unfortunately, we were recently raided by the German police, so I arranged with Philippe Baucq to have you brought here instead."

"Will you be back tomorrow? We can chat a bit more about good old Norfolk."

"That would be lovely, but I have to take a train to Antwerp with some of my nurses. Most likely, you will be on your way home before I return." She reached out and shook his hand. "It was such a pleasure to meet a Norfolk man. I wish you the best of luck in your journey home. I hope when we meet again, it will be on British soil."

* * * * *

Five days later, Edith returned from delivering the nurses to Antwerp. She was greeted at the door with enthusiastic tail-wagging by Jack. She talked to the excited dog as she unpacked her clothes, and placed her toiletries in the bathroom. Outside, she heard a truck rumble over the uneven stones, then the hoof beats of two horses, and the metal wheels of a cart.

Suddenly she became aware that a motorcar had approached and stopped. She hurried to the window to see it was a military motorcar. Two German soldiers with rifles over their shoulders climbed out. She made a hasty check around the room, searching for anything that could be used as evidence. She straightened up the crimson pillow. Rushing down the stairs, she opened the front door and stepped outside.

Elizabeth also saw the two soldiers and hurried to the hallway but the conversation between Edith and the soldiers was too subdued for her to hear. After a few moments, the soldiers left and Edith came back inside pale and shaken. Elizabeth was eager to welcome her home. She waited for Edith to say something, but her friend stood stunned and silent.

"What is it, Edith? Are they going to arrest us? Have they arrested someone else?"

Edith didn't answer but stared with unseeing eyes at the wall beyond Elizabeth. Elizabeth guided her friend to a nearby chair. "Come and sit down. I'll fetch you some water."

When Elizabeth returned, she offered the water to Edith, but she didn't take it. Elizabeth kneeled in front of Edith and held her hands. Looking up into her friend's tear-stained face, she said, "I've never seen you so upset. Please tell me what has happened."

Edith's voice was husky with emotion. "How can this be? It's impossible."

"What's impossible? Please tell me," begged Elizabeth, herself now in tears.

"It was torpedoed. The *Lusitania* was torpedoed by a German submarine while it was in the Irish Channel off the coast of Cork. It sank, taking thousands of lives with it."

Edith began to rock back and forth, reciting the 23rd Psalm. "The Lord is my shepherd; I shall not want. He maketh me to lie down in green pastures..."

"The *Lusitania* sank? Edith, please talk to me. Did they tell you if there were any survivors?"

Edith continued to rock. A knot in her throat made it difficult to get the words out. "Survivors? Yes, but not Marie. Marie didn't make it. She...drowned. They found her body washed up on the Irish shore."

She continued to ramble out the passage, "He leadeth me beside the still waters. He restoreth my soul."

"Marie? Which Marie?"

Edith stopped citing the prayer. "Marie DePage. She's gone. Just gone. It's horrible."

"Maybe they made a mistake in the identification."

"There were only six lifeboats of people and many were plucked from the sea by Irish fisherman. About seven hundred survived, but not Marie.

Edith felt as if she were being pulled down into a spiral she could not control. Lowering her face into her hands, she sobbed. She was not prepared for anything like this. The earth seemed to swirl beneath her. Thoughts of Marie and what this meant tumbled through her mind. *It is all wrong. Marie can't be dead. Not now. Everyone needs her. I need her. Antoine needs her. Her two boys need her. What happened to the funds she raised and those who depended on them? What about the promise that she and I would continue our work when the war is over? Marie was my rock. How can I go on without her?*

But Edith knew the world had changed. The sense of order was gone. Nothing, and no one, was spared in these unforgiving times. She felt as if she were on a dinghy out in the middle of the ocean, caught up in a dreadful storm, with nothing solid beneath her, and wave after wave washing over her. All she could do was rock back and forth and pray.

THE FRIENDLY FRENCHMAN

E dith lay half awake listening to the sounds around her. She heard the pounding of distant cannons in the predawn air and the bells of the two nearby churches that rang out five chimes. She could tell the differences between their rings. The bells of Sanctuaire de l'Enfant Jésus sounded from the right and always started first. They were deep and slow. The bells of Notre Dame de l'Annonciation came in next from the left. They had a higher pitch and a quicker chime. *Like the ones at the Norwich Cathedral that are ringing right now over my mother.*

When she opened her eyes, a slice of the early morning light pushed through the narrow opening in her curtains. Jack gave a squeaky yawn and drummed his tail expectantly against the rug by the bed, beating up little clouds of dust that danced in the shaft of morning light. She felt a chilly breeze blow in through a partially opened window. Fighting against the soreness in her joints, she propped herself up on one elbow, and slowly shifted her legs out from under the covers. Rubbing her hands up and down her arms to stay warm, she shuffled over to close the window and then sat back on the bed.

So many worries ricocheted around in her mind. *Will the ten nurses I escorted to Antwerp be safe, or did I lead them to their death? What should I do next? Marie is dead. The Germans are in charge of my Clinique and hospital. Our ability to rescue Allied soldiers is in danger. Elizabeth is upset. Why should I stay in Brussels if I can do no good? Maybe I should join Antoine and take over Marie's duties.*

She silently prayed. "My life is in your hands. Try me as You wish and I will come forth as gold, but please, Lord, show me the way."

She then addressed the expectant dog. "Time for breakfast. Then we will walk over to the new building. What do you say about that?" Jack's tail beat faster.

After breakfast, she was heading out when she was approached by two men. The tall man touched her arm and put his face close to hers. He spoke fluent French. "Madame, forgive me for approaching you, but we both need your help. I am a French soldier, and my friend here is English." He kept his voice low, and all the while his eyes darted around as if he were either looking for, or avoiding, someone.

Edith stared at him. He had a patrician's angular but handsome face. He was dressed in an ivory-colored linen shirt and striped trousers. The sun glinted off of his polished belt buckle. He lifted his trouser leg to reveal a bandaged ankle. "You see, I have been injured. It happened in the battle at Charleroi. I can barely walk; there is much pain."

His face grimaced, demonstrating his pain. "Please, Madame. I am told you are a kind woman who takes in wounded soldiers." He pulled the other man over to him. "My friend here is shell-shocked. We have nowhere else to go and are afraid we will be found and killed."

The other man was shorter and stockier, and was dressed in a gray suit. He spoke in English. "Please, we desperately need your help."

Edith motioned for them to move away from the potato farmers, who stood around doing little work. Jack positioned himself between Edith and the two men, his eyes fixed on them. When the men moved closer to Edith, Jack lowered his head, flattened his ears, curled his lip, and gave a low, rumbling growl.

The two men jumped away. "*Mon Dieu!*" said the tall man. "There is a devil in that dog!"

"No, he is just cautious. As am I. You have the code word?" asked Edith keeping a tight grip on Jack's leash.

"Code word? We were not told such a word. They only said a kind woman lived here who would help poor soldiers who needed a place to stay. Is that not true? Have we made so wrong a mistake?"

He backed away. "I apologize for begging for your help and will leave." He turned and leaning on his friend, slowly began to limp away.

"Wait. Come back. What are your names?"

"I am Georges Gaston Quien," said the tall man with a flourish of his hand, "and this is my friend. He is very much afraid to speak his name, so we call him Mr. X. You can understand his fear."

"Of course. In these times, one cannot be too careful. I think we can find a place for you." She led Quien to a room where another French soldier was staying, and the Englishman to where two English soldiers who had arrived the night before were staying. "The men here can be trusted. Rest well. I will see that the cook brings you some food."

When Elizabeth heard what Edith had done, she could hardly believe it. "You took in two men who did not know the code word? Remember the last time we did that? We found out the man was not a poor Polish workman but a German spy. And let's not forget about that Mr. Jacobs, or who ever he really was, who claimed he escaped from a German labor camp and then left pieces of paper in his room with German writing all over them. Edith, I beg you, get rid of these two. It's too dangerous to take any chances now."

"I know, but he says he is a French soldier. His ankle is too painful to walk on. How else would he have gotten that wound? I can't turn him back out into the street to be captured or shot. As soon as his ankle is healed, I'll move him out and the other man sooner. He looks like he is well enough to travel." She touched Elizabeth's shoulder. "I promise."

* * * * *

Quien had never enjoyed himself so much as now. This was even better than stealing motorcars and selling them to unsuspecting buyers. It had been a lucrative enough business until he got arrested and jailed that was. Otto Mayer agreed to release him if he took on this assignment to be billeted with pretty nurses and spy on their activities. It was an offer he couldn't pass up. The other part of the assignment was that he meet weekly with Mayer to report progress.

It was dark when he stopped in front of the gray government building on 24 Boulevard de Berlaimont. He passed the polished brass sign, *Geheimpolizei, Lieutenant Otto Mayer*, and walked down the dark hallway to where a dim light shone through a door transom. He knocked. "*Kommen*," came the low voice from behind the door.

"You are late. You were to be here at 20:00. It is…" Mayer looked at the clock on the wall "…precisely 20:12. I expect you to be prompt." He made a quick motion with his chin for Quien to sit opposite his desk.

"*Bonsoir*, Lieutenant Mayer." Quien looked around the office. "Congratulations. From the look of things, you are doing quite well."

Mayer rubbed his fingers against his forehead, trying to ward off a headache. It wasn't his idea to hire this French thief from St. Quentin prison, but he was told that Quien's fluent French and ability to trick people would get Mayer the information he needed. Mayer didn't like Quien, but Bergan was impatient for results, and he had no one else to turn to.

"Do you have information for me, or should I send you back to prison?"

"Information, monsieur? Oh yes, I have much to report." He pulled a flask from an inside pocket of his jacket and held it up. "May I? It has been a long day of doing police work."

Mayer nodded.

"I am so sorry," said Quien. "Where are my manners?" He offered the flask to Mayer. "Share?"

Mayer shook his head. Quien took a long drink from the flask and set it on the polished desk. Mayer removed it, handed it back to him, and wiped the desk where it had been placed.

Quien shrugged his shoulders, sighed, leaned back against the hard chair, and crossed one long, thin leg over the other. "Ah, yes, information. That is what you want." He noticed a speck of lint on his sleeve, removed it, and then looked up. "One cannot be too careful doing police work. It is very dangerous, as you know. I was thinking that maybe the pay is not adequate for what I am doing." He looked around at the thick drapes and framed pictures on the wall. "Maybe, since you are doing so well now, you could consider..."

Mayer's expression tightened. "I will consider nothing until you tell me what I need to know. Are they harboring enemy soldiers?"

"Oh, yes. They have them hidden all over—in the attic, in the coal cellar, and at the nurses' quarters." A wry smile formed on his lips. "Speaking of the nurses' quarters, there is a delicious peach of a Belgian student nurse who is quite willing to share her bed with me at night." He feigned a look of sadness. "You know, it gets so lonely."

"Does she know anything about the hidden soldiers?"

"She knows nothing about them. This is also true of many of the others who work there. Her only complaint is having to wear a stiff collar on her uniform."

"How many do they keep?"

"You know, when I tell the cook how her wonderful stew reminds me of my mother's cooking, she blushes and tells me how hard she works and how many she must cook for. So by simple calculation from day to day, I would say they keep anywhere from two to twenty men at any one time."

Mayer could feel his head pounding. "Who is responsible for this?"

"I am still working on that. You were right in thinking that the English nurse, named Cavell, is involved. Most likely, she is the leader of this cosy little group. I met her. Interesting woman. Older than the others. Smart, but surprisingly naïve. If you really want to know what is going on, interrogate her. I am sure you can find a way to trick her into talking."

Quien continued. "There is also a nurse named Wilkins. Pretty little thing, much too serious for her age and looks. I have won the trust of the other staff, but this one is shy about men and does not respond as the other women do. She needs a good man to loosen her up." He snapped his fingers. "With the right touch, which I have, I will win her over. It is just a matter of time. Once she is in my arms, she will sing like a canary. They all do."

"How many are involved with this treachery? How do they move them out of Brussels?"

"To be sure, there is still much more work ahead. I think the staff trusts me now, so in time, I will find the answers." He pulled out a long, thin cigarette, placed it in a sleek, wooden holder, lit it, inhaled, and blew the smoke upward. "French cigarettes are so much more refined than Belgian cigarettes. Belgian cigarettes are so uncivilized; they taste like pig dung." He held out his cigarette tin to Mayer. "Please?"

Mayer looked at the skinny cigarette.

"I have my own." He moved a glass ashtray over to Quien.

Quien continued. "There is more to this assignment than we anticipated. The women are smart, and the organization is complex. To be blunt, we agreed on a certain amount of time and money for me to do the job. It will take more of both."

"I am not one of your maidens to be played with, Quien. You have told me little more than what I already know. I need names and proof. I must know how their Underground network operates." He reached into a drawer and opened a metal box. "Here are more francs, but do not think for a moment that I will not have you arrested and thrown back in jail if you fail me. Go now."

Quien picked up the money thrown across the desk and smiled. He stood and stuffed the bills into his pocket. "I always thought you to be a reasonable man—reasonable and generous, but you worry too much. A poet once wrote, '*Where many fail, one succeeds.*' I know how to succeed."

* * * * *

The following morning, Elizabeth brought Quien his breakfast tray. "Tuck in. Your ankle is now well enough to walk. Your friend left a few days ago. Today is your turn."

— 53 —

"...BUT WAS LOATH TO PART"

Quien lifted his ankle up to the bed and rubbed it. *"S'il vous plaît,* Madame. It is so painful, I can hardly stand. I am still very sick. My stomach burns so much that I cannot eat your wonderful breakfast. I feel so weak."

Elizabeth put the tray on the bed. "Yesterday you were walking around and feeling quite fit. One of my nurses even thought you were following her. Were you?"

"Not at all. I did see your nurse. She looked so tired. I wanted to share my bottle of wine with her."

Elizabeth stared at him for a long, silent moment.

"I think I walked too much and the pain medicine has upset my stomach. Surely you can understand." Quien's eyes crawled over Elizabeth. He pulled his trouser leg up higher. "If maybe, as a nurse, you could rub my leg, it would feel so much better. Then I might be able to eat and gain enough strength to leave."

"Rubbing your leg will not improve your stomach. Drinking less wine might, though. I will discuss this with Mme. Cavell. She can decide if you need something to settle your stomach or your nerves."

He reached out and lightly touched her hand. "Your hand is so beautiful." She pulled it away. "I feel so much better when you are here with me." He patted his bed with his other hand. "Come and sit beside me. There is so much I want to know about you. Mme. Cavell is a fine woman, but she does not have your smile or your touch. If you sit here and talk to me, I might be able to eat just a little of this breakfast and rest for the journey. The sooner I eat and rest, the sooner I will be able to travel. Do you agree?"

"I'll send José to see to your tray. If you have not eaten any of it, it will be hours before we can bring you another meal."

"If you cannot stay here with a poor soldier who is wounded while risking his life trying to protect you, take the tray now. Go." He looked hurt and fell back against the pillow. "I must try to rest now. I could not sleep last night with such pain."

Elizabeth picked up the tray. With one swift movement of her foot, she slammed the door shut behind her. Edith saw her coming down the stairs with the tray in her hands. "Who isn't eating? Is someone sick?"

"That depends on what you call sick. The French soldier who was following Jacqueline around yesterday was told to pack up after breakfast and be prepared to leave today with the next group of soldiers."

Edith looked at the tray and back at Elizabeth. "And he chose not to eat before he moved out?"

"That would be too simple. He chose not to leave at all. He claims he is in too much pain to walk, and that his stomach is too upset for him to eat. He swears he wasn't following Jacqueline but admits he offered her some of his wine. He says he is too weak and tired to travel."

"We can give him something for his stomach, but I don't understand. Why isn't he anxious to get back to his family? Does his ankle look infected?"

"When I changed his dressing yesterday, it was healing properly. I see no reason for his delay."

"Let him rest today. Tomorrow I will discuss with him why he refuses to leave."

* * * * *

Later that morning, the cook was peeling potatoes over a bucket when she felt a warm hand on her shoulder. Behind her, a low voice said, "You work much too hard. I hope the nurses appreciate all that you do for them."

"M. Quien, how nice of you to visit me." She heaved up a bowl filled with potatoes and was about to dump them into a pot of water when he took it from her hands.

"Let me do that for you. This is much too heavy for a fine woman like yourself to lift."

He emptied the bowl of potatoes into the boiling water in the cast-iron pot and leaned over to inhale the aroma. "How can you make something so plain as potatoes into such a magnificent soup? And why so much? I heard Elizabeth say some of the soldiers were leaving today."

"Yes, but more will arrive tonight. They are usually brought in during the evening and are always hungry, poor things. I rarely can give them any meat now. All I have is this soup, some vegetables we grew in our garden, and black bread. It is tough as the stones, but it softens with the soup."

"Speaking of being hungry, I'm famished. I must have slept through breakfast this morning." He lifted his shirt. "Look, I am already thin as a rake. They feed us soldiers so poorly. If I lose any more weight, I will not be able to hold up my rifle when I am sent back to the trenches."

"You are much too thin. I have this bread and just for you..." She reached up into her cabinet. "...I have been saving this jar of jam. It is not much, but it will keep that skinny belly of yours filled until the noon meal. Besides, you are a good friend. I will miss you when you leave. Do you know when that will be?"

"I have not heard yet. How long are we usually kept here?"

"It could be a day or a week. I suppose it depends on how sick you are and how many guides they have."

Quien wiped a bit of berry jam from his mouth. He picked up the cup of black coffee and motioned with it towards the cook. "That blouse looks so charming on you. There are ladies in Paris who would love to own a blouse like that. Is it a special gift from your husband?"

"This? My sister gave it to me. It got too big for her when she lost weight." She smoothed down the blouse at the waist. "Do you think it suits me?"

"Absolutely charming. The horizontal red and white stripes emphasize your very womanly figure. Much too nice to be worn in this kitchen, where no one sees how beautiful you look. Of course, there are others here besides the staff who might see you wearing it."

"I cannot think of who that might be."

"What about the guides who come here to remove the soldiers? They must admire you. They must be so jealous of your husband. Are there many guides?"

"I do not always see them, except of course, to prepare a meal for them and those they are taking with them. One guide can sometimes be responsible for as many as six men. It is very dangerous work, you know. You will find that out when it is your turn to leave. They are very brave, these men. Their lives are always in danger. The Germans have spies everywhere." She pointed at Quien with a wooden spoon. "It is hard tell the difference between those who are honest and those who are spies working for..."—she shook her spoon—"...those Berlin vampires."

She stared into Quien's eyes. "But I know who they are. I can tell by looking into their eyes."

Quien gulped down the last of his bread, cocked his head, and smiled at her. "An hour spent with you is but a moment, but regrettably, I must bid you *adieu.*" He walked to the door, turned, and bowed to her. In a theatrical voice he said, "Now fitted the halter, now travers'd the cart, and often took leave; but was loath to part."

She pointed her spoon at him. "Are you quoting Shakespeare to me?"

"No, *ma chérie.* That is from *The Thief and the Cordelier*, written a long time ago."

* * * * *

E dith pulled out the four-by-six inch register she kept hidden in the pillow. She tried to remember the injuries of the two soldiers whose names she was about to enter but couldn't. So many had come through, some only staying overnight. In her small but precise hand, she wrote:

NO.	RANK	NAME	REGIMENT	ARRIVAL	DEPARTURE	WHETHER WOUNDED
50.	Pte.	Williams, H.	West Riding	Prob. June		Injuries not known
51.	Captain	Motte	French officer	End of June	About 4 days	Injuries not known
52.		Quien, Gaston	French	End of June	About 7 days	Probably ankle

As she was about to leave, Quien greeted her at the door, twisting his hat in his hands. "Mme. Cavell, I do so apologize for disturbing you."

"M. Quien. What a surprise. I do hope you are feeling better."

"My ankle pains me less."

"I have good news for you, then. We are preparing for you to leave with the next group by the end of the week."

"I am not sure I will be ready to leave by then."

"Elizabeth tells me your ankle is quite healed, and I understand from one of my nurses, who has seen you walking about, that you are doing well."

His hands worked at the soft cap. "As a soldier, I have learned to hide my pain. I am so embarrassed to ask you this. You see, I have no money. Everything I had was lost in the trenches. I want to get a letter out to my family. They have not heard from me for months, and I fear they may think me dead. I am so sorry to ask this of you, but my wife and children...I miss them so much." He wiped his eyes.

"Of course. Wait here," She went inside and returned holding a few francs out to him. "How old are your children?"

"One and three, both girls. Janine, the baby, was born with a twisted foot. My wife is not strong."

"I haven't much to spare, but I hope this helps. Also, here is a postcard. I want you to post it to me when you are safely out of Belgium, so I know you have made it. Sign it 'Cousin Lucy.'"

"*Merci, Madame.* You are so very kind to do this for me. I will never forget your thoughtfulness. I will tell my children of the wonderful nurses who saved my life."

That evening, while Elizabeth and Edith were eating supper, Elizabeth saw Quien pacing outside the dining room door. Quien caught their eyes and gestured for them to come over to him. They walked to where he stood. With his hands behind his back, he made an elegant bow. "I have a gift for the two beautiful ladies who have been so kind to me." With a flourish, he held out a bouquet of flowers, in each hand, to each woman. "*Pour vous,*" he said with a wide smile.

They took them but stood speechless. With the flowers hanging limp in her hand, Edith recovered first. "You told me the money I gave you was to contact your family."

"You gave him money?" asked Elizabeth.

"Only a few francs. He said he wanted to write to his family."

Elizabeth shook the flowers in his face. "Did you buy these with the money Mme. Cavell gave you?"

Quien gave a sheepish grin. "I wanted to do something special for you both to show my appreciation for all you have done. I did write a letter to my wife. It is a compliment to be given flowers by a gentleman. Are not beautiful women deserving of beautiful things?"

Elizabeth could hardly hold back her anger. "We can barely afford food and you buy flowers? How many loaves of bread and pounds of potatoes do you think those francs would have bought?"

Quien backed up and bowed again. "*Bonsoir.* I see I did not come at a good time. Please try to enjoy your gifts."

Elizabeth turned to Edith. "Get rid of him. I don't care how much the staff likes him or that José has named his newborn son after him, or that Grace wants to go to France with him. He must be gone by the end of this week, if we have to carry him across the border."

"You are the only one who dislikes him," said Edith, smelling the flowers. "Surely he is not the wolf you think him to be."

"If not a wolf, certainly a weasel."

Edith saw the anger in her friend's eyes and put the flowers down. "He will be out by the end of the week. I will see to it personally"

At the end of the week, against Quien's protests that he was not ready to travel, Edith saw that he was packed up and prepared to move out with the next group destined for Holland.

"We are well rid of him," said Elizabeth. "I hope I never see the likes of him again."

That evening, Edith dozed in the office while waiting for the guide, but by morning, none had come. She feared something was wrong but had no way to find out. A few evenings later, Philippe Baucq arrived with a rolled-up map sticking out of the top of his knapsack. "I've come to guide this group out of the country myself."

"It's too dangerous, Philippe. Please don't do this."

"It is no more dangerous than what we have been doing all these months. I studied the maps, and I think I can make it."

"Your work with the Underground newspaper is the only thing that keeps up the morale of the Belgians. You have a wife and two children. Send another guide," Edith pleaded.

"There are no more guides. They have all been killed. The new guards have reinforced the fences with live wires. One guide was electrocuted."

Philippe Baucq stopped and looked at Edith with a puzzled expression. "Have you heard about the new guard at the North Station in Schaerbeek who is lenient in examining the passports and papers? His name is Rammler or Rummel, and he walks with a limp. 'A war wound,' he told one of our men as he examined his passport."

"Was he tall and blond with a slight cleft in his chin?"

"That sounds like him. Do you know him?"

"He came to our Clinique with a severe thigh wound and quite sick from typhoid. His name is Karl Rimmel."

"Karl Rimmel. I will remember him. He may just come in handy one of these days." He put his hand on Edith's shoulder. "The truth is, we are coming to the end of our work here. German police are everywhere. I have prepared my family for what might happen. My wife knows I may be arrested at any time. We have made preparations if that should happen. I spoke to our oldest girl, and told her if the police question her about me, she is to tell them she knows nothing of what I do. I know it's dangerous but even Prince de Croÿ is sometimes serving as a guide now. *C'est la guerre.* What else can we do?"

JUST DO YOUR DUTY

E lizabeth was on her way to the kitchen to tell the cook how many people to prepare meals for that evening when she heard a familiar masculine voice.

"Mme. Wilkins, look who is here," said the cook as Elizabeth entered. "What a wonderful surprise to see M. Quien again. He has a special mission. Tell her about your new assignment, Gaston."

He winked roguishly. "*Ma petite colombe*," cooed Quien. "How delightful to see you again."

Elizabeth glared at him. "What are you doing back here? You were sent to Holland a week ago. Why aren't you on your way to your family?"

"You are as lovely as ever. I feel as if you and the wonderful staff here are my family," said Quien.

"What is your new assignment?" Elizabeth inquired in a neutral tone.

"I should not be telling you, because it is a secret mission, but you are such a good friend, I will take my chances."

Elizabeth crossed her arms over her chest, leaned against the table, and waited.

"When I got into Holland, the French officials there offered me money to return to Brussels as a spy for them. It is dangerous work, but I need the money for my family. I have word that my poor wife is living with her parents because she cannot afford to feed the children. I am a responsible man who wants to provide for his family. You can understand this."

"Do your mission somewhere else. You can't stay here," said Elizabeth, in no uncertain terms.

Quien gripped his chest as if he had been severely wounded. "The slings and arrows of an outrageous fortune." He looked over at the cook. "That, *mon cher*, is Shakespeare."

Elizabeth gave him a disgusted look and left to look for Edith. When she stepped into the Clinique, she was immediately confronted with confusion. Doctors shouted orders; nurses scurried around with basins and bandages; soldiers called out for help and moaned in pain. There was an odor of alcohol, sweat, pain, fear, and something else she couldn't identify. She searched the chaotic room until she saw Edith in the far corner leaning over a blood-soaked soldier who was violently coughing.

"Edith, could you step aside for a moment? I have to talk to you."

"Is it important? I can't leave him."

"Yes, very important. Gaston Quien has returned. He now claims he is working as a spy for the French officials in Holland."

Edith wiped her hair aside with the back of her bloody hand. "I'm sorry. I meant to tell you earlier, but this group of wounded soldiers were brought in and I couldn't leave. Quien came by this morning offering me flowers again. I didn't have time to talk to him. He said his foot became painful again, so he returned. He didn't say anything about working as a spy."

"He is right about one thing: he is a spy, but not for the French. I think he is a spy for the Germans. Please do not take him in again."

"Do as you wish, then, Elizabeth. Tell him to leave. Escort him out if you must, but I hope you are wrong, because if you are right, we may all be in serious trouble. Philippe guided Quien's group into Holland. He, and everyone who worked with him on that trip, may be in danger. There's nothing we can do now but to get a note to him."

"*Helfen Sie mir!*" called out the physician to Edith.

"Elizabeth, I must get back. They just brought in a group of German and British soldiers, and their injuries seem to be quite severe and haven't been sorted. I have to go. When I get back, I'll write a note to Philippe warning him of Quien."

Edith returned to the ward just as they brought in a man on a stretcher. His face was a deep red and he was coughing up a frothy sputum. She pressed a dressing to his arm wound just as he gripped his throat and thrust his head over the side of the stretcher and heaved. His nail beds were blue. She wondered if she had missed a chest wound and turned him back to examine him.

Both eyes watered profusely as he struggled to open his them. His gaze swam about the room unfocused until it lit on her hands tying a knot in the gauze, then traveled up her arms and to her face. His cracked lips curled into a stiff half-smile, and his eyes focused on hers. In a hoarse whisper, he gasped out the words, "G'day, Miss Edith. Fancy...meeting you here."

"Rob MacFarlane! My God, what happened?"

He broke out in a bout of coughing and wheezing. After a long, raspy breath he said, "Gas. The Huns are using it."

"What kind of gas?"

"Dunno." He broke out in a spasm of coughing, then wheezed to catch his breath. "It was green. Too late to run. Blinded me. Everything's blurry."

His pulse was too rapid to count. Respirations were forty per minute.

"Does your arm hurt?" Edith asked.

"Not now...that I have...my own...Florence Nightingale." He tried to move his wounded arm, but it remained lifeless. He stared at the limp arm in astonishment and then back to her, silently seeking an answer. She recognized the yellow-stained, disfigured fingers, now lifeless at the end of his mangled limb.

"Your arm is in a bad way. I'm sorry to say it most likely will have to be amputated."

He gave a weak smile through cracked lips. His breath emanated an odor of stale nicotine, dried blood, and vomit. "That hand was...no good anyway." His eyes darted around the room. "Where am I?"

"You have been captured and brought here. You are a prisoner now."

"Oh, God, no..." He fell back. His entire body jerked in a violent volley of coughing.

Suddenly the door flew open and three policemen holding rifles burst into the room. Edith looked up and saw one rifle was aimed at her. "You. Come with us." Edith straightened up and wiped her bloody hands on her white apron. She felt fear in the pit of her stomach but willed herself not to show it.

She was shoved out the doors, where another officer stood. His brow was furrowed beneath his cropped, military hair. "I am General Luttwitx, working under the orders of General von Bissing. You must stay here while we search these premises for enemy soldiers."

"I will be most willing to show you..." A hand was held up in her face. "*Nein.* If you want to be so helpful, watch for enemy soldiers not to escape."

Edith stared into the man's face. "I am a nurse, not a jailer. I treat wounded soldiers, no matter who they are. If your prisoners must be watched, bring in your own warden."

His cold gray eyes glared back. "Go back in there, but do not leave until I tell you." Before he left, he spoke quietly to the physician, gesturing toward her.

Edith's mind churned, trying to think how she could warn someone. The coal cellar. *If I can sneak down there, I can go under and up to the nursing office.* She saw the German physician move closer to her and knew he was following orders to watch her. Had they cleaned up after the last group of soldiers? Was anyone new brought in during the day?

The physician leaned over Rob McFarlaine, studied him a minute, and put his ear to the soldier's chest. He placed two fingers against the wounded man's wrist, then against the side of his neck, waited, and stood up. "He's dead." With a wave of his hand, he summoned the two stretcher carriers.

"Move the Aussie out of here." Edith felt the sting of tears. She stood momentarily transfixed, looking at the physician and then back at Rob, unable to believe what she had just heard.

"What killed him?"

"Chlorine gas. It fills the trenches so the men cannot breathe. It destroys their lungs. We have not seen it here before now, because most die from it in the trenches."

"That's horrible."

"War is horrible. Do not be so quick to judge us. The French started using gas against us months ago."

Edith knelt beside the lifeless soldier and ran her hand over his open eyes to close them. His face still warm, she felt the roughness of his sandy stubble against the palm of her hand. With bowed head, she silently prayed. The prayer was as much for those who might be found by the Luttwitx, as it was for the soul of the man who had just died.

A hand tightened around her arm and jerked her up. "Off your knees. He is dead. There is nothing more to do. Come with me." The physician led her over to the bed of a German soldier who gripped the sides of his bed and moaned in pain. The lower part of his right leg was angled outward. A bloody circle formed around a white shard that poked through his gray uniform.

"Compound fracture of the tibia and fibula. Prepare him for surgery." As the doctor turned to walk away, he said, "Don't pray over him. Just do your duty as a nurse."

Gas mask used in WWI.
(Photo by author in WWI Museum in Ypres, Belgium.)

— 55 —
THE MESSAGE

Elizabeth was able to explain everything to Luttwitx's satisfaction, although the few English soldiers staying in the building barely escaped. They were bought to the empty building next door until another hideout could be found.

Someday, thought Edith, *these "inspections," as the Germans liked to call them, will prove deadly.* To warn Philippe about their suspicions of Quien, Edith gave Jacqueline Van Til a note to take to him and money for a taxi to Schaerbeek, where he lived. The six-mile distance made communications with him difficult and slow. "Get this note to him straightaway. It is very important that he read it at once," Edith told the young woman.

Edith worried, not so much for herself, but for her staff, and her friends in the Underground. She had been able not to involve Grace, but she had no choice but to involve José, Marie, and the cook. She worried what her mother would think if she got arrested. Would she know that her daughter had remained steadfastly dutiful and patriotic? Edith decided to write to her mother again and give some hidden clues, but try not to alarm her. If she mentioned nothing about the Germans in it, it might get through.

Monday, June 14, 1915

My darling Mother,
Very many happy returns of your birthday & my best love &
good wishes. I have always made a point of being home for July
6, but this year it will not be possible. Even if I could leave the
country, to return takes a long while, for I heard that England
expects 2 months notice before giving a passport. It is still a
long while to your birthday but I am not sure of having another
occasion of sending this. Letters take a long time to arrive—I

still have no more recent news of you than your letter of Jan 24—except a word from a lady who crosses sometimes & says you are very well—for this I am grateful.

She paused. If she got arrested, her mother must know how to contact the right agency in Brussels.

Do not forget if anything very serious should happen, you could probably send me a message thro' the American Ambassador in London (not a letter).

Our new school is still unfinished and I see no prospect of moving in.

She missed talking with her mother and hated hiding behind veiled statements. She wanted to talk about the raids, the hidden soldiers, how brave Elizabeth was, the spies in the streets, and potato fields, and the dangerous Frenchman, but if she did, her letter might be censored, giving them all the proof they were looking for.

I should like to say more but leave all the interesting things till I see you again. I should be glad to know if Mr. Jemmett has sent me the £50 I asked for thro' the Embassy. If not, I hope he will do so at once—as we are needing money.

A knock interrupted her. "Come in," Edith called out as she blotted the ink.

The door swung open and Jacqueline rushed in. Her face was flushed and her brown eyes wide. Her hair was scattered about her shoulders and fell forward as she leaned over Edith's desk. Holding her side, Jacqueline blurted out the words in short phrases, trying to catch her breath. "So sorry...to rush in on you...but you must know what happened."

"Please, sit down. Let me fix you some tea. Tea has a way of calming the nerves."

Breathing heavily and still gripping her side, the younger woman sat stiffly on the chair. "No, thank you. I'm so sorry. I am here to tell you..." She gulped in some air and handed the note back to Edith.

"I could not deliver your message to M. Baucq…When I approached his house, I saw M. Quien there with a woman." She stopped and took a few more deep breaths. "After he left, two men, one in a military uniform and the other in civilian clothes, stood outside M. Baucq's house talking and pointing to it. I stayed hidden, then ran to a friend's house, but could not stay there either. They told me that just a few hours before, her husband and father were arrested."

"Arrested for what?" asked Edith, handing Jacqueline a handkerchief to wipe away the tears streaming down her cheeks.

"The police found out they had billeted a few French soldiers."

Nurse Jacqueline Van Til, who worked with Edith Cavell during the last five years. (Source: *With Edith Cavell in Belgium* by Jacqueline Van Til, New York, H.W. Bridges, 1922.)

— 56 —

VISIT FROM A PRINCESS

E dith felt as if she had no control over subsequent events. They slithered around her, slowly squeezing the life out of her. An unexpected visit from Princess Marie de Croÿ reinforced these feelings. She had once met the Princess's brother, but this was the first time she had met the Princess. Marie didn't look very much like her brother. Her face was small and narrow. Her chin was weak, and her eyes small and languid. She looked as if she had lived a pampered life and would crumble under the slightest pressure, but Edith knew nothing could be farther from the truth. The noble siblings had turned their château at the Bellignies into a hospital, and by sheer will power and courage, they had managed to rescue hundreds of soldiers behind the backs of the Germans.

"While I am so pleased to have finally met you, I do wish you hadn't come," said Edith. When she saw the alarm in the Princess's face, she quickly added, "Not because I don't want to meet you, but because I fear putting you in danger. They are very suspicious of our activities." Edith gestured out the open window. "See those men working across the street? We believe they are spies sent to watch us. And over there..." She pointed to the second floor of the building across the street, "...is the new German military headquarters for this area. They have guards on every corner and patrol the streets."

As Edith spoke, the Princess sipped on weak tea and looked around the prim living room with its stiff chairs and faded crimson pillow propped up in the corner of a worn divan. The drab walls were brightened by bookcases filled with books, and a picture of a cathedral. She looked back into the intelligent, blue-gray eyes of the nurse who had been her contact in Brussels all these past months. She had envisioned Edith taller and more robust, not the pale, thin woman with gray-streaked hair now sitting in front of her. She was aware, however, that Edith's calm voice revealed her fortitude and strong sense of purpose. The Princess cleared her throat as if to make an announcement. "Then you will understand why I came here. It is to say that we must stop our work. We, too, are being watched very closely. Search parties have gone through the château so often that we can no longer safely hide any more soldiers."

Edith sipped her tea. "I know about those inspections. We've had our share of them. In fact, we had to destroy many of my records for fear of them being found and used against us. I kept careful financial records, but now I don't know how to show Dr. DePage how the money was used."

"You need not worry. After the war, my brother and I will be your witnesses that the money was put to good use—that is, of course, if any of us are still here to bear witness to anything after this ghastly war." The Princess put her hand on Edith's. "My dear friend, we have done a good work, no, a great work. But I fear now that they are well aware of our activities, and we have no choice but to stop."

Edith could not help but think of the irony of circumstances that brought the two of them together. Here was an aristocratic Belgian princess who had grown up in a castle with every comfort and luxury, attended to by servants, living a life of wealth and culture; and a nurse who grew up living the plain and simple life of a vicar's daughter, who had drawn pictures to raise money for a Sunday school building, and had worked with London's most impoverished and destitute.

"Can we safely stop, then?" asked Edith. "I mean, are there any more men right now that need refuge?"

Startled at the question after the conversation they had just had, the Princess hesitated to answer her, and for an instant, she thought it best to lie. But when she looked into Edith's intense eyes, she knew she had to tell the truth. She now saw for herself what others had told her: it was Edith's eyes that revealed the power within her.

"Yes, there are."

"How many?"

"Louise Thuliez just found thirty soldiers near Cambrai."

Edith straightened and said, "We have no choice, then. We must continue. How can we live knowing we found these men, gave them hope for survival, and then abandoned them to be captured or shot? If they are killed because we were not there for them, we have betrayed their trust and their death is our fault."

The Princess looked out the window and saw two men leaning on shovels, smoking and glancing in their direction every few minutes. She shifted her gaze back to Edith. "If your suspicions about spies nearby are true, we cannot bring them here. If you will continue to direct the guides from here, I will contact Mme. Bodart, M. Baucq, and some of the others in our network, to find these soldiers another refuge. It will not be easy to move them out of the country. Many of our guides have been killed and friends have been arrested."

"Princess, we have seen some people outside Philippe's house who we believe are spies. I was unable to get this warning to him." Edith handed the Princess the message Jacqueline had not been able to deliver.

"I'll give it to him. I planned to meet with him after my visit with you today."

* * * * *

When Edith described to Elizabeth the conversation she had with the Princess, Elizabeth was fearful. "Please, Edith, you have done more than your part already. Look at how many lives have been saved because of you. She is right; it is time to quit."

"I've agreed to limit our involvement, but I cannot completely stop when there are men still desperate for help. Elizabeth, I don't take this situation lightly, but I simply can't sit by and do nothing. Can you? I can't live with myself knowing I turned my back on those men. Isn't saving people from sickness and death what we as nurses have vowed to do?"

Their conversation was interrupted by a loud and urgent knock at the door. Edith rushed to open it with Jack running behind her and barking. At the door, standing in the rain, was Ada Bodart, holding an umbrella. "I am so sorry to bother you. May I come in?"

Edith reached her hand out. "Of course. May I take your umbrella?"

"No, thank you. I cannot stay. I have urgent news to tell you."

"What is it, Ada?"

"The Princess de Croÿ was here earlier, is that right?"

"Yes, of course."

"And you told her you were being watched and that she should be careful?" Ada asked in a tense voice.

"All of that, and detailed directions as to how to leave here without being seen. Why?"

Water from Ada's umbrella dripped into Edith's shoes.

"Oh, dear," she said, as she leaned over and tried to sop the water up with her handkerchief. "I'm so sorry."

"Not to worry. The shoes will dry. Tell me about the Princess."

"She was arrested after she left here."

"Arrested! By whom and for what?"

"I don't know exactly. My friend overheard two men talking about it at *Chez Jules*. He could only pick out a word or two. One man spoke French, and the other spoke German. My friend knows French and enough Flemish to get the idea of the conversation. He said the German mentioned a man named Mayer and another named Pinkoff."

Edith and Elizabeth exchanged knowing looks.

"Did they say where they took the Princess?" asked Elizabeth.

"He was not sure, but he thought he heard them mention rue de Berlaimont."

"Rue de Berlaimont!" said Edith, her stomach dropping. "That's the new police headquarters."

57

LA LIBRE BELGIQUE

L ieutenant Mayer threw the newspaper across the table. The front page of *La Libre Belgique* fell with its headlines face up; "Belgians Demonstrate Pride on Independence Day."

"Who writes this meaningless garbage? I want it stopped. This rubbish incites them to defy us, and these childish demonstrations force us to pull our soldiers away from where they are needed."

Quien picked up the paper and read the article. "To be sure, it does do that, although 250 men gathering at the Place of Martyrs is impressive. I thought you knew that July 21 was the Belgian Independence Day."

"Yes, we knew about it. We put notices everywhere that all demonstrations on this day were forbidden. They not only defied our edict by gathering in public places, but also shut down their businesses."

Quien smiled, reached into his pocket, and pulled out a boutonniere of red, black, and yellow ribbons. He twirled it around in his fingers, and then held it out to Mayer. "A little girl was throwing these over a balcony at the Grand Place. Pretty little thing--the girl, not the boutonnière."

Mayer glared at it. "You are not here to bring me ribbons. Do you have anything to tell me, or should I have your worthless carcass thrown back in jail, where you really belong."

"Am I not doing what you asked? I gave you enough information about the Princess de Croÿ to arrest her," Quien said.

"For what good it did. I had to release her."

"Release her? Why release her when it took so much planning to arrest her? I am sure she is part of the Underground."

"True, but she is from an aristocratic family admired by the Belgians. If I had jailed her, their little demonstration would have turned into a riot. Not that I care much about killing the bastards or their princess, but it would only make a volatile situation much worse. We know where she and her brother are harboring fugitives, so we know where to find them. She denied everything, of course, but they will talk when we are ready. Those nurses will, too. We will soon close the noose," Mayer tapped the tips of his fingers together.

"Ah, yes, the nurses. You know, their new building is soon to be finished. I see them carrying furniture over to it." Quien paused. "You did know they were building a new nursing school."

"Of course. What of it?"

"That might be where they are hiding the enemy."

"I will send a spy over to say he is interested in renting a room for a generous price. Maybe they will want the money and show him around," Mayer said.

"Perhaps," said Quien, picking up the newspaper and holding it between himself and Mayer. Mayer grabbed and crushed it, then threw it in the wastepaper basket.

"Look at me when you are talking to me, Quien. Do you have any other information?"

"That newspaper you just threw away—the writing is good, yes?"

"I care nothing about how good the writing is. I want it to end," Mayer made a fist and almost pounded it on his desk.

In his most conciliatory tone, Quien said, "I was thinking, maybe the writing is too good to come from a common worker. It must be written by someone who is educated. Do you agree?"

"There are thousands of educated people in Belgium. Do you know something?"

"I have been watching a house in Schaerbeek for a few days. It belongs to an architect named Philippe Baucq. It is possible one of Cavell's nurses saw me there. If she did, I was with a certain beautiful woman and we…"

"Forget the woman and get on with it," Mayer gestured his impatience.

"I noticed that many people go there and leave with bundles under their arms. If M. Baucq is not writing this newspaper, I think he is printing it."

Mayer jumped out of his chair. "Tell me where this Baucq lives, and I will send my officers to arrest him."

Quien noticed Mayer's reaction. He leaned back in his chair and crossed one leg over the other. "You could do that and you will catch one traitor, but tell me, what is better than one traitor? Ah, two traitors, is it not? Does that interest you, or would you prefer to rush in and get just this one?"

Mayer sank back into his chair. "Of course two is better. How can we catch them?"

Quien twisted his ankle around to inspect his shoe. "Have I mentioned that I am out of francs? The soles of my shoes are getting thin. They will split the next time it rains, and considering how often it rains here...I need more francs. I had to hire an attractive escort so as not to look suspicious. She cost more than I had on hand, but she was willing to wait for her pay."

"I'm not paying for your escort," Mayer glared.

"Let me explain it better to you. If I do not pay her by tomorrow, she may not stay as quiet as she promised, and you will lose your chance to surprise the two I told you about. Word will spread. Your superiors will not be pleased if they hear that the man responsible for this annoying little newspaper escaped from under your nose. I understand you have been given quite a large sum of money to carry out this mission. It is Lieutenant Bergan's top priority, is it not?"

Mayer stared at Quien. Both became aware of the wall clock ticking away the seconds. A car outside backfired, then rumbled over the cobblestones. Mayer opened the side drawer, pulled out a tin, unlocked it, reached in, and slapped a handful of francs on the desk. "Here are your francs. There will be no more until I know you are telling the truth." He closed the box, placed it with exaggerated care back into the drawer, and leaned so close to Quien that Quien could smell his shaving soap. "Now, who is this other person?"

Quien picked up the money and counted it. "Is this all you can spare for the person who is about to give you enough information to justify your promotion? Did I mention that the nurses have turned me out? I am having difficulty finding a place to stay. This amount will not last very long."

"Do not trifle with me, Quien, or it will be the last franc you will ever hold. Maybe you should spend less time in bed and more out in the field. I can arrange for you to live temporarily at the German headquarters."

Quien cleared his throat. "You are much too kind. I will look around. There is another young woman who frequents M. Baucq's house. I have also seen her at the nursing school talking to Nurse Cavell. I think she is some kind of messenger. Whatever she is, I am sure she is part of the conspiracy. If you arrest both of them, I think you will find they will lead you to others."

"Get out there, and find out if this woman follows a schedule. When we know she is at Baucq's house, we will arrest them both." He stroked his chin in thought. "I need to find out more about this Nurse Cavell."

"I am told by a young nurse who works on her staff that Cavell is very close to her mother, who lives in the east of England. Do we know anyone in England who can visit the mother and find out more about her daughter's activities here? Maybe she has written her mother a letter, or perhaps some of the men she helped to escape have been in contact with her."

"I can arrange that. There is more than one way to skin this cat," Mayer leaned back in his chair, barely able to contain his impatience.

* * * * *

It was a warm evening on the first day of August when Louise Thuliez headed to Philippe's house, hurrying down the quiet, gas-lit streets. It felt like the evenings before the war. The air was filled with night sounds—a baby cried, a couple argued, a dog barked in the distance and another answered, a cat yowled from a backyard fence, and a distant voice sang to the chords of a guitar. The scent of freshly mowed grass wafted from the churchyard. Louise loved this city and everything about it. She used to bring her schoolchildren here on field trips.

It was late when she reached Philippe's house. She felt a wave of relief when the door opened and Philippe welcomed her in. He took her overnight bag and guided her up the narrow flight of stairs to the attic where his wife, Yvonne, his two children, and his two nieces were tying the newspapers into small packages.

"It is late," said Philippe. "We are almost ready for tomorrow's delivery. After breakfast tomorrow, we will discuss plans for moving the next group of soldiers out of Brussels. I spent the day printing up four thousand copies of the August edition. My head hurts and my neck is stiff. I am going to get some fresh air." He snapped a leash on his German shepherd, who wagged his tail in anticipation. "And my friend here also needs a break. I will be back in a few minutes."

He stepped out into the air, feeling the warm breeze brush by his face. The dog tugged at his leash.

"Philippe Baucq," said a voice behind him. It was more of a demand than a question. He whirled around, getting the leash wrapped around his legs. Six men in civilian clothes, hats pushed down over their eyes and scarves across their faces, stepped out from between the houses and grabbed his arms. His dog leapt up and down, barking at the strangers. "We have some questions to ask you," said the voice behind him.

"Let me take my dog back into the house. We can talk inside." He pulled his arms free from the guards and unwound the leash from his legs, but then hands clamped down on each of his arms as he half-walked and was half-dragged into the entranceway. The dog continued to bark. Once inside the house, he shouted, "I don't know what the police want with me. Why are you here? Are you going to arrest me?"

One of the men named Sergeant Pinkoff scowled. "Silence! Or I will close your mouth for you." He had a muscular build and was much taller than Philippe. Philippe noticed a disfiguring purple birthmark extending from his left ear to his nose.

Louise first heard the barking, and then Philippe's voice. She ran to the window and saw three strange men standing outside. "Police! Outside! They have Philippe."

"Quick!" said Yvonne. "Heave these out of the window. If they see us with them, we will all be arrested." Louise trembled as she tossed bundles of newspapers out of the open window on the side of the house. Yvonne tried to stack them on the ledge, but some of the piles fell, and broke open when they hit the ground.

Papers flew out from between the houses and into the road. One of them flew against the leg of one of the police officers. When he leaned over to pluck it off, he saw other papers flying out from the side of the house.

"Over here!" he called to the others. He ran to the side of the building. Just as another bundle fell, he reached out and caught it. "Get them! They are upstairs throwing newspapers out the window!"

Pinkoff pointed to Philippe. "You watch him," he said to the second policeman. To a third, he said, "And you come with me." They bolted up the stairs and burst into the attic, where they were surprised to see one child, three teenage girls, and two women with stacks of newspapers in their arms. Newspapers lay in random piles over the floor. Pinkoff recognized Louise as the woman who had recently entered the house. He removed his pistol from its holster and pointed it at them. "Everyone, downstairs."

The youngest girl began to cry. "Mummy, I'm afraid."

Yvonne hugged her and whispered into her ear. "Remember what your father told you."

Pinkoff questioned Louise and Philippe's family on their involvement with the newspaper and the resistance organization. He took notes on everything they said. He ransacked the house and confiscated anything of interest. By two o'clock in the morning, he had lists of names and addresses and a handful of correspondence.

"You and you," he said, pointing to Philippe and Louise, "come with me." He turned to the women. "The rest of you remain here, but I warn you, there will be a guard outside your house. Do not leave without permission."

At the police headquarters, he placed the many lists and stacks of correspondence on Mayer's desk. At Mayer's request, Bergan was also there, waiting for the police to bring back the suspects. "We'll put them in jail. It is late. We can question them in the morning," said Bergan as he shuffled through the pile of papers.

One letter especially interested him; the envelope looked somewhat official. He picked it up and opened it. It began, *Dear Philippe.* He scanned through the letter, which warned Baucq to be cautious because he was being watched by the German police. It was signed *Edith Cavell.*

58

A MAN WITH A COCKNEY ACCENT

L ouisa Cavell was worried sick for her daughter. She prayed Edith would escape from Belgium, and waited with apprehension for a letter saying she would be returning home. Many of the soldiers Edith had rescued came to Louisa's house and told her how Edith had nursed their wounds and saved their lives. Some brought her letters from Edith that said she was well, but Louisa knew Edith was hiding something. If Edith helped these soldiers to escape, why doesn't she escape herself?

It was early in August when the Chief of the Norwich Constabulary came to her house. Under the glare of the afternoon sun, sweat rolled down his flushed face. He removed his cap, and mopped his face with a wrinkled tan handkerchief. He tucked the limp cloth into his back pocket, pulled out an envelope from inside his uniform jacket, and handed it to her.

"Mrs. Cavell, this post was just delivered. It is from the MI5. I was told to bring it to you straightaway."

Her heart pounded like a mallet against her ribs as she ripped open the envelope. Was she being informed that Edith was wounded or even worse, had been killed? Her mind raced. No, that can't be. If any of it were true, the Chief Constable wouldn't tell her by simply handing her a note. She looked at his expression to find a clue as to what was in the letter, but his face remained expressionless. She unfolded the letter and her eyes scanned the neatly written words.

Brougham House, Crowthorne
BERKS
28 July, 1915

Dear Mrs. Cavell,
I am a member of the Ladies Committee who works with your
daughter, Mme. Edith Cavell, at the L'Ecole Belge pour les

Infirmières. Edith is an old friend of mine and I would gladly help her in any way I could.

I have a message from my husband, the Count de Borchgrave, who is still in Brussels, asking me to write to you to tell you not to speak to anyone about your daughter. I am told to warn you that a certain man with a reddish face, and a short moustache with a real cockney accent will visit you asking for information about Edith.

He will tell you he has a flower shop at Forest Hill in London. His inquiries will not be for the benefit of your daughter. He is working for the German police. You must send him off without speaking to him.

I have taken a great risk in contacting the police to get this message to you. I am sorry I cannot tell you more at this time. Please let me know that my letter has reached you.

Yours Sincerely,
Ruth de Borchgrave

Louisa remained composed as she read the letter. When she finished, she was surprised to see that her hands were shaking. She carefully folded it, and looked up at the Chief Constable. There was a tremor in her voice. "Is my daughter in danger?"

His tone was noncommittal. "I don't know enough about it to fully understand its measure. It was posted to my office with instructions to give it to you straightaway. Are you all right, then?"

She felt the blood drain from her face. Her knees weakened, as every bit of energy drained from her. Seeing her face turn white, he picked up the slight woman in one sweep, carried her in, and placed her on the settee. "Shall I fetch you some water?"

"No, I'll be all right. Thank you for bringing this to me. I would offer you some iced tea, but I need to be alone now and think about what this means."

"May I look in on you later?"

"No, this is a bit off your patch. You have enough to do. I'll call my son to come over."

After the Chef Constable left, Louisa clutched the letter to her chest. She thought of the bond that held her and her daughter together, no matter what the distance and circumstances, when a growing heaviness in her chest soon became a pressure.

Louisa tried to breathe the pressure away, but it persisted. Her arms felt disembodied from the rest of her and she couldn't lift them. The pressure turned into a pain that spread up into her neck and jaw. It was so intense that she couldn't speak. In desperation, she prayed to God to help her.

— 59 —
PAIN AND PROMISES

n oppressive summer haze lay heavy over the city as José and Jacqueline piled chairs and tables onto a cart they had borrowed from a neighbor. The heat sapped their energy, but this would be the last load of bulky furniture to haul to the new school and nursing quarters. José went looking for help to pull the cart while Jacqueline guarded its contents.

Elizabeth was packing up the last of the laboratory equipment when she saw Edith come in. She put the box on the floor and ran the back of her hand over her forehead. "Just a small breeze would help. I can barely breathe in this heat, but I'm just about finished here. You don't realize how much you have until you have to move it." She put her hands on her hips and stretched her back.

Edith looked into the box. "Please be careful with these glass tubes. Wrap each individually so they won't break. It's almost impossible to get new equipment now. If they don't arrive safely, you won't have much of a laboratory."

Elizabeth wondered about the use of "you" instead of "we."

"Two of my favorite people!" interrupted a voice from the door.

Edith turned to see the Prince de Croÿ coming over to them. "As are you one of mine," answered Edith. "Let's get out of this mess and go to one of the few places where you can still sit down without getting your clothes dusty." She led the prince out of the laboratory and into her office. He hefted a bag off his shoulder, dropping it to the floor with a thud, then flopped onto the divan leaning against the crimson pillow. "Do you know why I am here, Mme. Cavell?"

"If you are referring to the arrest of Philippe and Louise, I am sick with worry for them."

"Since you know this, you must also know that unfortunately the end of our work here has come." He removed the pillow from behind him and tossed it to the other end of the divan. "I assume you have destroyed all evidence that could be used against you."

Edith watched the pillow fall against the arm of the divan. "Everything was destroyed a long time ago. I'm certain they will find nothing, but if they know about Philippe and Louise, they must also know, or will soon know, that we are involved as well. I wouldn't be surprised if I were arrested any day now."

"I hate to agree with you, but you are probably right. Actually, that is why I am here. You understand that I must leave Belgium very soon. I beg you to consider doing the same. My sister insists on staying, but you could pack a small bag and leave with me. There are still people remaining who will help us over the border."

"Dear Prince, for me to try to escape is not only unthinkable but is also futile. I know the entire organization is collapsing, but I still have my work here. I had it before I started working with you, and I want to continue. There are so many things still undone, and my staff depend on me. They have been so loyal. What kind of message am I giving to them if I run away?"

"I agree." He stood up. Edith watched him pace around the room. When she first met him, she had thought he was a handsome man, but now his eyes were hollow, and his too-lean jaw was covered with several days of rough brown stubble. He rubbed it as he paced. "If you will not consider leaving Belgium, then you must hide. If you want to survive to finish your work, drop out of sight immediately. I see no other option. I know a few places where you can hide."

When he stopped pacing, Edith stood up to face him. They stood momentarily transfixed. He noticed how thin Edith was now. Her eyes were lined with fatigue, and her lips had thinned. Her face told a great deal about the pressure this war put on people. His sister had told him how she thought the extra work was taking a toll on Edith; now he saw what she meant.

He tried to fix Edith's face into his memory. Then he leaned over and hefted up the bag onto his shoulder. "Before I leave Brussels, I want to warn Ada and as many of the others as I can find. *Au revoir, Madame. Que Dieu soit avec tous.*"

Edith watched him disappear out the door. "And God with you."

After the prince left, Edith went to her room and collapsed onto her bed. Her friends were being arrested and now the prince was leaving

Belgium—the strain was getting hard to bear. She wondered when her own arrest would come or that of someone on her staff. She didn't care so much for herself, but she was responsible for the welfare of so many others. It crossed her mind that maybe once they were in their new nursing school and quarters, the German police might pay less attention to them.

She tried to mentally prepare herself for the worst. *If we are arrested, what will they do to us? What we did was not a crime. We didn't kill anyone. Maybe at the very worst, they will jail us until the war is over, then we can return and continue our work here. There are enough Belgian nurses to carry on in the meantime. The Committee has invested too much money and time to let the school fail, and they know how the hospitals depend on our trained nurses.*

Edith had always found solace in her meditation book. Reading it every evening had become a ritual. This evening, as she reached for the little green book, *The Imitation of Christ*, with the gold letters stamped on the spine, she felt a sharp pain across her chest. It was so sudden and crushing that it took her breath away. The book dropped from her hand and fell against the picture of her mother and both crashed to the floor.

She clutched her chest. She had felt twinges of pain in her chest before, but nothing like this. Sweat beaded across her brow and she felt nauseated. *Maybe I am having an attack of heat exhaustion.* She sat up and tried to will the pain away, but it was too intense. Falling back on one elbow, she saw her mother's picture, face up, on the floor and noticed there was a new crack in the corner of the glass.

"Edith, where are you?"

Edith thought she recognized the voice, but it sounded as if it came from far off down a tunnel.

Then the voice sounded closer. "Edith! What's the matter?" The familiar scent of lavender rose wafted through the air. She looked up to see Elizabeth standing over her. "Talk to me!"

Edith forced out two words through clenched teeth, "Chest pain."

Elizabeth piled up a few pillows and eased her friend back into a lying position. She rushed to the sink, saturated a towel with cold water, and placed it over Edith's neck and chest.

"Take some deep breaths," she said.

Edith closed her eyes and concentrated on slowly inhaling and exhaling. When she opened her eyes, the picture of her mother was back in its usual place. Elizabeth's face was clearer now. The pain eased and the nausea lessened.

"How long has this been happening?" asked Elizabeth.

"Only a few times, but nothing like this. It came on so suddenly."

"I should get a doctor."

"You'll do nothing of the sort," Edith whispered.

Edith saw the worried look on her friend's face and reached out and took Elizabeth's hand in hers. "I'm better now, really. It was probably just the heat. I'm breathing easier, and the pain is almost gone. Thank you for your help."

Elizabeth sat on the bed next to Edith and squeezed her hand. She couldn't hide her concern. "The stress of all that is happening is badly affecting you. Won't you at least consider leaving Belgium? I'll go with you. We can return after the war is over."

Edith's eyes studied Elizabeth's face. "Have you ever thought that maybe, just maybe, you should have gone off to Switzerland as you once planned? What have I brought you, Elizabeth? Misery, deprivation, and uncertainty? You are only thirty-one. You could have a whole new life ahead of you if you left now."

Elizabeth held Edith's trembling hands firmly in hers. "The truth is, I never wanted to go to Switzerland, not really. A young sailor I met earlier fancied me a bit. We wrote back and forth. When I approached you, I had just received a letter from him that made promises to me. It all sounded so, you know, exotic and exciting. But then I realized I didn't know him very well and started looking for a good excuse not to leave. You gave it to me.

"Edith, you promised me opportunities I would never find anywhere else. You said that my position as a novice nurse would grow into one of influence. All of that has happened and more. I could have left at any time, if not for Switzerland, for France or Italy. But this school was a dream and a vision I wanted as much as you did. Working with you here has been a privilege. I admire you, Edith; I always have. You symbolize everything that is good about nursing. You said back then that you needed me to help you with this work. The truth is, I needed you. I needed your strength, your compassion, your dedication and…"

Elizabeth leaned over and brushed her cheek next to Edith's, "…your companionship."

She stood up, straightened out her uniform, and giving an impish smile said, "Besides, I couldn't live in Switzerland. I can't yodel well enough, hate the cold, and I can't ski."

She walked to the door. "You're tired and should rest. I'll bring you back something cold to drink." Turning back, she added, "One more thing: I want you to know that it has not escaped by me that recently you have been speaking about the new building as if you will not be there to see it finished. Things are difficult now, but we will weather this storm as we have all the others."

As she walked through the door, she heard the words, "Promise me..." They were almost a whisper. She turned back to see Edith propped up on one elbow. Her head and shoulders were a faceless, dark silhouette, backlit by the soft glow of the setting sun. Edith's ghost-like features looked like a mirage shimmering in the light that would disappear if Elizabeth blinked hard.

"Promise you what?" she asked the shadowy figure.

"Promise me that if anything happens to me, you will take my place and continue our work here."

"No one will ever take your place. Not now, not ever. Now, please, rest up."

"No, that's not enough. Promise me, Elizabeth. I won't rest until you do."

The words came back as a whisper. "I promise."

After Elizabeth left, Edith sat for a few more moments. Feeling better, she stood at her bedside gauging how steadily she could walk. Still in her stockings, she wobbled a bit as she leaned over to pick up the crimson pillow to remove her register. Grabbing the back of her chair for support, she shifted over to the desk and placed the register on the blotter. She sat for a moment and wiped the sweat off her brow. After tucking the handkerchief in her sleeve, she picked up her pen and wrote:

No.	RANK	NAME	REGIMENT	ARRIVAL	DEPARTURE	WHETHER WOUNDED
66.	Mll,	Louise Thuliez	French civilian	Various times, Feb.—July		—
67.		Phillipe Baucq	Belgian civilian	Irregularly	1915	—

— 60 —

THE DREADED MOMENT

All that day, most of the activity had centered around getting the new buildings ready. A grateful Belgian female patient gave them a bunch of roses, and Edith wanted to make them last as long as possible. She took the vase to the pantry upstairs to put the flowers in fresh water. The open windows let in the sounds of the summer: the high-pitched squeal of cicadas, the roaring of an automobile engine, and the metallic clip-clop of a horse moving along the rue de la Culture. Church bells rang four o'clock. Hearing voices outside, Edith looked out and saw three men talking to Elizabeth while they pointed to discarded furniture piled on the sidewalk. Maybe they want to buy some of that.

Suddenly she heard a commotion downstairs. The door banged open. Feet scuffled. Jack barked in that high-pitched tone he used when something was wrong. A woman cried out. Edith heard a gruff voice say, "Don't move." Heavy feet pounded up the stairs. Two men in civilian clothes burst into room and grabbed her by the arms, causing the vase of roses to crash on the floor.

Jack jumped on one of the men. He kicked the dog aside. "Filthy cur!," Jack yelped as he went flying across the floor. He scrambled to get up and was about to leap back on the man.

"No, Jack! Down!" commanded Edith. Jack looked at her and then back at the men. Confused, he lowered his head, glared at them, and gave a low, rumbling growl. Edith's body stiffened when she felt a gun barrel pressed against the back of her head.

"Downstairs with the others. You are under arrest."

The voice was as cold and hard as the gun pressed against her skull. The men pushed her down the stairs and into the room where Jacqueline and five other nurses sat huddled in the corner. Next to them, Elizabeth stood frozen in place, Pinkoff's gun to her head. Edith's eyes locked onto her friend's and through that one exchanged look, each saw that the other understood the situation. They had shared this journey together, laughed together, fought adversity together, and now it all had come to this.

In a steady voice, Elizabeth said, "They are looking for British or French soldiers. They think we are harboring them here."

"I know of your activities, and I will find what I need to arrest you," said Mayer.

"That's ridiculous," said Elizabeth. "Have you, or anyone else, ever found evidence we are harboring enemy soldiers?"

Edith recognized the man with shoulders the size of boulders, meaty lips, and bushy red eyebrows. Mayer swaggered like a prizefighter, sneering at Edith and Elizabeth. "I will tear this place apart until I find the evidence. No woman will defy me. Your activity here is over. I will see to it."

While Pinkoff held the nurses captive, Mayer motioned for a third policeman to come with him. The two men burst into Edith's office. Edith heard drawers being pulled open and splintering as they were thrown against the wooden floor. Books were ripped apart. A few were flung out the window. Heavy leather boots crunched over the broken glass of the vase and picture frames.

Then Mayer descended the stairs and stood in front of Edith. He looked down at her. With the exception of one of the nurses who was sitting on the floor whimpering, everyone in the room was still. He held something in his hand. He had the look of a raptor who had finally caught its prey. With a smugness in his voice, he said, "I now have the evidence I need to arrest you. I found what you were hiding." He watched Edith's expression.

My God, he found the register! She thought.

With one quick motion, he dangled a square of paper in her face. His eyes glinted with victory. "Have you ever seen this before?" He held up a postcard. Edith recognized the name signed at the bottom as one of the soldiers she had assisted out of the country. He hadn't used the code name of "Cousin Lucy." She squared her shoulders and stared at the writing. Steeling her emotions against Mayer's question. "This is the first I've heard of this man. He must have got out of the country entirely on his own."

"That is interesting, because this person is thanking you for saving his life so he can return and fight the murdering Huns on another day. You can no longer deny that you have been helping British soldiers."

Edith was instantly conscious that this was the moment she dreaded and would remember it for the rest of her life.

"Mme. Cavell, you have helped an enemy soldier who promises to come back and kill more of our soldiers. You are aware of the notices we posted warning that anyone who harbors the enemy will be tried as a spy?"

"They are posted too high for me to read. I didn't think they had anything to do with me because I am not a spy."

His eyes were cold. "I have been suspicious of your activities for some time. My men have been watching you." He motioned to the uniformed guard. "Take her away." He pointed to Elizabeth. "And her, too. Keep a close eye on her. She has already tried to escape once."

A rough hand grabbed Edith's arm. Edith turned back to look at the nurses in the room. "Don't be sad, my children. Everything will be all right. We'll be back soon; be good and wise. Take care of Jack."

Mayer turned her around and pushed her out the door. She walked out proud and unsmiling. Two automobiles labeled *Geheimpolizei* waited at the curb.

Mayer motioned for Edith and Elizabeth to be put in separate motorcars. "Take her to the *Kommandantur* in the rue de la Loi," he said to the driver of Edith's motorcar. And to Elizabeth's, "Take her to my headquarters."

The vehicles rumbled off over the cobblestones, leaving a cloud of acrid gray exhaust swirling behind them. Two of the remaining nurses moved out onto the street to stare in disbelief at the disappearing cars. Both of their leaders had been taken away, and they were frozen with indecision. "What will we do without Mmes Cavell and Wilkins?" asked one nurse.

"Pray for their quick release," said another nurse with trembling lips. The curious crowd that had gathered outside gradually dissipated. The nurses stepped onto the stairs when an unfamiliar sound stopped them cold. They stared at each other with curious looks. Then it started again as a low, agonizing wail that swelled to a crescendo and then stopped.

"It's coming from upstairs," said one nurse. They backed out into the street and looked up to see Jack on the balcony. He stood with his forefeet on the rail, staring down the street where Edith had disappeared. The hair between his shoulder blades stood straight up. He threw his head back and gave another mournful howl.

Vintage postcard showing Edith Cavell's arrest and conviction.

— 61 —

"VERBOTEN"

I t was late that evening when an automobile pulled up in front of the nurses' quarters. Jack bounded down the stairs, anxious to greet Edith, but stopped short when he saw it was Elizabeth. As she leaned over to pat the saddened animal, her knees buckled. The German guard standing inside the door caught her before she fell and placed her flat on the floor, calling out, *"Hilfe! Ich benötige Hilfe!"* Jacqueline and two other nurses rushed to the door to Elizabeth's aid.

"What happened?" asked Jacqueline.

Elizabeth opened her eyes. "I felt faint." She struggled to get up. "Please help me to bed."

"But what happened? Are you hurt?"

"Not hurt, just exhausted."

Jacqueline helped put to her bed, while another nurse went for water. Jack padded along behind them to Elizabeth's room. He sat a short distance from the bed, his eyebrows shifting back and forth as he stared at her. Jacqueline handed Elizabeth the glass and pulled a chair to her bedside. "Are you able to tell us what happened?"

Elizabeth sat up and took the glass. "It was awful. Lieutenant Mayer, the big man with the red hair, questioned me for hours about taking in Allied soldiers. They threatened to jail me for assisting the enemy. They said they already knew we were harboring French and British soldiers because Quien, that miserable wretch, told them everything. I was right about him from the start."

She sipped the water. "They said they knew Mme. Cavell was giving soldiers money and finding them guides to take them out of the country. I kept saying I knew nothing of their accusations, and they let me go. Who is the soldier at the front door?"

"They sent guards to monitor us. We are not allowed to leave the building without their permission. We can move between our buildings, but cannot go outside."

"How is Mme. Cavell? When did she return?" Elizabeth asked.

"Return? She has not returned yet."

Elizabeth put the glass down. "You mean they still have her? We were questioned in separate places. I never saw her. Let's hope she will be back by the morning. I won't be able to sleep until she returns. They told me they transferred Philippe to the St. Gilles Prison. And that they arrested the Princess deCroÿ and are looking for her brother."

"And the schoolteacher, Louise?" asked Jacqueline.

"They got her, too. There are many others. They have all been imprisoned."

"Will they imprison Mme. Cavell?"

"She's too smart for them. They will get nothing out of her and will have to let her go; I'm sure of it." Elizabeth squeezed her eyes closed and then opened them wide, trying to shake off the tiredness. "I must get things ready for Mme Cavell's return tomorrow."

* * * * *

The next day, a German police officer walked up to the nurses' quarters. When Grace opened the door, he handed her a note. She immediately recognized the handwriting and tore it open.

My Dearest Gracie,

Let's hope you are not worrying about me—tell everybody I am quite all right here. I suppose from what I hear that I shall be questioned one of these days and when they have all they desire, I shall know what they mean do to with me. We are numerous here and there is no chance of being lonely. We can buy food at the canteen, but I should be glad to have one of the red blankets, a serviette, cup, fork, spoon, and plate. Not the best ones–also one or two towels and my toothbrush. In a day or two some clean linen. I'm afraid you will not be able to see me at present—but you can write; only know that your letters will be read.

Is Sister Wilkins free? I have been thinking of her since last night. Tell them to go on with the move as before. If Sister is there, she will know how to arrange everything. If   Jack is sad, tell him I will be back soon.

The day is rather long—can you send me a book and a little embroidery, also nail scissors, only a few things as I have no place to put them.

I will write again when there is anything to tell. Don't worry. We must hope for the best. Tell them all to go on as usual.

Edith Cavell

Elizabeth and the nurses were relieved to have received something from Edith. It didn't sound as if she were being treated badly. Elizabeth insisted that she would bring the requested items to Edith. "I have to see her to really know how she is," she explained to her staff. "I have questions about setting up the new buildings. If I am to be in charge until she returns, I must be able to talk to her."

By the end of the week, a new proclamation was posted on city walls including those outside the Clinique.

Verboten!

It is forbidden for any one, man or woman, to aid or hide men of English or French nationality in their home under penalty of death.
—*Per order of Baron Von Bissing*

INTERROGATION

dith's world was now filled with German uniforms, interrogation by men who hated her, and personal deprivation. After being subjected to hours of questioning, she was pushed into a motorcar.

"Take her to St. Gilles prison," said Mayer to the driver.

When the motorcar stopped, they pulled her out from the back seat. She was so exhausted, she could hardly walk. Two tall soldiers with black and red armbands and brass eagles on their collars escorted her to the prison gate. They stood before the brass sign, "Prison de Saint Gilles," waiting for the gate to be opened.

St. Giles, or Tir, National Prison, where Edith Cavell was interrogated and imprisoned. (Photo by author.)

She looked up at the forbidding stone edifice that was to be her home. This was the largest and most feared prison in Belgium. She had heard the stories of how prisoners were treated here. The arched entrance housed a massive oak and iron gate with fist-sized locks. On each side of the gate stood three storey-high circular turrets, from which the gray block wall extended in both directions. Built along the wall on each side were more turrets with slotted windows. It reminded Edith of a medieval fortress, built to keep the enemy in, not out. She surmised it was a symbol, not of justice, or even public protection, but of power and punishment. It served its purpose well.

Feeling dazed and numb, she would have stumbled on the uneven gray stone pavement had it not been for the support of the two strong guards gripping her arms. The hinges creaked and groaned as the gate was opened from the inside. She was led through a small, open courtyard and into a corridor lined with offices on each side.

A middle-aged, thick-necked German guard leered at her as she was brought to Bergan's office. He puffed waves of stale beer into her face as he groped her body for weapons. When he was done, he pushed a paper in front of her and handed her a pen. "Here. Sign. It is a record that you are here."

What will they do if I refuse to sign? Imprison me? Her upper lip curled slightly at her own joke. She bent over and signed.

They walked her down a long, dimly lit corridor. It smelled of rust, urine, feces, cabbage, sweat, and mould. It led to a circle, like the center of a wheel, from which other corridors spread out like spokes. She shuffled down another corridor and was brought to a standstill in front of cell number 23.

The iron hinges groaned when the door was opened. A heavy hand on her back pushed her through the door. One guard followed her in and went to the table. He unfolded it, showing her how it doubled as a bed. Saying nothing, he walked out, closing the door behind him with a heavy clank. She heard the metal key turn inside the lock, snapping the tumblers in place, and collapsed on the hard, lumpy mattress.

She was alone now. Totally alone. No guards. No questions. A thin stream of light squeezed through the iron bars of the slotted window high above her

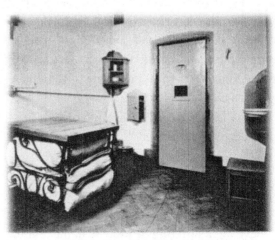

Edith Cavell's prison cell.

357

head and shone on the uneven oak floorboards, giving her just enough light to inspect her room.

A corner cupboard hung on the wall, with two shelves providing room for a jug, a bowl, and a mug. A single wooden straight-backed chair rested against a wall shelf where a basin and a pitcher of water had been placed. A round iron bucket with a cover sat in the corner. Edith cringed at the thought that this would be her toilet. On the wall opposite her, air vents and pipes were attached to a gas heater. She stared up at the crucifix hanging high up on the pasty tan wall over her bed. It made the cell look like a mausoleum.

A sudden surge of panic gripped her. To gain control, she leaned back, closed her eyes, and tried to ignore the odor of must and sweat emanating from the mattress. *I've smelled worse in the Whitechapel wards and during the typhoid epidemic.* She wondered what Elizabeth, Grace, and the others were doing. She missed Jack and ached to pet and reassure him. She thought of her mother and how Louisa would react to the news of Edith's arrest. *Maybe I will be out of here before she finds out.*

Edith judged the dimensions of the room to be about thirteen feet by eight. There was little room for what few possessions she would be allowed. She reminded herself that she had once lived in a tiny, unheated dormitory room, shared with three other nurse probationers. If she could do that, she could tolerate this.

She tried to rest, but her mind focused on the long hours of interrogation. She thought about how at first Mayer and Bergan were solicitous, offering her a chair and something to drink. Pinkoff, the man with the purple birthmark on his face, was less accommodating. They took turns, pummeling her with the same questions over and over, sometimes phrased differently.

She heard Mayer's gravelly voice in her head. "Have you taken any soldiers over the border?"

"No, I never have."

"Have you helped British soldiers escape and billeted them in defiance of German orders?"

"I helped the wounded and sick. I gave them food and clothing to relieve their suffering. It was the humane thing to do. I am a nurse. It was my duty. I would do the same for any soldier, even a German one. I have helped hundreds of German soldiers."

"We are not referring to German soldiers. We are referring to enemy soldiers, English and French. Did you care for enemy soldiers, fully knowing they would return to fight against Germany?

"I knew they were trying to get out of the country for their own safety. I did not know what they would do next."

Pinkoff paced nervously about the room; Edith never knew exactly where he was unless he was directly in front of her. She noticed that the purple birthmark on his face darkened when he felt angry or frustrated.

"Did you not receive five thousand francs from the Prince Reginald de Croÿ for your expenses in helping enemy soldiers to escape?"

Edith remained silent. The purple mark darkened. "You might as well admit it. He has been captured and confessed this to us."

"No, it was only five hundred francs." She realized too late that in her penchant for correctness, she had been tricked.

The purple mark lightened. His trick had worked.

"You might as well stop being evasive. We have all of your traitorous friends in custody."

"Which friends are those?"

"Ada Bodart, Princess Marie de Croÿ, Hermann Capiau, Louise Thuliez, Philippe Baucq, and about thirty more. They have all confessed to their part in this conspiracy—and your part as well."

It was a simple statement, but the horror of knowing that all of these friends were now imprisoned brought on a wave of disorientation. At least Elizabeth's name wasn't mentioned. Her back ached from hours sitting on a hard wooden chair. "I am so tired that I can no longer concentrate. I do not feel well. I have a headache, and I feel faint."

Back in her cell now, she reached for her paper and pen. When they had given them to her earlier, they warned her that whatever she wrote would be censored. Since Elizabeth might still be under arrest, she wrote to Grace, knowing she would share the letter with the others. She wrote telling them not to worry, asked about Elizabeth's safety, and for a few personal items. But she didn't include her last thought. *They haven't finished with me here.*

— 63 —

DECEPTION

F ive days after Edith's arrest, Elizabeth received a postcard from the prison warden. She read it over and over. *So it's true. Edith is being held in that medieval prison.* The note requested that clothes, linen, and personal items be brought to her. She had tried to deliver what Edith had asked for in her note to Grace, but had been turned away. Maybe now they would allow her to see Edith.

She went to Edith's room to gather up the items Edith has requested. Jack sat in the doorway and followed her movements with liquid, dark eyes.

"I know," she said to the depressed animal. "I feel the same way, but she'll be home in a few days." It felt like a violation to go through Edith's belongings without her being there. Tears formed as she picked out each item, treating it as if it were precious. She held Edith's meditation book, slipped a few francs between the covers, and went on to gather writing materials, embroidery, toothbrush, linen, towels, soap, skirts, blouses, and blankets. She filled two suitcases, then she and another nurse carried them the half-mile to the prison.

When she arrived, the two guards at the gate would not let her in. "Leave your suitcases here. We will bring them to your friend. What is her name?"

"Cavell, Edith Cavell. Please, may I see her? You can take the suitcases. I just want to see her, even if for just a few minutes."

The guards snickered. "My pretty little woman, you can visit me any time," said one guard.

"She is in solitary confinement," said the other. "No one is allowed to see her. Not even someone as pretty as you." He took one suitcase in a beefy hand, and touched her cheek with the other. Elizabeth pulled away, dropped the suitcases at his feet, and left with the other nurse.

The next day, Edith woke up at 5:00 a.m. to a trumpet blaring out reveille. At 7:00 o'clock, breakfast was pushed through a slot in the door. She drank the black coffee and brushed away a fly that droned over the single piece of dark bread. An hour later, a guard came around selling postcards and German newspapers. He offered to take any mail for posting and accepted food orders for the canteen. At midday, a bowl of potato soup and a glass of beer were slid in to her. An hour later, the dishes were collected and a second glass of beer was given out.

Edith found that supper wasn't much better. It consisted of coffee, dark bread, and a bit of cheese. At 8:45 p.m. a bell sounded. Fifteen minutes later a second bell signaled everyone to be in bed with their lights out. To ensure of compliance, a guard patrolled the corridors and shone a light through a hole in the door into each cell.

The next day, Edith was allowed to exercise for a half-hour in a circular courtyard. Before she left her cell, she was forced to wear a cowl over her head and face with two holes cut into it allowing her to see directly in front of her, but not to either side. Except for the guards, she was always alone, never seeing any of the other members of the Underground. When she returned this particular day, two guards came to her cell and commanded her to put the gray cowl back on. The rough linen cloth scratched against her face as she pulled it over her head.

"Where are you taking me?" Her question hung in the air unanswered.

When they stopped walking, she heard Bergan's voice telling her to remove the covering. Bergan sat on the edge of his desk, polishing his handgun. A cigarette burned in an ashtray next to him. Pinkoff paced in front of the desk with a cigar sticking out from the corner of his mouth.

Edith's eyes stung from the acrid clouds of cigarette and cigar smoke. There was a stillness to the air that sucked the energy out of her. She asked to sit near the open window to catch what little air floated in. She looked out of the dusty window at two guards laughing as they walked along the edge of the garden.

Was it just a week ago that I smelled the scents of flowers in the shade of my garden, with Jack sleeping at my feet? Nobody appreciates their freedom until it has been taken away. She looked back into the smoky room. The interrogation began.

"Did you deliberately give shelter to able-bodied enemy soldiers knowing they would return to fight?"

"No, the soldiers who came to me were severely wounded and were not well enough to fight."

Mayer held up the postcard he found in her desk. "And this? How do you explain that they found this in your desk?"

"I do not know who wrote that or how it got there."

"How many of your staff helped you?"

She swallowed hard and answered, "None, I alone was responsible for the care of these men."

Pinkoff strode over to the desk, put his cigar down, picked up a file, and flicked it open. He stared down at the neatly typed notes, then walked came so close to Edith that she could see the brown nicotine stains on his teeth. His eyes were hard, and his words were slow and precise.

"I am curious to know how many men you think you..." He referred back to his file. "... how do you put it?... 'helped who were wounded and sick?' All on your own, as a matter of duty, of course. How many?"

Her heart hammered as she stared straight into Pinkoff's eyes. "About two hundred." *And many more you will never know about,* she thought.

Bergan straightened up, snapped his pistol shut, and pointed it at Edith. He seemed momentarily transfixed. "How many?"

Edith saw a dangerous emotion in his eyes. He was coiled like a cobra ready to strike. *Is it shock or disbelief that I could have accomplished so much right under their noses? I am looking into the face of the beast I once feared, and smelling its breath, but oddly, I am no longer afraid.* She looked down at the pistol and spoke slowly and deliberately. "I helped about two hundred wounded men. They came to me seeking medical care; it was my duty as a nurse not to let them suffer."

"You expect us to believe you took in that many enemy soldiers by yourself. Do you think we are fools?"

"I was not needed in the hospital when your doctors and nurses took over. I had the time to take care of these soldiers."

At the end of the day, Pinkoff produced a statement written in German. "We have written down all you have said here. If you want it to go well for yourself and the others, I suggest you sign it."

"But it is in German and I don't understand what it says."

'Very well, we will accommodate you." Pinkoff handed it to his secretary. "Read this to her in French." Turning back to the small, thin woman, he said, "After he reads it to you, you will sign it." He drummed his fingers on the desk.

"Before I sign it, I want to be assured you will release the others."

"Every consideration for leniency will be given to them."

"Does the American Consulate know I am being held prisoner here?" She saw a quick exchange of glances flash between Mayer and Pinkoff.

"Of course," said Pinkoff. "Lieutenant Mayer has already written out a report for Mr. Whitlock."

Edith shifted on the hard wooden chair. The glare of the afternoon sun burned through the window. Sweat made rivulets down the middle of her back, causing her blouse to stick to her skin. She fingered a few strands of hair that hung over her face, and twisted them behind her ear. The interrogation was drawing to a close for this day, but she knew there would be another tomorrow and every day until she signed their confession. They told her it simply described her understanding of, and involvement in, the Underground activities that sheltered enemy soldiers and helped them leave the country.

The sooner I am out of this hot, smoke-filled, miserable office, the better. I'm not signing anything they don't already know. If it is true, that my signature will help the others, then I should sign it and be done.

The pen slipped out from her sweaty hand. She dried her hand against her skirt. Pinkoff's fingers drummed faster against the wooden desktop. After she signed her name, she was taken back to her cell.

* * * * *

Pinkoff and Bergan congratulated each other on a job well done. Pinkoff smiled as he read the last paragraph in the statement that had not been translated for Edith. "*I am aware that it is a capital offense under Paragraph 38 of the German Military Code which states: 'Any person who, with the intention of helping the hostile power to cause harm to German troops, will be guilty of the crime of Paragraph 90 of the German Penal Code and will be sentenced to death for treason.'*"

He waved the statement with Edith's signature in the air. "Von Bissing will be very pleased with this. It will ensure our promotion."

"And ensure her place at the execution wall," said Bergan, his mouth curled in contempt. "I should enjoy watching that arrogant Brit face a firing squad. We'll see how brave she is when she has eight loaded rifles pointed at her chest."

Pinkoff gave a sardonic smile. "The British soldiers are weaklings. They are already crumbling under our military power. When they see what we have done to one of their women, even one as well-known as this one, they will finally understand that we intend to win this war at any price. No one will be spared. Her death will break what is left of their spirits."

"Too bad she will not get to see it," answered Bergan, admiring the shine on his pistol. "What do you think will happen when Whitlock gets Lieutenant Mayer's report?"

"I do not think we will be hearing anything from Whitlock for some time. I said Lieutenant Mayer wrote the report. I didn't say he had submitted it," Pinkoff said with a sardonic grin.

— 64 —

LUCK OR FATE

Whitlock slammed the phone down. "This is incredible," he told his secretary, Hugh Gibson. "I just got word from the British Foreign Office in London—London, mind you—that the Huns have arrested a British citizen and are holding her incommunicado."

"Did they give a name?"

"It's Edith Cavell, the nurse in charge of the nursing school over in Ixelles. She's come to us a few times for help when she needed to get some of her nurses out of Belgium."

Brand Whitlock ran his hand over his hair and stopped to vigorously scratch the back of his head. "I can't believe it. I just can't believe it. They arrest a high-profile British citizen right under my nose and no one in Belgium tells me. What in the hell am I doing here? Selling bonbons?"

Gibson put down his pen, pushed aside the document he was working on, leaned back in his chair, and gave Whitlock his full attention. "I knew they had arrested a Belgian princess and a countess, but that's not under our authority. Have they gotten so desperate they are arresting women now? How did London hear about it?"

"That's another good one. Someone from Holland got word to London—from Holland, for Christ's sake. Had to be one of the Tommies who made it over the border. Anyway, they got hold of her sister's husband, who is a doctor. Wainright, I think they said his name was. He contacted the Foreign Office in London and asked if his sister-in-law had been arrested over here. And that's not all."

Whitlock scratched his head again. "The London office just heard about this a week ago. They are now telling me she has been imprisoned since the 5th of August. That was 26 days ago! They've got this poor woman, a Red Cross nurse at that, held in some goddamned hole somewhere and no one has seen or heard of her since. As the British representative, I should have been contacted."

"We can write a letter to the German authorities. I believe our contact is Baron von der Lancken, the civic general, who takes his orders from that old Prussian general, von Bissing. It's still early. I can get a letter over to him this afternoon." Gibson took out a clean piece of paper and dipped his pen in the ink. "I'm ready if you are, sir."

Whitlock paced back and forth, rubbing his chin. "Let me think about this for a minute. We have to word this delicately. Don't want to offend the miserable bastards, but we have to make it formal enough so that they know we mean business. Okay, start writing *'Your Excellency: My legation has just been informed that Miss Edith Cavell, a British subject residing at the...'* find out where she was residing..., *'is said to have been arrested. I request that you immediately...,'* No, too strong."

He tapped his forehead with his middle finger. "If we don't grovel a little, they'll get difficult. *'I should be greatly obliged if Your Excellency would be good enough to let me know whether this report is true, and, if so, the reasons for her arrest. Send the information that authorized this immediately...'* No."

Whitlock paced a few times. "Let's say..., *I should be grateful if Your Excellency would furnish this Legation with the necessary authorization from the German judicial authorities so that M. de Leval may consult with Miss Cavell, and eventually entrust someone with her defense.'* Can you think of anything else I should add, Hugh?"

"No, sir. I think it best to be brief."

"End with...*'I avail. Brand Whitlock.'* That should do it. Get this out as fast as you can, and let me know as soon as we get a reply."

Gibson blotted the ink. "I'll have it brought over to his office right away." He looked up at the pacing ambassador. "They wouldn't keep her locked up and then try her without a lawyer, would they? I mean, I've heard of them doing that with some Belgians and Frenchmen. Of course, they said they assigned a lawyer, but it was all for show; they never really got a decent defense. But she is a British citizen and a Red Cross nurse. What do you think they want with her? What did she do? Refuse to take care of a wounded German soldier or some such thing? I don't think she would have killed anybody."

"Oh, God, no. She's just a bit of a thing. The quiet type, but smart. Who knows what these crazy Huns do or why? They have another whole agenda with this *Kultur* claptrap. It's their excuse for everything, including starting this goddamned war in the first place. They've gassed thousands of soldiers to death, like so many diseased animals. What's the honor in that? It simply defies human decency, but that's what we're dealing with, and deal we will. We'll find out about this poor woman, and see what they intend to do with her. We have to get some legal counsel to her."

* * * * *

E dith was told she could write one two-page letter or a postcard once a week, and could receive mail on Tuesdays, after it had been censored by the prison warden. The hardest part of this whole situation was being separated from her staff and friends, especially Elizabeth. She ached to get back to the new school, to see it completed and set up the new curriculum. She missed her shaggy friend who was always at her side. There was so much she wanted to say, but dared not let it get into the warden's hands. On August 23 she wrote to Elizabeth.

> *My Dear Elizabeth,*
> *I am sorry you have had to wait so long for an answer from me.*
> *I have asked to see you but they have refused until after the*
> *sentence. So do not try any more–just write all you want to*
> *know, and I will reply on the first occasion.*
>
> *Many thanks for all your kind thoughts for me. I am sorry about*
> *our German maid deserting us but not totally surprised. We*
> *were warned about Marie for some time. I hope José and his*
> *family continue to be well.*
>
> *I'm sure you have many worries, but do not worry about me. I*
> *am quite well—more worried about the school than my own*
> *fate. Do not buy anything for me. I do very well with what I*
> *have. I hope all my things have been put away for safety—with*
> *camphor.*
> *As for Grace, I have been unable to communicate with her*
> *father. He owes us about 420 francs. I hope she will be allowed*
> *to stay—otherwise I cannot see what will become of her.*

Will you please send me my blue coat and skirt, white muslin blouse, thick gray reindeer gloves, gray fur stole, and six stamps. So sorry not to be allowed to see those who came on Sunday and brought me a meal. Tell José the Sunday meals are most appreciated.

Tell the girls to be good and work well and be tidy. My dear old Jack! Please brush him sometimes and look after him.

My love to you and the others.
Affectionately yours,
Edith

* * * * *

Whitlock called Hugh Gibson into his office. "Have we heard anything back from von der Lancken?"

"No, sir. I've tried to contact his secretary several times but my message was never returned."

Whitlock slammed his fist on the desk. "Damn those arrogant bastards! It's been eleven days since my last telegraph. Von Bissing is dragging his spurs on this one."

"I just received another message from the London Foreign Office asking about Miss Cavell. I told them you were out and that we would reply soon," said Hugh.

The pencil in Whitlock's hand suddenly snapped in half. "They keep asking me to report to them about Cavell. What am I to tell them? That she simply disappeared? How incompetent does that make me look? Bring your pen and paper in here. This time we'll be more direct. Send another telegraph off to von der Lancken. We can't let them get away with this. *"Brussels, 10 September 1915. It is with great disappointment that you have not…"*

Hugh stopped writing. "Sir, I think you should be a bit more diplomatic. A harsh tone will only make them more stubborn."

"You mean in spite of their obvious stonewalling of my request for information, I still have to kiss their ass."

"I believe that's about it, sir."

'Okay, we'll start out with the formality. '*The American minister presents his compliments to Baron von der Lancken* ...How's that for groveling?"

"It's a fine grovel, sir," said Hugh, smiling.

"But I'm not wasting much time with this. I want an answer back now."

"Yes, sir."

"*...and has the honor to draw His Excellency's attention to his letter of 31 August, in respect to the arrest of Miss Cavell, to which no reply has been received. As the minister has been requested by telegraph to take charge of Miss Cavell's defense without delay, he insists...,*"

He saw Hugh raise his eyebrows. Whitlock cleared his throat. "Delete 'insists.'..., *he would be greatly obliged if Baron von der Lancken would enable him to take forthwith such steps as may be necessary for this defense, and to answer by telegraph, the dispatch he has received. Brand Whitlock.*"

Two days later, Ambassador Whitlock finally got his response.

Brussels, 12 September 1915
To the American Ambassador

Sir:

In reply to Your Excellency's note, I have the honor to inform you that Miss Edith Cavell was arrested on 5 August, and that she is at present in the military prison at St. Gilles.

She has admitted that she concealed in her house French and English soldiers, as well as Belgians of military age, all desirous of proceeding to the front. She has also admitted having furnished the soldiers with the money necessary for their journey to France, and having facilitated their departure from Belgium by providing them with guides who enabled them secretly to cross the Dutch border.
Miss Cavell's defense is in the hands of the advocate Braun, who, I may add, is already in touch with the competent German authorities.

> *In view of the fact that the German Government, as a matter of*
> *principle, does not allow accused persons to have interviews, I*
> *much regret my inability to procure permission to visit Miss*
> *Cavell as long as she is in solitary confinement.*

> *Baron von der Lancken*

Whitlock threw the letter across his desk. "They refuse us any means to defend this woman," he said to his secretary. "If we can't defend her, she will be at their mercy. Ask our legal counsel if we can meet with him and figure out our options."

Gaston de Leval was a distinguished international lawyer in Brussels and had been assigned as Ambassador Whitlock's legal advisor from the beginning of his appointment. He was in his mid-fifties, and had dark eyes that stood out in a startling contrast to his head of white hair. Standing ramrod straight, he commanded a air of authority.

Both Whitlock and Hugh waited as de Leval read over the letter from von der Lancken. Whitlock leaned forward with a look of expectancy.

He watched as the lawyer's face drop into solemn seriousness. "*C'est ignoble!*" he said, removing his glasses and holding the frame in one hand. "It's wretched, because German law is not like Anglo-Saxon law. The Germans feel totally justified in arresting people without informing them of their offense. They believe there is only one right, one privilege, and that it belongs exclusively to the German officials."

The dapper lawyer continued to explain. "Gentlemen, in German law, the accused is not innocent until proven guilty. Quite the reverse. If she has been arrested, it is assumed she is already guilty. They will keep her incommunicado, while they go about gathering their evidence against her. It is impossible for the lawyer who is assigned to the case to prepare adequately. Generally, accused persons have no rights, not even a lawyer to put across their own

Gaston de Leval, legal advisor to Brand Whitlock, American ambassador to Belgium

defense. In Britain, this woman would be tried in a civil court, but under German law they can try her in any court they choose. Unfortunately, they have chosen to try her in a military court, where the military governor will be the judge."

Whitlock sat stunned. "But who is this Braun that was mentioned?"

"He is a Belgian lawyer who, like the rest of us, needs the work. I will try to talk to him, but my guess is that he will not be allowed to visit Miss Cavell. And they may not even allow him to speak openly in her defense."

"So what good is he, then?" Whitlock asked.

"If the Governor General feels so inclined, he can allow the defense to speak after the prosecution is done with his presentation and witnesses. If it appears that the sentence involves some breach of the military code, the case can be taken up through diplomatic channels after the trial. An appeal can be made. During that appeal, the defense counsel will be allowed to make a case showing that justice was not served."

"What's the chance of proving that?"

"In view of the fact that Miss Cavell has already signed a statement admitting she is guilty of harboring enemy soldiers, very small." The lawyer rubbed the bridge of his nose and carefully replaced his glasses, one earpiece at a time. Then he inserted both letters into a file, closed it, and placed his hand over it as if he were about to take an oath. "Have you seen the statement they say she signed?"

"No, I just heard about it today."

"Then I will try to get a copy of it. Did this nurse understand German?"

"I'm not sure. She is highly intelligent, but I doubt she knew enough German to read or understand a legal document."

"It is quite likely that they wrote it in German, gave her their own translation of what was written, and got her to sign it without her truly knowing what she was agreeing to."

Gibson stopped writing for a minute and looked up. "We were able to get that clergyman off a while back. Why can't we do the same for this nurse?"

De Leval raised his hands in a gesture of uncertainty. "The difference is that the clergyman was an American. America is not at war with

Germany, at least not yet. That American had the good fortune of being arrested right after 128 Americans drowned on the *Lusitania*. The last thing Germany wanted was another incident that would push America into war. Miss Cavell, unfortunately, is a British citizen, and right now, their hatred for the Brits is quite strong. They have nothing to lose by imprisoning or even executing her. In fact, they would relish the opportunity to do so. They will do anything to weaken the spirit of the Brits, and what better way than to make an example of a popular British nurse who defied them? We are really up against it."

"Do you think von Bissing will be presiding over this case?"

"Possibly, or it will be the new military Governor General, who just arrived at the beginning of this month."

"Is he any more reasonable than von Bissing?"

"I am not sure, but probably not. He is General von Sauberzweig, another old Prussian like von Bissing. We are still trying to find out more about him."

"So, von Bissing or this Sowberzing, or whatever his name is, will also impose the sentence?"

De Leval responded, "The penalty is determined by a kind of judge advocate and prosecutor. It could be whoever is appointed, but I assure you, he will be hand-picked by the Governor General, who does not want any embarrassing surprises in his court, especially in a high-profile case such as this one. So it is safe to say that the sentence will be determined by the Governor General and the judge advocate before the trial starts. There will be a second hearing where the sentence will be imposed by a jury of military officers."

The chair squeaked as de Leval lifted himself up. He walked over to the shelves lining the wall to his left. He picked up a small copper box, studied it, and held it out to Whitlock. "Do you know what this is?"

Whitlock took it in his hand and studied it. "It looks like a tobacco box of some kind."

"Exactly," said de Leval. "I have a collection of them." He took it back from Whitlock's hand, placed it in the precise place from which it had been taken, and picked up another. "Some have religious themes, but many of them, like this one, were presented to soldiers by their kings during the Hundred Years' War. Not many of these survived, because ver few of their owners survived the war."

De Leval leaned against his heavy desk, facing Whitlock. "Your Miss Cavell may not survive this war either. Are you prepared for that?"

"Not if there is something we can do about it."

"There will be nothing much that you, as the American ambassador, can do even if you are representing England. International and German law have tied your hands."

Whitlock picked up a copper tin. "But some soldiers did survive, didn't they?"

"Yes, survival is a matter of luck or fate."

"Is it possible you could approach Thomas Braun and request that you take over Miss Cavell's defense?"

"Possible, yes. Is it likely that he will turn it over to me? Probably not, but I will try to persuade him. His father, also a lawyer, is defending the Princess de Croÿ. He understands and speaks German as well as French, which may be why he was assigned this case."

"Thank you for that. I know this isn't an easy situation for you." Whitlock looked over the row of copper tins, perfectly lined up on the shelf. "It's disturbing to think that a war could actually last a hundred years. Let's all pray this one doesn't last that long."

De Leval took the box from Whitlock's hand, set it back on the shelf, turned, and scrutinized the faces of the two Americans.

"The outcome of anyone who gets caught up in war's atrocities is always a matter of luck or fate."

— 65 —
THE VISIT

E dith reached for a ball of red thread to finish the rose she was carefully embroidering onto a dresser scarf. She was measuring out the length of thread against her arm when the cell door opened and Elizabeth rushed toward her with outstretched arms. Behind Elizabeth stood Otto Mayer, watching the two women as he leaned against the closed door with his arms folded across his chest. Edith dropped her sewing when she felt Elizabeth's arms around her. The warm softness of Elizabeth's closeness enveloped her in ecstasy.

"Elizabeth! Is it really you? How were you able to…"

"I let her in," interrupted Mayer. "She has been requesting to see you every day since your arrest. I thought it best to let her see that you are alive and well."

Elizabeth pulled back, inspecting Edith. Their eyes locked onto each other.

"Are you all right? You look so thin and pale. Are they feeding you?"

"The light is dim here, so I get very little sun. The food isn't the same as our cook's, but it will do. The meals you send over every Sunday are very much appreciated." Edith stared back at Elizabeth as if trying to burn every feature into her memory: her thick hair piled on top of her head, her dancing eyes, her heart-shaped lips. There was so much to say, and she didn't know where to start. "How are the new school and Clinique coming along?"

"Oh, they're finished; totally set up and functioning. We've all moved in. Some of the nurses left for other positions, but all of the probationers have stayed on. We started teaching a Red Cross class for the public."

"And how is my dear, dear Jack?"

"He misses you terribly. He keeps running back to the old rowhouses hoping to find you. We often have to go over and bring him back. Sometimes José has to carry him because he refuses to leave."

Edith cleared her throat trying, to fight back the tears. After a moment of awkward silence, she regained her composure. "I do so love the roses you sent me." She held up the scarf she was embroidering. "As you can see, I am copying one of them into my embroidery. They have stayed fresh for some time, but I'm afraid the chrysanthemums wilted in this dim light."

"As long as you don't wilt."

"You know, Elizabeth, the end may soon come. We must be prepared for all the possibilities."

"Please don't say that. You can't give up, not now, not after all we have been through together. We all need you to return, especially me. The nurses ask after you every day, and often talk about what will happen when you return. There are so many things they want to show you. Your work must continue with you there."

"I pray for them every day, but I must tell you that this waiting and uncertainty has put great strain on me. I've done my duty, and now they must do theirs." Edith's glance flickered over to Mayer, who shifted his stance. "Isn't it ironic that people so dedicated to doing their duty can end up on such opposite sides?"

She saw Elizabeth's eyes begin to tear. As the droplets ran down her friend's cheeks, Edith gently brushed them away with her hand. "My dear, dear friend. We have traveled a marvelous journey together. Now you must learn to carry on without me. You have to find your own place and reach for your own destiny. You must be strong for yourself, as well as for the others. They will look to you for leadership."

Elizabeth looked at Mayer. "Can we spend a few moments in privacy? What harm will it bring? We can't go anywhere."

"I agreed to let you in only if I remain present. There is concern that you will pass pills to the prisoner to make her sick, or end her life. She must be alive and well enough to stand trial."

"I would never do such a thing. What a horrible thing to say." She looked back at Edith. "What trial? What are they trying you for?"

"I have confessed to everything. I told them that I, and I alone, hid French and English soldiers and aided them to recover and flee the country."

"But you are not a spy. Many others have done the same." She turned to Mayer. "When will she be tried?"

"The date has not been set."

"The American legation knows of her arrest?"

"They have been informed."

She looked back to Edith. "Have you heard from them yet?"

"I've heard nothing from the consulate, nor have I seen a lawyer. You are the first person I've seen from the outside since I was arrested."

"You have no lawyer? How can that be? You can't be tried without a lawyer to defend you!"

"A lawyer has been assigned. This not a subject we can continue to discuss," said Mayer.

Edith touched Elizabeth's arm. "I am fine, really. I was so tired when I came here, and now I am rested. I have my meditation book and my sewing. Please tell everyone that I miss them so very much, and urge them to do well in their studies."

Just then a loud whistle sounded overhead, and an explosion shattered in the street. Debris and shrapnel splattered against the wall. A siren sounded and loud voices were heard. A dog howled as if in pain and then abruptly stopped. The three looked up at the window and around the walls, as if expecting them to cave in at any moment.

"It is enemy activity. You have seen that she is well. We must leave now," ordered Mayer.

They hugged for one last moment. Edith took Elizabeth's hand. "Do not worry, my friend. Be strong for both of us."

"If I am allowed to return, is there something you wish me to bring you?"

"I have no room for anything more. Just seeing you is more than enough."

Mayer gripped Elizabeth's arm and pulled her away from Edith. As he shoved Elizabeth out the door, she turned for one last look. Edith met her eyes. Nothing more needed to be said. They communicated a meaning that transcended language.

After the cell door closed, Edith leaned over and wept into her hands. The scent of lavender rose lingered on fingers as she cupped them to her face and inhaled deeply.

I don't regret my confession if it means they won't arrest Elizabeth. Had I not confessed, even more would have been arrested. My biggest regret is not what I did but that I was forced to stop. I knew someday I would face the consequence, but denial would have been useless and would only have diminished the meaning of what I did. There are greater laws than the ones I broke, and they are the ones I follow. I hope I have the strength to face whatever befalls me. I will never let them see me break down. She smiled to herself. The surprise is not that I was caught, but that it took them so long to catch me and they still don't know the half of it. I confessed to two hundred soldiers, but in fact there were hundreds more.

I hope people do not make more of this than what it is. I am not a martyr, but a nurse. I took a vow to help those in need. Everyone must face the moment when they are asked to stand for something they believe in. I hope I will be remembered less for who I and more for what I stood for.

She took out her meditation book and in pencil, placed an X beside Chapter 16 to mark her place. She reread the last verse in the chapter.

...we ought to bear with one another; comfort one another, help, instruct and admonish one another. Occasions of adversity best discover how great virtue or strength one hath. For occasions do not make a man frail, but they show what he is.

She placed a double line beside these last two last sentences, then closed the book and held it to her chest. "Please, God," she prayed. "I am Your servant. I do not know what You have in store for me, but I accept Your will, whether it be my freedom or fate. Please, Lord, let no harm come to Elizabeth and the others. Give them the strength to carry on the work You sent me here to accomplish."

At the end of the week, Edith was again allowed to walk outside in an enclosed area. She kicked at a few leaves that gathered in small piles, and noticed the change in the air as summer faded into fall. Vibrations of distant cannons often broke the silence. *It's the end of September, and the war still continues. When will it end? Will my captors be the victors or by some miracle, will the boots they keep pressed to our necks be removed?*

Another figure entered the exercise area. He held out his hand. "You are Mme. Cavell, the matron at the nurses' training school?"

She recognized his accent as Belgian. "Yes, do I know you?"

"I am Sadie Kirschen, the lawyer assigned to defend you. The previous lawyer assigned to your case, Thomas Braun, has resigned, and your case was reassigned to me. I must know more about your situation, so I can defend you in whatever way possible. We should go inside and talk."

Just then, Otto Mayer burst into the courtyard with two armed guards. "You are not allowed to be here. It was a mistake that you were let in."

"But I must see my client to prepare an adequate defense. Please, just for a few minutes," pleaded Kirschen.

"No minutes. It is the rule. She is not allowed visitors."

With rifles drawn against him, Kirschen was escorted out of the prison.

— 66 —

THE LETTER

G eneral von Bissing walked around his desk, trying to decide what to pack. He picked up the marble ashtray, placed it in the wooden box, retrieved it, and put it back on the desk. *Too heavy,* he thought. He reached down into the bottom side drawer to pull out a bottle of Russian vodka, which he nestled in the box between a scarf and a starched shirt. The only thing that raised his spirits was thinking how recent events would soon lead Germany to victory. *We have conquered the Russian army. We won both the battles at Champagne and Artois. The western front will be next. The British army is depleted, and those left in the trenches are weary. Soon the Kaiser's troops will be marching into Paris.* Von Bissing was proud of what his country had accomplished. It had cost them hundreds of thousands of lives, but those men had gladly sacrificed themselves for the Fatherland. They died with honor and pride.

He opened the top drawer of the polished sideboard, reached in, and pulled out a uniform dress jacket. While carefully placing it in the box, he heard a knock on his door.

"*Kommen.*"

Baron von der Lancken entered and stood at attention, waiting for permission to speak.

"You have something to tell me?" asked von Bissing without looking up.

"I have a letter here of some importance addressed to you. It is from the Nurses' Training School in Ixelles."

"I am busy packing. Read it."

"It is dated October 3.

To His Excellency, Baron von Bissing, Governor-General in Belgium

---

Excellency,

We, the undersigned nurses of the clinic situated at 32 rue de Bruxelles-Uccle, Brussels (formerly 149 rue de la Culture), humbly take the liberty, on consideration of your benevolent intentions towards the whole population, of approaching Your Excellency in the hope of shortening the term of imprisonment of our matron, Miss Cavell, who was arrested on 5 August 1915, and, if there were any way practicable, of procuring the suspension thereof.

We would make it known to Your Excellency that Miss Cavell has superintended our clinic for eight years, and has won, by her self-sacrificing work, lasting recognition in the service of charity from all her patients, as well as her staff. Confident in the benevolent reception which your Excellency will recognize our sad position, and graciously set our minds at rest concerning the fate of our esteemed matron. In this hope we beg to assure Your Excellency of our lasting gratitude."

Von der Lancken dropped the letter on von Bissing's desk. "It bears the signatures of seventeen nurses."

Von Bissing picked up the letter, scanned it, and handed it back to von der Lancken.

"What am I to do with this? The governorship of the War Council has replaced me with General Sauberzweig."

Von der Lancken picked up the letter. "I have been assigned to serve under his command. He will almost certainly ask my opinion about this letter. What do you suggest I tell him?"

"It does not matter what I have to say, and frankly, I doubt that he will ask for anybody's opinion, but if I had a choice in this matter, I would tell him to find her guilty and send her to a military hospital in Germany. It is a fitting sentence to make her care for the very soldiers she plotted against. Executing her will only arouse the Belgians and lead to even more treachery. They will form another Underground to replace this one."

"You and I have been working together here for many months. If I could ask, General, why are they removing you from the command of the War Council and giving it to General Sauberzweig?"

"You do not know?" Von Bissing's sword clanked against his thigh as he took his seat at his desk. The drawers scraped along the sides of the desk as he pulled each out for one last inspection. "It is simple. The Kaiser wants this war to end, and he believes I have been too lenient. Victory requires total suppression of all resistance, and as we have just found out, I have not accomplished that."

"But you just broke up the Belgian Underground and put thirty-four of the traitors in prison. I do not understand."

"Evidently it was not enough. I am told I was too slow in discovering the treachery that has cost us German lives. They said..." He looked at the German flag hanging by the door as if to gather courage. "They think that if this single British woman can operate as effectively as she has over the past nine months, then I am too weak and will not judge her without mercy."

"General Sauberzweig is now in charge of the army and will bring in his own officers. Who knows? In time, he may even have me totally removed, too."

"I hope it never comes to that. I heard he is replacing Herr Mewes with Dr. Eduard Stroeber as the military prosecutor," said von der Lancken.

Von Bissing looked up. "Oh, yes, *Kriegsgerichtsrat* Stroeber. How fitting. He is the lawyer they call the "Hanging Judge," because he always gets his convictions granted."

Von der Lancken stepped in front of the old general's desk. "If I could suggest, General, while you are still in charge of the military trials, perhaps you should hold court and try this Cavell woman separately. The interest in her case is high. It is only justice that since you arrested her, you should be the one to conduct her trial. Turn the others over to General Sauberzweig and Dr. Stroeber later. You can then say you have finished what you set out to do. And what of Mr. Whitlock? Who will report this back to him?"

Von Bissing answered his colleague. "We have kept much of the information away from Mr. Whitlock to prevent him from creating an international incident out of this. But it is not my business now. I wash my hands of it. She, and the thirty-three other traitors, are now General Sauberzweig's responsibility. Let him deal with the American consulate."

He placed both hands on the chair arms and pushed himself up. He waited a minute to straighten his back, then reached in the box to pull out a clothes brush. He brushed invisible dust and lint off the shoulders and arms of his jacket, placed the brush back to the exact place where it had been in the box, and walked over to the window. He watched a woman in a black shawl holding onto the hand of a youngster and pulling him across the street. An ambulance with the Red Cross insignia painted on its side bumped down the street. An old man leaned forward as he pulled a cart filled with bulky furniture on stiff wooden wheels. A small brown dog, with head and tail down, padded along behind the cart.

Von Bissing turned back. "I am looking forward to turning the military responsibility over to someone else. I will have enough to do with the rest. Take the box to the motorcar waiting outside."

Von der Lancken picked up the letter and held it out to the departing general. "But what of this letter?"

Von Bissing opened the door and stepped through it. "Give it to the new governor of the War Council. It will be his first item of business. It is no longer in my hands."

— 67 —

THE TRIAL

O n the morning of October 7, Edith tucked her white muslin blouse into her blue cotton skirt and slipped on her blue coat. To deflect any additional attention away from the school, she had decided against wearing her nurse's uniform. *How ironic. These are the same clothes I wore when I first came to Brussels. At that time, my life in Brussels was just beginning. And now, I wear them when my life might soon be coming to an end.* She reached over and fitted a hat onto her head, adjusting the two feathers that stuck out at an angle. *Might as well go in style.*

The guards brought her to the main entrance where the others who had been arrested stood in rows of twos. Once her eyes had adjusted to the morning light, she saw her friends for the first time. They looked around at each other, sizing up the changes that had taken place. They were a shabby and pathetic-looking lot, pale from the sunless interior of their dingy cells and weary from the monotony of solitary incarceration. Their eyes exchanged silent messages of hope, support, desperation, and fear. As their names were called, they were loaded into a van and a motorbus. Once the van was full, four helmeted soldiers, with rifles in hand, entered the van and settled themselves on the last few bench seats. The door was slammed shut from the outside.

"No talking," warned the guards.

The diesel engine turned over a few times and then caught. The van lurched forward, parting the curtains just enough for Edith to see branches with leaves hanging in bright swatches of gold. A flower market displaying buckets of white, yellow, and red, chrysanthemums passed by.

Life out there is so filled with color, she thought. A clump of white on the hem of her skirt caught her attention. She reached down and plucked it off. It was some of Jack's fur. She held it tightly in her fist, closed her eyes, and pictured Jack lying next to her. *If only I could hold him just one more time*. She opened her hand and watched the tuft float to the floor.

"Oh God, I am so frightened," whispered a woman to her right. Edith shifted her gaze to the woman. She was about forty and had the expression of a person viewing a theatrical tragedy.

"What have you done?" asked a man sitting next to her.

"I lodged some Englishmen."

"Nothing else?"

"No!"

He touched her arm. "Then don't be frightened. You will not be shot."

"Are you sure?"

"Quite sure. In these times, that's all that matters, isn't it?"

Edith wondered why the man was so confident and hoped he was right.

"No speaking! *Verboten!*" shouted a guard into the dark interior of the van.

The van and motorbus drove through the open spiked iron railings of the Parliament House and circled round the enclosed courtyard. The doors opened, and everyone clambered out onto the uneven, rounded cobblestones. They stared around at the splendor of the three-story government building.

Marching in pairs through a back entrance, they were led up a narrow staircase and out onto the floor of the Senate Chamber. The first thing that struck Edith was the brilliant blaze of red. The carpeting was a river of red. The sea of chairs were upholstered in red velvet, their backs covered with a red cloth emblazoned with the gold emblem of the Lion of Belgium. *It's an ocean of blood.* She wondered how much of it had been spilled because of decisions made here. As the seat of Belgian political power, it was here that wars were declared and leaders were voted in and removed from power. Now, it was being used by the Germans for military trials. She wondered whose blood would be asked for next.

Once Edith's eyes had adjusted to the interior light, they swept around the room. It was circular, with columns that held up a semicircular balcony. Looking up into the balcony, she saw uniformed officers holding up field glasses to their eyes to stare down at her and the prisoners who were being herded into seats to the left of the thirty other prisoners sitting in a semicircle of rows to the right. Edith wondered what they had done.

Edith, Princess de Croÿ, Philippe Baucq, Louise Thuliez, and two others were directed to the benches immediately in front of the podium. Guards sat between the prisoners, preventing them from communicating with each other. After guards and prisoners had been seated, witnesses for the prosecution were brought in and seated behind them. Ada Bodart recognized one of the witnesses as her fourteen-year-old son. She waved to him to get his attention, but the guard slapped her hand down. The boy's dark oval eyes shifted to his mother and then away. Four lawyers filed in with briefcases in hand and sat behind the witnesses. The lawyers had not been allowed to discuss the cases, or even to see the prisoners before this day. Edith took a quick look at her lawyer and wondered how he could present a defense strong enough to sway the judges without knowing why she was arrested.

After everyone had settled, the prisoners were made to stand. Lieutenant General von Sauberzweig was the first to enter. He marched down the aisle from the back of the room. He was tall, with strong

The Senate Chamber in which Edith Cavell's trial took place.

shoulders and a purposeful stride. A Prussian ex-cavalryman, he wore polished black, knee-high riding boots. Light from the skylight glistened off the sword that swung at his side to the rhythm of his step. Like a king before his court, he marched up the five stairs to the upper podium.

Von Sauberzweig's angular face sported a waxed mustache that thinned out across his narrow cheekbones. His deep-set eyes scanned the room, and then turned to the soldiers who stood erect on each side of him. At his nod, five elderly judges, all military officers, filed in and took their places around the table in front of the lower podium. Their pressed uniforms were heavily decorated. All wore Iron Crosses at their necks. Two of them set monocles to their eyes.

Dr. Eduard Stroeber strode in from the left. He heaved a briefcase onto the podium, removed his helmet, and ran his hand over thick, black hair that was slicked down and parted precisely in the middle. Giving the impression of strength and determination, he looked every inch like a knight entering a battle in which he was sure to be victorious. This was his court; it was where he would display his well-practiced skills.

This room was more opulent than any Edith had ever seen. The walls were decorated with richly painted murals representing events in Belgian history. Corinthian columns rose up like sentinels around the balcony. Gilt frescoes and white alabaster busts of former leaders of Belgium contrasted with the dark, richly carved wooden wall panels that rose high above and behind the podiums. Over the panels, a clock encrusted with gold carvings displayed the time: 8:05. Edith followed the beam of light from the clock up to the skylight dome that was surrounded with paintings of the coats of arms of the nine original provinces of Belgium. She looked back at the line of her fellow prisoners and noticed the stark contrast between the opulence of the room and the pathetic appearance of her friends. *None of us looks worth saving.*

After a brief swearing-in ceremony, a soldier moved to the front and called out the names of each prisoner in turn. Stroeber was the first to speak. He placed a monocle in his right eye and introduced himself. Like a finely-tuned machine built for accuracy and precision, his words were deliberate and exact. He spoke in German, which was immediately translated into French. He addressed Edith first. "Edith Cavell, *aufstehen.*"

"Edith Cavell, levez-vous," said the French translator. Edith stood.

A silence pervaded the room. Everyone knew it had all come down to this moment. Stroeber's stare bored into Edith's blue-gray eyes. She could feel herself wilting under his gaze.

"From November 1914 to July 1915, you lodged French and English soldiers, including a colonel. You helped Belgians, French, and English of military age by receiving them at your nursing home, and giving them money and the means to return to the battle."

As he spoke, Edith felt the inside of her body tremble. She felt diminished in this enormous room. Even though there were thirty-three others in her situation, she still felt alone. Fear overtook her as she realized how these accusations must sound to those who would be judging her and determining her fate. Her knees began to weaken. She gripped the edge of the banister in front of her. The heat of the room felt like a heavy blanket weighing her down. A wave of nausea swept over her and sweat dampened her upper lip and neck. She had a sudden urge to run. *What if they caught her and shot her? She would be no worse off. At least it would be quick.*

She looked about the room for an avenue of relief. Something glittering, high up on the wall behind the podium, caught her attention. Edith's eyes followed a beam of light that shone down from the glass dome to a panel depicting gilded angels. They seemed to hover over the proceedings below, their gleaming arms beckoning to her. *Angels are sent as messengers from God! In the garden of Gethsemane, an angel had appeared to Christ to strengthen Him at a time of weakness. These angels are messengers from God to tell me He is also watching over me. I will not dishonor my God. I will look the beast in the eyes and not be afraid.*

She heard Stroeber's words, hard as granite, directed at her and then the translator's interpretation. "Is this so?"

A peace and serenity came over her. She straightened up and looked directly at him. With little expression in her voice and an unyielding stare, she breathed in the thick, hot air and answered, "Yes."

"With whom were you working when committing these acts?"

Edith called out the names of those who worked directly with her in the Underground.

"Who was the head, the originator of this organization?

"There was no head."

He shook his head in disbelief. "Was it not the Prince de Croÿ?"

"No, the Prince de Croÿ confined himself to guiding men out of the country and providing them with a little money."

Stroeber strode back and forth behind the podium. He obviously enjoyed being a prosecutor, and like an actor playing his role, he let his voice slide from low, soothing tones to louder, sharper ones. It was dramatically effective.

He raised his arm and pointed at her. "Why have you committed these acts?"

Edith did not flinch. "At the beginning, I was sent two Englishmen who were in danger of death; one was badly wounded."

"Explain what you mean by 'danger of death.'"

Edith's body was weak, but her voice was clear and firm. "Had I not taken them in, they would have been shot."

"Once these people crossed the frontier, did they send you news that they had arrived?"

"Four or five did so."

He asked about Baucq's role and that of some of the others. Then he asked her if she had known that her activities had directly helped the enemy.

"I was not preoccupied in aiding the enemy; but did want to help any men who came to me. Once they crossed into the frontier, they were free to go wherever they chose."

"How many people have you helped ?"

"About two hundred."

Stroeber couldn't resist a short dramatic pause. Then he thundered, "Two hundred! You helped two hundred men of military age escape from Belgium?"

There was an audible gasp from the five military judges. One judge, who had been scribbling everything down, stopped writing. They looked around at each other. A second one nervously smoothed his mustache, and a third dropped his monocle.

"This must be an overstatement. Did you really help as many as two hundred men?" asked the judge as he placed the monocle back to his eye.

"Yes."

"And were they all English?"

"English, French, and Belgian."

There was a silence as the meaning of this was taken in by the judges. Finally, another judge blew out a gust of smoke from his cigarette. Talking through the smoky haze, he asked in a mocking voice, "Did you not realize how foolish you were to help the English? They are so ungrateful for acts of charity."

"No, the English are not so ungrateful."

"How do you know that?" insisted the judge.

"Because some of them have written back to thank me."

Stroeber gave the judges a conspiratorial look, but Edith had no idea of the significance of what she had said.

"You may sit down."

Edith looked up at the clock. It was 8:09. Her whole interrogation has taken four minutes. Stroeber continued to question each of the prisoners individually. Louise Thuliez was next. Philippe Baucq followed, then Ada Bodart. Each were questioned about statements they had previously signed, most of which had been distorted in translation.

After interrogating the first six prisoners, Stroeber lectured for two hours in German. Edith could tell from his gestures and expressions that the trial was not going in their favor. She picked up on the word *Todess-trafe* several times. From the French translation into *pénalité de mort*, she knew it meant "death penalty."

At 4:00 p.m. the judges asked that witnesses be called. Lieutenant Bergan was the first. Holding a prepared statement, he read, "I swear that my examination of the prisoners has been conducted with all scrupulousness and in a fair and conscientious manner. All of the confessions have been made in the presence of witnesses. The prisoners' statements were read back to them and were signed only after they fully understood and accepted the charges as written. We placed no pressure on the prisoners to extract confessions." He looked to Stroeber for approval and got it in a nod.

"In your investigation of these Underground activities, do you believe they were highly organized and deliberately helped men of military age to return to their ranks?" asked Stroeber.

"I am of the firm opinion that this was a highly organized affair. All of the accused deliberately helped in returning soldiers to the ranks of the Allies. There were two headquarters engaged in this work. Princess de Croÿ and her brother worked one at their chateaus in northern France, where the fighting took place. Their other headquarters was in the south of Brussels and was headed by the woman Cavell sitting here before you."

After this testimony, the judges whispered among themselves, frequently referring to a book with a green cover. Edith assumed it was a manual of some sort, containing the German military code of rules. When the judges finished reviewing the book, a second witness was summoned. A boy, dressed in black and with black curly hair, rose when called on.

"What is your name?"

"Bodart, sir."

"Have you no parents?"

"Yes, he does. I'm his mother!" called out Ada Bodart.

Stroeber pounded his fist on the podium. "You will be quiet during this testimony! Guard, if she speaks out again, remove her until this witness is done." He turned back to the boy, who now looked bewildered. "We will continue, but I warn you that if you lie, you will be sentenced to ten years of hard labor. You know it is a sin for a Christian boy not to speak the truth, do you not?" The boy gave a silent nod.

Stroeber tapped the podium with the tip of his fingers, emphasising every word. "Now. Have you ever seen Philippe Baucq bring bundles of the newspaper *La Libre Belgique* to your mother's house for distribution?"

The boy looked at his mother with tormented eyes, then back to the prosecutor. He cleared his throat and gave a weak, "Yes."

"And is it true that you have seen that same man trace out routes for escaping soldiers to take to reach the border out of the country?"

The boy swallowed hard. "Yes."

Ada Bodart put her hands to her face and wept.

Philippe Baucq jumped up. "I protest this questioning! This boy speaks English. His mother is Irish. He does not understand what you are asking him." A guard grabbed Philippe's arm and tried to wrestle him back into his seat, but Philippe did not stop. He raised his free hand in the air for emphasis. "I have never marked out a route for fugitives. The boy does not understand. I have only traced out a route they might have taken. It was their choice. There's a difference." Another guard took Philippe's other arm and forced him down.

"If you speak out again, I will have you removed," threatened Stroeber. He turned to the boy. "You are dismissed."

The boy suddenly bolted from his seat, ran to his mother, and threw his arms around her. "I'm so sorry, mother. They made me say everything."

Ada hugged her son and ran her hand over his thick mop of black hair. "I know, I know. I love you. You are a good boy. You did what you had to do."

A guard wrenched the boy from his mother. Edith wiped her eyes with the back of her hand, knowing that this might be the last time Ada and her son would ever see each other.

It was 7:00 p.m. when von Sauberzweig adjourned the court. The prisoners were marched back out in pairs with a guard on either side. The daylight had long since given way to an overcast evening. Edith welcomed the cool air as it brushed against her face. Like scattered ashes, dried leaves swirled around her feet as she was herded back into the van. Since Edith and Ada were loaded in first, they sat the farthest away from the guards. Edith put her hand on Ada's and whispered, "I'm so sorry about your son. I'm sure he didn't mean any harm. He was..."

Ada jerked her hand away. "He was frightened into saying what he did. He is just a boy and didn't understand the consequences, but you did. Why in bloody hell did you give them our names? Did you not understand what you were doing?

General Von Sauberzweig, the trial prosecutor.

You sealed our fate. That's what you did. You might as well have put a gun to our heads yourself."

Edith accepted the rebuke and bit the inside of her lip. "Ada, you may think me mad for doing so, but it was useless to do otherwise. They already had all of us nailed. How do you think we all got arrested? I'm just as keen as you are to get out of this alive, but they told me they already had the information, and insisted that if I lied, it would go badly for all of us. What I said was merely a formal confirmation of what they already knew."

Ada frowned. "The prosecutor is going to ask for the death penalty for many of us. You didn't have to help him do it."

"You must know by now that this whole horrid trial is nothing but their excuse to do what they want with us. They want to make an example of us to others who are also resisting. Our only real hope is if our solicitors can speak well enough on our behalf tomorrow, or if Ambassador Whitlock can somehow intervene by creating a political stir. But other than that, we are helpless, no matter what we say or don't say."

Ada cupped her face in her hands, and wept. "I may never see my boy again. What will happen to him?"

"Silence! No talking!" called out one of the guards.

Edith arrived at her cell to find her supper sitting on the table. She dipped half of the dry, dark bread into the cold soup and saved the other half for the next day's trial. She washed it down with weak, cold coffee. Then she filled the basin with water from the pitcher and washed up.

Exhausted from the day, she slid under the thin covers of her bed. Images of the trial flashed through her mind, raising questions. *Will my lawyer be able to bring in witnesses to speak on my behalf? Is the American ambassador working diplomatically behind the scenes? Is Ada right for being angry with me? Did my testimony go badly for all of us? Father said to always speak the truth, but what happens when that truth is twisted by evil men for their own ends? I've been deceitful these last nine months, but is it really deceit when the purpose is to save lives?* She wished she could talk this over with her father. He always knew the right thing to do.

Her eyes burned and her body ached. She needed to rest both mind and body. If she could hardly concentrate today, it will be even worse tomorrow if she didn't sleep. In a half-hour, there would be a signal around the cells to shut the lights. She sat up and took out her meditation book, flipped through the tissue-thin pages, and read:

> *Labour but now a little, and thou shalt find great rest, yea, perpetual joy. If thou continuest faithful and fervent in thy work, no doubt but God will be faithful and liberal in rewarding thee. Thou oughtest to have great hope of getting the victory; but thou must not be secure, lest thou wax either negligent or proud.*

Edith marked the passage with heavy double lines in the margin. She prayed to God for courage and strength to face the next day's trial. Then the vision of the angels looking down on her in the Senate Chamber flooded into her mind. *It's a sign that God is protecting me.* These thoughts enveloped her like comforting arms. A car roared down the street in front of the prison and backfired, but Edith did not hear it. The demons had released their grip on her. The book slipped from her hands. Exhausted, she fell asleep.

— 68 —

ALL THE PROOF WE NEED

T he next day, the trial continued up in the Chamber of Deputies, a room in the same building as the Senate room but smaller, with a semicircular table and chairs facing the lower and upper podiums. Again Edith and those considered to be the most guilty were placed in the front with guards between them. The guard to her right smelled of smoke and beer. He sat with his with his legs splayed and an elbow pushing into Edith's side. Behind the prisoners sat a row of lawyers.

Edith looked around the room. Gone were the golden angels that had so comforted her the day before. This room was plain, with no balcony, no onlookers, no tapestries or massive murals, nor gilded clocks. Edith thought of the irony of being tried in this room because she remembered that it was just a year ago when King Albert stood at this very podium and declared to his worried people that "a people who defended their freedom could never die."

The proceedings were less formal. Von Sauberzweig and Stroeber entered together from the side of the Chamber. The judges emerged after them and seated themselves at a table placed between the podium and the prisoners. Stroeber, dressed in a pressed and fitted uniform, opened the proceedings.

After thanking the police for their excellent efficiency in arresting "those who would do harm to Germany," he held a folder into the air, waving it as if it were a loaded gun. "We have all the proof we need right here. These prisoners deliberately helped fugitive soldiers and men of military age to cross the border. They sheltered these men, gave them false identity papers, and sent them to Brussels, where they were taken in and guided to Holland. They arranged for guides to receive them and help them return to France or England. The Prince de Croÿ and his sister retrieved soldiers from the battle lines at the western front and brought them to Miss Cavell's institute in Brussels to be lodged and guided out of the country. Philippe Baucq worked out the routes and distributed *La Libre Belgique*, a newspaper that incited insurgencies against the German government. He also handed out military information to the Allies, exposing the German army to great danger."

For the next three hours, he ranted against the accused, repeating the witnesses' statements and information he had presented the day before. Edith and the other prisoners were bewildered because he spoke entirely in German; Stroeber refused to have his diatribe translated into French because, "it interrupts the flow of my speech." Like an actor on the stage, he never tired of the sound of his own voice, changing inflections for added drama.

He pointed to Edith and those seated near her. "These wretched people have exposed our military to grave danger. We do not know how many of our brave soldiers have fallen as a consequence of their evil plotting. What they have done is nothing less than treason. High treason."

Stroeber held up the small green book Edith had seen on the judges' table the day before. "Here in the German Military Code, their punishment is clear. According to paragraph 68, 'Whosoever, with the intention of helping the hostile power, of injuring German troops or any allied to them, is guilty of one of the crimes listed in paragraph 90 and will be sentenced to death for treason."

He snapped the book shut and leaned closer to the judges. Lowering his voice, he spoke slowly and deliberately. "Among the crimes listed in paragraph 90 is 'conducting soldiers to the enemy.' Therefore, I not only recommend, but demand, that the court pass the sentence of death on these traitors." He read off the names, giving the court each one of his final recommendation.

"Baucq, *Todesstrafe*. Cavell, *Todesstrafe*. Bodart, *Todesstrafe*. Libiez, *Todesstrafe*. Capiau, *Todesstrafe*. Thuliez, *Todesstrafe*." Each recommendation rang out like a death knell until all nine names were spoken. Finally, he said, "For the Princess de Croÿ, ten years of penal servitude, and for the rest, long terms of imprisonment with hard labor."

No one needed a translation of what Stroeber had just said. Edith felt crushed by his words. Hadn't she heard that they would not execute a woman? What had gone wrong? Why had her lawyer not defended her? Still needing confirmation of what she had just heard, she looked around to see the reactions of her friends. Baucq's elbows were on the table, his face in his hands. He looked devastated as he peered through his fingers. Thuliez appeared dazed as if she couldn't grasp the reality of what she had just heard. Libiez turned white and began to squirm. Another prisoner screwed up his face as if he were a creature caught in a painful trap, and one simply fainted.

The judges averted their eyes from the prisoners and seemed uncomfortable with the recommendations. The room fell silent as each person began to process what had just happened. Stroeber stood motionless. His eyes burned with the zeal of an athlete who had just scored a victory. Finally, he called on Avocat Sadie Kirschen to begin his defense.

In addition to Edith, Kirschen was also representing five others. The only time he had to prepare his defense was during Stroeber's lengthy diatribes. He had never been allowed to talk to any of the prisoners before the trial; he had not even been informed of the charges. He started with Edith.

The small man stood up and began. "Mme. Cavell is a woman whose whole life has been devoted to humanity. Working with the Red Cross, she ministered to both Allied and German soldiers. When presented with wounded English soldiers, it was natural for her to want to help them, considering her nationality. She is an unfortunate victim of circumstances and her own dedication to nursing. She took vows to help those in need. How could she now act against those vows? She was not deliberately sending men to the enemy to be recruited back into Allied armies. Holland is not an enemy of Germany. All she did was to help people reach the border. What they did after that was not in her control."

Kirschen looked at Stroeber, who sat behind the podium shuffling through papers, then shifted his gaze to the judges. Three looked in his direction. One was lighting a cigarette while another was flipping through the pages of the green military book. Hoping to get their attention, Kirschen raised his voice a little higher. "It would seem that a psychologist would be better fitted to try this woman than military judges, because they would understand how impossible it is for her to resist what is her natural instinct—to help others. The men she aided were all in danger of being killed."

Stroeber suddenly jumped up and interrupted Kirschen. "This is not true under German law."

"Mme. Cavell is English, and does not know German law. Never did she think that she was acting on behalf of England or against Germany. I challenge the prosecutor to prove that any of the men she helped went back to fight for the Allies. Mme. Cavell has been under intense stress. I truly doubt the number of men she claims she assisted into Holland. If I could have had her dossier before the trial, I could have more easily proved this to be true." He turned to Edith. "Mme. Cavell, please stand."

Stroeber broke in. "You are insulting! I can prove everything I presented here."

"For sixteen years, I have practiced as a lawyer. I know that insulting the prosecutor or the judges will not help my client. It is difficult for me to plead in defense of Miss Cavell in German, when my own language is French and I have not been allowed to discuss the case with her before-hand. But I am trying to defend a woman who has just been threatened with the death sentence."

Stroeber sat back in his chair, crossing his arms across his chest, and stared at a spot high up on the wall.

"If she must be condemned," Kirschen continued, "let it be for attempted rather than actual treason. It certainly is not high treason." He turned to Edith. "Do you have anything further to say in your defense?"

Edith stood tall and calm and spoke with sober deliberateness. "When I first turned my attention to this work..."

Stroeber jumped up. "Yes, yes, you have told us all that before. Sit down."

Edith was stunned. "I have nothing further to add then. I made my own defense to the court yesterday, and it still stands."

Kirschen addressed the judges. "I ask you to remember that this woman has spent her life in devotion to the sick and wounded. More than one German soldier owes his life to her. It would be morally wrong to condemn such a woman to death. If you must punish her, then imprison her until the war is over. That would be the only justifiable punishment and would render her harmless."

Kirschen continued to defend each of his five clients. When he was finished, Stroeber stood and said, "The decision of the judges will be told to you in due time," but gave no indication of when that time would come. Von Sauberzweig declared the court out of session and, along with Stroeber and the judges, marched out of the room. In the course of two days, thirty-four people had been accused of crimes, in a foreign language, with inadequate defense.

* * * * *

B rand Whitlock was dashing out of the door when his phone rang. He hesitated, but thinking it might be Mr. Hoover, he turned back and picked it up.

Listening for a few moments, he exclaimed, "What do you mean you can't find him?"

"I've called his office and house and he does not respond," said de Leval on the other end.

"Damn it! How far away can he be? It's important that I speak to Kirschen about yesterday's trial. I've got the American ambassador in London waiting for word to pass on to the British consulate, who will send it over to Cavell's brother-in-law, who is breathing down their necks. Keep trying to find him, and when you do, leave word with Hugh. Today is Hoover's last day here, and of course, he's trying to cram everything in at the last minute. I don't know when I'll be back, but Hugh will know how to get in touch with me."

"Kirschen probably won't do business on the weekend."

"To hell with the weekend. I'm working; he can as well. This is too important to wait until Monday. If this trial went badly for Cavell, we will need all the time we can get to appeal on her behalf."

Whitlock pulled out his pocket watch, stared at it, and then snapped it shut. "Look, I'll phone Hugh and have him get a quick letter off to Ambassador Page. That will hold him off for a while. At least he'll know we're working on Cavell's case. Leave Kirschen a note to call me if you can't get him on the phone."

Next, Whitlock phoned Hugh Gibson. "Hugh, any word yet on the Cavell trial? No? Can you believe de Leval can't find her lawyer? No, he's gone! Vanished somewhere. Look, do me a favor. Dash off this letter and teletype it over to Mr. Page in London so he'll know we are working on Cavell's case. Ready? 'Sir: Upon receipt of your telegram of the 27th of August, I took the matter up with the German authorities, and learned that Miss Cavell had indeed been arrested on a charge of "espionage." The Belgian attorney appointed to defend her before the military court called me several times and promised to keep me posted with regard to the case.'"

He paused. "Do you think we should tell him about Cavell's confessions? I agree with you. Write, 'Unfortunately, it seems that Miss Cavell made several damaging admissions. There appeared to be no ground upon which I could ask for her release before the trial. I will write to you as soon as there is any further development.' That should hold him until we learn more from Kirschen."

Throughout the day, de Leval tried phoning Kirschen and even went to his home, but was unable to find the Belgian lawyer. Finally, he left a note on his door: "We are inquiring about the recent trial of Miss Cavell and the other prisoners. It is important that you please contact me as soon as you read this."

A neighbor saw him at the door and approached him. "Are you looking for M. Kirschen?"

"Yes, do you know where I can find him?"

"You will not find him here. He most likely went to his villa, where he spends most weekends."

"Do you know where his villa is?

"No, monsieur. He stays with someone who breeds and trains shepherd dogs for war purposes. It is somewhere west of Brussels. That's all I know."

The next day, just as Whitlock was finishing breakfast, he got a call from Hugh. "Sir, there's a nurse from the training school at the office. She says she was told the prosecutor has asked for the death penalty for Cavell and eight of the others."

Whitlock threw his napkin on the table. "How did she hear this?"

"She said it came from one of the other lawyers."

"Call the prison governor, or whoever you can get over there, to find out if this is true. Get de Leval to reach the lawyer who talked to the nurses, and find out what he actually said. Any word from Kirschen yet?"

"Not yet."

"Damn him! He promised to keep us informed!"

That afternoon, Whitlock got a call from de Leval. "Brand, I spoke to the other lawyer, who tells me the nurse is correct—the prosecutor did ask for the death penalty for Cavell and eight of the others. He said it went badly for Cavell because of her written confession, but he also said it looked like the judges were in disagreement over the sentencing."

"Good work, but bad news. We can't let this happen. What do you think about contacting von der Lancken?"

"He is not an easy person to contact, especially on a Sunday night. Well, none of them are actually, but I will try to reach him. At the very least, I will try to get permission to visit with Mme Cavell."

"Keep me informed. I'll follow up with Hugh."

Whitlock paced for a few minutes trying to think of what action he should take; then he called Hugh back. "I heard from de Leval. Things look bad. The prosecutor did ask for the death sentence. The German authorities promised to keep me informed; I shouldn't be getting this information secondhand. Were you able to find anything out?"

"From what they told me, it doesn't matter what the prosecutor recommends. The only thing that matters is what the judges decide, and they're not likely to pronounce for another few days."

"We had better keep Ambassador Page informed. Draft a letter about this and telegraph it over to him. Tell him the German authorities have assured us that no official sentences have been pronounced, and that I shall use every means in my power to prevent them carrying out any severe penalty."

"Yes, sir."

"Do we know how much time we will have between the pronouncement and the sentencing?"

"No, but we do know the Germans aren't known for their patience. If I had to guess, it wouldn't be long, days maybe."

"We need to be prepared for a possible bad outcome. Write petitions for pardon to General von Sauberzweig, General von Bissing, and Baron von der Lancken. Appeal to their generosity and humanity and ask them to commute the sentence of death in Cavell's case. De Leval is going to try to reach von der Lancken tonight to see what can be done to save her."

— 69 —

ONE IS FOR SORROW...

E dith returned from the trial so weary that she could do nothing but unfold her bed and collapse into it. How much her universe had shrunk. At first she had welcomed the rest, but now, like a sailor too long at sea, she felt the monotony set in. Where once she had handed needles and threads to world-famous surgeons to mend human bodies, now the only needle and thread she touched were the ones used for embroidery. A few months ago, she had led a school of nurses. Now she was being led around like a badly behaved dog. The questions from her students were replaced by the inquisitions of her captors. The challenge of keeping wounded soldiers alive was replaced with the challenge of keeping herself alive. Her friends' laughter were replaced with the cries of prisoners in other cells. A cold dampness seeped through the walls; she pulled the covers over her shoulders for warmth and began to doze.

A clang and a scrape at the door jolted her awake. A guard shoved her supper tray through the open slot in the door. She slid off the bed and picked up the tray.

"The lights will be kept on all night tonight," said the guard.

She leaned down and peeked though the slot.

"All night? Why so?"

"One of the prisoners in the trial today just hanged himself. We have orders to keep a close watch on the rest of the prisoners who were at that trial."

"That's terrible. Who was the poor man?"

The guard did not answer, merely stated, *"Gute Nacht.* Good night."

Hanged himself. The words lingered in her mind. Who was so desperate and hopeless as to commit such an act?

Thoughts of death whirled around her mind. What mattered most to her about death was that it meant separation from those she loved and the work she hoped to finish. How would her mother accept her death? It disturbed her to think that she had caused her mother distress.

Edith recalled the last time she and Louisa had been together. It was the previous summer when she had returned home to celebrate her mother's birthday. They were sitting in the kitchen sipping iced tea, when her mother brought over an album. She recognized it as the one Edith had given her mother when she had been a girl of just seventeen. In it, were twenty-four of her best drawings of flowers, leaves, and trees, many sketched from their garden. She remembered feeling the glow of satisfaction when her mother gave her an approving smile. It made the weeks of work all worthwhile.

"I will treasure this forever," her mother had told her. It was at that moment that she realized how much she appreciated her mother. Her arms now ached to hold her, and tell her how much she loved her. She felt a tug of guilt when she thought of how, in spite of her mother's pleas, she had returned to Brussels. She reached for the weak coffee on her tray and gulped it down, hoping it would comfort her. If she had any regret over her actions in the last nine months, it was that they might have consequences that would devastate her mother.

She tore off a piece of stale brown bread and placed it in a container to keep it away from the occasional mouse. For some time now, two crows had made a daily morning visit to her window. They often fought over the bits of bread she tossed to them. The last few mornings, however, only one crow had appeared. She had watched the plucky bird hop over to the bread, turned its head sideways for a quick inspection, then pick it up and fly off. She loved the swagger of the black bird, but wondered where the other one had gone. *One crow is for sorrow*, she thought.

She remembered when Edward had first told her the ditty about counting magpies or crows. It was the summer when they walked together along the flower-lined lanes of Suffolk that led to the beach. A round of deafening cawing came from a murder of crows gathered at the edge of a group of trees. Edward had stopped and looked up at the fluttering and chattering birds gathered in the branches. "Do you know how to count crows?" he asked her.

"I jolly well do." She pointed to the birds high up in the trees. "One, two, three…"

Edward laughed. "No, not like that. Father taught me. It's a way of telling the future." He took her hand in his and lifted it so they pointed up at the crows together. "One crow is for sorrow. Two crows are for joy. Three for a girl, and four for a boy." He moved in closer and kept pointing. "Five is for silver. Six is for gold. Seven..." He stopped for a moment. "Do you know what seven is?"

Edith guessed. "Seven means you go to heaven."

"I'm sure you will, but no, seven stands for a secret, never to be told. Eight is for a wish and nine..." He pursed his lips and looked impish. "....and nine is for a kiss." He turned to look at her directly. "I think we counted nine crows."

She felt the wind tug at her straw hat and blow it off her head. It bumped and rolled down the road. She took her hand away from his and ran to pick it up. "You just made that up," she called back.

"No, honest," he protested and ran to catch up with her. But she was too fast for him and made it to the beach before he staggered up to her, gasping to catch his breath.

Guessing at their future was a favorite topic of discussion with Edward. "What do you want to do when you grow up?" he asked her.

"Someday, I am going to do something useful. Something for people, I think, especially those that are hurt, helpless, or unhappy."

"I want to do that too. Why don't we do it together?"

"This is something I must do for myself." Seeing the hurt in his eyes, she added, "And you will do the same. I would only get in your way."

Years later, they had a similar conversation. He recalled what she had said that day at the beach. "You once told me that you wanted to do something useful for people. Do you think you have done that?"

Edith now visualized that angular face of his, so much a feature of the Cavell family. "I think I am doing a good deal of that right now," she had told him.

"But Edith, we miss you so much. I miss you. Don't you want to be with me and the rest of your family?"

Edith now remembered hugging him and saying, "Edward, you are so dear to me, but I must finish the work I started."

He had been her best friend for so many years. She had known he wanted to be more, but she also knew she could never step over that line with him. She wondered what he would think about her being jailed and tried for helping Allied soldiers to escape. She had kept her promise over the years and had written to him when she could. What could she now say or do to let him know she still thought of him? She glanced over at her meditation book. It was such a comfort to her; maybe it would comfort him. She picked it up, opened the cover, and on the flyleaf wrote, "*Love to E.D. Cavell.*"

She disliked eating alone. She should be used to it by now, but meals had always been a time of sharing for her. While finishing the last of her potato soup, she remembered the meals and times shared with Elizabeth. She had learned how Elizabeth's eyes were a gallery of her every mood. They could radiate with passion, glow with love and understanding, or turn dark with doubt or anger. A language had grown between them that needed no words. Edith couldn't imagine the past years without Elizabeth. She had always feared that someday Elizabeth would leave, and she would have to go on alone. Now it looked as if the opposite might be true.

She finished the last bite of bread and sip of coffee. As she put the tray aside, her eye fell on the crucifix hanging on her wall. Christ also cared for humanity, and look how he had suffered. She reached for her meditation book hoping to find some words of solace. The pages fell open to Book IV, chapter IV. She glanced down at it, and then picked it up and held it closer to read the small print.

> *I am racked with grief of heart. I am burdened with sins. I am*
> *troubled with temptations. I am entangled and oppressed with*
> *many evil passions; and there is none to help me, none to*
> *deliver and save me. But Thou, O Lord God, my saviour, to*
> *whom I commit myself and all that is mine, that Thou mayest*
> *keep watch over me and bring me safe to life everlasting.*

To what did this passage refer? Was it her feelings for Elizabeth? Had God looked into her soul and was now chastising her for what He saw there? Tears filled her eyes. She reached for her pen and drew three heavy lines next to the paragraph.

Edith whispered, "Forgive me for my sins, oh, Lord. I am but a broken vessel, undeserving of the mercy I ask of Thee."

She settled back on her bed and tried to sleep, but doubts and regrets kept her awake. She wondered if she had been too harsh and unbending sometimes with her nurses. It is time to make amends. With the blanket around her shoulders, she perched herself on the wooden chair, took out a pen and paper, and began to write what might be her final letter to them. *If only I had spent more time with them. She pondered over the right thing to say and finally started.*

10 October 1915, Prison of St. Gilles

My Dear Nurses,
It is a very sad moment for me when I write to make my adieus to you. It calls to my mind the fact that the 17th September was the end of eight years of my direction of the school. I have told you on various occasions of those first days of the difficulties that we encountered. Even the choice of words for your hours such as "on duty" and "off duty," etc, were all new in the profession in Belgium.

She wrote about the present hard times and the progress that had been made. She urged them to keep up their devotions for spiritual strength, not to gossip among themselves, and to cultivate a sense of loyalty among themselves. Being satisfied that she had said all she needed to, she ended with,

If there is one among you whom I have wronged, I beg you to forgive me. I have been perhaps too severe sometimes; but never voluntarily unjust, and I have loved you all much more than you thought.
My best wishes for the happiness of all my girls, those who have left the school, as well as those who are there still, and thank you for the kindness that you have always shown me.
Your devoted directress, Edith Cavell

* * * * *

Unable to find Kirschen all weekend, de Leval sought out the one person in the German military he knew best—the Baron von der Lancken. He brought with him a letter from Whitlock asking for mercy, should the judges sentence Edith to die. But when he arrived at the political ministry building, he was told that von der Lancken was unavailable.

De Leval persisted. "Is there someone else in authority that I may speak to? It is of the utmost urgency."

"It is late in the evening," protested the guard, but realizing de Leval would not easily be deterred, he agreed to take him to Mr. Conrad, one of the German political ministers. When Mr. Conrad came to the door, de Leval did not wait for casual introductions. He blurted out, "I am the legal representative of the American and British consulate. Please tell me, is it true that the prosecutor has asked for the death penalty for the nurse Edith Cavell?"

Conrad leaned against the door frame with his arms folded across his chest. "Herr Stroeber has asked for the death penalty, not only for Miss Cavell, but also for eight others."

De Leval handed him Whitlock's letter. "Please, it is imperative that you take this to the Baron von der Lancken on behalf of both consulates."

Without unfolding his arms, Conrad looked at the outstretched hand holding the letter. "I am sorry. I do not have the authority to take responsibility for a letter from the Consulate. You must take it to General von Sauberzweig yourself. But I assure you, such measures are premature. The judges have not pronounced their sentence yet. I will keep you informed when that happens."

De Leval slid the letter into the inside pocket of his jacket. "When do you expect that to be?"

The political minister yawned and put his hand on the door to close it. "Not for a few more days—Tuesday, or Wednesday maybe."

"In the meantime, please grant permission for me and her minister, the Reverend Stirling Gahan, to see Mme. Cavell. Surely no harm can come of it since the trial is over."

"Such visits must be approved by Baron von der Lancken or General von Sauberzweig. It is late now; go home. I will speak to them on your behalf tomorrow and let you know."

With that, Conrad he closed the door, leaving de Leval standing alone with no other option but to go but home.

70

THE DECISION

I t was early morning when De Leval, tired from a restless night, climbed out of bed. He opened the curtains and looked out to the street below, his eyes narrowing against the brightness of the morning sun. He watched an old man urging a large, shaggy, black dog to pull a wooden cart filled with earthenware jugs. The jugs rattled against each other as the cart bumped over the cobblestones.

De Leval dreaded what this day would bring and was resentful that Kirschen had not been in contact with him after the trial. He now realized his mistake in not attending the trial himself.

He dressed, finished a quick breakfast, and then phoned Brand Whitlock. The phone rang once and then was disconnected. He drummed his fingers against the desk and phoned again. A weak voice answered the phone.

"Brand, is that you? You sound strange on the phone. Must be a bad connection."

There was a long pause on the other end of the line. "It's not the connection. I'm off my game today. I don't know what hit me, but I can hardly lift my head off the pillow."

De Leval hoped his irritation did not show in his voice. His fingers tapped faster. "Shall I call a doctor?"

"No, I'll see how I feel in a few hours. What did you find out?"

"Conrad did not say much last night except to confirm what we already knew. He promised he would follow through with our request, and inform us when the sentence was handed down. Maybe if you call him today, it will put a little more weight behind what we asked for."

"It would be best if Conrad didn't know I'm ill. I don't want him to see me being weak. I'm hoping that if I stay in bed for the morning I'll get over this. Please, follow up for me and make the calls. See if you can find that miserable lawyer who disappeared after the trial. He has to come home some time."

De Leval waited until noon to call Conrad at the German political ministry. After the usual formalities he asked, "Have you been allowed to grant us permission to see Mme Cavell?"

"I already told you that you cannot visit with her until the final judgment has been made."

"I must tell you, the American and British legation is very disappointed with this decision. It is our responsibility to represent her, and we can hardly do that without being able to talk to her. There are diplomatic considerations here." De Leval then realized that veiled threats would only annoy Conrad and that the Germans had no desire to inform England of anything. He softened his voice. "When do you expect the judgment to be made?"

"As I explained to you last night, not for another day or two. Most likely tomorrow. Even then, no action can be taken until the Governor General is in agreement and signs the final disposition."

"And her pastor? Surely there is no harm in her receiving some comfort from a pastor of her own faith."

"There are three Protestant clergymen assigned to the prison. If she feels the need for spiritual guidance or comfort, she can ask to speak to any one of them."

"It is imperative that we know immediately when the sentence has been passed. We want to prevent an international incident."

"As do we. I will keep you informed when I know more."

A chill crept up de Leval's spine. Something about this was not right. Actually, nothing about it was right. If only Cavell had not confessed to assisting English soldiers to cross the border. The truth was, with the exception of a flimsy postcard, they had no other evidence against her. Without this, the charges would be "attempted" treason, which would carry a lesser penalty. She did not personally escort soldiers across enemy lines and Holland was not at war with Germany. If she had been the only person arrested, he would believe she was being targeted for being English, but the truth was, the Germans had also arrested her French and Belgian colleagues and charged them with the same crimes.

Since he promised to keep Whitlock informed, he called him back.

"Are you well enough to speak, Brand?"

"Yes."

"Sorry to bother you when you are in such a bad state, but I have just spoken to Mr. Conrad."

Whitlock's voice was muffled as he spoke through a handkerchief he held to his nose. "When can we see the Cavell woman?"

"Sorry, he refuses to let anyone, even her pastor, see her. He insists no judgment will be passed until tomorrow, and then we can see, but Brand, I have a bad feeling about this. I think we should assume they will agree to Stroeber's death sentence, and request a pardon for her now."

De Leval heard the Ambassador blow his nose, "Oh, God. Let's hope it doesn't come to that. I'll have Hugh help me write it up. And what about Kirschen? Any luck finding him?"

"Not yet. I will go back over to his house. If I cannot find him, I will contact one of the other lawyers at the trial. Shall I call Mr. Gibson for you?"

"No, you have enough to do. I know where to reach him."

De Leval called Kirschen's office and was told that he would not be in until late that afternoon. He thinks more of his dogs than defending a woman about to be condemned. He made a mental note to avoid doing business with Kirschen in the future. Then he telephoned a lawyer named Dorff, who had defended Capiau and Baucq at the trial.

Dorff responded immediately. "I have not made contact with Mr. Kirschen since the trial. I must say, he made a very good plea for Miss Cavell, using all the arguments that could be brought in her favor before the court. But as you know, it was difficult to adequately defend her without knowing the nature of the charges, or being allowed to confer with her before her testimony began. It was also difficult because she was tried in a military court instead of a civil court. Even so, I was surprised that the prosecutor asked for the death sentence. It seemed harsh considering the circumstances. It is all very disturbing. Probably Mr. Kirschen felt the futility and frustration of it all and took a long weekend off."

"Nonetheless, he should have spoken to someone in the legation before he left. Have you any information when the final sentences will be announced?"

"I received a call from the German *Kommandantur* informing me they will be deliberating at least until Tuesday. There were over thirty prisoners on trial, so I would be surprised if they came to a conclusion even that soon. Do you agree?"

"It seems so, but to be honest, I fear the worst for all the prisoners, but especially for Mme. Cavell. The Germans hate the English and will do anything to demoralise them. I worry that they see her as a means to punish the English and intend to make an example of her to the Belgians. I doubt they will spare the woman who has made them look like fools for nine months."

De Leval called Whitlock to tell him what the lawyer had said. "Have you written the letter asking for a pardon yet?"

"Hugh is finishing it up in the office. I am feeling a little better, although my head is still swimming when I try to stand. Anyway, I also had him send a letter to Ambassador Page in London telling him what we know and explaining that we had done everything possible to secure a fair trial."

* * * * *

That afternoon, in a back room of the Parliament Building, a swirling cloud of cigarette smoke hovered over the five elderly military judges. The judge with the monocle agreed that Cavell's crime should be punished but thought that paragraph 90 of the German Penal Code did not provide strong enough grounds to execute her. He held the little green book close to his face to read. "See here. It says, 'guiding soldiers to the enemy.' She certainly helped soldiers to escape, but she did not personally guide them to the enemy. She should be tried for sabotage but not high treason. She did not murder an officer or the sovereign of Germany. Nor did she attempt to overthrow our government."

Another military judge spoke as a trail of smoke emanated from his lips. "I disagree. What difference does it make? She saved two hundred enemy soldiers, who could return to their ranks to kill our soldiers. Do you know how many of our soldiers could be killed by that many enemy soldiers? She aided and abetted the enemy, and that is equivalent to attempting to overthrow the government. She deserves to go before the firing squad."

A third judge listened intently while writing everything down. Then he stopped writing, stroked his chin, and seemed to weigh the problem carefully. He gestured with his pen. "I agree she should be punished, but we do not want to create an international incident. The American ambassador Whitlock will go back to President Wilson and report on what we do here. We do not want to give the Americans a reason to get involved in the war."

The second judge ground his cigarette into the ashtray until all that remained was a splatter of ash. He gave the third judge a disapproving look and spoke with the huskiness of a heavy smoker. "The Americans are not going to go to war over the death of one British woman. Twenty-five percent of Americans are German. Our ambassador there, Herr Dr. Albert Zimmerman, has kept us apprised of the American attitude. He tells us that their message to Wilson is to stay out of the war. If he became involved with this war, it would end his political career."

There was a thoughtful silence. Then the fourth judge spoke out. "If we execute her, we cannot condemn her alone. She should be executed with some of the others, so they cannot accuse us of singling her out. And if we decide to do it, we should do it quickly before Whitlock can inform the American and English governments and create a reason to protest." His mustache parted slightly with a thin smile. "But frankly, I think it would be better if we simply send her to a German prison. That will keep her from influencing anyone else. We could keep her in solitary confinement so she could not contact anyone. It will achieve what we all want to accomplish, and serve as an example to other dissidents. And if she dies in prison, then all the better. Her blood will not be on our hands."

They all turned to General Sauberzweig, who sat at the head of the table, intently watching each officer as he spoke. The clock above their heads ticked off a long, silent minute as each man felt the tension of making this decision. Finally Sauberzweig cleared his throat and straightened up in his chair. He spoke in a slow deliberate voice. "This Englishwoman has created an embarrassment for our military. In doing so, she has tarnished the good name of our Kaiser. If you find her guilty, there is no other choice than to pronounce the sentence of death. If we let this Englishwoman live, others will take up her cause. The Americans do not care about an old woman who is not their own. Even if she were one of theirs, they would not go to war over her."

It was the statement of a man who felt so sure of himself that he saw no reason to back up his claims. He stood up, placed his hands flat on the table, and leaned over. The light flashed off the Iron Cross that dangled from his neck. His piercing eyes raked across the face of each judge. "Do any of you have children?"

All but one nodded.

"My son, my only son, was blinded by an English soldier. His military career is ruined. He will have to struggle for the rest of his life to put food on his table. For all I know, the bullet that blinded my son might have come from the gun of one of those English soldiers whom this Englishwoman rescued. How many other German sons have been killed or wounded by those same soldiers? And they are still out there, killing our sons. It could be your son next, and then yours." He pointed at one judge, then another. "She must be put before a firing squad so she feels what my son felt when a bullet hit his face. Only she should feel the bullets go through her traitorous heart."

He stood straight up and straightened his tunic with a quick tug. "The Kaiser wants us to protect the Fatherland from the enemy. This treacherous woman, and those who helped her, are our enemies. The Kaiser has a vision that there be one world, under one ruler, one people, one language—all of Europe united under Germany. We must take hold of our destiny or be willing to accept our place as a fallen empire. For traitors, there can be no other sentence than death. The Kaiser expects this of us, and we must not disappoint him. Victory means annihilation of all resistance. *Kultur* must prevail."

WWI German Iron Cross medal forged by the British as an anti-German propaganda medal. The words 'FOR KULTUR' is a scornful pun on the Kaiser's claim to be spreading culture.

71

"*TODESSTRAFE*"

W hen Edith heard the heavy prison doors open and slam shut, she knew they were gathering up the prisoners and would soon be coming for her. She dreaded what might come next. Putting her sewing aside, she threw a coat around her shoulders to protect her from the chill of the rainy day. The metal key slid into her cell lock. As the door creaked open, she heard one guard mutter under his breath to the other, "Five have got the death sentence. The others got hard labor." He motioned to Edith. "Come with us."

Looking down the long, bare corridor, she saw far off the silhouettes of two figures. By the way they walked, she thought that one was a guard and the other a prisoner, but she couldn't make out who it might be. She turned to one of the guards. "Where are you taking me?"

He shoved her forward. "You will find out soon enough."

She remembered the days when she walked miles every day between the Clinique and the hospital and thought nothing of it. Now she ached as she walked down the long corridor leading to…to what? She searched the faces of the guards for a clue, but their eyes gave nothing away.

At the end of the corridor, all the guard said was, "Turn left. Assembly hall." He pushed her through a door.

Her eyes surveyed the large room. About thirty prisoners were directed to form a semicircle around the back of the otherwise empty room. She recognized each as someone who had been tried along with her.

Louise Thuliez's thin frame was covered with a coat, hat, and mittens. Her straight hair, normally pulled up in a roll, randomly stuck out, giving her the appearance of a scarecrow. She gave Edith a quick nod and a faint smile. Edith returned the gesture of recognition.

Then her eyes were drawn to Philippe Baucq, who stood in the front. He was in constant motion, shifting his weight, folding and unfolding his arms, and running a hand over his head and neck. She moved to stand behind the line. Looking beyond those in front of her, she saw Ada Bodart coming through the door with an expression of bewilderment. When she recognized the others, her face relaxed.

Four more prisoners entered the room and found their places with the others. Many of the prisoners were half-dressed, as if they had been yanked from their cells without warning or preparation. They instinctively huddled together as if to seek protection from what was about to come. There was a low murmur of subdued voices. Most stood with heads bowed except for a furtive glance now and then. Edith felt weak and leaned against the back wall for support.

Acting as if he were the host of an elegant party, Stroeber appeared with a flourish in front of them. His leather boots clicked against the tile floor as he walked to the middle of the room and faced the prisoners. He looked resplendent in his crisp gray uniform. His leather belt and holster were highly polished, his mustache waxed and trimmed.

A small parade of figures filed in behind Stroeber. First came the tall, red-faced Lieutenant Bergan, who stood in anticipation of performing any task Stroeber asked of him. Behind Bergan entered a German chaplain, walking with his head down and hands clasped in front of him. Two German officers followed next, with guns on their hips and holding rifles across their chests. They positioned themselves on each side of Stroeber.

With an arrogant smirk on his face, Stroeber stared at the pitiful group of prisoners through a monocle. He wagged his fingers at Bergan. Seeing the gesture, Bergan immediately reached into a portfolio, pulled out a paper, and handed it to Stroeber. Stroeber snapped it up with a flourish and held it out in front of him with both hands. Seeing him poised for an announcement, the prisoners stopped moving, and the room fell silent. Stroeber began to read from the paper, sounding as if he were bestowing awards.

"Philippe Baucq: *Todesstrafe*."

There was a universal gasp and everyone immediately turned to look at Baucq. Philippe's face flashed an expression of pain, and his knees buckled. Two men on each side of him caught him as he was about to crumple and held him up.

"Louise Thuliez: *Todesstrafe*." Louise shuddered and slumped over a bit. When she straightened up, her cheeks were flushed. She searched faces around her with a pleading look in her eyes.

"Louis Severin: *Todesstrafe*."

"Countess de Belleville: *Todesstrafe*."

Stroeber stopped, searched the crowd, and finding Edith, his eyes locked on her. His lips curled into an cynical smile. She looked back into his eyes and held them with the full force of her compelling gaze.

"Edith Cavell: *Todesstrafe*."

Edith's heart began to pound and a tightness gripped her throat, making it difficult to breathe. She slumped against the wall.

For the others, Stroeber announced the sentences of twenty, ten, or three years of hard labor. When he finished, he surveyed the prisoners and smiled. He had gotten what he wanted from the judges. He had known he would. He always did. His success as a prosecutor was well known in Germany, but now everyone in Belgium would also remember his name.

"Interpret," he commanded as he snapped the paper over to Bergan. Bergan took it and translated the sentences into French. But no one needed the translation; they all knew from the trial what *Todesstrafe* meant. Finally, Bergan lowered the paper and asked, "Do any of you have anything to say?" His question was met with stunned silence. "You may appeal your against sentences in writing."

One prisoner immediately pulled a paper out of his pocket, stepped forward, and handed Bergan an appeal for mercy addressed to the military Governor General. The prisoner next to Edith leaned over and whispered, "Make an appeal for mercy."

She shook her head. "It's useless. You see, I am English. They want my life."

Stroeber clicked his heels together, spun around, and marched out the door, leaving Bergan and the chaplain to face the distraught group.

"*Vive la Belgique!*" yelled Philippe. Two guards immediately grabbed him and pushed him out of the door. Other prisoners took up the chant. "*Vive la Belgique! Vive la Belgique!*"

Bergan backed away, fearing he might have a riot on his hands. "Take them back to their cells!" he barked at the guards.

Still stunned, Edith did not move away from the wall until the German pastor, Reverend LeSeur, took her by the elbow and led her out of the hall and into a side room. Edith leaned against the table and then turned to face him. "How much time do I have?" The abruptness of the question made LeSeur blink a few times. He cleared his throat.

"Unfortunately, I have been given the difficult task of telling you that you only have until tomorrow morning. The execution will take place at the Tir National Firing Range in Schaerbeek."

Her body slackened against the table, and her eyes glazed over for a few seconds, then refocused on him. "I understand."

LeSeur took her hand in his. "I am at your disposal for pastoral services any time you need me, day or night."

"Thank you. I expected this."

"Please, can I not show you some kindness at this difficult time?" He saw her blue-gray eyes looking at his German uniform. "Please do not see me as a German, but only as a servant of our Lord and Saviour. I place myself at your disposal."

She withdrew her hand. "I have just one request. Would it be possible for me to write to my mother in England? I gave her my promise that I would do everything in my power to inform her of my circumstances, and I want to keep my promise. She expects this much of me."

"If you give me your letter, I will do my best to see that it is delivered. One more thing. If you prefer to receive the final sacrament from a pastor of your faith, I know the Anglican pastor in Brussels, the Reverend Stirling Gahan. Would it please you if I asked him to come and administer the Holy Sacrament to you?"

Edith's eyes widened, and for the first time, a faint smile briefly flashed across her lips. "Yes, I would so appreciate your bringing him to me."

"I..." his voice trailed off. Looking for courage to continue, he fidgeted with his glasses, cleaned them with his handkerchief, replaced them, and then continued. "I...that is...it is my duty to stand at your side to the very last unless you would rather Reverend Gahan be there instead."

"No, that will not do. He isn't accustomed to...to such things."

"I am not accustomed to such things either. With your approval, instead of meeting you at the firing range, I will come here and escort you there."

"That is most kind of you," Edith said in a calm voice.

LeSeur motioned for the guard to take Edith back to her cell.

Edith struggled with how to explain to her mother all that had happened. She wrote a letter describing the recent events, and ended it with, *"my biggest regret was leaving you, but be assured, I do not fear dying."*

Next she wrote to Elizabeth.

Please take charge of my will and dispense my belongings to my family. My dear, you have been so kind to me, and I thank you for all you have done. I hope people will think of me as a nurse who tried to do her duty. I am not afraid."

And last, she wrote to Grace.

I want you to have my wrist watch. It has always been close to me, and will now be to you. I pray to God that He will keep you in His tender care. Forgive me if I have been severe at times. Remember that I loved you, and love you still. If God permits, I shall watch over you, and wait for you on the other side. I am neither afraid nor unhappy.

She put the letters aside and reached for her prayer book. Inside the flyleaf she wrote:

Arrested 5 Aug.1915.
Imprisoned at St. Gilles 7th October 1915.
Condemned to death on 8th Oct., with four others.
Dies at 7 a.m. on Oct.12, 1915.

She stared at the last entry and thought. People wonder all their lives when and how they will die. Will it be sudden or will they linger with illness? Will they be alone or surrounded by those they love? Will they be in some foreign place or in their own bed? How odd it is to know the exact time of my death, where it will happen, and how. *I had hoped to live long enough to see the full success of my work, but I am resigned now that others will have to see it for me. I pray that I will be remembered, at least for a little while, as one of the founders of this school. My work will live on in the nurses whose lives I have touched, and that is more than most people can hope for.*

With her mind at peace, she packed up her few belongings. When she came to the two vases of dying roses, she kissed the red rose Elizabeth had given her. She emptied the vases of water, but could not bring herself to throw the limp roses away, so she placed them on top of her bundled belongings. How appropriate that they are red—the color of love and bloodshed. Not knowing whether Reverend Gahan would be allowed to see her or not, she completed her prayers and climbed into bed. She was ready for the next morning.

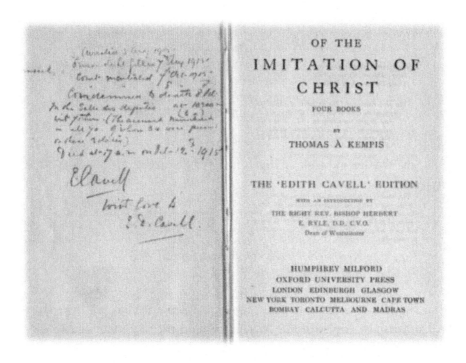

Meditation book, *The Imitation of Christ*, used by Edith Cavell.
(Photograph of author's copy of the book.)

72

"PATRIOTISM IS NOT ENOUGH"

The evening light darkened early to a somber gray. Nurses at the Institut huddled around a hearth heated with the few bits of coal available. Even this new building could not keep out the dampness of the rain. It was seven o'clock when one of the nurses looked out the window to see a man running up the walkway to their door. He gripped his coat closed with one hand and anchored his hat with the other. When he got closer, they recognized him as the lawyer who was also a member of the Institut's board of directors.

Hoping for good news, the women ran to the front door to welcome him. He stepped inside, stamped the rain off his shoes, and pulled off the wet, shapeless hat. Their hopes of some encouraging news sank when they saw the expression on his face. For a moment he stood there, water dripping off his nose and coat onto the bare wooden floor. Finally, in a hoarse voice, he whispered, "Poor child! Poor nurses."

"When?" asked one of the nurses.

"Tomorrow morning. At dawn or possibly even before."

"That's impossible! How do you know?"

"I overheard them talking at the Parliament Building."

"Oh, God," said Van Til. "She is lost to us forever."

Suddenly Elizabeth entered the room.

They ran over to her. "Have you heard? It's Madame. They are going to…"

Elizabeth held out her hands to the others. "I was just told. This is dreadful! I was giving a lecture for the Red Cross when I was called out and given the news. How can they do this? How can they even think of…?" Elizabeth choked before finishing the sentence. She paced aimlessly, her eyes darting from one person to the other. "There must be something we can do. I must find someone who can help us save her…" She ran weeping out of the room and disappeared.

The nurses waited for her to compose herself and return but when she didn't return, they could not think of what to do besides go to the prison.

"Maybe they will tell us it isn't true," offered Miss Buck, a new English nurse. "At least they may let us see her. She shouldn't be alone now."

"But shouldn't we wait for Mme. Wilkins?" asked Van Til.

"Where did she go?" asked another nurse.

Nurse Van Til reached for her coat. "Maybe she is already at the prison. We should go there, too."

The four nurses ran through the rain until they got to the great gates and turrets of the St. Gilles prison wall. They approached the guard. "We know it is late, but it is very important that we speak to Superintendent Marin. It concerns Mme Cavell."

The guard stood at the gate under a small arch. He looked miserable in the cold rain. He gave them a long look. "It is late. Come back tomorrow."

"No, it is of the utmost urgency that we see him now," insisted Van Til.

The guard saw the faces of the distraught nurses and without further discussion, motioned through a small window for the gate to be opened from the inside. Another guard met them inside the gate and escorted them to the office of the prison superintendent.

Mr. Marin looked up from his paperwork at the four women in his office. Recognising them as nurses, he tapped his tobacco-stained fingers on the desk. "I will tell you what I told the nurse who was here earlier. No one is allowed to see the Cavell woman except the pastor."

"Nurse? Was it Mme. Wilkins?"

"Yes, she has been here many times before asking to see your Mme. Cavell."

"Is she still here somewhere?"

"She was very upset, actually hysterical. She fainted, and I carried her to the couch to recover." The nurses gave each other worried looks.

"Where is she?"

"The Anglican pastor, Reverend Gahan, said he knew her and that he would take her to his home. He said his wife would take care of her until he returned from Mme. Cavell's cell."

"He is there now?"

"He is. Our chaplain made a special request for him to visit."

"Then it is true? What we heard, I mean. Mme. Cavell is to be executed tomorrow morning?"

Marin's fingers tapped faster. "Considering the other nurse's reaction, I hesitate to tell you anything more." He stood up and approached the women. "But I will be honest. Yes, it is true. Tomorrow morning. At dawn."

Van Til, the Dutch nurse, lowered her face into her hands and began to cry. Miss Buck held a handkerchief to her nose. The fourth, a Polish nurse, flung her arms around Van Til. Van Til looked over the nurse's shoulder to the superintendent. "Please, can we see Mme. Cavell? It can do no harm now. Just one more time. Surely you cannot deny a condemned woman some solace from her friends."

"I have my orders. There are two guards on duty at her cell. Only the pastor is allowed to see her. He will provide all the solace she needs. I will give her your goodbyes." He looked up at the clock. "It is nine o'clock. There is nothing you can do now. Go home."

They turned away. "We had better look after Mme. Wilkins," said Miss Buck.

They hurried through the rain to Reverend Gahan's house, where they were invited to come in by his housekeeper. Mrs. Gahan came into the room and greeted them. "I've been expecting you. Please come in. Your friend, Elizabeth Wilkins, was brought here an hour ago in quite a state of hysteria. I gave her a sedative, and she is resting now. My husband is still at the prison administering the last rites to Miss Cavell. The German chaplain at the prison arranged for him to see her. Please sit and I will get some tea to warm you up."

* * * * *

Reverend Gahan had left home immediately after he received the note from Reverend LeSeur. His heart pounded all the way to the prison. What should he say to a woman who would be shot to death only a few hours from now? Would she be distraught? Vindictive? Highly anxious?

When he arrived at her cell, Edith stood to greet him. "Good of you to come, Stirling. I had hoped we could have met again under better circumstances."

He was surprised by how calm she was. He felt his muscles relax and his anxiety ease. He pulled the chair in front of her, sat down, held both of her hands in his, and looked into her luminous blue eyes. "Edith, I am so sorry for all of this. I came to minister to you. Are you prepared to meet God tomorrow?"

She smiled and squeezed his hands. Her voice was calm and almost detached. "Stirling, my good friend, I have no fear of what tomorrow will bring. Death is just death, nothing else. I have seen death so often that it is not strange or fearful to me. It is a great honor to give my life for my country, and I am willing do it. I am prepared to meet my God on the other side."

He noticed how gaunt she had become. "You look so pale. Have they treated you well?"

"They have all been very kind to me. I thank God for these ten weeks of quiet before the end. Life has always been so hurried and full of difficulty. This time of rest has been a great mercy."

"They will not get away with this. There will be much said about this atrocity. I will personally see to it that what is happening to you will be known throughout England. This will not be hidden from the rest of the world."

"It is most important to me that my family knows I died with my soul offered to God. It seems that each warring group claims to have peace and justice on their side. But peace achieved through war does not lead to peace. Victory through violence leads to further violence and war. Standing as I do in view of God and eternity, I realize that patriotism is not enough. I must have no hatred or bitterness towards any one."

Gahan sat beside her on the bed, set the chair in front of them, and placed the vessels containing the host and wine on it. With tears in his eyes, Gahan asked for her confession. After she gave it, he offered her communion and anointed her forehead with oil.

"May the Lord Jesus Christ protect you and lead you to eternal life." Then he tucked the vessels back into a black, leather pouch and turned to her. "The hymn *Abide with Me* was written by a man suffering from tuberculosis just before his death. I believe the words are fitting for us now. He began to sing:

> *Abide with me; fast falls the eventide;*
> *The darkness deepens; Lord, with me abide.*
> *When other helpers fail and comforts flee,*
> *Help of the helpless, O abide with me."*

On the last round, Edith joined in with him:

> *Hold Thou Thy cross before my closing eyes;*
> *Shine through the gloom and point me to the skies.*
> *Heaven's morning breaks, and earth's vain shadows flee;*
> *In life, in death, O Lord, abide with me."*

"How can I be sure that heaven will be open to me after death?" asked Edith. "I am a sinful woman and so unworthy."

Gahan touched her hand. "Remember the thief on the cross? He also felt he was unworthy, but our Saviour's words to him were, 'Today thou

Stirling Gahan's Communion set, used on the day he visited Edith Cavell. (Owned by Martin Gahan, Stirling Gahan's grandson .)

shalt be with me in paradise.' Jesus forgives and admits all those who have been pardoned into His blessed presence."

Edith's shoulders visibly relaxed. "Then I will be free. Being confined as I have is almost like being dead while I am still alive."

He looked at her through misty eyes. "We shall always remember you as a heroine and as a martyr."

"Please don't think of me as a martyr. Think of me simply as a nurse who only tried to do her duty."

"I had better go now, as you will need to rest."

"Yes, I have to be up at 5 a.m."

They moved together to the cell door and stood face to face, holding each others hands one last time.

"Goodbye, my friend."

Edith squeezed his hands. "We shall meet again."

Gahan pressed them back. "Yes, we shall. God be with you."

* * * * *

As soon as Gahan arrived home, the nurses, who had been waiting for him to return, crowded around him.

"How is she?" asked Miss Buck.

"She is fully prepared for the…ordeal tomorrow. She has made her peace with God."

"Is she sick? Elizabeth said she looked so pale when she last saw her."

He handed his coat and hat to the housekeeper. "She told me her life had been hurried and full of difficulty, but that the rest these past weeks was a great mercy."

"How she must hate the Germans for this."

"Quite the contrary. She said she wanted no hatred or bitterness towards anyone."

He looked up to see all four nurses wiping their eyes. Van Til sobbed openly.

"She is really quite brave and calm," he assured them.

"Is there anything we can possibly do to help Madame? Anything at all?"

"I can think of only one last thing." He walked over to his closet and put his hat and coat back on. "Come with me to the American consulate and make a strong case for a reprieve. The Germans do not want to do anything to incite America to join England in this war."

Van Til wiped her eyes. "Do you think it will help?"

"Maybe; it has in the past."

— 73 —

THE APPEAL

Hugh Gibson's desk was piled with a mountain of administrative paperwork. He got up and walked around his desk, trying to figure out the best approach for organizing the paper stacks. He picked up a paper on top of one pile, read it, shook his head, and placed it back on top of another. He pulled out his pocket watch: eight o'clock in the evening. Even if he spent the next few hours working, he would never be finished by tomorrow; he felt overwhelmed.

Suddenly, there was a rapid knock on his door. Curious as to who would be seeking him out long after curfew hours, he opened the door with papers still in hand, and found himself staring down into five sets of anxious eyes. "Please come in." The four young women and the minister hurried into his office.

The minister spoke first. "We apologize for the lateness, but we have a matter of utmost urgency. We must see Ambassador Whitlock."

Hugh placed the papers in his hand back on the nearest pile. "I'm afraid that won't be possible. Mr. Whitlock is ill. No one can see him."

The four women looked at each other in bewilderment. "Please, we are desperate for his help," said Jacqueline Van Til. "We do not have much time. It is about our matron, Mme. Cavell. They have condemned her to die tomorrow morning. Please, you must help us! There is no one else to turn to!"

Gibson furrowed his brow. "Surely you are mistaken about this. I have been in contact with Mr. Conrad at the prison every few hours. He has assured me that no final disposition has been made and promised to inform me immediately when something was decided. He thought that might be tomorrow."

The four women broke out in tears. "Tomorrow! Tomorrow will be too late!" said Miss Buck. "They are going to execute her tomorrow morning. Please! Do something! Make an appeal for clemency! They will listen to you. You are our only hope."

"How do you know this is true?"

Gahan explained how the nurses had learned of the final verdict, how the German pastor had confirmed it and had broken the rules so Gahan could see her. "She was told she will be executed by a firing squad at dawn tomorrow."

Gibson pounded his fist on the desk. "This is outrageous! If it's true, they have been lying to us all along! They have arrested others for the same crime and not executed them. What do they think they are doing? Please, sit down. I'll call our legal adviser to go over and help Mr. Whitlock write a letter to the Baron von der Lancken." He paced about, holding the phone's cradle in one hand and the earpiece in the other.

Jacqueline only heard the parts of the conversation that took place when he turned in her direction.

"...Yes, it's urgent. Get him to write a strong letter of appeal...I know it's late. He can't come here...Because he's sick, that's why. We haven't much time...I'll have my driver pick you up and bring...then bring you here with the letter... the Spanish and Dutch ambassadors?... Good idea. I'll call them next."

Gibson turned to the huddled group of nurses. "M. de Leval and Ambassador Whitlock are putting together a strong letter of appeal and de Leval will meet us here. I'll call the Spanish and Dutch ambassadors to join us. It will add weight to our appeal. Maybe we can threaten them with an international response."

He rang and spoke first to the Dutch ambassador and then to the Spanish. Finally, he placed the earpiece back onto the phone cradle. "The Spanish ambassador, Marquis de Villalobar, has agreed to join me in making an appeal. Unfortunately, the Dutch ambassador, Maurice Van Hollenhover, has refused. He said the neutrality of his country would make an appeal illegal."

Hugh Gibson guided the women and the reverend to comfortable chairs and a table. "Wait here, while we go to see von der Lancken. He is our best contact with the Germans."

Jacqueline Van Til looked up and noticed a sculpture of a large golden eagle hanging on the wall over their heads. Its outstretched wings seemed to hover protectively over them. The sight of it made her relax a little. She sank into the chair, unfolded the handkerchief twisted in her hands, and wiped her eyes. Gibson threw on his jacket, straightened his tie, and rushed out the door.

Just as they were about to enter the motorcar, de Leval arrived. Gibson held out his hand. "Let me see Ambassador Whitlock's letter."

De Leval handed him the folded letter. Hugh unfolded it and held it in the dim light of the street lamp. His eyes darted over it:

Baron von der Lancken

Your Excellency:

I have just heard that Miss Cavell, a British subject and consequently under the protection of my legation, was this morning condemned to death by court-martial.

If my information is correct, the sentence in the present case is more severe than all the others that have been passed in similar cases tried by the same court, and, without going into the reasons for such a drastic sentence, I appeal to Your Excellency's feelings of humanity and generosity in Miss Cavell's favor, and ask that the death penalty passed on Miss Cavell be commuted, and that this unfortunate woman not be executed.

"God, I hope this works," said Hugh as he shifted the letter for more light.

Miss Cavell is the head of the Brussels Surgical Institute. She has spent her life alleviating the sufferings of others, and her school has turned out many nurses who have watched at the bedside of the sick the world over, in Germany as in Belgium.

At the beginning of the war, Miss Cavell bestowed her care as freely on the German soldiers as on others. Even in default of all other reasons, her career as a servant of humanity is such as to inspire the greatest sympathy and to call for pardon. If the information in my possession is correct, Miss Cavell, far from shielding herself, has, with commendable straightforwardness, admitted the truth of all the charges against her, and it is the very information which she herself has furnished and which she alone was in possession to furnish, that has aggravated the severity of the sentence passed against her."

Gibson looked up at de Leval. "Do you think this will make a difference?"

"It should, she was the only one who was truthful. That should count for something."

It is then with confidence and in the hope of its favorable reception that I have the honor to present to Your Excellency my request for pardon on Miss Cavell's behalf.

I am too ill to present my request to you in person, but I appeal to the generosity of your heart to support it and to save this unfortunate woman from death. Have pity on her!

Brand Whitlock
Ambassador to the United States of America

Hugh folded the letter and stuffed it into his inside jacket pocket. "If this doesn't work, nothing will."

He slid into the back seat of the motorcar and gave directions to his driver. "Take us to the Baron Lambert's, where Villalobar is dining, pick him up, then drive to the German Political Ministry."

"Yes, sir." The driver slid the engine into gear, felt it lurch forward, and rumbled over the cobblestoned streets. After picking up Villalobar, they stopped in front of the German Political Ministry building. The diplomats flung open the doors and rushed up the front steps.

"Wait here!" Gibson called back to the driver. Not seeing any light coming from the windows of the building, they pounded on the heavy oak door. It was opened by a military orderly holding a rifle across his chest.

"*Halt! Wer sind Sie?*"

The men showed him their papers. "We are the American and Spanish ambassadors, and this is our legal adviser. It is urgent that we see Baron von der Lancken."

"He is not here," said the orderly in German.

"Then where is he? It is of utmost importance that we talk to him tonight."

"He will be back in the morning. I will tell him you have come."

"No! We absolutely have to see him tonight. Now!"

"Not possible."

Villalobar stepped forward and looked down at the orderly. "Listen, the Baron requested that we notify him if we had urgent information. We are following his orders, and he will not be pleased that you did not bring us to him. Do you really want to disobey the Baron's direct orders?"

The orderly lowered his rifle. "I cannot tell you where he is, but I can try to bring him to you if I can find an available motorcar."

"Use ours; it is just outside."

Gibson hurried down the stairs to the waiting driver and opened the door. "Take this man to wherever he wants to go. Do not lose sight of him. When he finds the Baron von der Lancken, bring them both back here. Understood?"

"Yes, sir." The driver looked at the German soldier, still holding his rifle, and gave Hugh a questioning look.

"It's all right," said Hugh.

Two hours later, von der Lancken strode back into the Political Ministry building with two men in German uniforms. He introduced them. "This is Count Hurrach and the Baron von Falkenhausen." He removed his blue-gray overcoat and black leather gloves, handed them to the orderly, and seated himself behind his desk. He motioned for the two uniformed men to sit to either side of the desk, and for Gibson, de Leval, and Villalobar to sit facing him.

Hugh Gibson thought von Lancken's smile had all the warmth of a rattlesnake. After straightening each of his cuffs, von der Lancken cast a critical eye over Gibson's wrinkled coat and skewed tie.

"Tell me now, what is so important that it cannot wait until the morning?"

Gibson reached inside his coat pocket and took out Whitlock's letter. "Your office agreed to inform us of the final decision concerning the English nurse, Miss Edith Cavell. We have just heard the horrifying news that a decision was made hours ago, and that she is to be shot tomorrow morning. I have a note from the American ambassador, Mr. Whitlock, appealing for clemency on her behalf." He handed von Lancken the letter.

Von Lancken unfolded the letter and quickly scanned it, then threw it across his desk. "I know nothing of this case. In any event, even if she has been condemned today, no sentence of death would be carried out as quickly as tomorrow morning. It is disturbing that you would give credence to any report that did not come from my office. Any information that does not come from me is merely rumor. Do not bother me with false claims."

Hugh Gibson expected stalling, and even refusal, but not outright denial. He began to sense that von Lancken was putting on a performance for the two officers. If he challenged him too strongly, the German would go on the defense. But if he didn't, Edith Cavell would be shot within eight hours. Gibson shifted his stance. "We have every reason to believe our report is correct. If you do not believe it, please make the proper inquiries. It is possible you have not been fully informed."

"And who are your informants?"

After a long pause, Villalobar leaned forward and said, "We cannot divulge our sources, but we have every reason to believe they are quite accurate. Please look into it for yourself. Call the prison."

"As I said before, even if this were true, it is impossible that such a sentence could be put into effect within so short a time. It takes days of preparations. An entire firing squad must be formed and officials must be present. I suggest that we all go home and discuss this case in the morning after we have all had a good night's rest."

When Hugh leaned forward, he smelled whisky gusting off von Lancken's breath. He surmised that they had interrupted him while he was eating and drinking, maybe more. "Tomorrow morning will be too late. I beg you to call now and inquire. If I am wrong, we will apologize and go home."

"All our government offices are closed now. There is no one to ask."

De Leval's eyes locked onto von Lancken's. "We have had enough of your deception. You made promises to us that you have not kept. You made this woman inaccessible to anyone who could reasonably defend her. Your prosecutor convicted her before she ever appeared in what you called a 'trial.' No more deception. I know that you can call anyone you want, whenever you want, for whatever reason you want. If you are not hiding anything, call the judge who presided over the decision."

Von Lancken reached for the phone. A few minutes later, he slowly set the earpiece back in the cradle. His voice was somewhat contrite. "It seems that your sources were correct. Your Englishwoman is to be shot early in the morning."

Hearing this, Gibson burst out in anger and frustration, "What is there to be gained in shooting a woman? In the past, the sentence of death has only been imposed on those charged with espionage. That is not what Miss Cavell has been charged with. The sentence imposed on her does not fit the crime. This woman is no spy. She has been managing a nurses' training school and clinic, and teaching physicians in a well-respected hospital. For God's sake, she has cared for hundreds of your own German soldiers under the flag of the Red Cross. This act of cruelty will bring you more harm than good."

There was a flicker of sadness on von Lancken's face. "It is already settled. I cannot help."

Gibson leveled an accusing finger at the German. "Your political department has failed to comply with repeated promises to keep us informed of the progress of this trial, and its outcome. You have deliberately allowed your department to deceive the office of the American ambassador. When the rest of the civilized world hears that you shot a woman, a Red Cross nurse at that, what effect do you think it will have on your cause? What will people think of German *Kultur* then?"

Count Harrach interrupted Gibson. His meaty lips curled up in a sneer. "I am quite confident that the effect will be excellent."

Gibson could not contain himself. "You think so? How excellent was the effect when the civilized countries heard you burned down Louvain, executed its scholars and priests, deported 10,000 of its people, and burned 300,000 of its ancient manuscripts? How about the effect of your blowing up the *Lusitania* and drowning over a thousand innocent people, including women and children? Shooting this woman will only stir up more horror and disgust for your so-called *Kultur*. It will rank with your other atrocities. You have deliberately taken on a policy of subterfuge with the American ambassador. This execution and how you have handled it, might even incite the United States to join with England against you. Is shooting one Englishwoman worth taking that risk?"

Count Harrach shifted himself up in the chair. "Americans are weak. I am not convinced they would go to war over one old Englishwoman. I think I speak for all of the German officers and the Kaiser when I say we would rather see Miss Cavell shot than have harm come to the humblest of our German soldiers. My only regret was that we do not have three or four more old Englishwomen to shoot."

"Is this what German *Kultur* is all about? Shooting women? Call your headquarters," said Villalobar, "and lay the case before the Kaiser. See if he is willing to test America's patience by slaughtering this woman."

Von Lancken turned to Villalobar. "I cannot do that. I am not a friend of my sovereign, as you are of yours. I must remind you that the military governor of Brussels is the supreme authority in matters of this sort."

"Then call General von Sauberzweig to find out if he has already ratified the sentence, and if not, if there is any chance for clemency. We have no intention of leaving until we have heard directly from him."

Von Lancken's eyes shifted from Villalobar to Gibson, then to de Leval, and then back to the two officers. "If I contact him, I expect you to honor his final decision without further argument." The three men remained silent. "Since you have not disagreed, I will take your silence as consent." With that, von Lancken got up and left the room.

An hour later he returned, sat down, and faced his three visitors. "I have spoken to our military governor. He wants me to assure you that his actions in this case were taken only after intense deliberation, but that the character of Miss Cavell's offence was so grievous that the death penalty is imperative. He regrets to inform you that he must decline your ambassador's appeal for clemency."

"Then call the Kaiser. A woman's life is at stake here," shot back Gibson.

"Even the Kaiser himself cannot intervene." Von Lancken threw the letter across the table to Hugh. "Here, take back your letter. This meeting is over."

Gibson didn't pick it up. "Could you at least give Ambassador Whitlock's note to General von Sauberzweig as a matter of diplomacy?"

"I have read the note and will pass the contents on to the General."

Gibson reached over and picked up the letter. "When you destroyed the city of Antwerp, I crossed the lines at the request of your Field Marshal to look after German interests. Since you have invaded this country, we have never asked a favor from the German authorities, so it seems incredible that you would decline our request to delay this execution for even one day. You conducted her arrest, trial, and sentencing with trickery and deception, which is nothing short of an affront to human civilisation. Why are the German authorities so eager to execute her? You said yourself that to schedule an execution so soon after the trial was impossible and unprecedented."

Von Lancken looked down at his desk and shifted an ashtray over to von Falkenhausen, who was lighting a cigarette. Count Harrach dropped his hands to his lap and did not look up. Baron von Falkenhausen blew a cloud of smoke toward the ceiling. Gibson looked at each of them, waiting for an answer, but he was met with silence. He asked again. "Why are the German authorities so anxious to execute this middle-aged nurse? Is it because she is English that you are so unbending?"

Baron von Falkenhausen brushed a bit of cigarette ash off his tunic and tapped his cigarette on the ashtray. "She is not the only one who will be executed tomorrow."

De Leval looked puzzled. "I understood the executions of the other four have been delayed because of their appeals."

"That is true for three of them. The fourth will be shot at the same time as your Cavell woman."

"Who?" asked de Leval, shocked to be hearing this for the first time.

"An architect named Philippe Baucq."

"Philippe Baucq? The father and sole provider for three children and a wife?"

"Just as the Englishwoman did not think of the consequences of her treachery, neither did he. They will both be examples to anyone who helps the enemies of Germany."

Hugh now realized that no effort or argument would change the sentence.

Outside, the church bell was sounding midnight when the three men finally left to face the group of nurses who were waiting for their return. The thought tugged at Gibson that von Lancken was not himself in agreement with the final verdict, but could not persuade von Sauberzweig to accept Whitlock's appeal. He also realized why they wouldn't agree to wait one more day. Because in that one day, we could have had President Wilson, the other heads of states, and the Hague all roused to protest.

The slick black leather crackled in the cold as the men slid onto the seats of the motorcar. Hugh directed the driver to return to the American ambassador's residence. His breath formed a circle of mist on the window as he watched the Political Ministry building slide away.

"Heard them talking," said the driver.

Hugh looked at him. "Heard who talking?"

"The military orderly and that tall Jerry official Lucken or whatever they call him. We found Lacken in one of those seedy little theaters that entertains German officers. The orderly you sent to get him tried to make him leave but he wouldn't budge until the play was over. Must have been quite a play. I heard them talking about a second Jerry—a von Sauber-schweig, I think they said his name was. He was at one of those estaminets where the drinks are cheap and the women are easy, if you know what I mean. The first Jerry didn't want to disturb the second one because they said it would make him angry, and it wouldn't make any difference because they knew they could never get him to leave."

Gibson looked at de Leval. "Do you think von Lancken actually ever spoke to von Sauberzweig about the letter?"

"I had the feeling von Lancken was caught off guard on this," said de Leval, "and that he would have preferred a compromise of some kind. But with those two wolves at his side, who probably report to Sauberz-weig anyway, he knew that the General he would rain hell on them for disturbing him in the middle of a liaison with a female. I think von Lancken might have tried, but gave up. I cannot imagine confronting this drunken military governor."

"Oddly enough," added Villalobar, "I felt as if there was something else he wanted to say but did not dare to speak out of turn. I mean, what power does he really have other than to do the bidding of von Bissing and Sauberzweig? With von Bissing pushed to the back, he has to deal with the mad dog they sent here to reign terror on the Belgians. This is Sauberzweig's first test case, and he has to show he is worthy of the Kaiser's trust."

"After seeing Count Harrach and Baron von Falkenhausen, I think both von Bissing and Sauberzweig had better look over their shoulders. What cold-hearted bastards they are," said de Leval, rubbing the condensation off the window to see outside.

Gibson felt a headache begin to pound in his temples. He rubbed his forehead vigorously, hoping it would dissipate the pain. He wished he could run to some place away from the misery of this war. *How can I explain all of this to the nurses waiting for me at the ambassador's office?*

The minute he walked in, the nurses stood and instinctively moved closer together. He saw that Elizabeth Wilkins had joined them. Mrs. Whitlock was leaning over a tray of tea. He was relieved to see that Reverend Gahan and his wife had remained to support the nurses in any way they could. This would be helpful when the nurses heard what he was about to say.

There was no way to break the news gently. He could tell from the looks on their faces that they had read his own dejected expression and knew, even before he spoke a word, that the news was bad. He walked over to face the group and took Elizabeth's hands in his. "I'm sorry, the meeting did not go as we had hoped. We tried everything, but they would not accept Ambassador Whitlock's request for an appeal."

Elizabeth's lips quivered as she tried to control her speech. "Did you plead with the military Governor General?"

"We were not allowed to see him, but we did visit with von Lancken, who brought our letter to von Sauberzweig's attention, but he was unable to persuade him to accept our plea for leniency."

"There must be someone else we can talk to," pleaded Miss Buck.

"We tried to get them to contact the Kaiser but von Lancken refused," said de Leval. "He said it would do no good because all power in this decision has been given to von Sauberzweig."

Elizabeth fell back into the chair and sobbed. Her eyes were red and swollen from the hours of weeping, and her face was ashen. She rocked back and forth, repeating to herself, "Where there's life, there's hope. Where there's life, there's hope."

On the return trip to their living quarters, the group of nurses tried to accept that their beloved directress would never return.

— 74 —
PREPARATIONS

J acqueline Van Til sat on Edith's sofa, wrapped herself up in a blanket, picked up the crimson velvet cushion, and hugged it to her chest. Miss Buck stood by the coal stove in the corner and rubbed her hands over it for warmth. She removed her coat and shook the wetness from it. Elizabeth got just inside the door before she sank to her knees. "Oh, God! Oh, Lord! Please give me back my mistress! Take my life away if you will, but give her back to me!"

The Polish nurse, who had entered behind Elizabeth, cradled her in her arms. They rocked back and forth together, tears streaming down their faces. "We have done all that we can do. Her fate is in God's hands now," she said. But Elizabeth could not be comforted and continued to cry that God should take her life in return for Edith's.

Van Til noticed how much Elizabeth had aged since Edith's imprisonment. Her hair, once golden blonde with cascading curls, was now a dull, colorless hue and hung limply along the sides of her face. Her body seemed frail, as if the very life in it was ebbing away. She wondered what would happen to Elizabeth when Edith was gone. The nursing school and Clinique had come to depend on Elizabeth as a light that reflecting Edith's vision to the others. It seemed at times that Edith's own voice spoke through her.

No one moved to go to bed. No one could sleep. They simply sat in the parlor and wept together until they could weep no more. Elizabeth was helped to a chair, where she mercifully fell, exhausted, into a fitful sleep.

At five in the morning, they all put their coats on, walked through the darkness to the prison gate, and rang the bell to be let in. Mr. Marin, the prison superintendent, met them at the gate. Miss Buck's voice was choked with emotion. "Oh, please give her back to us. We need her to be with us. Please help us. She has been punished enough."

"Your Madame is a very brave woman and has prepared herself for the end."

This was met with more sobs. Not knowing what else to say to the women, who refused to leave, he offered, "If you wait for a while, you might possibly catch a glimpse of her when the motorcar carries her out through this gate."

* * * * *

That evening, Colonel Bulke knew that his tour of duty in Brussels had gone on much too long. He had been told early on that the war would be over in six months, but it had raged on for fifteen months with no end in sight. Brussels was becoming a cesspool of starving people with horse carcasses rotting in streets that were filthy with excrement and garbage, old women with thick ankles dressed in black, dirty-faced children in rags, and dark, mealy bread. Even the beer was watered down.

He had just been granted a week's leave of absence and planned to spend it in Frankfurt visiting his wife. He had packed his bags a week ago, but often went back to replace one pair of trousers or shirt for another. Now he set aside one uniform, spotless for when he greeted her, and rewrapped a teapot he had bought for her. He was thinking of the *Roggenmischbrot*, sugar beets, Weissbier, and sausage his wife would prepare for him.

Then Bulke received a call from the Military Governor, ordering him to plan for two executions at dawn the following morning, the day he had expected to leave. He fought back the feeling of anger over this disappointment.

He looked over his check-list. The prison supervisor had been instructed to have a minister available for both prisoners. The physician, Dr. Gottfried Benn, had been notified to be at the Tir National Firing Range in Schaerbeek. Von Sauberzweig had already informed Herr Stroeber and his secretary, Captain Behrens, about the executions and requested their presence. The last thing Bulke had to do was to assemble two firing squads, each with eight men. He called Lieutenant Bergan's office to make the necessary arrangements.

When this is over, he thought, *I will be on the next train to Berlin and then on to Frankfurt.* He set his watch, coins, and keys on the side table next to his bed. He slipped off his boots and polished them, along with his holster and belt. It was midnight when he poured himself two fingers of whisky mixed with water, lit a cigar, removed his tie, opened his shirt, and settled down in his armchair. He thought about making love to his wife. It would be a welcome change after the prostitutes at the military brothels. They relieved him, but never fully satisfied him. Would he carry his wife to bed immediately when he arrived, or would he wait until after they had eaten a fine supper and had a few drinks together?

75

BETWEEN LIFE AND DEATH

A slot in the rusty metal door opened and the German guard passed the breakfast tray through it. Edith opened her eyes to a still dark morning. She slid her feet out from under the covers onto the wooden floor and felt the cold seep through. In spite of all that had happened, she had never thought this day would come, not really. How could it be that an hour from now, she would no longer feel the morning's chill, never see another sunrise nor hear her mother's voice again? She moved the breakfast tray to a table. *It's best I go through this on an empty stomach.*

A narrow window high up on the wall grudgingly cast an angular square of a faint diffuse light over the cell below. She removed her nightgown and bundled it with the rest of her belongings. After balancing Elizabeth's two wilted red roses on top of the bundle, she dressed in her navy-blue nurse's uniform. In a motion so familiar to her that it had become instinctive, she pulled the starched white cuffs straight and buttoned the stiff collar. Looking into the faded mirror, she positioned the gauze cap on her head and tied the strings under her chin. Eight years ago, when she had designed this uniform, she never thought it would be the last thing she would wear. *I was proud to live in this uniform for the past eight years; now I will be proud to die in it.*

At 6:00 a.m., she reached for her meditation book, *The Imitation of Christ*, and wrote in the flyleaf, *"Died at 7:00 a.m. on Oct. 12, 1915."*

When the German guard opened the iron door to her cell, he found her kneeling beside the bed with her hands folded and resting on a small black book. He placed his hand on her shoulder. "It is time, Mme Cavell."

Outside her cell door, the German chaplain LeSeur waited for her. "Come with me," he said and held her arm to guide her through the prison corridors. As she passed the Belgian and German officials and jailers, they bowed to her. She acknowledged their tribute with a slight nod of her head. The corridor led to an open courtyard. From another doorway, she saw the architect Philippe Baucq being led out to join her. The fiery patriot never showed fear, not even now on the day of his execution. He reached out his hand to the German sentries and called out, "Let us bear no grudge." A few gave a slight wave back.

Two gray military motorcars waited for the prisoners in the courtyard with their engines running. Edith was instructed to sit in the back seat of the first car between two armed guards. The car with Philippe and his guards followed. The wheels of the two motorcars crunched over gravel and stone as they made a slow circle in the courtyard and headed for the great wrought-iron gates. Two guards unlocked the gates and shoved them open. They stood at attention on each side as the motorcars went by. Suddenly a blue cape, fluttering like a giant bird, caught Edith's eye. She heard a frantic voice crying out, "Edith! Edith!"

It was Elizabeth! She stiffened and fought the urge to turn and see her dearest friend just one more time. *If I turn to look at her, I will break down.* She bit the inside of her lip. *I will not let them see me in tears. They will think me weak and interpret my tears as remorse or regret and not as my grief over losing my dearest friend.* She covered her mouth with her hand and forced herself to look straight ahead.

Her car lurched and bumped over the cobbled streets slick with the predawn dew. Edith looked for the last time over the city she had loved and served. Eight years ago, when she first arrived, the streets had bustled with civilian motorcars. Now, gray military cars rattled over them. Back then, the sidewalks had burst with color from the flower vendors' stalls. Now, the empty shop windows stared out like the vacant eyes of a cadaver. Then, big, handsome Belgian horses stepped high as they pulled sleek, open carts filled with well-dressed patrons visiting on holiday. Now, the few horses that had not been confiscated or eaten by the Germans were old and boney or rotting on the streets. She watched the chimneys exhaling smoke into the steely clouds. *Strange to think that the sentence was announced only ten hours ago, and now I will not see the sun set on this day.*

Edith had once heard that some people who were about to die had their lives flash through a kind of review, but her mind did not do that.

Instead, everything present became more intense. She felt a strange dissociation between her mind and her feelings. Intellectually, she knew she would not be returning from this journey, but emotionally, it was difficult to believe. The car bumped over open holes in the road; Edith had to grip the edges of the seat to keep herself from sliding into either of the two guards. To steady themselves, the guards gripped the side arm straps.

The cars headed north toward Schaerbeek down a wide boulevard lined with beech trees, past the Parc de Bruxelles. She remembered bringing children here to play when she was a young governess for a wealthy Belgian family. One time, they had played a game of questions. "What do you most wish for?" asked one of the children.

"Why, what every English person wants; to be buried at Westminster Abbey, of course," she answered.

Now she saw the absurdity of that answer. She would not be buried in Westminster Abbey, or even in her own country. *I will be buried in a desolate dirt and rock firing range in a foreign country that is being destroyed by war. No matter, as long as my soul is safe with God.*

They passed a row of houses and then turned left. Her motorcar bumped down a cobblestone walkway and into a bowl-shaped firing range as large as a sports playing field, and stopped. The engine was turned off, and the two guards motioned her to get out. Standing on the yellow clay earth, Edith took in everything around her.

The entire area was closed in by dirt and stone mounds, the largest of which was at the front. Oak and maple trees grew on top of the other three mounds, preventing a clear view from surrounding houses. A light breeze blew a clatter of dead leaves in a circle around her feet. She looked up at the skeletal branches of the bare trees and inhaled the moist air. The mixture of the damp earth and fallen leaves had a sweet, fresh odor, but standing here made it feel dense and close.

The scene before her had a dreamlike quality. Ahead, two wooden posts had been driven into the ground about fifteen feet apart from each other. Behind them, at the foot of the hill, two graves gaped open. A simple wooden coffin rested next to each. Two groups of eight soldiers stood at attention in perfect lines facing each post. The butts of their rifles rested on the ground; their right hands gripped the barrels.

Philippe's car pulled up behind hers. She felt Chaplain LeSeur's hand on her arm as he guided her to one of the posts. Behind her, Philippe was accompanied by another chaplain, who led him to the second post. Her hands began to sweat and she rubbed them against her skirt. She fought to show no hint of fear to her executioners. Standing in front of the pole, she looked ahead and saw the prosecutor, Herr Stroeber, standing between the two firing squads. When their eyes met, he turned his head away from her gaze as if something else more important had caught his attention. Behind him stood a large crowd. Edith swallowed hard. How many witnesses does it take to confirm that two helpless people are dead?

LeSeur faced her and gripped her hands in his.

"May the grace of our Lord Jesus Christ and the love of God and the communion of the Holy Ghost be with you forever. Amen."

Edith squeezed back. "Please ask Reverend Gahan to tell my loved ones that I believe my soul is safe, and that I am glad to die for my country."

He released her hands. "I will also tell them you were brave to the end."

He looked over to Colonel Bulke and gave a slight nod. Bulke touched the sleeve of the soldier standing in line next to him and handed him a rope and blindfold. Private Rimmel took them and walked up to Edith.

At the other post, Chaplain Leyendecker stood facing Philippe with his back to the firing squad. As he ministered to the condemned man, Philippe called out, "Comrades! In the presence of death, we are all comrades!"

Colonel Bulke wrenched him back to the post. "No more of this," he growled in his face. Philippe gave him a wry smile. "What are you going to do about it? Shoot me?"

Bulke spat out the words, "If you want to prove your patriotism, die like a man." Then he handed the soldier standing at the end of the second firing squad another rope and blindfold.

The soldier walked over to Philippe. "Hands behind your back."

"No. No ties. And no blindfold. I will die watching the sun rise over my beautiful country."

The soldier looked to Bulke for direction. Bulke nodded back to him. "Let him be. He will not be going anywhere."

Rimmel tied Edith's hands around the post behind her. When he turned to face her, Edith noticed a cloud come over his expression. They searched each other's faces. Recognition struck both of them at the same time. She remembered caring for him when he had typhoid. Rimmel remembered her as the nurse who had saved his life and who looked like his mother. A tic made his upper lip quiver, and he ran the tip of his tongue over his upper lip to stop it. His eyes scanned her face— oval-shaped, with brown hair streaked with silver and pulled up on top; thin lips, fair skin; intense, deep-set blue-gray eyes, webbed at the edges; angular features bearing her British heritage.

"It is you. How can I do this?" His eyes pleaded with her for absolution.

She looked back at him with total comprehension of what he was feeling. In a calm voice, she said, "Karl, I am at peace. Be at peace with me. I have done my duty. Now you must do yours. Put on the blindfold."

He saw tears glinting in her eyes as he reached up to place the blindfold. His fingers fumbled with the knot; his jaw clenched so tight that it ached. Then he turned, straightened his shoulders, and stepped back into his place in the firing line.

Bulke watched the soldier's hesitancy with the eyes of a hawk. He made a mental note to deal with Rimmel later. He nodded to the prosecutor to continue. With all the confidence of a general who had just won a battle, Herr Stroeber turned to face everyone and read the sentences. After his words were translated into French, he addressed the two firing squads.

"You must execute these people without remorse. By their own admission, they have been justly tried and have been found guilty." He moved closer to the eight men who would be executing Edith and looked directly at Private Rimmel. "Have no worries at the thought of shooting a woman. She committed crimes of a heinous nature and must be punished."

Two crows strutted along a branch of a nearby tree, as if to mock the prosecutor. They squawked down at him with bragging confidence as if issuing their own orders to the humans below. When Edith heard the two crows, her cousin's words echoed from a corridor in her mind. "One is for sorrow. Two is for joy." *This is a joyous time. I will soon be with my God in paradise.*

Rimmel fought to control the slight dizziness and feeling of nausea that overcame him. Stroeber's words had affected him like a vague, miserable sickness. He gulped down a throatful of acidic bile. His mind snapped through past images like the repeat of rifle shots. Pain from his leg wound; the smell of carbolic acid; a woman's hands cleaning him with cool cloths; his mother's voice, or was it the nurse's voice? "You must rest." The odor of soap; a dark blue uniform—a nurse's uniform, or was it his mother's domestic uniform? His mother's Bible. "A memory of me always with you"—a picture of a rose on his Bible—the nurse smiling at him, "I pray you will blossom like this rose."

The images flashed through Rimmel's mind in no particular sequence; they shifted and played back again. *If I do this, I will never have peace. The only peace that truly matters is having peace with my own conscience. My soul will never have peace with God. This is not "Kultur." It is not patriotism. It is madness. This is brute force executing two people simply because it can.*

Colonel Bulke raised his arm. "Ready."

Sixteen men snapped up their rifles and placed them in shoulder position.

"Aim."

Sixteen rifle bolts snapped into position, ready to be fired.

Rimmel looked through his rifle sight at the blindfolded woman tied to a stake in the ground. He tried to focus on her, but her image shimmered and his mother's face appeared. He blinked and swiped his eyes over the shoulder of his uniform and looked again. He saw his mother, a domestic servant in her work uniform, coming home after work, reaching into the pocket of her blue uniform. "Karl, I brought you a surprise." Her wrist was cuffed in white when her hand pulled out a shiny red apple and held it out to him. Childish fingers reached for it.

Karl's hands and arms trembled. The rifle shook so badly he could no longer hold it. It burned in his hands, flew into the air, and landed on the ground. He stepped away from it as if it were a lethal snake and looked straight ahead. His voice cracked with emotion.

"Sir, I cannot fire at this woman. I feel sick. Permission to leave."

76

SEVEN BELLS

C olonel Bulke swept both arms up in the air. "*Halt!* Stop!" Fifteen soldiers drew back their rifles. Still at attention, their eyes shifted between Rimmel, their commander, and each other. Bulke walked over to Private Rimmel and leveled a hard look at him. Rimmel's lip continued to quiver but he looked straight ahead. In one quick motion, Bulke pulled out his revolver, put it to Rimmel's temple, and fired. A crimson halo exploded out from the point where the bullet entered. Rimmel's eyes flew open in surprise; his body wavered for a few seconds and then slowly crumpled to the ground.

Bulke shoved his revolver back into his holster. "This is how we treat mutiny," he announced to the remaining soldiers. He pointed to the two men who were standing to either side of Rimmel's body. "You two, move this traitor out of the way." The two soldiers stepped out of line and turned the dead private onto his back. Grabbing his hands and feet, they dragged him a few feet, laid him next to Edith's open grave, and returned to the firing line leaving a trail of blood behind them.

Bulke looked up and saw a soldier standing in the crowd of witnesses. He pointed to the soldier. "You, come. Stand here." He pointed to where Rimmel once stood. "You will shoot this woman when I give the order. Understand?" The soldier stepped up to the empty place in the firing line. "Yes, sir."

"Do you have a problem with that?"

"No, sir."

The bell tower of the nearby church began to peal out the time.

One bell.

Bulke swiveled back into position, facing the two firing squads and called out, "Ready."

Edith heard the bells, but time had now stopped for her. The chiming church bells transported her back forty years to her father's church in

Swardeston. She was just nine, and gathering dried autumn flowers in her mother's garden. It was before breakfast. She snapped off some Queen Anne's lace and held it up to the early morning light. She studied the delicate spidery brown skeleton left behind after all the flowers had fallen away. It looked like the fine woven reeds of a basket. She was fascinated by the precise symmetry. *I will draw this for Mother.*

Two bells.

"Aim!" Sixteen rifles snapped into action.

She looked up from the spent flower and saw her father coming toward her. His arms were outstretched, beckoning her to come to him. The flower bobbled in her fist as she ran to him.

Three bells.

"Fire!" Two salvos of eight shots rang out at the same time. Philippe called out, "*Vive la Belgique!*" and pitched forward.

Her father's strong arms wrapped around her and lifted her up. She felt weightless. She saw her father's smile and moved her face close to his, felt the smoothness of his cheek after a fresh shave, and inhaled the fragrance of soap and shaving lotion.

Four bells.

The volleys echoed back and forth around the dirt and stone walls. Edith's body slumped forward and slid to the ground.

"You must come with me," said her father. His voice was deep and strong. She felt safe with him. He always knew the right thing to do. He carried her in his arms through the garden into the morning light.

"Father, we are going away from home. Mother will miss us for breakfast."

"Edith, my precious daughter, we are going home, and when we get there, we will wait for her to join us."

Five bells.

Gray smoke from the rifles floated in circles and hung suspended in the air between the soldiers and the two victims.

Suddenly, the dead flower in her hand came to life. It burst open, with delicate white flowers. She looked at it with surprise, then looked around the garden. It had changed as well. All the flowers had suddenly blossomed: blue hollyhocks, pink roses, white lilies, red geraniums, yellow daisies, and primroses. The bushes were full and green.

Six bells.

The two crows screamed out and flew to a tree further away. Suddenly, there was a collective gasp. A murmur ran through the onlookers. Edith's body was moving as if trying to raise itself.

"*Mein Gott!* She is still alive!" called out LeSeur.

Edith heard a crow calling out in the distance. Was it one crow calling out twice or two crows, each calling out once? She couldn't tell, but it didn't matter because a pathway of light had opened up before them and drew her attention away from the sound. She wriggled out of her father's arms onto the ground and ran into the brightness. "Father, hurry! Look at the beautiful sunrise!"

Seven bells. Then silence.

Bulke swiveled around and saw Edith's body moving. He strode over and stood looking down at her. Drawing his revolver, he took a steady aim at the center of her forehead and fired. Her body fell back and her hair fanned out on the ground.

Dr. Benn ran to her body. He leaned over, put his stethoscope to her chest, then looked up at the astonished soldiers and witnesses and shook his head. "She's dead."

The murmur from the onlookers got louder. In disbelief of what they had just witnessed, they looked around at each other for confirmation. Dr. Benn walked back to his place next to LeSeur and spoke softly so no one else could hear. "There are only three bullet holes in her chest." LeSeur looked puzzled for a moment, then understood what the physician was saying.

"So five of them shot wide," he responded.

"Yes. We must not speak of this to anyone."

When they looked back at Edith, a radiant sunrise flashed over the horizon, bathing her body in a bright golden light.

Edith heard a far-off voice shouting something and then a shot, but she felt nothing. She took her father's hand. Their feet glided over the garden pathway and into the brightness. Never before had she felt such peace and joy.

Bulke reholstered his revolver and turned to face the eight soldiers standing in front of the dead woman. He pointed to two of them. "You two, help Dr. Benn with her body and close the grave." He pointed to the next two soldiers.

"You two, dig a grave for this traitor," he said pointing to Rimmel's body. Bury him next to her. It will be his punishment to spend eternity lying next to an Englishwoman."

He walked over to the second firing squad, pointed to two soldiers, and ordered them to bury Philippe. Finally, he called out, "Dismissed!"

Stepping away from the activity, he brushed the dust off his tunic and looked down at his watch: 7:10 a.m. Still early enough for him to catch the 8:00 a.m. train to Berlin and then home to Frankfurt.

"How the Germans murdered Edith Cavell." At the execution site. (vintage postcard.)

Edith Cavell's grave at the execution site in 1915.

77

Aftermath

THE NEW YORK HERALD

OCTOBER 22, 1915

"HAPPY TO DIE FOR MY COUNTRY"
MISS CAVELL'S LAST WORDS

*American Envoy Tricked by German Officials When He Fights
to Save Miss Cavell. Report of Mr. Brand Whitlock declares
promise was broken when she secretly was condemned to
death. Ill in bed, he pleaded to have sentence commuted.*

*English nurse admitted to aiding allied wounded soldiers to
escape. Germans warned of reprisals by Mr. Benson, Secretary
of the Legation. Bishop of London calls woman's death
"Greatest crime in history."*
*The horror spread throughout Britain at the shooting by
Germans of Miss Edith Cavell, "The Florence Nightingale of
Brussels," the noble Englishwoman, whose last words, as
reported by the American Minister of Belgium, in an official
report were, "I am happy to die for my country" was voiced by
the Bishop of London yesterday.*

*The cold-blooded execution of this Englishwoman who, as a
Red Cross nurse, had cared for hundreds of wounded German
soldiers and rescued hundreds of Allied soldiers was shot by a
Brussels German official within hours of the completion of her
trial while the American and Spanish Ambassadors were
pleading for her life.*

*Addressing the wave of indignation to avenge her death, the
Kaiser is defending the act to soften the condemnation.*

"What did we do wrong?" Brand Whitlock asked Hugh Gibson as he placed the paper on his office desk.

"I don't know. Maybe we should have had our own representative sit in on the trial, or maybe we should have appointed a different lawyer."

Whitlock raised the coffee cup to his lips, gulped down a mouthful, and then curled his hands around it. "We weren't given much of a choice, were we? We did have de Leval looking over things. Have you spoken to him since the execution?"

"I heard from him yesterday. He said Sauberzweig had a copy of the *London Times* with our reports printed in headlines over the front page. Since the Huns can't threaten you, he said they are threatening to send him to a concentration camp in Germany for reporting on the Cavell case."

Whitlock reached over to Gibson's cup with the coffee pot. "Have another cup. It's good ole American coffee. Not that sludge the Belgians call coffee."

"Thanks. You know, de Leval wasn't the only person to report this story. When I sent in my report to the American ambassador's office, it

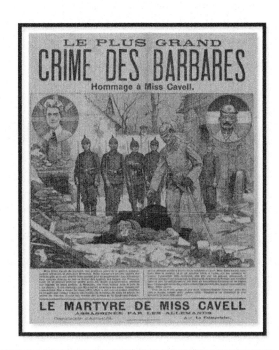

French poster depicting the execution of Edith Cavell by the Germans. "The most atrocious crime by the barbarians. Homage to Miss Cavell."

was forwarded to the British Foreign Secretary, who sent the whole lot of it to the press. That's when it got published in the *London Times*. It's just now getting around to the American newspapers."

"And also the French newspapers. Have you seen this one?" Whitlock threw over *Le Petit Parisien*. Gibson picked it up and began to read out loud.

"The assassination of Miss Cavell. The crime denounced by the whole world."

He looked up. "It's an article reprinted from a London newspaper. Word gets around." He continued to read. "Even the horrible attack on the *Lusitania* did not move the English people as much as the details officially given of the execution of Miss Cavell. Who is going to avenge the murder of this magnificent woman? The Bishop of London said, 'The iniquities committed by the Germans in Belgium and the crime which destroyed the *Lusitania,* will ever be remembered in history. But the cold-blooded act committed against this woman because she harbored refugees is never to be forgotten.'"

He pushed the paper back over to Whitlock, who coughed and then blew his nose into a handkerchief. "Sorry, I came to the office to catch up but I'm still not completely over the grippe or whatever it is." He spoke through his handkerchief. "I hear they are honoring her on October 12, which is Trafalgar Day. It is a special English holiday to honor war heroes over in Trafalgar Square."

Headline of Edith Cavell's death in the *New York Times*.

Gibson reached into his briefcase and pulled out another newspaper. "I saved the best for last." He arched an eyebrow. "*It's the Kölnische Zeitung*, a German newspaper. I got it from de Leval yesterday, who wrote out the translation. I'm better at his handwriting than you are, so I'll read it. It's entitled '*Justice or Chances*.'"

He walked over to the window for additional light and cleared his throat. " 'A pompous memorial service is taking place in St. Paul's Cathedral for the English Nurse Cavell, who has been executed in Brussels. Those present at the service will include a representative of the king, as well as heads of state. Some people have started street collections in slotted cigar boxes to aid the Cavell Fund for a memorial. The English press cannot refrain from publishing articles of the most abusive character against the Germans.'"

"That's not bad coming from the Huns," said Whitlock. "I'm surprised it isn't worse."

"Before you speak too soon, let me read you the rest of it. 'Everything seems to indicate that the Cavell case has made a very deep impression on the public feeling in England and that public opinion has been greatly incited in order to use the execution of a woman to forge a moral weapon against Germany. We are gradually getting used to the fact that the English and American press have joined in the howling of the London wolves. It is in an undignified manner that the English beg for

Campaign to recruit volunteers using a poster depicting Edith Cavell's death.

the pity of the Americans. One has no choice but to be disgusted about the false conclusions contained in the English propaganda. We hope this will serve as a warning to other Belgians who would consider harboring criminals against our state.'"

Whitlock exclaimed, "False conclusions? What false conclusions? They took a 49-year-old nurse, tied her to a pole, and shot her in cold blood, and they call the English press reports of her death 'undignified?' Outside of Germany, there isn't a single person in Europe or America who would read this story without feeling the profoundest horror and pity. *Kultur*, my ass."

"Actually there is one person who disagrees with you, and he lives in America."

"Not President Wilson." Whitlock stated.

"Of course not. I think this just might be the straw that breaks the camel's back, or in this case, *Kultur's* back. Up until now, Wilson has been able to keep the U.S. out of the war, but having Cavell's story illustrate what is happening over here might just be the thing to rally the American people to support England, even if twenty-five percent of them do have Germanic ties."

Whitlock leaned over to tuck his handkerchief in his back pocket. "So, who is it that would disagree with me?"

"It's Alfred Zimmerman, the German Under-Secretary for Foreign Affairs. If you think the German newspaper was bad, listen to how Zimmerman dances around to justify it." He pulled out another paper from a folder and handed it over to Whitlock. Whitlock put his reading glasses on, held the paper up at arms length, and read:

> ***"Arthur Zimmerman on the Execution of Edith Cavell***
> *It was a pity that Miss Cavell had to be executed, but it was necessary. She was judged justly. We hope it will not be necessary to have any more executions."*

Whitlock looked over the edge of the paper. "Well, he's getting his wish. There's been such a backlash about shooting Cavell that they have now stayed execution for the 33 others."

Whitlock continued reading:

It is undoubtedly a terrible thing that a woman must be executed; but consider what would happen to a state, particularly in war, if it left crimes aimed at the safety of its armies to go unpunished simply because they were committed by women. I have before me the court's verdict and I can assure you that it was gone into with the utmost thoroughness, and was investigated and addressed to the smallest detail."

"Tell that to her lawyer, who never got a chance to work up a pretrial defense. Hell, he never even got a chance to talk to her."

The result was so convincing, and the circumstances so clear, that no war court in the world could have given any other verdict, for it was not concerned with a single emotional deed of one person, but a well-thought-out plot, with far-reaching ramifications, which for nine months succeeded in doing valuable service to our enemies to the great detriment of our armies.

He scanned the rest of the paper and then put it down. "How does this man sleep at night? Seems like he missed a few facts, but why let the truth get in the way of a good excuse?"

Gibson looked down at a German regiment marching down the street, let the curtain fall back, and returned to his seat near Whitlock's desk. "You mean something like how the punishment didn't fit the crime? The Germans have since taken care of that. They just posted a new edict changing the law under which she was tried to include the word "death." Nothing like committing the crime and then creating the laws to justify it."

"Hugh, I'll be returning home in December for Christmas. While I am there, I plan on having a long talk with President Wilson and will straighten out the misconceptions in Zimmerman's report. Wilson should know how our pleas for Cavell's clemency were ignored. Her death is a blatant violation of human rights. The world is at war over here, and Americans are sitting with their hands over their ears. This might be just the incident that will stir up public opinions to convince the president to support the Allies."

* * * * *

Private Robert Mapes dropped his newspaper. His cheeks flushed, and his shoulders slumped. He slid his hand over his face.

"Supper is on the table. Tuck in!" his mother called from the kitchen.

Not hearing a response from her usually hungry son, she wiped her hands on her apron as she walked into the living room. "Robert? What's wrong?

He held the newspaper up for his mother to read.

"It's Nurse Cavell, Mother. They shot her. How could they do that to a woman—a nurse?"

"What nurse? Who shot her?"

Sweat from his hands smeared some of the print as he handed over the newspaper.

"Here, read it for yourself."

She took the newspaper and read out loud:

*"**NURSE CAVELL EXECUTED BY GERMANS.***
The story of the killing of Nurse Cavell by the Germans in Brussels is reverberating throughout the civilized world. Sir Edward Grey is confident that the news of the execution of this noble Englishwoman will be received with horror and disgust, not only in the Allied states, but throughout the civilized world."

She looked over to him. "Who is this Grey bloke?"

"He's the Foreign Secretary."

She continued to read.

It seems his prediction is correct. 'This is savagery,' reports neutral Holland. 'The peace of the future would be incomplete and precarious, if crimes like these escaped the justice of peoples,' writes the Paris Figaro. *'The killing of Miss Cavell will be more expensive than the loss of many regiments,' said the* New York Herald.

Nurse Cavell, a Red Cross nurse at the Berkendael Hospital, met her demise when she admitted to rescuing 200 soldiers and helping them escape, although sources say that number is too modest and that the actual number is closer to 1,000."

"A thousand soldiers. Good Lord!"

"Yes, and I'm one of them. I took a bullet in my ankle and couldn't walk. She took me in, tended to my wound, and helped me make it to the border. Were it not for her, I would have popped my clogs long ago."

Evelyn reached out and put her hand on her son's knee. "Why didn't you tell me this before?"

"Because we were all sworn to secrecy. We had to protect her identity and not speak of what she was doing. We feared for her safety because so many of us depended on her for our lives. The war over there is horrible."

Evelyn's eyes welled up as her son spoke. After a few silent moments, she looked back at the paper. The print wavered in front of her eyes as she silently read on.

Dr. Benn, the physician who attended to her at the execution, commented, "She was the bravest woman I ever met, and was in every respect the heroine her nation has made of her. She went to her death with a poise and bearing which is quite impossible to forget."

Feelings are most intense in the United Kingdom, where this tragedy was the theme of many pulpit references recently. On October 29, a memorial ceremony will be held in her honor at St. Paul's Cathedral, where it is expected 10,000 voices will join together to sing, "Abide with Me," the hymn Nurse Cavell recited the night before she died. The Prime Minister and a representative of King George will attend. They are reserving space for nurses from hospitals all over London.

Another memorial ceremony is planned in Norwich Cathedral, near where she grew up in Swardeston. The Nursing Mirror, for which she wrote as a war correspondent, urges the institution of a Cavell Cross for Heroism, a decoration for women only.

This will settle the matter, once and for all, about recruiting in Great Britain. The best memorial to Edith Cavell will be the determination of her fellow citizens to put aside self in willing service to their country.

"There will be no need now of compulsion," said the Bishop of London. Response has been overwhelming. Enlistment centers report that recruitment has tripled with men seeking revenge for the magnificent woman who gave her life to rescue others. Continual recruiting meetings are being held at the base of Lord Nelson's monument in Trafalgar Square.
In Nurse Cavell's native village, every eligible man has joined the Forces. A tide of enthusiasm has set in which has not yet waned. Similar enlistment activity is being experienced in Ireland, Scotland, Australia, New Zealand, Wales, and Canada.

Even wounded soldiers are pressing their physicians to approve them fit enough to go back to the firing line. "I will go back willingly to avenge this great woman's death," said one veteran soldier. "If she can die like a man for our country, so can I. If she were a soldier in the King's service, we'd be pinning the Victoria Cross on her chest."

That the Germans are conscious of the extremely bad impression their actions have produced in neutral countries may be judged by the apology prepared in Berlin and sent to London from Amsterdam. In an interview with the Associated Press of America, the Home Secretary, Sir. John Simon, will address their excuses. Pleas for mercy from the American and Spanish consulates were ignored.

A proposal for a national memorial has been suggested. She died as she lived, with the courage of a loving heart.

On the same page as the article, Evelyn noticed an advertisement with Edith's picture that read "*Murdered by the Huns. Enlist in the 99th and help stop such atrocities.*"

Mapes pounded on the arm of the sofa, sending a puff of dust spiraling up into the air. "This isn't over, you know. The Huns aren't going to get away with some damned weak apology. We won't forget this. It's going to be the sorriest thing they ever did, mark my word. They'll find out they will be much worse off dealing with one dead Nurse Cavell than with a hundred live ones."

78

October 1921–The Ceremony

E lizabeth boarded the train to Norwich and settled back on the raffia cloth seats. She pitched forward as the train lurched off. Gradually, the clacking of the metal wheels on the rails fell into a rhythm that had a mesmerizing effect on her. She gave in to it and closed her eyes.

Scenes from the past flashed across her mind. She remembered as people had crowded along the railway line to pay their last respects to Edith as her coffin made its way from London to Norwich. Children, eyes filled with tears, threw flowers onto the track. Men with black armbands stood with hats held over their chests. Soldiers stood stiff at attention, hands to their brows in salute. Women dressed in black, with heads bowed, wiped their eyes as the train passed. Many strained to catch a glimpse of Edith's coffin, draped with the Union Jack.

Little did I know when I left London for Brussels that first time that we would both be returning on the same route, under very different circumstances.

She opened her eyes and sat up, but the shadows of the past continued to haunt her thoughts. It was two years ago, the spring of 1919, when she was told Edith would be exhumed and returned home. Disinterred. The word was sickening. It represented the finality of death because only the dead get disinterred. She knew Edith would have wanted her remains sent home.

Elizabeth replayed those last few minutes of Edith's life in her mind. What was Edith thinking as she stood there, tied to a stake, waiting for the end of life as the bullets crashed into her chest? Did she think of Elizabeth and the nurses she was leaving behind? Or of her mother, father, sisters, and maybe even Edward? Or that she would be buried forever in foreign soil and be forgotten? Knowing Edith, she would pray that God would accept her into His kingdom.

Elizabeth remembered pleading with God over and over again, but it was not to be. She winced when she recalled seeing Edith on that last morning, sitting in the back seat of a black military motorcar disappearing from her. *Didn't she hear me calling out to her? Why didn't she turn around?* She had needed that one last look from Edith that would have acknowledged their deep friendship. She remembered silently pleading, *Please look at me. Remember me as I will you, forever.*

She reached into her pocketbook and pulled out a slip of paper she had found in Edith's belongings and copied it. She read from the worn paper:

> *Storms may gather, O love, my love,*
> *But here shall thy shelter be*
> *And in my arms, my dear, my dear,*
> *The sun shall come back to thee.*
> *The winter of age, O love, my love,*
> *For us no shade shall bring*
> *But in thine eyes divine, my dear, my dear,*
> *For me, 'twill always be spring.*

"Ticket, miss?"

Elizabeth jumped at the voice. "Oh, yes, of course." She snapped open her purse, pulled out her ticket, and handed it to the conductor.

"Going to Norwich?"

"Yes."

She watched the conductor punch a hole in the ticket. "Visiting family or friends there?"

"One very good friend."

"It will take a few hours, so relax and before you know it, you'll be greeting your friend with open arms."

She gave a non-committal shrug. "Not exactly, but thank you."

A woman in a long skirt and ragged shoes came through with bunches of flowers bundled in her arms. "Last of the season," she called out as she offered them for sale to the passengers. She stopped in front of Elizabeth. "What will it be, Luv? Asters, carnations, roses, sunflowers, or daisies?"

"Two carnations, please." She reached in her purse and passed a coin to the woman.

"Thank you, Luv," said the woman as she handed her a red and a white carnation, then continued down the aisle. Elizabeth twirled the stems in her fingers. The red and white color brought back the images of Edith's flag-draped coffin, covered with red and white carnations in the shape of a cross, being carried into Westminster Abbey. Everyone on the streets stood hushed. Her casket, hoisted on the shoulders of soldiers inched forward to a steady, slow drumbeat as it was carried into the Abbey at the very site where monarchs were crowned, kings and queens were joined in matrimony, royal babies were christened, and those who held in the highest regard by Britain were eulogized as their remains were laid to rest. It was the British Holy of Holies.

Her train pulled into Thorpe Station in Norwich, belching out a cloud of steam as it came to a halt. When Elizabeth was last here, Edith's coffin had been carried off the train, placed onto a horse-drawn gun carriage and slowly moved up the Prince of Wales Road to the Norwich Cathedral. Elizabeth remembered how difficult it was to be there, yet she would have had it no other way.

Edith's coffin was carried into the church by some of the same soldiers she had rescued. The Bishop of Norwich gave the eulogy. "She was glad to die for her country and had no fear of death, having been in touch with it so often." Even the German chaplain, Reverend LeSeur, had attended and emphasized that she was a "a very brave *Fräulein*." The Bishop had said that she taught us the same lesson of forgiveness that Christ had when He forgave the sins of the thief on the cross next to Him.

Tomorrow there would be another ceremony, but for now, it was quiet in the city of Norwich. Elizabeth made her way outside behind the cathedral to Edith's grave. She had heard that King George had wanted Edith buried in Westminster Abbey, but her family had wanted her closer to home. She placed the red and white carnations on Edith's grave and then sat on a bench facing it. The solitary grave seemed like an anticli-max considering all that had happened since Edith's death.

It was marked with a simple stone cross. Inscribed in stone beneath it were the words:

To the pure and holy life of Edith Cavell
who gave her life for England, 12 October, 1915
Her name liveth forever.

It felt good to be here close to Edith. She often found herself addressing Edith in her thoughts and occasionally out loud when no one was around. It was the only way Elizabeth could handle the loneliness. Maybe loneliness wasn't the right word—more like aloneness. Nothing replaced the shared vision, the commitment, or the closeness she had experienced with Edith. She had felt so alive then. Edith had inspired her to create and accomplish the impossible. Now, her life felt more like a faded photograph.

As the sky was beginning to darken, she addressed the square of freshly planted pansies over the grave. "The Kaiser admitted he would have been better off losing an entire regiment than to have executed you, Edith, my friend. He actually admitted that shooting you was the worst mistake he made during the war. You brought the leader of Germany to his knees. I should tell you that he transferred Sauberzweig to the Western Front. Oh, and Colonel Bulke, your executioner, was mysteriously shot. They never found out who did it.

"Edith, I want to hate the Germans for what they did to you, but I know you would never approve of that. You would tell me that loathing them would sink me to their level of hatred and evil. After the war, the Belgians arrested Quien, you know. Jacqueline Von Til and some of the other nurses identified his picture for the police when they captured him."

She paused and sighed. "I was so very upset when you chose death over life, but Jacqueline was probably right when she said your ultimate goal could only have been met with your death. She said the governing body of the nursing school would have considered your actions not fitting for a nurse and would not have let you return to your post, at least not for a long time. That alone would have crushed you."

She didn't notice an elderly man, dressed in a black suit, limping down a narrow pathway behind her. He stopped next to her. Bent over and leaning on a cane, he said, "I come by here every day. I've never seen you here before."

"I'm just visiting."

"I always know when it is the anniversary of her death. That's when they plant the pansies."

"They are quite lovely. She loved flowers. Did you know her?"

"Everyone in Norwich knew her. If they didn't before she died, they rightly did after."

"What did you think of her?" asked Elizabeth.

"She saved the life of my nephew, Sergeant Jessie Tunmore. He was one of the pallbearers who carried her coffin to this cathedral for her final laying to rest. There were many soldiers who came home because of her."

"I remember your nephew. He came to us with another fellow, a Private Lewis. I remember he convinced Edith he was not a spy by identifying her picture of this cathedral. He saved both their lives by doing so."

Edith Cavell's funeral at Norwich Cathedral.

The old man looked over to the solitary stone cross, where a crow had landed. It looked down at the carnations, crowed twice, and flew off.

"Not a very fitting grave, is it?" asked the man.

"It is as her mother wished. She thought it should resemble the graves of fallen soldiers."

"Her poor mother. She died a few years after her Edith's death. It broke her heart. There was some talk that Edith deserved what she got, because she took care of enemy soldiers and deliberately broke the law. Her mother never stopped defending her." He stepped a few feet closer to Elizabeth and faced her. "What do you think of her?"

Edith Cavell's final resting place behind Norwich Cathedral, Norwich, England. (Photo by the author.)

The question unlocked a torrent of emotions in Elizabeth. What could she say? That she loved her? That her departure had left her with a crushing weight of despair and sadness? That for the rest of her life she would be haunted by thoughts of what else she could have done to save her? That memories of Edith kept her awake at night so often that the days became exhausting?

The bells in the cathedral tower began to ring out the time: six o'clock. She thought about how often Edith would have heard those chimes while growing up. She shifted her eyes from the cross back to the man.

"So many things come to mind. What stands out is that she loved her work and everything about it. To Edith, it was not work; it was a calling. Even if she had never gotten become caught up with the war, what she accomplished would have distinguished her as one of our greatest nurses."

Elizabeth stood up, smoothed out the wrinkles in her skirt, closed the collar on her coat, and repositioned her hat. "It's getting cold and late. Will you be at the ceremony tomorrow?"

"Of course. All of Norwich will be there."

* * * * *

The next day, Elizabeth approached the great arch at the entry to the cathedral. Standing in a straight line on each side of the entrance to the cathedral was an honor guard: representatives of the British Red Cross, nurses from various training school, soldiers from the Norfolk Regiment with multi-colored military medals pinned to their uniforms, flag bearers, members of the Salvation Army, a few older veterans—one leaning on crutches—and other military groups whose uniforms she didn't recognize. To one side, about to enter the cathedral, was the white-haired Bishop of Norwich, resplendent in his richly colored brocade and satin robes.

When Elizabeth stepped inside the cathedral, she was shocked. Every seat was filled. She searched for an empty place and finally found one half way down the central aisle. People moved over, allowing her to squeeze in. She looked around at the solemn faces and judged that at least a thousand people had gathered here to be a part of this memorial ceremony. Her seat vibrated when the organ began to play. She heard the liquid movement of the bishop's satin robes as he walked down the aisle past her, and stepped up into the pulpit. He invited everyone to stand and sing the first hymn.

Now the labourer's task is o'er:
Now the battle day is past:
Now upon the farther shore
Lands the voyager at last.
Father, in Thy gracious keeping
Leave we now, Thy servant sleeping.

There the tears of earth are dried;
There its hidden things are clear;
There the work of life is tried
By a juster Judge than here.

With the exception of an occasional cough, Elizabeth marveled that so many people could be so quiet. The bishop read a passage from the New Testament that admonished people to "put away bitterness and anger together with all malice." Then he put the Bible aside, gripped both sides of the pulpit, and spoke.

"Edith Cavell was forced to make a painful and fatal decision. It was the same decision that the Good Samaritan made when he stopped to help a man who had been beaten and left on the side of the road. Two others had already passed the poor man by, but the Samaritan stopped and put himself at risk of being attacked.

"Her nursing instincts told her to take the risk, in spite of the consequences, for the good of humanity. Perhaps there was a sense of adventure in her, or some may say, even defiance. But there is no doubt that she knew what she was doing was dangerous, and certainly illegal. It was the same willingness to take a risk that every man took when he put on a soldier's uniform and lifted his head above the trenches. It is the same willingness to turn the cheek to danger for the good of others.

"Just as Christ did when He gave His life on the cross, she has shown the world that good can indeed overcome evil. That fateful decision and willingness to take a risk for humanity has sparked new hope and life in all of us. I exhort you that we must all learn to face the dangers of our lives with the calmness of Nurse Cavell. She has given us all a powerful reason not to fear the consequences of taking a risk that will help others. When our hearts beat faster in the face of responsible risk-taking, then we know that we are fulfilling our God-given calling in the same way that our own Norfolk Edith chose, and we have joined hands with her.

"Edith Cavell brought life and hope to thousands who were desperate. Her defiance of the enemy and ability to accept her lot and face death with her head high has inspired thousands of others, indeed, some even sitting in this cathedral today."

A soft murmur rose from the seats. The woman next to Elizabeth put a flowered handkerchief to her nose. Further down the aisle, a man wiped the back of his hand over his eyes. The bishop continued.

"Like other Christian martyrs, she was able to look death in the face and move through it. In doing so, she died into the future. Her death sparked responses that went from outrage to a call to action. It was a call that millions heard and responded to. It was a call that most certainly influenced the direction of the war from defeat to victory. As shown by today's honoring of her life, she continues to inspire us, and I suspect will inspire many more in the future."

Something the bishop said snapped in Elizabeth's thinking. She now realized what Edith's life and death was all about. Certainly the nursing school was a part of it, but not the whole. The whole was a bigger picture. Bigger than her work in Brussels; bigger than anything Elizabeth could have known. She now realized it was not Edith's destiny to live long enough to see the flourishing of her work. Nor was it destined that Elizabeth should persuade Edith to stop rescuing soldiers, because it was not in the divine plan that Edith be stopped.

Great waves of questions and answers flooded into her thoughts. Edith had a very powerful destiny—greater than Elizabeth could have imagined. It all made sense now. Like Christ in the Garden of Gethsemane, Edith had accepted her fate and submitted herself to it. What if she had never lived? What would have happened if she had gone home at the outbreak of the war as everyone urged her to do? What if she had not made that fatal decision to take in those first two English soldiers? And what if she had given up her rescue efforts when Elizabeth urged her to do so?

What if the trial had been fair and Edith had not been executed, or if found guilty, had simply been put in prison? If she had been hidden away in a German prison, would there have been the same outrage, and zeal to avenge her death? Would thousands of soldiers, possibly even millions, have joined up to avenge her death? Would America have entered the war? It was the American ambassador who brought this injustice to the attention of President Wilson, and it was the anger of Americans, in response to reports of Edith's death in the newspapers, that pushed the President to get involved.

If Edith had not died as she had, would there have been a very different outcome of the war? Could one woman, a nurse, have made that much of a difference?

Elizabeth knew now that there was nothing she could have done, or should have done, but to support her friend in her journey. She smiled to herself. *My dear friend, you not only taught us how to live, but also how to die. You could never have known that your decision to do your duty would change the course of world events. I thought your death was a tragedy, but in truth, it was a triumph.*

Elizabeth felt a great burden lift from her. Maybe it was time she put aside the shadows of the past and turn the page in her own life. Edith would want that. She thought of Edith's final resting place behind the cathedral, with its carpet of multi-colored pansies and smiled.

Sleep well, my friend.

EDITH CAVELL MEMORIALS
AROUND THE WORLD

Although it is unusual for a novel to include a Memorials section, I added it because, while doing research on Edith Cavell, I was struck with how many of them I found from all over the world. I thought that if I were so impressed, my readers would be, too. If you find others, please contact me and we will periodically do an update.

—Terri Arthur

England

- A 40-foot statue of Edith Cavell by George Frampton was erected in 1920 to the right of Trafalgar Square near the Lord Nelson column, London, UK. Engraved on Cavell's statue are the words: *Humanity, Sacrifice, Devotion, and Fortitude*. On the back is the British Lion trampling on a serpent, symbolical of Envy, Spite, Malice and Treachery, and above it are the words, "Faithful unto Death."

- The statue of white marble, an emblem of Purity, shows Nurse Cavell standing erect in her nurse's uniform. On the base is the inscription, "Patriotism is not enough. Edith Cavell. Brussels. Dawn - October 12, 1915."

Every year, nurses from the Royal London Hospital lay a wreath there. London, England.

♦ On the anniversary of her death, a memorial service is held when members of the Royal British Legion lay a wreath at her grave outside Norwich Cathedral, Norwich, England. The Edith Cavell Memorial statue by Henry Alfred Pegram was placed outside the Erpingham Gate, Norwich Cathedral, 1919, Norwich, England.

♦ The Edith Cavell public house, Tombland, Norwich, England.

♦ Maidshead Hotel next to the Norwich Cathedral was once called the "Cavell Home," Norwich, England.

♦ A successful London play about Edith Cavell was staged in London in the 1950s.

♦ Radio Cavell (1350 AM) broadcasts to staff and patients on the Royal Oldham Hospital Charity Radio.

♦ The first roll of honor from the Royal College of Nursing. In 2010, Yvonne McEwan created a listing of the deaths of British, Irish, and Dominion nurses in World War I.

♦ An Edith Cavell War Memorial was placed by teachers, pupils, and friends of her old school in Laurel Court, Peterborough Cathedral, Peterborough, England.

♦ A car park in Peterborough's Queensgate shopping center bore her name until 2011, when it was renamed as a color. Peterborough, England.

♦ A blue oval plaque bearing Edith Cavell's name was placed outside the Cavell House in North Somerset, England. This house is now a bed and breakfast. She spent some of her childhood here. Clevedon, Somerset, England.

♦ There is a dedication on the war memorial on the grounds of Sacred Trinity Church, Salford, Greater Manchester, England.

♦ The Cavell Van is the prototype passenger luggage van that transported her remains from Dover to London during her repatriation.

♦ A memorial window was placed in St. Mary's Church, depicting Miss Cavell in prayer. It is entitled "Fragile Martyr." Parishioners of St. Mary's hold a Cavell Flower Festival each year. A stone cross memorial also stands outside the church. Swardeston, Norfolk, England.

Belgium

♦ An inscription on a bronze memorial, naming Cavell and 35 other people executed by the German army at the former Tir National Firing Range in Schaerbeek, Belgium.

♦ The Sanatorium Edith Cavell, Obourg, Belgium.

♦ The *Commission de l'ecole belge d'infirmières diplômées* (the Belgian school of nursing) commissioned sculptor Armand Bonnetain to produce a bronze medal commemorating its former director and treasurer, Edith Cavell, and Belgian Marie DePage. Bonnetain's busts of the two nurses remains one of his most accomplished works, completed in 1919. On the reverse are the words: "1915-Remember."

♦ Plaque commemorating Edith Cavell on a block of flats near St Pieter's station in Ghent. (Photo by Nick Miller, Norwich, England)

Australia

♦ There is a carved marble with cast bronze relief panels of Edith Cavell in the the Shrine of Remembrance, 1929, Melbourne, Australia

♦ An Edith Cavell Memorial Plaque depicts German firing squad executing Nurse Edith Cavell, St. Kilda Road, Melbourne, Victoria, Australia.

♦ The Edith Cavell Trust was established by the New South Wales Nurses' Association, which provides scholarships to nurses in New South Wales, Australia.

♦ A building is named after Miss Cavell at the University of Queensland, Australia.

Canada

- Mount Edith Cavell, a peak in the Canadian Rockies, is named for her in Alberta, Canada.

- A bronze memorial dedicated to Edith Cavell was designed by Florence Wyle and placed outside the Toronto General Hospital, Canada. The inscription reads, "Edith Kavell (sic) and the Canadian nurses who gave their lives for humanity in the Great War. In the midst of darkness, they saw light. Lest we forget." Toronto, Canada.

- A hanging glacier and a mountain were named after her in the Jasper National Park, Alberta, Canada.

France

- A beautiful sculpture of her, *Monument de Miss Edith Cavell*, stood in the Tuileries Garden and was destroyed by Adolf Hitler in 1940, Paris, France.

- A bas-relief of Edith Cavell, destroyed in 1940, was in the Museum of Jeu de Paume, Paris, France.

Scotland

- Cavell Gardens, Inverness, Scotland.

United States

- A stone memorial statue by Canadian sculptor R. Tait MacKenzie stands in the garden behind the Red Cross National Headquarters in Washington DC, USA.

- A book was written in 1917 by Alice L.F. Fitzgerald, entitled *The Edith Cavell Nurse from Massachusetts*. This nurse was paid for and sent to work with the British Expeditionary Force to serve in France in 1915. This is her diary. A medal was manufactured in Boston honoring this event. Boston, Massachusetts, USA.

- There is a memorial stained-glass window dedicated to Edith Cavell in Manhattan Cathedral, New York City, New York, USA.

- There is an Edith Cavell chapter of the Daughters of the British Empire in Houston, Texas, USA

- The Edith Cavell Nursing Scholarship Fund, a philanthropy of the Dallas County Medical Society Alliance Foundation, provides scholarships to exceptional nursing students in the areas surrounding Dallas, Texax, USA.

- A YWCA camp is named after Edith Cavell (Camp Cavell) in Lexington, Michigan, USA.

- Cavell Park is a playground in northeast Minneapolis, Minnesota, USA.

- American artist George Bellows (1882-1925) drew *The Murder of Edith Cavell* in 1918. It was rendered for a series of twelve lithographs he produced depicting atrocities committed by the German army in Belgium. It is now in the Princeton University Art Museum in New Jersey, USA.

MEDICAL FACILITIES

England

- University of East Anglia, Norwich, named its School of Nursing Sciences and Midwifery Centre the Edith Cavell Building when it opened in 2006, Norwich, England.

- Her Majesty Queen Elizabeth the Second, opened the Edith Cavell Hospital, in Peterborough, England, UK, where she received part of her education in1988.

- The Cavell House Care Home Middle Road, Shoreham-by-Sea is in Exeter, England.

- A wing of Homerton Hospital, Hackney, was named after Edith Cavell, London, England.

- There is the Edith Cavell Surgery in Streatham, London, England.

- A ward in the Whittington Hospital in Archway, London, England, is named after Edith Cavell.

Belgium

- A hospital in Brussels, Belgium, is named the "Institut Medical Edith Cavell." A nurses' training school is now called Ecole Edith Cavell in the Brussels borough of Eccle, Belgium.

Canada

♦ Cavell Gardens Care Home. The site was Edith Cavell Hospital from 1955 to 2000, Vancouver, Canada.

♦ A wing of Toronto Western Hospital, Canada, was named after Edith Cavell.

♦ The Edith Cavell Care Centre is located in Lethbridge, Alberta, Canada.

♦ The Cavell Building, Quinte Children's Treatment Centre, and Regional School of Nursing are located in Belleville, Ontario, Canada.

Australia

♦ A building at the Medical School, University of Queensland, Australia, is named after Edith Cavell.

♦ The Edith Cavell Trust was established by the New South Wales Nurses' Association, which provides scholarships to nurses in NSW, Australia.

New Zealand

♦ The Edith Cavell Home, Hospital, and Retirement Village are located in Sumner, Christchurch, New Zealand.

♦ There is the Edith Cavell Memorial Hospital in Paparoa, New Zealand.

STREETS

England

♦ Edith Cavell Drive, Steeple Bumpstead, England.

♦ Cavell Street, running next to the London Hospital in Whitechapel, where Cavell trained, was formerly known as Bedford Street, London, England.

♦ Edith Cavell Way, Shooters Hill, London, England.

♦ Edith Cavell Close, Openshaw, Manchester, England.

♦ Edith Cavell Court, Kingston upon Hull, England.

♦ Cavell Road, Dudley, West Midlands (formerly Worcestershire), England.

♦ Cavell Road, Norwich, England.

♦ Cavell Walk, Stevenage, England.

♦ Cavell Way, Maidenbower, Crawley, West Sussex, England.

- Cavell Way, Pendleton, Salford, Greater Manchester, England.

- Cavell Road, Billericay, Essex, England.

- Cavell Close (this has been demolished), Woodbeck, Nottinghamshire, England.

- Cavell Drive in Bishops Stortford, Hertfordshire, England.

- Cavell Drive (Queen Alexandra Hospital), Portsmouth, England.

Belgium

- Rue Edith Cavell / Edith Cavellstraat, a street in Uccle/Ukkel, Brussels, Belgium.

- Edith Cavellstraat, a street in Ostend, Belgium.

France

- Rue Edith Cavell, Le Havre, France.

- Rue Edith Cavell, Vitry sur Seine, France.

- Avenue Edith-Cavell, in Nice, France.

- Avenue Miss Cavell, Saint-Maur-des-Fossés, France.

- Rue Miss Cavell, Arques, France.

- Avenue Miss Cavell,St-Maur-Des-Fosses, France.

- Avenue Edith Cavell, Hyères, France.

Canada

- Edith Cavell Boulevard, a road in Port Stanley, Ontario, Canada.

- Cavell Drive in Winnipeg, Manitoba, Canada.

- Edith Cavell Boulevard, a road in Port Stanley, Ontario, Canada.

- Cavell Avenue in the Danforth neighborhood of Toronto, Ontario, Canada.

- Cavell Avenue in Etobicoke, Ontario, Canada.

- Cavell Avenue in Guelph, Ontario, Canada.

Australia
- Cavell Street, West Hobart, Tasmania, Australia.

New Zealand
- Cavell Street, Dunedin, New Zealand.

- Cavell Street, Reefton, New Zealand.

- Edith Cavell Bridge at Arthur's Point, near Queenstown, New Zealand.

- Nurse Cavell Lane, Paparoa, Northland, New Zealand.

Tasmania
- There is a Cavell Street in West Hobart, and a Cavell Square in Hobart, Tazmania.

United States
- Cavell Street, Westland, Michigan, USA.

- Cavell Avenue, in Trenton, New Jersey, USA.

- Cavell Avenue, Twin Cities, Minnesota, USA.

Portugal
- Rua Edith Cavell, a street in Lisbon, Portugal.

South Africa
- Edith Cavell Street in Hillbrow, Johannesburg, South Africa.

Mauritius
- Edith Cavell Street in Port Louis, Mauritius.

SCHOOLS

England

♦ Edith Cavell Lower School in Bedford, England

♦ Cavell House, dark blue house at Jersey College for Girls, Jersey, England.

♦ Cavell Primary School, Norwich, England.

♦ Wymondham College has a boarding block named after Edith Cavell, Norfolk, England.

♦ Cavell House, blue house at Sheringham High School, Norfolk, England.

♦ Cavell House, red house at Cliff Park Junior School, Gorleston, Norfolk, England.

Australia

♦ Cavell House. The fourth, blue house of St Aidan's Anglican Girls' School, Brisbane, Australia.

Canada

♦ A middle school closed in 1987 in Windsor, Ontario, Canada.

♦ An elementary school later renamed to S.F. Howe, Sault Ste. Marie, Ontario, Canada.

♦ Edith Cavell Regional School of Nursing, in Belleville, Ontario, Canada.

♦ Edith Cavell School, Moncton, New Brunswick, Canada.

♦ Edith Cavell Elementary School, Vancouver, British Columbia, Canada.

♦ Edith Cavell Elementary School, St. Catharine's, Ontario, Canada.

India

♦ Cavell House at Queen Mary School, Mumbai, India.

♦ Cavell House, Pratt Memorial School, Kolkata, India.

♦ Edith Cavell House, green house at Barnes School, Deolali, India.

Argentina

♦ Northlands School Cavell House, 1920, Olivos, Argentina.

OTHER TRIBUTES

♦ Edith became a popular name for French and Belgian girls' after her execution. The French chanteuse, Édith Piaf (1915-1963), born two months after Cavell was executed, was the best known of these.

♦ A successful film called *Dawn* depicted Miss Cavell's story in 1930.

♦ A geological feature on Venus is named the Cavell Corona.

♦ A number of flowers and plants are named after her: a variety of rose first bred in 1917, a lilac and a peony in 1916, and an apple tree.

♦ On the anniversary of her death in October, a memorial service is held at the Norwich Cathedral when members of the Royal British Legion, the Red Cross, Belgium, the Royal London Hospital, and many others lay a wreath at her grave.

♦ In 2013, an American Red Cross nurse, Terri Arthur, laid a wreath from the American Red Cross, the first American wreath to be placed since Cavell's reburial here in 1919.

♦ Vintage postcard depicting the murder of Edith Cavell at the hands of the Germans.

AUTHOR'S NOTE

For the most part, the events depicted in this novel actually took place; they are matters of historical record, and I have adhered closely to the accounts of historical documents. I have exercised creative license with respect to a few minor characters and situations, but have tried to keep my additions scrupulously consistent with the known facts.

Previous studies of Edith Cavell's life and work struck me as providing a rather thin historical context, so I have woven historic events into her story that must surely have affected both Cavell and those around her. To enrich the accounts of her nursing experiences, I did extensive research into the nursing profession and nursing practices during World War I. The injuries described in the novel, for example, are typical of World War I and most likely resemble those that Cavell was called upon to treat.

Historical opinion is divided that Rimmel—or Rammler, as he is sometimes called—actually existed. True, very little is known about him, but since I found a postcard depicting his disinterred body lying next to

Cavell's, I chose to accept that he was a real, not a legendary character, and to portray his character in a way that counterbalances the brutality undeniably displayed by many other German soldiers. He was also prominently written in the book,

Postcard of a young German soldier who died from a bullet wound and was disinterred from a dissident's grave in Schaerbeck, Belgium. Photo was taken by Dr. Vanderven of Schaerbeck.

Dawn, by Captain Reginald Berkeley, M.P. The 1930 movie on Edith Cavell was based on this book. Other details of Cavell's final moments are likewise open to dispute, and not everyone will agree with my rendition of it, which is based on pictures, drawings, and vintage postcards.

The diary in which Cavell kept the names of many of those she rescued was not found until forty years after her death by her sister's servant. It is now in the Imperial War Museum archives, along with many of her letters.

I told Edith Cavell's story in a novel format because it gave me the opportunity to dramatize her thoughts and feelings—something that many previous accounts of her life and work have failed to do. Cavell is often depicted as emotionally distant, repressed, reserved, stiff, formal, or starchy. I disagree. I believe she felt and loved deeply, even passionately, and was very much in touch with her own emotions and those of the people around her. However, she was a woman of the Victorian era and her behavior was constrained by the conventions of those times; we should not judge her deportment by today's norms of conduct and self-expression.

If, after reading this book, you feel that you have experienced her amazing journey, I will have succeeded in what I set out to do.

For more information:

Please visit the website: www.Fatal Decision-EdithCavell.com or find us on Facebook under Edith Cavell

ABOUT THE AUTHOR

I nspired by the images on a set of vintage postcards, Terri Arthur set about learning more about the life and death of a British nurse, Edith Cavell. A nurse herself, Arthur was surprised to learn that none of her nursing colleagues were familiar with Cavell's amazing story or knew how it had influenced World War I. Arthur also discovered that none of the books about Cavell had been written by a nurse and felt strongly that as a nurse, she could throw fresh light on the life and career of this extraordinary woman. After many years of research, which included two visits to Belgium and four visits to the United Kingdom, she wrote this historical novel based on Cavell's heroic career.

Arthur was invited by the nurses of Norwich, England to join them in the memorial ceremony honoring Edith Cavell at the Norwich, Cathedral in October 2013. Representing the American Red Cross, Arthur is the first American to have been so honored. She is referred to as the "American Cavellite" by the Norwich nurses.

Born in New York, Arthur is a long-time resident of Massachusetts and has served as a nurse in hospitals on Martha's Vineyard, Cape Cod, and Plymouth. She is also a volunteer for the American Red Cross. In addition to her nursing, she holds a BS in Education and Biology, and an MSM in Health Business Management. Also an entrepreneur, Arthur created and manages Medical Education Systems, Inc. a business that provides continuing education to nurses, doctors, and medical personnel.

Terri's email:
terri.arthur@gmail.com

Author laying a poppy wreath on Cavell's grave at the Norwich Cathedral in Norwich, England during the memorial ceremony.

481

BIBLIOGRAPHY

Books

Anonymous. *A War Nurse's Diary: Sketches From a Belgian Field Hospital*, New York: Macmillan, 1918.

Beaumont, Harry. *Old Contemptible*, Hutchinson of London, 1967.

Beck, James. *The Case of Edith Cavell: A Study of the Rights of Non-Combatants*, Dodo Press, 1915.

Berkeley, Capt. Reginald. *Dawn: A Biographical Novel of Edith Cavell*, New York: J. H. Sears, 1928.

Boston, Noel. *The Dutiful Edith Cavell*, England: Norwich Cathedral, n.d.

Brown, Gordon. *Courage: Eight Portraits*, London: Bloomsbury, 2007.

Bryce, James. *Report into German Atrocities in Belgium*, December, 1914 - May, 1915. Commissioned by the British Government headed by Prime Minister

Cammaerts, Émile. *Through the Iron Bars: Two Years of German Occupation in Belgium,* Project Gutenburg, 1917.

Clark-Kennedy, A.E., *Edith Cavell: Pioneer and Patriot*, London: Farber and Farber, 1961.

Collier's Photographic History of the European War, New York: P. F. Collier, 1915.

Collins, Sheila M. *The Royal London Hospital: A Brief History*, Whitechapel, London: The Royal London Hospital Archives and Museum, 1995.

De Leeuw, Adele. *Edith Cavell: Nurse, Spy, Heroine*, New York: G.P. Putnam's Sons, 1968.

Dossey, Barbara Montgomery. *Florence Nightingale: Mystic, Visionary, Healer*, Springhouse, PA: Springhouse, 2000.

Evans, Jonathan. *Edith Cavell*, Whitechapel, London: The Royal London Hospital Museum, 2008.

Ferguson, Niall. *The Pity of War: Explaining World War I*, The Penguin Press, 1998.

The Friends of Edith Cavell. *Edith Cavell: Her Life and Her Art*, UK: Royal London Hospital, 1990.

Gay & Fisher. *The Commission for Relief in Belgium*, California: Stanford University Press, 1929.

Gibson, Hugh. *A Journal From the Legation*, London: Hodder & Stoughton, 1917.

Grey, Elizabeth. *Friend Within the Gates*, New York: Dell, 1960.

Heyman, Neil. *Daily Life During World War I*, London: Greenwood Press, 2002.

Higonnet, Margaret R. *Nurses at the Front: Writing the Wounds of the Great War*, Boston: Northeastern University Press, 2001.

Hill, William Thomson. *The Martyrdom of Nurse Cavell, The Life Story of the Victim of Germany's Most Barbarous Crime*, London: Hutchinson, 1915.

Hoeling, A. A. *Edith Cavell*, London: Cassell, 1958.

Horne, John and Kramer, Alan. *German Atrocities 1914: A History of Denial*, New Haven and London: Yale University Press, 2001.

Judson, Helen. *Edith Cavell*, New York: Macmillan, 1941.

Kellogg, Vernon. *Headquarters Nights: A Record of Conversations and Experiences at the Headquarters of the German Army in France and Belgium*, Boston: Atlantic Monthly Press, 1917.

Kempis, Thomas A. *Of the Imitation of Christ, Edith Cavell Edition*, U. K.: Humphrey Milford Oxford University Press, 1920.

Luckes, Eva C. E. *The London Hospital (1880-1919)*, U.K.: The London Hospital League of Nurses, 1958.

Myers, J. W. *Dr. Myers' Medical Advisor*, Philippi, W. Va.: Myers Remedy, 1916.

Neillands, Robin. *The Old Contemptibles: The British Expeditionary Force, 1914*, U.K.: John Murray, 2004.

Richardson, Nigel. *Edith Cavell*, London: Hamish Hamilton, 1985.

Ryder, Rowland. *Edith Cavell*, London: Hamish Hamilton, 1975.

Van Til, Jacqueline. *With Edith Cavell in Belgium,* New York, New York: W. Bridges, 1922.

Upjohn, Sheila. *Edith Cavell: The Story of a Norfolk Nurse*, U.K.: Norwich Cathedral Publications, 2000.

Vinton, Iris. *The Story of Edith Cavell*, New York: Grosset & Dunlap, 1959.

Whitlock, Whitlock. *Belgium: A Personal Narrative*, New York: D. Appleton, 1919.

Wilmont, H. P. *World War I*, London: Dorling Kindersley, 2003.

Woodham-Smith. Cecil, *Florence Nightingale*, USA: McGraw Hill Book, 1951.

Zuckerman, Larry. *The Rape of Belgium: The Untold Story of World War I*, New York University Press, New York and London, 2004.

Zwerdling, Michael. *Postcards of Nursing*, Philadelphia: Lipincott Williams and Wilkins, 2004.

Film Media

Line of Fire: Mons. DVD. UK: Cromwell Productions, 2002

The First World War Remembered. DVD. London: Imperial War Museum. n.d.

The Battle of the Somme. DVD. London: Imperial War Museum, 2008.

Newspapers and Journals

Davis, Richard Harding. "The Burning of Louvain." *New York Tribune*, August 31, 1914.

"The Death of Edith Cavell." *The Daily News and Leader* (London and Manchester), n.d.

"For Belgian Wounded: Mme DePage Obtains $80,000 here for Field Hospitals." *The New York Times*, April 18, 1915.

"Whitlock Makes a Report: News of Sentence Was Kept from him for Several Hours." *The New York Times*, October 22, 1915.

"Officials Defend Cavell Shooting." *New York Times*, October 25, 1915.

"Sculptured Memorial to Edith Cavell-Miss Cavell's Memory Honored." New York Times, November 24, 1918.

Beck, James M. "A Second Review of the Case of Edith Cavell." *New York Times*, November 14, 1915.

"King Honors Miss Cavell." *New York Times*, May 11, 1922.

"Four German Bullets Killed Nurse Cavell; Body to be Taken to England Tomorrow." *New York Times*, May 12, 1919.

"Happy to Die for my Country" Miss Cavell's Last Words" American Envoy Tricked by German Officials, When he Fights to Save Miss Cavell." *New York Herald,* October 22, 1915.

"German Under Secretary Justifies Killing of Nurse." *Fort Wayne Journal-Gazette,* October 25, 1915.

Paul, Pauline and King, Kathryn M. "Remember Nurse Edith Cavell." *Orthoscope,* Winter Issue, 1992.

"The Execution of Miss Cavell: A Memorial Service." Prime Minister to Attend. Germans Give Apology." *The Standard,* October 25, 1915.

"Miss Cavell's Case." *The Dacatur Review,* October 26, 1915

Nursing Mirror, London, May 1, 1905, April 25, 1908, August 8, 22, 1914, April 17, May 15, 1915, June 19, 1915, September 19, 26, 1914, October 13, 1914, May 22, October 23, 30, 1915, November 13, 27, 1915. Copies obtained at the Royal College of Nursing Archives, Edinburgh, Scotland.

La Libre Belgique. Bibliotheque Royal, Brussels.

"Edith Cavell." *The British Journal of Nursing,* December, 1930.

Holder, Victoria, L. "From Handmaiden to Right Hand—The Beginning of World War I: Edith Cavell." *AORN Journal,* September, 2004.

Strayer, Charleton Bates. "A Shock to Humanity." *Leslie's Illustrated Weekly Newspaper, Public Opinion,* November 11, 1915.

"WWI - The Rescue of the Starving," *Antiques Digest, Old and Sold,* n.d., 1918.

"RMS Lusitania: The Fateful Voyage." *First World War.com,* August 11, 2001.

"Arthur Zimmerman on the Execution of Edith Cavell." *The First World War.com,* 12 October, 1915.

"The Late Madame DePage." *Nursing Mirror and Midwives' Journal,* June 5, 1915.

"The Edith Cavell-Marie DePage School of Nursing, Brussels." *The British Journal of Nursing,* March, 1933.

Letters written by Edith Cavell, copies obtained at the Royal London Hospital Archives, Whitechapel, London, UK and the Imperial War Museum, London, UK.

Websites

"Edith Cavell." Wikipedia, URL: http://en.wilkipedia.org/wiki/Edith_Cavell

"The Case of Edith Cavell." URL: http://greatwardifferent.com/Great--_War/Cavell/Cavell_00.htm

Lockkeeper.com "Edith Cavell." URL: http://lockkeeper.com/short/cavell/index.htm

"Typhoid in Maidstone in 1897, Health and Medicine." URL: www.kented.org.uk/ngfl/subjects/history/medhist/page30

Brugmann, Chu. "Antoine DePage" (1862-1925), translated version URL: http://www.chu-brugmann.be/fr/histo/depage.asp

"Mme Antoine DePage (Marie Picard), Saloon Class Passenger." The Lusitania Resource, URL: http://web.rmslusitania.info:81pages/saloon_class/depage_marie.html

"Hague Conventions (1899 and 1907)." Wikipedia, URL: http://en.wilkipedia.org/wiki/Hague_Conventions_(1899_and_1907)

"WWI, War Encyclopedia-H, Hague Convention." URL.: http://www.ww1according.tobob.com/wcH.php

"Marie DePage: The Lusitania Resource." URL: http://mslustania.info/pages/salon_class/depage_marie

"The Use of Poison Gas." *WWI Document Archive*, April 22, 1915, URL: http://ww1.lib.bya.edu/index.php/The_Use_of_poison_Gas

"Nurse Edith Cavell, The Testimony of Pasteur Le Seur." URL: http://www.chamberlin.plus/cavell/leseur.htm

Benn, Gottfried. "The Physician at Cavell's Execution." Wikipedia, URL: http://en.wilkipedia.org/wiki,Gottfried_Benn

CPSIA information can be obtained at www.ICGtesting.com
Printed in the USA
BVOW08s0539160416

443478BV00007B/10/P